The Brown Mud Of Jericho

By
T.F. Platt

First published by AuthorHouse 04/14/04

ISBN: 1-4140-4723-1 (e-book)
ISBN: 1-4184-3626-7 (Paperback)

This book is printed on acid free paper.

Dedication

This work is dedicated to my family.

Introduction

As in all books of the Jericho series, The Brown Mud Of Jericho and its characters are fiction. The books are written in honor of the author's grandfather, Clarence Groner, and the author's mother, Edith Marie Groner Platt. The geography used in the books is similar, however, to that of the community in Michigan where Clarence Groner and Edith Marie Groner Platt and T.F. Platt, and others of the Groner and Platt families, resided through much of their lives. The books aren't in any sense biographical, although Clarence and Edith for a time lived on a road called Jericho Road and Clarence did work briefly in a paper mill nearby.

Early twentieth century Michigan is the setting for The Brown Mud Of Jericho. The tale opens during that first night after the return of Clydis and Edith to the little farm on Jericho Road.

Clydis and Edith had escaped the talons of the villainous woman and made it home but they still feared for the safety of Edith. The villainous woman was still loose. The outcome of Clarence's impending courtroom trial also hung over them. They worried, too, whether Clydis would be accepted into the community. And, further, Clydis was doubtful of her own ability to rear Edith.

Their story is flavored by colorful, often humorous, characters who share in the dread of a muddy road. The muddy road is symbolic to situations of suspense, romance, humor, horse rustling, kidnapping, terror, tragedy, passion, woe, and triumph. While coping with the situations, Clydis gradually becomes indispensable in the community, but her friendship finally leads to a compromising situation at the little farm on Jericho.

The Brown Mud Of Jericho is the second of the Jericho Books by T. F. Platt, following on the success of his first book, If We Make It To Jericho. The Jericho stories are intended for adults and young adults. The tales aren't lewd and they omit cussing.

Acknowledgement

The author wishes to thank family members and friends; notably Rena Baker, Michael Baker, Buck Platt, Helen Platt, Violet Robinson, and Jim Robinson, who have read one or more of Jericho Books prior to publication. Their comments have been helpful and appreciated.

Chapter One

Throbbing pain brought Clydis awake. She'd fallen asleep on top of Clarence. His arms held her fast to his chest and they locked her head to his. Oh how good it had been! Over a year she'd been away. And now home again. Oh how good! But in slumber his embrace had pinned her. He clung more tightly in response to her gentle push up from him. Gosh it hurt! After a silent, hopeful count of three, she thrust violently up from him. Her momentum threw her onto the floor, her head crashing against the dresser drawer wherein Edith slumbered. Niagara Falls roared and crashed inside her head. Her head was weighted by rocks as she tried to raise it. Her face grew numb. Oblivion claimed her.

Floating.

Floating, but her head lagged behind, too heavy to float with her body.

Warmth graced her ear and she pressed against it. Oh, much better. "Clydis, Clydis."

Warmth caressed her ear, her body, her being. Slowly, her head throbbed less where she clobbered it. To escape from her mother, she, with Edith in her arms, had dived under a moving train car and emerged in the clear but with her scalp crushed and torn. Now he held her. Oh, how good! Oh, how good.

"Clydis, Clydis." Warmth at her ear. His warmth. She pressed against him, wanting more of him.

"Clydis, Clydis." Away from the train and with Edith clutched tightly she ran and ran until exhaustion plunged her into sharp stones and gravel on Cross Road. With arm and forehead cut deep and viciously scrubbed, she'd stood in the road crying out to God, to Clarence; trying to come home.

Now terror consumed her. "Edith! Edith!" Her mother coming, coming to regain her project, coming for Edith.

"Edith! Edith!" Her screams pierced the cool air of the bedroom.

His forehead beaded sweat. "She's here. She's here," he said, his lips at her ear. "Oh, my darling, she's here. She's alright. You're alright. You're home. You're

1

here with me. Oh, thank God, you're home." He held her, his hands caressing. With body and soul he felt her stiffness abate, replaced by shivering warmth which filled him, united them. She sobbed and sobbed as he held her, caressed her, kissed her, smoothed her matted hair.

Her wavy brown hair, still matted by blood, had stiffened and was half covered by a stained white bandage. He knew she cared for it and preferred it in shoulder length freedom to be cuffed by the gentlest zephyr yet held tame by a delicate ribbon, but now its matted snarls he smoothed with his fingers, muttering in her ear of her beauty. She leaned to him firmly, her five foot seven with the curves of Venus de Milo slotting perfectly to his slender body. "I'm frightened." Her lips brushed his ear. Hold me. Hold me," she muttered. "Don't let her get Edith."

She bolted up from him, "Edith! Edith!"

Edith slept peacefully in a blanket lined dresser drawer. They'd escaped from Mrs. Klinert with naught but the clothes on their backs, making necessary the makeshift sleeping arrangement. She slept with her new rag doll beside her and with a tiny pretty hand clutching her dad's red shirt, which was her blanket. He helped to lift Edith into her arms and he carried them into the living room, her one hundred thirty pounds no challenge for his slender composition, seating them in the wide armed chair. "Rest," he said. His lips brushed her forehead. In the dim moonlight he saw her face serene and her eyes clearing as lightly she patted Edith. Edith slept with her head nestled against the naked chest of her mother. "Be right back." He hurried after blankets and her medication.

Nervously he administered four UpJohn aspirin tablets and a swallow of laudanum. Upending a table, he slid it behind the chair and propped her head against it with pillows. Cuddled under the blankets, still patting Edith, she rested.

He stood naked beside them, shivering; head to toe of his five foot eleven aquiver, looking lovingly at them radiant in the moon swept room, rubbing his arms. Cold? Oh, my gosh! Rushing to the kitchen, he added fuel to the Detroit Company potbelly.

Seeing she'd drifted asleep, he grabbed a blanket and plopped onto the couch, not inches from them, and was soon in slumber, his curly brown hair pressed to the pillow, the blanket pulled tight around his emaciated body.

Clydis awoke from time to time, each time finding comfort in seeing him there, feeling for him, shuddering in recall of the strapping one hundred eighty pound man she'd known, that she loved, knowing she'd driven him to emaciation, yet still warmed by the deep sparkle in his brown eyes. She'd tried not to love him. Her mother's plan was for her not to ever love him. Him the oaf, the clod, she'd selected for her daughter's mate. The mate was to be toyed with then flippantly abandoned, and herself to go on with Edith. Edith was to be reared by ladies to be a lady. Reared as had been Clydis, reared enisled of societal influences, shielded from all but her tutors and Mrs. Klinert, the tutor extraordinary.

She hadn't known her mother was insane. She'd thought she deserved the physical and mental brutality dealt her by her mother throughout her youth. For Edith she'd thought it'd be different. She'd be there to help Edith, to protect her, to help her learn the lessons.

They'd left the farm on Jericho, speeding toward Grand Rapids and Kalamazoo, at last free of him, ready to begin the training of Edith. But already, even before they'd reached Kalamazoo, she'd missed him. But she'd thought him little to sacrifice for Edith. Repeatedly, day by day, she'd told herself that.

In Austria she began to lose Edith. Mrs. Klinert, at first little by little, but soon abruptly, wrested her from Clydis, limiting Clydis' parentage to nursing and diaper changes. Clydis had begun plotting their escape from the villainous woman. Not until in Manchester, England, did she see a way; but her mother caught her and that evening Edith had screamed. The innocent Edith, her very own child, was to receive the punishment for any infraction committed by Clydis!

Her mother, she'd realized upon hearing her daughter's scream, was insane, and probably had always been. Instantly, she'd realized her own innocence, now seeing the reality of penalties exacted on her by her mother throughout her youth. Her mother stayed within feet and inches of Edith at all times, affording not a moment's private intimacy between Clydis and Edith, nor any chance for escape. She'd fought the impulse to simple take Edith and run, knowing by her own counsel she'd be caught and that likely Edith would be taken from her; and herself declared an unfit mother.

Because escape was impossible, complete cooperation with Mrs. Klinert she'd seen as her only aegis for Edith. Hating herself, loathing her mother, she'd faked cooperation, even to a relentless condemnation of Clarence, which her mother seemed to especially enjoy. And she'd succeeded in shielding her precious, loving, innocent daughter throughout their sojourn in Europe and in New York and finally had shielded her all the way back to Leadford, Michigan, ending not two miles from the farm on Jericho Road, not two miles from Clarence. Her heart had pounded and pounded while in Leadford, wanting so much to run, but she'd forced herself to plan, to plan, to plan, and finally they'd made it back to the farm on Jericho, to Clarence, to home. And now she sat in the wide armed chair, feeling better with the effects of analgesics and with Edith cuddled and with Clarence near. From outside the window a half moon bathed the room in dim silvery light. The light fell on Clarence asleep on the couch, lighting him as though God were pointing him out, showing him off. Tears cruised down her cheeks, knowing how much she'd hurt him.

She saw Clarence as the being closest to God on Earth, not believing that God could ever punish anyone, that he could only be supportive, forgiving, loving, because that's how she saw Clarence. Never had he asked why she'd gone away.

Instead his full attention was to their being back and that they'd go on together. "Together," he'd said, "we'll help Edith grow. We'll do it together, Clydis. We'll just do it." Oh, how she loved him!

Now, suddenly, a new view, a frightening view, filled the window. She shivered, dragging her eyes from it, but now the wide armed chair began to taunt her. She'd sat in it hour after hour, day on day, watching along Jericho, waiting for them, they who would take her away. That day she, with Edith clutched jubilantly, had hopped into a Ford, beginning their lives apart from him. She dragged her eyes from the window but the chair gripped her, holding her to the awful memory.

"Edith! Edith!" her mind screamed.

But Edith was safe in her arms. Safe now. Safe! Oh, how good.

Softly she patted Edith.

Now thoughts arose to consume her soul, shielding her mind from the pain of her wounds, and of the wide armed chair and the window. Her lips quivered. She knew nothing of normal child rearing. She'd never been a child, never had seen any child reared. The privilege was denied her. How could she rear Edith? "We'll just do it," Clarence said. And he said they'd learn by observing others, others like the Jameses, and they'd learn by listening to Ma and Pa. Ma and Pa, she treasured, they'd done a good job of it, but she knew not the Jameses or scarcely anyone else!

Her eyes looked up, cruised to the south wall of the room. Beyond the wall, on down the road, she knew that Billie cuddled Clydene. She'd met Billie, had instantly liked Billie but again hope was thwarted. Billie would expect to learn from her, not she from Billie! Melancholy dragged her down, down, down.

She'd stayed aloof, not wanting acquaintances, not desiring that anyone learn anything about her. Due to her reading aloud the scriptures, they'd seen, she'd realized proudly, that she was a remarkably gifted person; albeit a cold one. At that time, she'd desired no friends.

Tears drifted slowly down her chin, spattering Edith.

Chapter Two

At the first glow of daybreak Ma turned into the driveway and flowed up the drive to the power shed. Morley Perkins, landlord of their farm on Jericho, and master gardener, was tucked tight in behind Ma and before he'd pulled to a stop, Claire James, with Trella Mead beside her, pulled in past the little arborvitae tree that during the previous day they'd named for Edith. Behind Claire, Jane Toberton turned her heavy team of stamping Percherons, their heads bobbing, nostrils steaming, into the yard. Lorraine Benson rode in astride a livery horse named Boliver. Boliver labored under a prodigious pack tied behind the saddle and close on his tail, Clifford James guided his husky Clydesdales.

Clydis and Clarence stood on their rear stoop. Old Sniffer had signaled 'friendly, all is well' and they'd looked from the kitchen window. Clarence realized at once what was taking place. "They're for you," he said reaching her hand, "and Edith."

Clydis looked on in wonder. She felt her heart pounding at the base of her throat. Her face white, she moved tightly against him and he folded his arms about her. She wanted to cry, to shout with joy, to run to them and to hug them. She hadn't known them. She'd remained aloof from them, but they were there, there in the yard for her, for Edith, for Clarence. "Thank, God," she breathed on his neck. "Oh, thank God for such people."

The mere mention that "Edith had no coat, no clothes for that matter," had started it. Grandma Emma had gone to Trella Mead's house after she and Robert had left the farm on Jericho the previous evening. Hoping for an early start the next morning, she'd expressed the need for cotton cloth for Edith's diapers. The truth of Clydis' and Edith's condition emerged as Emma visited with Trella who owned the yard goods store. Trella had taken it from there.

She telephoned Claire James first because she guessed that Claire and Clydis were about the same size and build. Claire telephoned Lorraine Benson, asking her to take her shift at the shop so that she could help Clydis. Lorraine would hear none of it, suggesting that Trella close the store at least for the morning. Trella agreed, realizing at once Lorraine's compassion.

Lorraine had just finished a beautiful set of percales for their bedstead. Without hesitation, she spread one of the sheets on the floor and began pulling out bureau drawers. Her very best under things went onto the pile, and were followed by dresses and stockings and shoes. "Tie these," she'd said to Ed. The second sheet also became a bundle, a bulky one, because it contained a high chair. The chair had been Naddy's, loaned to Lorraine; Lorraine was four months pregnant.

Clydis clung to Clarence, her legs weak, her back shivered, knowing her hair was a mess, not knowing what to do, wondering how this'd all happened. Her heart thumped and she tried to swallow its beat down from her throat.

In addition to Trella Mead's efforts, the Toberton household had been a beehive since hearing that Clydis and Edith were in trouble. Helgie Perkins had arrived at the Toberton's on that afternoon to midwife for Billie. Billie was okay now, but for being a bit surly because they told her to stay put, that they would handle it, that she, they promised, would get to see Clydis and Edith soon enough. The Tobertons were very concerned for Billie and newly born Clydene, especially Clydene, because three of them had suffered the loss of their baby within a week or two after its birthing. Jane, Molly, Satin and Helen, wives of Rik, Tom, Pal, and Sid, heaped a farm wagon with clothing, house cleaning equipment and household goods. Hearing of the Toberton efforts from Helgie Perkins when she returned to the mercantile in town, Lorraine sent her son, Joseph Marvin Benson, to let them know of their similar efforts.

Now, Joe Marvin Benson was seated next to Clifford James when he edged the Clydesdales in beside Jane's Percherons. Jane looked over at Joe Marvin. "Good morning pilgrim. Are you the camp cook? Or is it you're the set up man?"

Joe smiled over. "Well, I sure planned on set up," he declared, "but cooking?" He grabbed his abdomen, feinting illness. "You'd be asking for it."

Seeing their scurry, hearing their banter, she struggled to know who they were. Some, the Tobertons, she recognized but could put no name to a person. Her wounds smarted and ached; threatening to numb her yet her soft brown eyes darted to one and another in the yard. Her eyes sparkled with tears as she discerned Ma skipping gaily about in the brightening rays of the morning sun. And of the big man whose smile now reached her, her brain struggled: Mr. Clifford James?

Satin, Jane, and Clifford hoisted a husky tripod from the wagon and soon had it located in the middle of the south lawn. Joe Marvin unloaded the wheelbarrow then rolled the cook pot into it. Within minutes the soup cooking station was set ready for Molly and Helen.

An automobile moved, snapping her eyes to its driver. Her smile grew radiant as she recognized Morley Perkins, grinning proudly, driving onto the lawn with his load of vegetables.

He began paring the potatoes, onions, carrots, rutabagas, and tomatoes, all in far greater abundance than they'd need, tossing them into the cook pot. Molly and Helen set up a second cook stand for boiling sweet corn. They would return later to help Morley. Claire, Lorraine, Jane, Molly, and Trella quickly unloaded Clifford's wagon. The big man looked over at them and he exchanged a friendly wave with Clarence as he and Joe Marvin Benson hopped up behind the Clydesdales. Due at work and school, Clifford and Joe stopped briefly near the arborvitae and looked back across. What they saw goose bumped Joe. More than happiness, really, it was honor. Honor and gratitude such women as these were possible; not realizing, as Clifford did realize, that such women were standard issue. The horses whinnied, their steamy breath warming the frosty air, as Clifford started them back toward town.

Sniffer'd given his all is well bark when the cars and horses were arriving, but was obviously astonished at seeing the yard fill up. Hurriedly he sniffed each of them before running quickly off to wait out the calamity with his friends. Bunny, Toad, and old Jude were glad to see him coming. The home horses and Sniffer added their opinions to the melee as the women began their assault on the house.

Naddy James was the first to arrive at the stoop. She'd tugged Clydis' skirt. Clydis glanced down at her and placed a hand on her shoulder. She and Naddy were pressed back into the entry as the women filed in with their bundles of goods and cleaning utensils. Molly Toberton even had a coil of garden hose dangling from her shoulder while her hands grasped one end of a bed for Edith. She and Helen maneuvered the bed into the kitchen. Naddy still held to Clydis' skirt. "Please, can I?" Naddy pleaded. Clydis knelt beside her.

"You must be Naddy."

"Edith," Naddy said, "can I see her?"

"How wonderful of you," she hugged Naddy. Straightening, her head roaring, vision blurred, she took Naddy's hand. "Come with me," she said. "We'll go and see Edith."

Edith was soundly asleep in her dresser drawer crib; and soaking wet, the pillowcase diaper having failed dispassionately at containment. Naddy ignored the moisture as she began to rock the rocker, Edith in her arms. Edith's eyes popped open and she looked up at Naddy. She puckered to cry but then calmed, taking assurance from Naddy's sweet young voice as she began to tell her of her dolly who can close her eyes to go to sleep. Clydis pulled the pillowcase from a pillow. "Come, Naddy," she said. "You can help me change her."

She and Naddy'd become a team. Clydis was greatly relieved for she would have something to do. She would care for Naddy and she for her. They would be together. And together they would care for Edith.

A baby carriage had like magic appeared at the bedroom doorway and Clydis popped Edith into it. Naddy gleefully pushed it toward the kitchen.

Dozens of diapers were stacked on the kitchen table when they arrived there and Grandma Emma Groner was busy at the stove preparing scrambled eggs and oatmeal. And at the side sink, Helen had attached the garden hose. The hose had been Helgie Perkins' idea. She and Morley used it to water their garden, taking water from the kitchen sink faucet. The hose was rapidly disappearing out the window as Molly had grasped the far end of it, pulling it into the yard toward the cook pot, the washing machine, and their scrub and mop buckets.

Grandma, Clydis saw, gratefully, had taken charge of the kitchen. And Trella Mead, whom Ma introduced, had charge of sorting the clothing into piles, each a different category. Edith would have her turn at wearing Naddy's clothes. Naddy had outgrown them and Claire had given them to Lorraine. Now Lorraine's baby, many months from now, would be privileged to wear the clothes handed down from Edith. Clydis changed Edith into a downy soft diaper while Naddy selected the dress for her to wear.

Edith sat in her sparkling high chair wearing a large bib over her pretty red dress. She held a spoon in one hand while with the other she held scrambled eggs and between crammed in mouthfuls of the eggs, Grandma spooned in the creamy sweetened oatmeal. Taking a seat near Edith, Naddy reached for toast.

Clydis looked on; shaking, wanting to cling to Edith, knowing not what to say, what to do, feeling unworthy, overwhelmed by their goodness. Molly Toberton walked up to her and touched her arm. In turning to look at her, Clydis met her smiling face. "We heard you read at church," she said. "We know you're a good person."

Clydis smiled. She gave Molly a hug, held her close.

"Just relax," Molly said. "We're having fun."

Clydis sat down to the oatmeal Ma had set for her.

"Pa?" she asked, looking at Ma.

"Stayed in town. Working on a project. He'll be along soon. He'll not miss out on lunch."

She reached toast toward Clydis.

Clydis touched her hand, sharing warmth with Ma.

***

Pa Groner'd worked hard on the knot free quarter sawn oak window ledges for Emma, making them twice the normal width because she planned to set plants on them. He'd but to varnish and they'd be ready to install. Carefully he placed the cardboard pattern of a workhorse on a window ledge and next to this figure he placed a cutout representing a gentle mare. Ram and ewe, he placed also, and a hen and a rooster and two each of dog and cat and pig, and on until he'd crowded as many pairs as possible onto the window ledges. He held each figure tightly while he traced around it with his soft leaded pencil, then he was ready.

Emma had drawn the figures for him the last evening, before she'd decided it best that she visit Trella Mead. Trella gladly opened her shop for Emma to get cotton cloth for Edith's diapers. But her visit had soon grown into a project, that of arranging the warming for Clydis. Pa hadn't gone to the warming because he'd traced the figures onto the ledges, but had no means for cutting them out. He saved two of the ledges to use in building an ark. The ark would have a door in its side that hinged, thus serving as both a door and a ramp. And the roof of the ark would be hinged so that Edith would open the lid and see inside. At daybreak, right after breakfast, after Emma left for the warming, he carried the boards down the street.

Benjamin and Hanna Haimmer owned a small furniture shop with their living quarters partitioned behind it. "Oh, I hope she's all right," Hanna said, looking out the window.

Benjamin looked. "He's her grandfather." He studied, then, "Carrying something. Boards. I hope he stops in."

Robert walked on toward the front of the shop, passing the way he had by plan, hoping they'd see him. He sat down on a bench out in front, but had barely settled when Benjamin opened the door.

"Good morning. Come in. We're just at breakfast."

"I shouldn't be bothering you so early." Robert glanced down at the boards he held in his lap, then up at Benjamin. "I can pay," he said. "It's for Edith."

"Groner, isn't it?" Robert nodded, yes. "Robert, is it?"

"Yes. You go on back and finish your breakfast."

"Not without you, Robert. Please, join us for coffee."

Over coffee, and a roll or two, Robert explained his project. While he talked, Benjamin studied the beautiful oaken boards. To Benjamin a beautiful project was not possible if one began it with inferior wood. Benjamin liked what he saw here. During the conversation the Haimmers were able to confirm their suspicions. The baby and her mother had, indeed, been prisoners. "It just didn't ring as a normal family arrangement," Hanna said. "They drove right by here twice a day, some days more, it just didn't ever look right to us the way they were arranged."

Robert explained about their making a rag doll for Edith and about Edith's choosing her dad's red shirt for her blanket. "They were obliged to come away with naught but the clothes on their backs, certainly bringing no blanket nor doll nor any toys." He mentioned too that Clydis was injured and he remarked to being proud of the way the womenfolk were pitching in to help. Clydis had mentioning that Edith had liked to play with the animals of her ark set. "She said that Edith liked the giraffe but that she broke the neck off of it."

"I wish I'd known about the warming," Hanna said as she looked hungrily at the wood, and she glanced over at Benjamin.

She needn't have glanced at him. She'd glanced at him because she loved him, and then she said, "I believe I can finish out that table," wanting to be sure he'd caught her fever.

He'd already caught her fever while wondering how he could get her to catch his. Communications were established, and Benjamin smiled: "We can get to that table after a while. I've heard about a little lady who needs toys. Mayor Kroust cannot be all that rushed for his table."

***

Any job too big for him to do was the job little Harold James wanted to do. Empty, the wheelbarrow had pushed quite easily, wobbly but quite easily despite the inconvenience of the handles held at the height of his shoulders so that the courageous little six-year-old could keep its legs off the ground. He filled the wheelbarrow with chunks of firewood then his feet dug into the turf as he struggled and strained to lift and move the darn thing, but he couldn't budge it. Clarence'd been minding the door, mainly just holding it open and, between times, when he saw his chance, he'd struggled to remove the spring from it. At last he succeeded and promptly swung the door wide open and propped it flat against the outside of the entry. As he looked up, his eyes fell upon the struggling little Harold. "Guess you have your hands full," he greeted Harold as he walked over.

Harold didn't wish to give up his charge. "We need it for the fire," Harold gasped, trying once more to move the heavily loaded wheelbarrow. His feet dug in. His face grimaced, putting his all to the task.

"I'd guess you've earned a ride on this one," Clarence assured him as he removed a few of the hard maple chunks. He'd created a place for Harold to sit and without further ado, hoisted him up onto it. "Hold tight now."

Harold held tight, enjoying his ride. They were a team by then and Clarence was grateful. It would keep himself out of the way, give him something to do.

Soon, Clarence knew it was past the time for Harold to be in school, but he didn't mention it to Harold. He was sure that Harold liked school, but was certain, as well, that no greater lesson could be had by anyone than the one he was immersed within. Cheerfully they continued their toil with the wood.

Only once before had Claire James seen anyone start the Alamo engine that powered the electricity generator. Her brother-in-law, Charley, had started it with no apparent trouble last winter on a day when her family had been to visit Clarence. The Jameses were building a house down the road a bit from the Groners. They'd visited Clarence so that Charley, the house builder, could study the electrical and plumbing set up. As though she were Charley, she entered the power shed. A minute or so later, the Alamo burst to life, its loud wheezy chug-chug adding its industry to the vigorous day. At the sound of the engine, Clarence

10

looked over in time to see her nonchalantly stroll from the shed, as though for her this was an everyday occurrence. Seeing Clarence, she walked part way over to him. "How long do I leave it run?"

"It'll be about an hour. I generally cut it when the needle reads forty. Seems to be about right; also it's the time I'm usually done with chores and no longer wish to hear it."

"I thought so," she said.

"Don't be dissuaded," he said. "They're talking about putting a line out here from town. Telephone, too."

"Great," she replied, obviously pleased to hear about it. She'd walked on over to Harold.

"How goes it, big guy?" Harold smiled. He drew back, however, when she decided to run her fingers over his hair, as all moms seem impelled to do.

He held back still farther from her as if expecting the next treatment to be humiliating. He closed his eyes and, sure enough he got it, the old wet apron hem therapy. She'd managed to find a speck of dirt on his cheek. "Naddy's going with us," she told him. "We're going down to visit Mrs. Toberton and to see her baby. You're welcome to come with us."

"I really should stay and help Clarence. We're going to cut up the meat and throw it in."

"You're sure?"

"Dad will be here, too. He's coming for dinner."

"Okay, big guy. You be careful now. I'll see you later."

The Percherons were soon leaving the driveway pulling a wagon. The women had loaded the living room couch on board and the wide armed chair. Lorraine was seated in the chair holding Edith with Naddy sitting on an arm of the chair holding to Lorraine and looking down at Edith and chatting with her. Claire James, Grandma Groner, Trella Mead, and Clydis were seated on the couch. Satin handled the team. They were as one, a spiritual unity headed down Jericho to visit Billie and Clydene Billie.

During the past two hours Morley'd been sleeping. He'd protested at the time, but they would hear none of it. Lorraine knew he'd been up most of the night. She'd been out during the wee hours along with the other ladies, still loading Clifford's wagon. She'd been surprised to see Morley driving from the doctor's office. Helgie, Morley's wife, was the community midwife and one of Helgie's patients Lorraine had realized, was having a difficult time of it and needed a doctor. "You've worked all night," she scolded him. "Now, you lay down here."

Morley'd plopped on the horse blanket that she'd found in the barn and had been sound asleep before Helen could get a pillow under his head. They'd covered him with several layers of blankets. Awake at last he looked around as though bewildered. "Lordy," he remarked, having fixed his eyes on Clarence.

11

"Sorry, I . . ."

"You had me worried, Morley," Clarence joked. "I was about to wake you. What was I supposed to do with these peppers?"

"Peppers?"

"These green ones."

"You'd think I have to just explain every little thing to you. It's a wonder you just didn't sit there and eat um."

"I did eat one."

"Well, let's throw the rest in the soup."

Chapter Three

Looking from the kitchen window Molly Toberton saw they were putting the finishing touch to the soup. She and Helen had tidied the bathroom and were working in the kitchen while the others visited Billie and Clydene Billie. "We can put the corn in anytime, Morley," Molly said as she approached.

As she sat on a campstool and began husking the sweet corn, Clarence marveled at her vitality. For country folk the workday began long before daybreak with chores, which at the Tobertons included the milking of twelve cows. Breakfast was typically a hardy one and breakfast was followed by an early start in the fields. Late afternoon was again chore time and time to eat heavily at supper. As they were into the fall of the year, sundown would find them ready for sleep, but he knew that the women had ignored sleep to prepare for the warming and that by any measure Molly should be tired, yet Clarence could not keep up with her husking the corn.

Helen joined them at the cook site. "I hope she reads to them," she said as she began to husk an ear. Clarence had heard Clydis read during a Good Friday prayer meeting long ago and he knew what she meant. Clydis had read from the scriptures and Clarence had held up Edith, a tiny babe then, so that she could see and hear an angel speaking.

***

Billie heard them, a large group of them! Expecting only Clydis and Edith, her eyes darted about, checking to see if the room was sufficient to receive guests who were strangers. Grandma Tillie Mae placed Clydene beside her and left the room, meeting the visitors in the kitchen. "How is she?" someone whispered.

Tillie Mae said, "You're welcome. They're fine."

Oh, my! How many are there? And they'll all come in!

Clydis and Edith were the first to enter the room.

She kissed Billie and she brushed her hand across Clydene's velvety black hair. "Billie, she's so absolutely beautiful. May I hold her?" Billie looked about to cry yet managed to nod her head toward Clydene and to lift her babe toward Clydis. Gently holding Clydene Billie, talking softly to her mother, Billie's worry lines began to fade, but returned full force upon seeing a face she didn't recognize. Who?

Clydis introduced Lorraine Benson. After that the room filled with a warmhearted populace that kept Billie at the edge of tears due to happiness and pride. Within the bevy of kindness little Clydene was in high demand as each waited patiently their turn to cuddle her.

Naddy followed Clydene around person to person, sharing her with each of the ladies. Edith toddled along with Naddy. Finally Edith and Naddy placed their company with Clydene on Billie's bed. Claire watched over them as Naddy chatted with Billie.

While in England, on one of her surveys about town looking for an escape route, she'd happened onto the grave of Pocahontas in a small church cemetery. She'd recalled that Clarence'd mentioned Indians abiding in the Leadford area and quickly she'd developed interest in Pocahontas and read about her in a London library. After she'd met Billie, and seeing that she was expecting, Clydis'd penned a story for her about Pocahontas. That story she'd left behind during her escape with Edith but she'd stolen moments to rewrite it while the women were resurrecting the house. The room suddenly hushed.

Clydis had commenced with reading from a small notebook she'd taken from her coat pocket without any of them realizing she was about to read. The facts about Pocahontas she'd gleaned from a book by Smith. But she'd embellished the account with some imaginative rendering of her own and she read her story as though Pocahontas was speaking.

Pocahontas told of her life as a little girl living in an Indian village, later to live in a fort with whites. She married one of them and they had a beautiful baby. Several of the women had heard her read at church and weren't surprised at her ability, yet they were as spellbound as the others. Before she'd finished the passage little Naddy crawled from the bed and up onto Clydis' lap. Clydis had trained as an elocutionist in New York and in Britain. She was thrilled that she could please them.

***

"Ready!" Jane called from an open window. Clarence hadn't been inside the house all morning, and was glad for the excuse to go in. Harold ran ahead, wanting to be first at whatever she was ready to do.

The Detroit potbelly was disassembled down to its body and legs and ropes were tied beneath the base of it and fashioned into four loops. Harold rushed over and grabbed one of the loops. Molly, Helen, and Jane each gripped a loop. Clarence took Harold's hand from his loop, but held onto Harold's hand. "Hold me steady, now, you hear, Harold? This won't be easy." Harold did a fine job of steadying Clarence as they lugged the potbelly into the living room.

Just before noon, Clifford James, in step with the women returning from Tobertons, swooped in past Edith's tree. Clifford helped unload the wagon, placing the couch and the wide armed chair on the lawn near the front steps. Edith went inside the house, lunch and naptime for her, while Naddy and Harold gleefully began jumping on the couch.

Suddenly Naddy's yell pierced the tranquil air! Drawing adults as a magnet, and all of them tore after old Sniffer.

"Kitty! Kitty!" She caught onto Sniffer and began yanked meanly at him, tears streaming her face. "Kitty! Kitty!"

Harold jumped, trying to latch onto a lower limb of the maple, intending to climb for the calico cat Sniffer'd treed. "Kitty! Kitty!"

Clifford enfolded his trembling daughter. "Don't worry. We'll get Kitty down," he said. "Clarence, if you take the dog into the house a minute, the cat will come down."

The cat rode every day with Clifford and was as much a fixture with him as was his leather apron and his pistol. He delivered freight from the railroad. Clifford upped his Clydesdales. The cat streaked from the tree to resume its place on his leather apron. He placed the cat in its box under the seat.

"Soups ready!" Helen yelled.

The kids streaked to join Clifford who was first behind Clarence.

Clarence downed fours ears of the corn and as many bowls of soup. The corn was really ripe, perhaps even over mature for some people, but just the way he liked it. Boiled to perfection then dipped into a crock of melted butter, followed by a light sprinkling of salt, the corn could not have been more satisfying.

Morley'd gone to fetch Helgie and Pa while the sweet corn boiled and they arrived in time for dinner. The women gathered around Helgie to hear about Bell Thompkin's ninth. Bell'd had a difficult time and they wanted to hear about it.

While the discussion of birthing was going forth, Clydis drifted over to Clarence and took his hand. She led him over to the wide armed chair. They stood beside it.

"I don't want the chair," she said. "Last night, during the night, after you'd fixed me up in it, I became frightened, recalling the awful consequences it'd led to."

He looked at it a moment then squeezed her hand fondly. "I'm sorry you were scared. But, dear, it's a different chair now. It's not the awful chair anymore. It's the chair we'll sit in when we read to Edith."

She returned his squeeze, holding close to him, feeling better. Softly, her voice tickling his ear, "It is a different chair," she whispered. "We'll keep it. It's the chair we'll sit in while we read to Edith."

During that night, Clarence returned to work, joining Red Toberton. They went about the work more by habit than cognition, his mind on Clydis and Edith, Red's on Billie and Clydene. At three-thirty, he sent Red on home to be with his family. Now toiling alone, he found himself fretting that Mrs. Klinert would return in the night to grab Edith. "Ridiculous!" he told himself, knowing that Sniffer was on guard and believing Clydis would tear her mother to shreds should she brazen an attempt to get Edith. Upon the impetus of those brave thoughts his mind drifted to pleasantries.

Foremost were his recollections of the day just past. Clydis had been treated as a friend; a friend in need and they'd left no doubt in her mind. She was an accepted member of the community. Continuing his muse, he envisioned his little family functioning and growing as a part of community, of neighbors, of friends; and his step was light as he moved through the factory with an oil can.

About to oil the rollers of a conveyor belt, he paused, and his head snapped toward the factory door. Moments later he was standing on the loading dock, his eyes straining up Moppit Hill, boring off toward their home on Jericho. What is it? What is it? His arms swung at his sides, his fists clinched, his body leaning toward Bunny's stable, but with his first step toward home he suddenly felt calm. Still in wonder, his head shaking side to side, he resumed his work.

He fought to stay calm, to keep his head, to do a good job. But shortly his hand shot out, grabbing the telephone. "Midge, ring Morley Perkins."

Helgie answered. "Clarence, I knew it'd be you. They're okay. Marshal Rockney's over there. He said if you called for you to stay put. They're okay."

"What happened?"

"We heard Sniffer growling and barking so we called Rockney."

"They're okay?"

"Yes. Morley just came in. Marsh tore out here and called to Clydis. She said they were okay so Morley just came back in to tell me. Marsh and Sniffer are looking around the yard. Our yard, too. They're okay. He hasn't seen anybody, but he's looking real good. He said you needn't rush home from work."

"Well, I sure want too. Thanks, Helgie."

Nervously, he set back to work. Not walking now, running. Running from one task to another. As he rushed into the boiler room, John Purley Benson grabbed him. "Clarence!"

A limp rag now, he grabbed John Purley. "John Purley. Oh, my gosh, I'm scared!"

"Midge called dad. Dad's a deputy, did you know? On call automatic whenever the marshal's called away. Dad woke me. I figured you'd want to get home. I've saddled Bunny. Strawflower's about done in."

They found no trace of Mrs. Klinert but knew it had to've been her. Arriving home, he'd found Clydis with Edith cuddled in the wide armed chair. Teeth clinched, she'd looked up at him. "She tried it. But she'll never get Edith. She'll never get Edith."

Gently he brushed her bangs from her crinkled forehead and held his hand there. He kissed the top of her head.

Her hand came up to rest upon his. "Sniffer warned us."

"He's the best dog in the world."

"We must keep him inside after this, when you're gone. She might shoot him."

"Sure, we will. And I'm going to stay home, too. I'll not return to work until I can do so without being scared out of my mind."

***

He didn't know why Clydis and Edith had gone away. For over a year, while they were gone, he'd pounded his brain trying to figure it out. Now he could see that it hurt her to talk about it. Hurt? No, it's terror! Those scars, he just knew, it was about them. He could imagine it taking a long time for him to find the answers. Not that she wouldn't explain it if he'd ask, but to ask sent her into terror and the terror centered upon Edith. He'd already seen that scars weren't on Edith so he guessed Mrs. Klinert wanted to hurt her, rather than that she had, but she'd hurt Clydis! He'd seen the scars on Clydis.

In intimacy he'd seen them. "What happened?" he'd said. She'd glared at him and he'd shivered, himself afraid. For fear that he'd lose her, he'd not again asked, but now he could, but he couldn't. When reminded of her past she became terrified, but for Edith, not for herself? Quandary tossed him in the night. But touching her calmed him; and she didn't seem to mind his touching her. Contented, he could sleep. And then sometimes he felt warmth during his sleep and he'd come awake and feel her touching him, but she'd be asleep. The touch. Oh, how wonderful. And after several days he came to realize that recalling the touch was enough to calm him no matter the time of day nor the distance from her. Then he knew why Clydis touched him. And he knew he could return to work.

***

The Moppit mill made thousands of pounds of paper every day. Each working day Pal Toberton hauled huge rolls of it to the box plant in Grand Rapids or to the rail yard for shipment elsewhere. Clarence was in charge of maintenance and utilities at the mill. He didn't make paper nor did any of his crew. Their work made it possible for the others to make paper. Clarence worked a ten-hour shift, six days a week, his shift overlapping that of John Purley's and Red's. As well, his crew included Tom and Rik Toberton such that two of the daily eight-hour shifts were doubled manned.

He'd begun his work at the mill during his sixteenth year, after he'd completed all eight grades at the one room school. Before that, he'd worked with Pa collecting rags and paper for the mill. They'd become acquainted with Hermes Luke in connection with delivering the paper and rags, and Hermes hired Clarence as mill sweeper. Before hiring Clarence, Hermes and his brother Raymond, with Red Toberton part-time, carried full responsibility for mill maintenance and utilities. Age and illness forced Raymond into retirement. Hermes, Red, and Clarence handled the job until Hermes died at it. Hermes had trained Clarence to replace himself so Clarence'd become boss; to Red's relief. Often times the work was a mind boggle and as often they'd work overtime, sometimes nearly living at the mill. Even a normal shift pained Red. At the time of Red's hiring, he was crippled, one leg shortened and the knee stiffened by a she bear while he was cutting wood and, though he did his work well and that he liked, and needed, the work, he'd been glad when Clarence became the boss. With Clarence back, routine returned at the mill, but time was ticking. The mind boggle lay ahead. No one knew when. Tick, tick, tick, tick; Clarence braced himself.

As if problems that could arise at any time at the mill weren't enough, a cloud more ominous than the mill lay over him. A while back, long before she and Edith'd returned, he'd barged into the Klinert residence to try to see them, to talk to her, to get her to see that he loved them and that he wanted them to come home, but in the effort a vase was smashed. And a list of charges far exceeding the smashed vase was filed against him by Lucious Klinert. Clarence was under arrest. Free now on his own recognizance, he fearfully awaited his trial in Judge Barley's court.

Fine thing for a deputy!

And he wished he weren't a deputy. Marshal Rockney had sworn him in during the summer. That act was intended to enlist Clarence's help in a case Rockney was working on. A man professing to be a minister, the Right Reverend Simon E. Lowgo, had laid hands to Billie Toberton, a Potawatomie Indian princess and wife of Red Toberton. As a friend of the Tobertons, Clarence knew more about the case than did Rockney so they'd worked together to resolve it. In complication to the issue, Red Toberton had been shot in the leg. Then while gimped in one leg due to the she bear and while wounded in the other leg by Rockney, Red had set out for Missouri in an effort to find and kill Simon E. Lowgo. The situation had resolved by now, Red was home and Lowgo in prison, but the marshal was reluctant to release Clarence as deputy, stating that he still needed him. Clarence hadn't wanted to serve as a deputy in the first place. But his respect and admiration for Marsh Rockney, a family friend, had bonded him to service.

Crippled in both legs, Red was in constant pain and Clarence knew it. Doctors associated with a Grand Rapids hospital had told Red they could, they believed, help him. It would be a difficult reconstruction and would put him out of work for several months. It would mean longer hours at the mill they all knew, and were willing, yet he hated to lose Red. He felt a keen personal desire to be home as much as possible with Edith and Clydis. He loved them and he feared for their safety, yet to spend more time with them meant delaying Red's restoration. "Darn it! Am I acting like a tyrant?"

And was he taking undue advantage of Ma! In his youth she'd been taken from them with TB. Now finally, and by God's grace, she'd remitted and was home but he worried that she was doing too much. By five-thirty every morning she cruised in past Edith's arborvitae driving her sprightly little Jeffery Rambler. A spry little lady with salt and pepper hair, she served as Clydis' wake up alarm clock, as if one were needed. Edith had become an early riser and no sooner had Clydis changed her than she'd toddle into the kitchen to greet Grandma. Clarence was party to those scenes only through his imagination for by the time he came in from chores Ma and Clydis'd have breakfast ready for him, and he'd see Edith gleefully mauling hers. Likely as not, Ma'd already be busy at the darning basket by then and the women's conversation would be of the impending day's work. Besides doing the perpetual laundry, they'd canned a quarter of beef and half a hog in the week or so Ma'd been coming; and he'd told Pa he'd see to it she'd not overdo! He should've known better than to make such boast to Pa, and he told him so, and Pa'd just smiled his soft appreciative smile and nodded his head. "Your Ma's always been a doer," Pa said.

Clarence tried to remember her working so hard, but he couldn't. His memory was of her love. Gosh, he'd missed her when she went away, and he'd tried not to cry, but he did some and he knew Pa knew it. Pa'd said, "She'd want us to just keep on doing the best we can, son." And he'd seen that tears twinkled Pa's eyes. That'd been the fall Pa'd given up his job as a section hand on the Pennsylvania railroad and had began his daily toil collecting paper and rags for the Moppit mill. Once a month he'd go to Battle Creek to see his Emma and once a year, in the fall before school set it, he'd go with Pa. She'd be frail and tired, her eyes blank, anxious, but she'd be smiling for him. That's how he remembered her to be, but in his compassion for her he'd missed her strength. Now he saw her as one of the strongest, grittiest, people he'd ever seen; and knew she'd always been that way. Well the meat's canned so now maybe she'll slow a little, he thought, and his thinking went on to include an appreciation for Dr. Laird.

Laird, without being asked, had come out to the house to remove Clydis' stitches, ending one dread.

The Groners had dreaded going to Leadford. The event of stitch removal was to be their first foray into town since she'd returned. Laird's appearance made the trip unnecessary and they'd breathed a sigh of relief, but knew that soon they'd have to venture into the Klinert den. Ma and Pa, Helgie and Morley, and others, including Marsh Rockney, had willingly ran errands to meet their need for groceries and other items from town, yet he worried that Clydis was going stir crazy and would soon not be able to resist leaving the farm.

Already she was taking walks with Edith and Sniffer around the yard and buildings and she'd said the leaves should to be raked. She wanted to go outside despite the fact that upon several occasions recently Sniffer had barked his throaty "Wrolf! Wrolf!" Her confidence had bolstered each time they'd found nobody outside ready to grab Edith and again she'd lamented their need to rake leaves.

Chapter Four

A raw wind blew across Kent County, stripping naked the trees in the north yard of the small farm on Jericho, except for one leaf. The leaf fluttered in the wind for a time in defiance of the fall season, but seasons are relentless, the leaf ephemeral and finally the wind claimed it. The leaf sailed to the privet hedge and clung there.

A little girl going on two played in the fallen leaves near the privet. Her mother raked the leaves, lifting them to the wind and the wind carried them to the privet. Edith laughed and squealed with glee as she chased the leaves.

On the other side of the privet lay Jericho Road and across the road stood a dense stand of naked sumac. Behind the sumac along the edge of the field, her footfalls softened by the young winter wheat that the field had sprouted, there cautiously approached a villainous woman. The woman was drawn toward the gleeful chatter of the little girl who played in the leaves beyond the privet. That was as close as Mrs. Klinert had been to the little girl. On previous attempts an irascible contemptuous dog had barked, but on that day the dog did not hear her, did not bark, and the woman crept closer until she stood not thirty feet from the little girl.

The little girl's attention was drawn to a single leaf lodged in the privet. The leaf was basically russet brown in color but still held a generous blush of dark red. Edith toddled toward the leaf.

Sniffer lay in lee of the wind near the house. He watched as little Edith reached for the leaf. "Gammer," she said. "Gammer. Gammer." Old Sniffer's eyesight was poor, but his hearing and sense of smell were keen. The wind had carried her sound and scent away from him and the rustling leaves had hidden her from him, but now he saw her. "Wrolf! Wrolf!" his bark was throaty as he sprang to his feet. Clydis joined Sniffer in a mad dash toward Edith.

Beyond the sumac the figure slinked away and crept furtively down along the sumac that bordered the wheat field. Nervous, she walked swiftly to where her

Franklin stood with its motor idling. The car was hidden from Cross Road by a row of thornapples and from the present view of Clydis by the sumac and by a knoll in the wheat field. Moments later the car rushed from the farm lane which served the field, careening onto Cross thence back toward Leadford.

"Gammer." Edith babbled as Clydis picked her up. Edith had a leaf clamped between her thumb and the hand of her mitten. She brushed the leaf against her mother's face.

"Oh, did you find a pretty leaf," Clydis cooed to her. "Leaf," Clydis pronounced distinctly.

"Eff," Edith repeated. She held onto the leaf as Clydis held her close and dashed for the house, Sniffer beside them.

Clydis, Edith, and Sniffer rushed into the kitchen where Grandma Emma sat with her darning basket and one of Clarence's holed socks. She looked up and smiled at seeing their rosy cheeks. But her smile quickly dimmed as she saw the determined stern look in Clydis and as Clydis lowered Edith to the floor, Grandma caught her eye and was afraid. "Eff." Edith toddled over and held the leaf toward her grandma. "Eff."

Grandma smiled down at her. "Pretty leaf," she said.

In a moment Clydis emerged from the pantry, a box of phosphate wooden matches in her hand. "I'll be out for a while," she explained. "I have leaves to burn."

Emma said, "It's too windy, isn't it, to burn leaves?" Her lips pursed as she studied her daughter-in-law.

Clydis stood her ground. "My mother was out there beyond the hedge. Within feet of Edith. I will not wait longer. I'll burn the leaves in the privet."

Emma nodded agreement. "You might also ask Morley and Helgie who owns the field. The owner may agree to our removing the sumac as well."

"I will, but I cannot wait longer on the hedge. The leaves have blocked it, making it difficult to detect anybody approaching from that direction." Clydis left the kitchen carrying the matches.

She struck her match near the mailbox at the south end of the hedgerow. Her fire was within reach of the Perkins yard and home, sixty feet distant across the road. The hedge stood six foot in height. Leaves were lodged in it and piled beside it. Within minutes the flames towered skyward and smoke rolled toward the Perkins home and toward Leadford. Morley and Helgie were alerted by the odor of smoke and the crackle of angry flame as it snapped through dry leaves and brush. They ran from their house and took their place beside Clydis. The group managed to keep the flames under control at the south end of the hedge row, short of the mail box and of Edith's arborvitae, sparing the Perkins property, but by concentrating their efforts and vigilance there, they compromised the sumac. Flames jumped the road and roared through the sumac toward Cross. Along Cross the westerly wind

22

greatly advantaged the flames, sending a holocaust toward Leadford.

Seeing smoke in the distance, fire chief Will Bean came out to investigate. His area of concern was the town of Leadford and, obviously, the blaze was beyond the town limits. And the river, bordering the town from Lead Bridge to Lower Lead Bridge would offer a measure of protection. But he spoke his concern: "Provided the sparks didn't leap the river." There were moreover several field margins, and small wooded areas that could enable the blaze to reach residences further north along the western side of the river. Bean became increasingly concerned as he watched the bellowing smoke. The town owned a horse drawn tanker with its hand operated pump in addition to an independent tank wagon for bringing extra water. Bean positioned his small force of six men at the town limits facing the blaze. Their anxiety peaked when at the corner of Jericho and Cross he saw the flames soar upward. Spark invested smoke towered into the sky. Bean chose a gap in the field border, where a farm lane served the field off Cross, to begin a backfire. His men also positioned on Cross and began shooting precious water at the oncoming flames.

In less than an hour's time, the conflagration was brought under control. The smoke blackened, tired, thirsty fire fighters stood by their meager equipment, much relieved. "Refill the tanker," Bean directed. He would take no chances with this one. The west wind still shot sparks into the air and here and there little blazes were springing where moments earlier the fire had seemed dead.

The fighters with the pumper pulled into the field and started up that side of the blackened way putting out any smokes as that went. Clydis had hurried across the wheat field angling ahead of the fire as it burned along Cross. She carried a broom.

She'd traveled far in her effort to out distance the conflagration. Thus Bean saw her coming from the east, her way opposing the route the blaze had taken. Her broom now little more than a stub and with her hair and eyebrows singed, she walked right up to Bean. Bean, thrilled to be confronted by a beautiful young woman, was stepping foot to foot as she approached. He worried and he wondered what he should say to an obvious heroine who had fearlessly fought the blaze. He was dearly shocked when the first words she uttered to him were: "The fire's my fault. I lit it."

At once disgusted, "Burning leaves?" He hated leaf burning. Every fall he'd fought such fires and dreadfully often he'd been obliged to fight the fires, a house or another building, lit by the fires. Clydis looked far less beautiful to him now. Just another thoughtless fool hearted leaf burner. They never learn. Sadly but sharply, he said, "You should've known better." He glared at her. "We risked our lives."

"I know, I know. And I'm sorry." He continued his glare. "The blaze is my fault. I want you to send out the marshal. There are mitigating circumstances."

23

"Chief, there're tracks in this field we didn't make!" one of the fire fighters shouted. "Automobile tracks!" Will Bean and Clydis moved swiftly over to investigate.

"These the mitigation you spoke of?"

"I believe so," she answered.

"I'll send out the marshal."

***

Marshal Rockney's main frustration thus far in his day had been an encounter with Purvis, attorney for the Klinerts. Purvis had insisted that Clarence Groner be returned to Rockney's lock up. Lawyer Purvis was himself suffering frustration, his frustration caused by Lucious Klinert.

Klinert was fuming two frustrations. His first had been that the divorce of his daughter, Clydis, from Clarence Groner had not occurred because on the day before the court date set for the procedure that moon eyed lovesick daughter of his ran back to that ridiculous clod. Okay, that part may be over, he told himself, but he still had the lecherous scoundrel. Make no mistake about that, he thought. When we finish in court on the other charges, the scamp will be left totally destroyed!

He knew that Mrs. Klinert had counted heavily on the outcome of the divorce, anticipating that it would sever forever Clarence's influence over and his rights to Edith. Edith had been Mrs. Klinert's project, her second chance. She felt that she'd failed in her attempt to make a lady, in her image of a lady, of Clydis. Now she'd lost Edith. When he'd first learned of his daughter's defection, Lucious touted: "Fear not, love. You'll shortly have them back." His thought was to the upcoming trial. He'd filed a long list of charges against Clarence. Certain his son-in-law would be imprisoned, he'd said to her, "Patience, my love. You'll have them both returned shortly," but the boast had cheered her little more than he'd been cheered by his present frustration.

At the time that Clydis ran back to that carnal scamp Klinert had been in Detroit closing a land deal which would lead to his owning an automobile factory. The outcome of his dealings in Detroit had greatly pleased him. Now for some real fun, he'd thought while on his trip back to Leadford. Upon his arrival he'd been sobered but momentarily because of the divorce failure. His wife had muffed that, but no matter, the trial would ruin Clarence Groner. Groner would soon be incarcerated and for a very long time. Lucious had implored Purvis to hurry ahead on the trial procedure.

Purvis had driven to Leadford and reviewed the evidence file on Clarence Groner. As Marsh Rockney'd predicted, Purvis saw that the case against Clarence held nowhere near the potential his client, Lucious, was counting upon. Earlier that morning Rockney had waxed content that Lucious would drop the charges against

Clarence. Now Purvis had thumped Rockney's desk, demanding emphatically that Clarence be returned to the lockup to await his trial!

The hard-boiled attitude of Purvis was a ruse. Purvis had already decided they should drop the charges. He'd pointed out to Lucious that the vase Clarence had smashed the day he entered the Klinert home was not a priceless vase from India, as Mrs. Klinert claimed. It was a nice vase, beautiful and beautifully crafted surely, but a vase which could have been purchased at modest cost in Mexico. Further he told Lucious that his forceful entry charge was weak in that Clydis had let Clarence into the house and that she'd later abetted his departure from the premises. Lucious recklessly vent his extreme frustration: "If you've no guts I'll get another attorney," he bellowed. "I want him put away for life!"

Purvis'd had no option but to press Rockney. In frustration Rockney'd called Jason Plinkly, Clarence's attorney. The two attorneys were in session presently. Rockney could do nothing but sit in thwart, waiting to see what the legal system would require of him regarding Clarence.

***

Rockney was much relieved when smoked-soiled Chief Will Bean entered his office to fill him in on the fire. "Thanks, Will. I'll take it from here."

Frustration was put at bay. Rockney was lighted by the fire set by Clydis. Eagerly he gathered his evidence bags and his plaster powder and charged to the wheat field. His investigation led him all the way up to the Groner yard.

Just arriving home from Moppit, Clarence received his first shock upon seeing that while he was away at work a fire had threatened the Perkins home and his own. Secondly, he was shocked to see Marshal Rockney poking around in the ashes. "My gosh, Marsh, what happened? Is Edith all right?"

"They're okay, Clarence. Go in the house. Stay there please. I'll be along in a few minutes."

Clydis and grandma filled him in on the reason for the fire. "You did right, Clydis," he assured her.

"Emma, you'll need some sheets of paper a ruler and a pencil," he greeted upon entering the kitchen and seeing her there. "I want a drawing of this front yard to the middle of the road. I want an overlapping sketch, beginning with the hedgerow and extending into the wheat field. I want a sketch of the wheat field's north side, the sketch extending from the middle of Cross and covering the roadside and the wheat field extending about a hundred feet into the wheat field. Clarence, you help your mother. Clydis, I want you outside a minute."

Emma had produced her sketches by the time Clydis explained the situation as it had been in the front yard. They returned to the kitchen where Rockney filled in the sketches with numbers indicating various locations mentioned by Clydis.

"Gerff," she said, poking him with the oaken giraffe she held. He looked down at her, but kept writing, intent on accuracy in the statement Clydis would sign. "Gerff," she insisted. Marsh glanced at her.

"Nice giraffe." He kept at his writing; and was soon finished with it and could turn his full attention to Edith.

As he sat on the floor next to the beautiful child, his thoughts returned to an incident now nearly a year past. "No. You listen!" Clarence had yelled back at him. "I want to tell you. Tell you about her." What on earth drives this man, he remembered himself thinking. "She has brown hair," Clarence had said, "and it's curly and it jiggles just a little when she moves. Her face is soft and chubby and pink and her legs look strong. I'd bet she can walk real well." Marsh'd looked at him wondrously. "That's why I went, Marsh. I didn't get a chance to hold her, even to touch her, but I saw her, Marsh. Don't you see? I love her." Marsh understood then why Clarence had barged into the Klinert home. His barging in had led to the present charges against him, but Marsh understood the reason for Clarence's rashness. The reason was with him now. "Orse," she said, holding it toward him.

"Horse," Marsh confirmed. He wished this could be his final chapter of the day. Reluctantly he rose to his feet, his hand touching her bouncing curly brown hair. "Thank you. She's a beautiful child. I'll be on my way."

Chapter Five

The morning sun shined brightly from a clear azure sky. Clarence stood shivering while he talked with Molly and Tom Toberton. It was a deceptively cold November day, 1906. The sun shined brightly, but it was cold, make no mistake. He edged toward the house with its warm cheery kitchen as they talked. "Bradley Hinds had talked of clearing all of that along his field anyway," Tom was saying. "We'll be seeing him about his cow, so I'll mention it. I'm sure he'll be glad it burned."

"Do you think Morley will give up his brindle?" Molly wanted to know.

"I'd miss that old Guernsey myself," Clarence answered. "But I'm agreed you should ask it. I'd bet certain that Morley'd sell her if you said I'm agreed to it." They were entering the kitchen, Clarence with the brindle's morning milk contribution sloshing in his bucket.

He began cranking the milk through the cream separator. "We'd want to buy that too," Molly said. "New is it?"

"Had it a week. Works good." As he turned the crank rich yellow cream poured from one spigot while pearly white milk streamed from another. "Morley takes the cream to Jennifer Faygard. Roger motorized the churn she uses to churn butter." He grinned up from his cranking. "We get butter in trade."

Molly nodded thoughtfully before saying, "Papa Clevis Harold will manage the operation, but we'll all be involved in both dairy and farm," she went on to explain, "and our men will keep their jobs at the paper mill." Butter could be good business, too, she thought.

Of the wives, Molly had natural acumen for business. Clarence encouraged them. "It sounds like good thinking." She nodded, a finger on her chin. Molly's smooth dark, nearly black, hair topped her height of five foot four inches, making her taller than Billie by and inch. Helen was barely taller than Molly, but Helen was much slighter in build than were her sister dairymaids. In contrast, Jane, at six foot, towered over three of the wives, but stood but a bit taller than Satin. The

Tobertons where intelligent and they were hard working people. A glance at Molly confirmed his thoughts. He knew the dairy would succeed, but struggled with the courage to tell them of a mind boggle looming at the mill.

"I'll do my best to keep you guys off overtime." His cranking stopped, the separator wound down. "But you'll be on forty eight hour, or more, weeks for a while." Molly's eyes bugged.

"The flutter wheels?"

"Yes, two flutter wheels to lighten the load on the water wheel, so the wheel can generate electricity. More electricity than we'll need, by the way, Molly, so a line will go to the north, toward you."

"We're getting set up with the dairy as though we'll have electricity. Tom guessed that a line may come to us either from Leadford or from Moppit mill." Tom had slipped his arm around her waist.

"We figured to buy a used refrigerator car to use as our cooler," Tom said.

Clarence raised an eyebrow. "Sure, we know," Tom agreed. "It will be a tough job lugging it home from Leadford, but this winter when the road is frozen we plan to drag it home." Clarence could picture in his mind the magnitude of that adventure. He looked forward to his being involved in it. "We've ordered the refrigerator car. It'll soon be here."

Edith toddled into the kitchen with her doll clutched under an arm, its limbs flapping. She held a giraffe by its neck and was chewing on its rear legs. "Gerff," she greeted, holding her arms toward Molly. Molly lifted Edith to her lap. Edith held the giraffe close enough to Molly's eye to nearly touch it. "Gerff." She pushed the doll toward Molly's face. "Dollie wet." Molly's head craned rearward.

"She'll want to select a clean dress for her doll, Molly." Bacon sizzled. Edith climbed down from Molly's lap and hurried to her stack of doll dresses. Selecting a green one, she toddled back to Molly. The dress matched Edith's. Both were fabricated from printed feed sacks, the yard goods having been supplied by Grandma Emma Groner.

Soon Edith was deep within her poached eggs and milk toast. Old Sniffer sat beside her high chair patiently waiting for any spill that might come his way. He was just reaching for a generous plop of soggy toast as the Toberton's were leaving.

"Wish you luck," Clarence said, "and you remember, I want to help with that train car."

"The dairy is a wonderful idea," Clydis said.

***

Marsh Rockney by that time had arrived at the Klinert residence armed with a search warrant and was to arrest Mrs. Klinert. He'd enlisted the help of Deputy Ed Benson and of Tulip Board. Tulip's restaurant supplied food to the occupants of Rockney's lockup. Tulip would help Rockney during the time Mrs. Klinert was caged up. He couldn't hold her long, he knew, unless Clydis pressed charges.

Rockney didn't expect Clydis to press charges. However misguided and dangerous her mother was, and had been, the child seldom suffered duress sufficient to charge the parent. Bradley Hinds had charged Mrs. Klinert with trespass of his wheat field but the action wouldn't be sufficient to keep her locked up. His thinking was that by holding her even temporarily, he might convince Mrs. Klinert that her best discretion would be to leave town, desisting her quest for Edith.

***

Having failed in his attempt to have Groner jailed, attorney Purvis had driven back down the plank road to his home in Kalamazoo. No sooner had he arrived than his phone rang. "Get back up here," Lucious insisted, "these fools have incarcerated my wife."

Too tired to drive his car all the way back to Leadford, Purvis took the train north from Kalamazoo. He slept soundly on the train, not even awakening during the station stop at Grand Rapids, and arrived at Leadford with a backache and a stiff neck just after noon. Appalled that nobody met his train, he walked miserably over to the Klinert Ford agency. Looking up from some paperwork were John and Henry Clout of the sales staff, so Purvis was met at the agency door.

"Good afternoon, Mr. Purvis. Henry and I need to be ready to ship by two this afternoon to catch the south bound. We're moving the Power Wagon inventory to Detroit. You may want to wait in the kitchenette. If we can be of any help, feel free to call on us. A telephone, by the way, if you need one, is here in our office."

"Thanks."

In the agency kitchenette he perked coffee. Now seated at the table with his mug of scalding black elixir, he looked around the small room.

A child's crib caught the corner of his eye. Moving to the other side of the table to ease his stiff neck placed the crib directly in front of him and the doorway to the show room was in view to his right. Looking past the rear of a Ford he could see across the showroom to the outside door of the agency. Returning his scan to the kitchenette he saw that the foot of the crib was guarded by shelving upon which toys and clothing for a female child were neatly arranged. In front of the crib, between it and the table, a lounge chair was located. Purvis suddenly felt as though something crawled upon his back! An evil presence pervaded and coffee spilled as he jumped from the chair.

He didn't want to believe where his thought had taken him. She would be a prisoner here, he thought again as he again scanned the room. This chair and the lounge were guard stations. The child was the prisoner and had been guarded by the grandmother. Ridiculous, he told himself. "Purvis you're tired, disgusted, and you hurt all over. Now, get smart for gosh sakes!" He went into the room next door and took a seat with the Clout brothers.

"He's moving the Power Wagons, you said?"

"Yes. Well, we haven't sold any since selling two more to the paper mill. The trucks do better on firm ground. There are a lot of wood-paved streets in the big cities and a lot more industry, of course."

"I've been in conference with the Grand Rapids city council and with the Kent County board," Purvis said. "They plan to have the best system of county roads in the state; all leading to Grand Rapids, of course."

"Henry and I think it'll not only improve the sale of trucks, but even more so, cars."

"You're thinking right."

Henry caught John's eye, catching a slight nod from him, before turning to Purvis to ask: "Mr. Purvis, may we confide in you?"

Purvis arched an eyebrow. "Yes," He smiled, "and with client confidentiality privileges."

Purvis had a keen nose for business, seeing them indeed as clients. He'd seen them in serious contemplation; and now waited, finding no surprise as Henry said, "We'd like to buy this agency."

"Oh." He peered at them. "Why would he sell?"

"We think he isn't happy here. Family trouble mainly, as we're sure you know about; and we haven't sold a single car nor have we serviced or repaired a single car since Mrs. Groner left here with baby Edith. Yet we look across and see that Faygard's doing a landslide business servicing or repairing our Fords. It looks to us like a boycott of the Klinert agency. We think it's likely he'll decide to sell and get out."

John handed Purvis a sheath of papers. Purvis scanned through the neat columns. "I'll back you fellows." All smiles, they settled back. "Lucious will be here soon. I'll meet with him in his office. If he mentions selling out, I'll tell him that I know of some good prospects."

***

Lucious Klinert began his first automobile sales agency in Clyde, Michigan selling Oldsmobile and Rambler. He did well with the agency despite there being very few roadways appropriate to travel except by horse or oxen. He was a respected man in the town, but not an admired one; better respect than love had become his motto. He was ambitious and his ambition would drive him far.

Coupled with him was Mrs. Klinert, summer festival queen three years running, who had no interest in the automobile business except the wealth and opportunity it prevailed them in the hands of Lucious. They'd left Clyde seeking grander horizons, their only remaining legacy of their hometown being Clydis. Clydis was born in Kalamazoo, far away from the little burg of Clyde, yet the town had inspired her name. By age three Clydis was attended by her first tutor, teaching posture, proper dress and mannerisms, her rearing to be spent separate from mundane society; as Mrs. Klinert envisioned royalty ladies to have been reared.

Clydis had been strictly Mrs. Klinert's project. But after they'd moved to Leadford to open the Rambler and, later, the Ford agency, her project began to impede business as it expanded to include Clarence; and later, to include Edith. Lucious'd had enough. He wanted out. Not just out of Leadford, but out! Out of all of it. He planned to have Purvis encourage the levy of an attempted kidnap charge upon his wife. Having been so charged, nobody could wonder as to his reason for divorcing her. As far as he was concerned, their sojourning the grand horizons was over.

Lucious had his mind made up by the time he was meeting with attorney Purvis. "I want to see Groner hang," Lucious expounded.

"The case against him just isn't there," he tried again to explain. "I'm again recommending that you drop the charges against Clarence Groner."

There are the three things, besides the Groner trial, that I want you to do," Lucious ranted. "Get her charged with kidnapping, arrange my divorce, and sell the agency."

"Lucious, it is way beyond by good conscience, let alone my ability, to foster her arrest for kidnapping. I'll have nothing to do with that." He went on to say, "And as to a divorce, I will not negotiate that either." Lucious glared at him. "Lucious, you're being far too rash, in my opinion." Lucious continued to glare. "Give the situation some time, Lucious. That's my recommendation."

"I'll divorce her whether or not the other," he expounded. "I've had all of her business disrupting miserable projects that I'm going to stand." Purvis knew that he meant it.

"I'll see to moving the agency," he assured Lucious. "It'll not be hard to find a buyer. And that is credit to you, my friend. You really know how to do business." Lucious smiled and nodded his head.

"That's twelve so far I've started," he said. "I even started agencies in Paris and in London, Manchester, and Salzburg. I've sold my agencies at a good profit except for here in this backwoods hick town. The people's yen for bicycles, as you may know, caused road improvements. But presently, cars are causing road improvement and road improvement causes car sales to increase, but you must start with cars. But, I admit it. I started hick Leadford too soon. But she had it by that time in her fool head that Leadford was the ideal locale for a next chapter of

31

her lubricious project. Now you see what's happened. I want out. I mean out and away from her."

***

At the farm, Clarence had no thought for the Klinerts. Indeed, he'd decided even to sit a spell. Just sitting was a new experience. He hadn't known the pleasantry of idle time. Yet since Clydis and Edith had returned he hungered for it. And reprieve was in order, he felt, before tackling the mill's new boggle. Often times his job was far more than a full time job. But, by gosh, maybe? With the cow in more capable hands, the Tobertons, even chores wouldn't be so rigid. He sat idly sipping a cup of creamy lukewarm coffee, Edith drawing his attention as she splashed in her No. 3 tub. She sat jabbering and splashing with her tin cup in one hand and her saucepan in the other. Suddenly his ears perked. Did she? He listened. She sure is! "Clydis," he called, leaning nearly out of his chair. "Come and listen. She's talking a sentence."

Clydis came from the bedroom lugging a hamper of dirty clothes. As she approached, she smiled proudly down at Edith. "What did she say?"

"'Pan all wet,'" he bragged. "Clear as a bell."

Clydis thumped down the heavy hamper. "After this, we do the wash every week. That way the hamper will not be so heavy." She pulled out a kitchen chair and sat upon it, then strained her ears toward Edith.

"Eaith take a baph now. All wet. Play in water. Cup." She held up her cup then poured water on her chest, giggling as it poured over her little round belly. "Bewwie wet," she giggled. Her parents were spellbound, rapt, eminently happy and so very proud of their orating daughter.

"Woof, woof," Sniffer told them of friends passing the arborvitae. Clydis began to dry Edith and to reach for her clothes. "It's Ma," Clarence said, looking out the window near the side sink. "Naddy's with her."

Naddy rushed into the kitchen with a hand clutched to old Sniffer and with her free hand waving her doll. "Your grandma's here too," she announced. "I rode in her car." As she was talking she hurried on toward Edith. "I've come to help take care of Edith," she said. "Can I?"

Grandma Groner'd arrived right behind her, in time even to catch the door before it had time to close. "She sure can scoot!" grandma complained. "I was going to teach her to knock."

"No matter. You're both always welcome."

"I've brought our washing. I'll help with yours along with ours. We usually wash once a month, but if you are going to wash every other week or two, why we won't have much each time." Ma was feeling somewhat guilty having brought the burden of their wash into an already busy household.

32

They would have insisted that she simply bring the wash and they would do it along with theirs, but they knew she wouldn't hear of an arrangement so generous. "Clarence has it fixed up so well here that it's no trouble," Clydis bragged as she looked at the new pipe and faucet at the side sink.

He'd installed a pipe running down from the water heater. The heater was located in the bathroom upstairs. The pipe ran along the kitchen ceiling then down the wall to the sink. And he'd tapped into the sink drain such that the wash water would run out into the yard with the sink water. "Morley said we'll put in a dry well out there," Clarence nodded. "Then run a line so that the waste water drains into the field. It'll be a separate line than the one from the septic tank." He was proud of his engineering insights, much of which was fringe benefits of his employment.

Emma and Clydis were soon busy at the washing. Naddy and Edith had taken over the living room by then and his own idle time was beginning to worry him. Must be something, he thought, but they wouldn't want me messing with their wash. Deciding to go outside, he'd no sooner commenced with pulling on his boots than Morley bustled into the kitchen carrying a packet of papers.

"Helgie and I've been talking," Morley confessed as he laid the packet on the table. "A year or so ago, I wouldn't have considered it, but now we know you folks better. You're a good family and you care about the place. Even got a tree for Edith. So we were hoping you may wish to buy the place." He looked worried. Wondering what they would say. "We'd really like to be sure you'll always be our neighbor," he finished seriously.

Clarence was astonished. He looked over at Clydis. He'd thought to ask Morley about buying it ever since she'd returned and had dedicated a tree to Edith, but hadn't broached the subject knowing they were poor. He looked over at Clydis.

"We want it," she said as she turned off the washer.

"Clydis," he began, "we may not be able to."

"Pour the coffee," she ordered.

They were soon gathered around the table. From the living room they could hear a lively game of peek-a-boo. Edith's squeal of delight was only marginally more audible than Naddy's merry giggle. With that music as background, Morley went over his calculations with them. " . . . And so that's why we're asking four thousand."

Clarence had never dreamed of so vast an amount. He'd only known pennies, nickels and dimes all of his life. Even recently, now that he was a boss at the mill, his thoughts had swollen only to dollars and sometimes dreamily perhaps even to hundreds of dollars. Thousands of dollars! He hadn't before stretched his mind to think about numbers of such vastness. His depression was obvious as she looked at him. "I wish we could," he mumbled.

"We can," she said. "We'll go to the bank. I'm sure they'll listen."

"But we'd owe money," he reminded her. But he was looking at Ma as he said it. He and Pa'd had no debts in all of their lives, having always preferred to wait until they had the money in hand before spending any of it.

"Opportunity has knocked," Ma said.

"The mill's been depositing part of my pay, but I don't expect that is much," Clarence fretted, still looking at Ma, astonished at her comment. He glanced at Clydis, she smiling hopefully, and then returned his sad gaze to Morley.

"Well, you folks think about it," Morley said, somewhat dejected. "I won't sell it to any one else." He rose to leave. "I'll leave all these papers with you."

After Morley'd left Clarence sat at the table a while longer. He could see into the living room from where he was seated. The girls were parading around and around the chicken wire fence he'd constructed around the potbelly. Naddy would let Edith catch up. Edith would grab her and giggle and yell then Naddy would hurry around the potbelly to rush up behind Edith and grab her and tickle her and they would both laugh and giggle. He wondered who owned the strip of land between them and Jameses. But for it, they'd be next door neighbors with the Jameses. Any land not owned by somebody was likely still owned by the railroad. He'd ask the banker. We're going to buy it no matter what it costs, he thought bravely. Clydis and Ma are right. He pressed his feet firmly to the floor. "Opportunity has knocked and we're gonna answer."

He was surprised later that afternoon to find that he had more than enough in the bank to pay for both parcels. While Edith and Clydis were away he'd drawn only ten dollars a week of his pay. Pay not drawn each week the mill deposited at the Farmers bank. He was surprised to learn, banker Leevy being on the board of directors at the mill, that he'd arrived at the top of the pay scale and that he was profit sharing, a privilege granted to department heads, bosses so called. Leevy also told him that he was in line for some sixty thousand dollars or more that Hermes had left him. The Hermes money would become available to him after Hermes' brother Raymond passed on, the arrangement being provided for in the wills of both Hermes and Raymond. "But you can borrow against this if desired," Leevy told him.

Clarence sat spellbound before Leevy's desk. He had intended any savings he could accrue to be used in keeping track of Clydis and Edith, intending to pursue them all of his life if necessary so that he could tell them that he loved them and that he wanted them to come home. He would tell Edith, too, that she was named from Matthew and that her name means woman and that her first name, Edith, meant Goddess of Battle, an Anglo-Saxon name, but now he rejoiced knowing that he would be with them forever. His mind had been so fixed on getting them home or, that failing, pursuing them forever that he'd not considered his own material wealth, hadn't sensed its growth. Now he sat with swimming mind before Leevy's

34

desk. He reached out his hand and Clydis took it, squeezed it, and he drew strength from her. "We'll take it," he told Leevy, "both parcels."

***

At the time the Groners were in the bank Rockney was in his office trying to think of some way that he could delay his release of Mrs. Klinert. He'd seen the Groners outside and that little Edith was with them. He sat chatting with Tulip Board, just any thing to chat about. Finally, with the Groners safely inside the bank, he said, "It's time, and I see Purvis is on his way over. I'll get it done. "

"You'll pay for this," she promised as he opened her cell door.

"You're free to go. All charges have been either dropped or not brought." Mrs. Klinert glared at him.

Attorney Purvis had been in to talk with her earlier that day. He'd recommended that false arrest charges were not in order and, further, the evidence against her still would stand. The weed samples Rockney had collected matched those in her car, the wheat field, and on her clothing. The heel prints found in the field and caste in plaster by Rockney matched her shoes. Plaster casts of the tire tracks matched her tires and that Benjamin and Hanna Haimmer had seen her go past their furniture shop at about the right time for her to be returning to town; and she had looked disheveled to them when she drove past.

"You're lucky to be out of jail, Mrs. Klinert." he confided in her as they entered the street. "I would not press your luck just now." She remained silent. "And I recommend that you leave this town as soon as possible."

She stopped, peered at him. "I'm free to leave town then?"

"Yes, but go no where near Jericho Road."

"Nothing is keeping me in this town now but the trial which will incarcerate that carnal whelp forever is there?" They resumed toward the Ford agency.

Presently they were seated in the kitchenette. "Ma'am, I take it that nobody has informed you about the state of the evidence against Mr. Groner." He carefully explained the situation to her.

"We'll be dropping the charges," she said. "I'll inform Lucious of that and he will, and I mean it, he will listen."

That evening she and Lucious thrashed out their differences. She wouldn't contest the divorce if he'd drop all charges against Groner. She wanted nothing more, she said than to get out of that hick town.

Those decisions were made in November 1906, just several days before Mrs. Klinert began her stalk of Naddy James.

Chapter Six

The Clydesdales stamped their impatience. "Easy, hold a minute. Ruby! Stand." Clifford tugged gently back on her reins. The horses blew, sending jets of condensation into the chill November air. It was the last day of school before Thanksgiving and the first of her solo walks from the freight depot near Lead Bridge to the Meads shop, four blocks distant. Claire was in Meads watching a clock while he sat upon the seat of his freight wagon beside Naddy. The calico cat was cuddled in his leather apron. She reached over and tickled the cat's chin. The cat purred and wriggled, wanting more. He checked his Hampden railroad pocket watch. "It's time, Naddy. Ten minutes before one." Naddy climbed excitedly, proudly down from the high seat of the massive Studebaker freight wagon. "Be careful, now," he cautioned as she began her solo journey.

The Jameses were building a house out on Jericho Road, the next place south of the Groners, but, to no fault of Uncle Charley James, the work had gone slowly. Charley was called repeatedly back to his home near Bruin City. At first they would have been upset with him had he not gone home because Flora had given birth to a charming son whom they'd named Rylus. But after that a power company began to log off two tracts of land, one to be the site of Rogers dam, while the other was destined to be Croton dam. Charley's loggers were pressed into service and his saw mill began operating day and night seven days a week to cut timbers for the construction of buildings, bridges, and roadways. Charley just couldn't get the house on Jericho finished.

Clifford and Claire James believed that children should be thoroughly indoctrinated as to hazards and safety precautions of town navigation. He watched his daughter on her way.

Along in front of the Ford agency there was no boardwalk. Naddy stepped along the edge of the display lot. Unseen by Naddy or her dad, a furtive figure peered from the agency windows, and followed Naddy's every step past the agency. As she stood intently watching from her window, Naddy struck her as a child tolerant to the rigors of training. She watched Naddy keenly, guessing her age to be about the same age as Clydis had been when she'd received her first tutor. I wonder, she thought. I wonder. She'd need to be removed far from her present environment; to Europe, obviously, probably Austria would be best. She would require isolation; and perhaps a beating or two, but I wonder. After all she is free from the diapers and would be beyond her impulse to eat like an animal; and she would be young enough to soon forget her original parents. Mrs. Klinert drifted deep into thought regarding Naddy.

Marshal Marsh Rockney also chanced to see Naddy as she was making her way up the boardwalk. He was very proud of Naddy and of her parents. If they'd all take the time, he thought. And his mind also dwelt on a different possibility; Tulip Board, but he mustn't think of her now. He watched after Naddy with interest as though he were her parent. He was very proud of Naddy and, suddenly he realized, very much in love with Tulip.

Their plan was that as Naddy crossed Ferndin Street she'd enter the viewing radius of her mother. Knowing this, Clifford sent his team on their way. The team strutted onto Front and proceeded with their load of parcels on up Front toward the intersection with Main. Claire glimpsed his going but for a frantic instant Naddy was still not within her sight; they'd have to adjust their timing a bit. With relief, Naddy walked into view a moment later. Just mere seconds past one o'clock, she entered Meads shop to be greeted warmly and proudly by her mother.

As Clifford moved his team onto Front Mrs. Klinert hurried from the agency, without coat or hat, to stop beside a car parked in the display lot. She watched Naddy's progress all the way up Bridge to where she entered Meads. Shivering now, she hurried back inside the agency. Five minutes later she emerged driving the Franklin. She drove the car past Meads where she turned onto East and drove toward the Klinert residence in the northeast section of town. She turned around in her drive then followed Sprocket back to Bridge. She drove across Bridge then cruised along River, a block south of Bridge. She flowed past the alley that bordered Rockney's office and the Farmers bank.

One of these two, either the street or the alley, she thought; and she was hopeful that the James family's ridiculous training of the, far more capable than they reckoned, child would continue. Dull as they are, it probably would continue and on one of these corners, on one of these corners I'll be waiting. She returned to the Ford agency.

Sky Ferndin from his mercantile had also noticed Naddy's walk. Good idea, he thought and no sooner had he returned to his duties than he saw Mrs. Klinert hurrying without coat or hat back to the Ford agency. Crazy coot, he thought; but a darn pretty one; look at that walk would you. And to think she's such a kook. Darn it, Sky, he scolded himself. You have troubles enough without that. But I wonder when, or if, it could ever happen to me. His mind scanned the single women in town: Trella Mead? No, too old, and she'd never been more that strictly business in her dealings with him. Tulip Board? Right age. Smiles sometimes, but doesn't appear to have eyes for me. Some of us, it seems, are not destined for marriage. But he wondered about Mrs. Coats. Her husband had died, leaving her to run the Ellington store. By gosh, I believe I just should go and, one businessperson to another, see how that store is doing.

***

Marsh felt a sensation that he thought must be hunger. Why else would he be ambling toward a restaurant, he reasoned; but other thoughts nagged: She's too young. It'd ruin her life. Spoil her chances for the right man.

He recalled, though he tried not to recall, a time some thirty years past when a waitress had grabbed his attention. Nothing materialized and he soon knew the reason for her lack of response. After Emma and Robert, he at least twelve years her senior, were married Marsh had boarded a train for St. Louis. He trained as a detective in St. Louis but within two years he'd found himself back in Leadford. He soon became the town marshal and after a time Emma had become simply the wife of his friend Robert. He'd never begrudged Robert. He thought highly of both Robert and Emma and, of course, of their son Clarence.

Maybe some day things will be different, he told himself. Maybe some sweet thing would want me. But then, who could want a lawman as a mate? From just outside the restaurant he could see that three train cars were backed deep down into the siding. They rested near the Lower Lead Bridge. He would check them out, but first he'd be busy with Tulip's famous steak, egg, pancake meal that she served at any time.

Tulip opened at six each weekday morning through Saturday and on Sunday the restaurant opened at noon. Each day the business closed at six in the evening. She ran the place with two cooks and two waitresses, herself doubling in either capacity. To order one of her three standard meals one held up one, two, or three fingers. Rockney displayed his right index finger. Tulip nodded and she smiled at him from the kitchen. A moment later she was approaching his table with two cups of coffee.

"Good afternoon, Rockman," she greeted as she slid out the chair across the table from him. "It'll be about five minutes."

"Take five," he advised her. "I'm in no hurry this afternoon." She reached out to pour cream into his cup at the same time as he reached for the cream. Their hands brushed ever so lightly, sending warmth through his body. "I've plenty of time," he continued. "I heard Purvis advising her to leave town."

"That would be a relief," she said. For the Rockman, she thought, but didn't say it aloud. She knew he'd had enough of Mrs. Klinert. The Rockman did not like his hands tied. Legally, they were. He could do nothing about her because there were no charges against her, yet he believed she was criminal. He'd turned a criminal loose, lending him no comfort. "What you need," she said, "is to wrap yourself around a good meal." She smiled at him over her cup as she sipped from it. "You look drawn out, Rockman," she sounded serious. "When do you sleep?"

"I'm like you."

"I cannot believe that," she said across from him. "At six tonight, I'm out of here. Twelve hours a day are mine and twelve hours a day are the restaurant. What twelve hours of any day are yours?"

Marsh smiled across at her. He didn't answer her question. His was a life of unexpected events. He dealt with them expeditiously and well. He knew the importance of his job and he was never off his job. He kept the peace by being there. Tulip had heard talk from patrons that because the crime rate was very low in the marshal's domain, a permanent lawman may not even be needed, not realizing that his mission was to ward off crime. One did not wish for a second go around with Rockney. He seemed to miss nothing. "Have you heard anything about those train cars out there?"

"One's a refrigerator car," she explained. She was a capable observer and listener with a developed instinct for hearing the information Marsh may need to hear about. "It belongs to Tobertons. They're starting a dairy out at their place. Had you heard that?'

"No."

"Molly and Helen were in here yesterday. They've worked out a deal with Sky to store milk in his cooler. You know, forward thinking, he built in far greater capacity than he needed when he installed ice cream. We all lease storage space from him. Sky's will become the place in town to buy milk and cream and butter and such. Sky tells me that he's expanding again, this time to include a meat locker. I don't know what the town would do without Sky." She looked at him. "Or without you, Rockman."

Rockney smiled. He looked over her shoulder to see his meal coming. She wished the smile was for her, but she'd heard the waitress approach. At best she would be obliged to share his smile with meal No.1. Better than nothing, she thought. Look at me, Rockman, her mind pleaded. I want you to just look at me. Finally their eyes met. Warmth flowed through Marsh Rockney. Searing heat flowed through her. They'd not looked this way to each other before, but now they knew.

"They're going to lug it out to their farm," she said.

"This is going to be difficult," Rockney said.

"We can do it," she said.

That day had turned out to be the happiest of Rockney's life, and of hers. They need not say it. They knew it. Between them they knew it and for once in their lives they would be selfish, sharing with no one. From that moment they were Marsh and Tulip. They were one and would be one forever.

***

Roger Faygard had been servicing Rockney's Oldsmobile when from outside his shop he heard Clifford James talking to his team, holding them. Over the sounds of his work, Roger could hear fragments of Clifford's talk. He wondered as to what was taking place, but kept to his task of adjusting Marsh's tappets. It was unlike Clifford to halt his team where he had as there were no businesses there for Clifford to make a delivery. Thinking that Clifford may need a repair, he'd moved to the other side of Marsh's car in time to see Naddy begin her walk. He had then watched Naddy a moment. Clifford upped his Clydesdales and as the team and freight wagon rumbled past his shop Roger and Clifford smiled and waved. They were great friends, as most people were with either of them. He could see up the street to where Naddy had arrived at Meads. Roger and Jennifer had worried too while their youngster was learning his way around town; and they'd been lucky. Jill having been older when they moved into town had taken it upon herself to teach her sibling. Roger'd returned full attention to his work.

In another few minutes, Roger finished the job on Marsh's car. Automatically, his mind set to the next project. A Ford needed grease and an oil change. He was surprised to see some one's feet sticking out from under the Ford as he approached it.

The feet, about half size to Roger's, turned from side to side, first one foot then the other, then both. Then one would be raised, pulled by a flexing knee, then strained out straight again. "Be sure you're going counter clockwise with it; to the left," Roger cautioned.

The boy struggled a moment longer. "I'm getting it . . . got it!" he answered. Oil gushed from the crankcase, pouring with a black syrupy splutter into an oil drain pan. The boy swung out from under the car.

"How much oil are you going to put back in?"

"I don't know."

"Who are you?"

"Marvin. Marvin Edward. We just moved here."

"How old are you, ten?"

Marvin stood up straighter, stretched up as far as he could. "Eleven," he answered, "nearly twelve."

"You should be in school. There's school today. After that you get off for Thanksgiving. Then you go back three weeks until you get off for Christmas. Then you're off until after New Years day. Didn't you know that?"

"I went there this morning, but I'm not going back. I want to work on

40

automobiles." He was shifting foot to foot, his eyes pleading.

Roger's mind raced, searching for a solution. His scan of the shop came to rest on his oil rack. Come over here he directed. They walked over to the rack. "It took me a time to mark this stick," he explained to Marvin. "It's marked off in quarts and is accurate as long as we always use the same drain pan. The pan you used is the correct one. If we don't know how much oil we need to put back into the car, we measure the amount of oil we took out. We put that amount of oil back in then check the oil level in the crankcase; usually find it to be a bit low, then we carefully bring the oil level up to the engine's full mark. That way we never put too much oil back in; it's hard on the engine to have too much oil." Marvin listened intently. "But usually we don't need to go to all of that because we already know about the car we're servicing." While he was talking Roger'd walked over to his service desk.

"It's all in here," he explained, holding up a book. "This is the Ford book. We keep track of everything in here. You see other books for Olds, Rambler, Franklin, and on. And we keep account books and we keep customer records."

"I want to work on automobiles," he said, his moist pleading eyes firm upon Roger's. "I don't want to go to school."

"The best thing, and only thing, I'll do for you," Roger emphasized, "is equal time. You can't work for me one hour unless you've been in school at least one hour. You understand that?"

"She beat up Raymond Perkins something awful."

"That's no reason. You don't know but what he deserved it."

"It's because he couldn't read."

"Everybody needs to know how to read. You can't fix cars even unless you can read. I showed you the record keeping. And you got to read about each kind of car, each part of each kind of car." Marvin now had tears in his eyes.

"I can do arithmetic."

"That's necessary too." Roger picked up a booklet about Fords. "Read this," he said, pointing.

"Th, th, th he hee." What in the world, Roger's mind raced.

"Is that how Raymond reads, too?"

"Yes."

"And she beat him for it?"

"He hit her back."

"Hit her back?"

"Then she really beat him. Near killed him with a stick."

"Don't ever clobber a teacher," Roger cautioned him. He studied Marvin a moment. He saw a boy with a great deal of spirit, and a boy who needed help. "I want you to meet my wife," Roger said. "I'm sure she'll agree to this. You work for her the same amount of time she works with you. You work for me no more than the amount of time you spend in school. My wife can teach you to read. She taught me. We were kids then, but she taught me no less. We have a baby now, name's Fred, and we have three other children; two you'll meet at school although one is younger than you. The other one is Meggy. She's three. So my wife's real busy upstairs above here," he glanced upward, "where we live. That's why you need to help her when she helps you."

Marvin began to smile. "Yes, sir," Marvin assured him. "Thanks, sir."

"Roger."

***

Early on the afternoon that Marvin began his training with Roger, other training was being discussed. The wind had calmed by then, allowing the sun's lubricating warmth to stir one's blood and one's feet. At least it had Billie's. Clydene was tucked in beside her on the seat of the buggy. The matched team of light chestnuts felt the warmth as well. They'd broken into a smooth loping mile-busting gait and Billie let them travel. She and Clydene had decided that a visit with Clydis and Edith was in order. Sniffer signaled friendly, incoming, no problem, as the team sped past the arborvitae.

Clydis, bursting with pleasure, was standing on the rear stoop waving to them as they pulled in. Edith clung to her mother's skirt. "Hi. Hi. Hi." Both ladies were greeting at once.

"We're so glad you've come."

"We've been wanting to get here, but the air has been cold," she chatted as she tethered the team. "We can't let cold stop us. So I bundled us warm. We are warm enough. It is a pretty day." Clydis was holding Clydene by this time and had knelt down so that Edith could see her.

"Dowie," Edith remarked.

"Baby," Clydis corrected. "Clydene."

Finished with tethering now, Billie reached her arms toward Edith. "Baaie."

"Baby," Billie confirmed, picking her up. "You are talking well," she congratulated as they trooped into the warm kitchen. The ladies continued to hold one another's baby as they took seats at the table. "Your head is well," Billie said as she studied Clydis. "You are very pretty."

Clydis smiled, appreciating the compliment. "The doctor says the red color as well as the lumpiness may go away in time. How have you been, Billie, dear?"

"Fine. I have too much milk. It drips out. Itches me."

"I wasn't as lucky. We had to supplement with a bottle." Billie looked at her, confused.

42

"Suppl . . .?" Clydis realized her mistake.

"I didn't have so much milk."

"Oh. You be glad," Billie giggled, looking down at her bosom, knowing her under garment would be soaked. "You will see why I have come," Billie said. "To see you and Edith, yes. To show you Clydene and me, yes. But also, I need your help," Clydis was at once curious and wanting to help. "I do not know enough words," Billie confessed, "and I can write only 'Red', 'Billie', and some words. I can't write 'Clydene'. I want to write my baby's name."

"I'll help you," Clydis assured her, "and you have helped us by taking the cow. The cow is not a worry to Clarence now. Especially these days at the mill, he has enough to think about."

"Our men work long," Billie said, referring to the work at the mill where Red and his brothers were doing double shifts. Clarence, however, was nearly living at the mill.

They were reordering the mill's power system to flutter wheel impetus while gearing the water wheel's might to an electricity generator. John Purley too was nearly living at the mill. The men would be several days working their overload, themselves too busy, worried, tired out, to think but fleetingly about their lonely families. Their families, missing them, were concerned for them, and were pulling together to stave the stress of their absence. Thus Clydis was more than usually pleased to see Billie while Billie was overjoyed to be with Clydis.

The babies fell asleep in their mothers' arms as the ladies talked. The darlings were soon snuggled together in Edith's bed.

Clydis opened a book of bedtime stories for children and read each of the stories to Billie. Then she helped Billie through the stories. Clydis spelled out 'Clydene Toberton' on a paper along with several other words for her to practice. Billie learned so quickly that Clydis was amazed that she hadn't already developed the skills. "I am going to school now," Billie said proudly. "I want to go before, but we could not."

"Oh, why not?"

"We were hidden." Clydis was astonished. Hidden? Billie continued: "We lived in the old way. My people did not go to the west. We stayed and we lived by the rivers in the woods. My people wished to be Indians still; like the way Indians always have been."

"Oh. That sounds like a nice way to live. I wish I would have done that too."

"Chief Roughwater came to tell us about powwow. We go to powwow. One day we met Red in the woods. The next powwow Red and I are wed. I love Red right away. I am eighteen now." Clydis mentally calculated, guessing: Married at fourteen?

"You are very capable, Billie. I like teaching you to read and write." Clydis folded the writing project and placed it inside the book. "When Clydene is a little bigger you will read the stories to her," Clydis said, handing the book to Billie.

Billie giggled, the book clutched to her abdomen, her eyes on Clydis. "I will do it well," she said.

"Billie," Clydis said. "I'm troubled too. I need your help. I do not know a thing about horses. I haven't touched a horse. I cannot ride a horse. I cannot drive a buggy."

"Oh! Yes, I will help you," Billie said delightedly. "Tomorrow or the first good day, I will come and get you."

Clydis knew that Ma would be visiting in the morning to plan the upcoming Thanksgiving and Christmas arrangements. "Could it be tomorrow," she said. "Grandma Emma could drive me to your house in her car."

"Oh, yes, golly," Billie giggled.

In too soon a time, it seemed to them, Billie was on her way home, Clydene, still soundly asleep, tucked beside her. The air was crisping rapidly as the sun was seeking its rest and the horses, plodding at first, recognized they were on their way home and picked up their pace. Billie pulled her scarf tight around her face leaving but a slit for her vision and she let them travel.

Morning dawned crisp and clear. The sun, fully orbed, looked hot but served only to bring the unwary out of doors. Once outside the cold slowly penetrated, soon filling one's whole being with a desire for fireside warmth. Pa wished it would snow. One felt warmer with a blanket of snow. The little Rambler left a cloud of steamy air behind it as Emma drove slowly toward Jericho. There is nothing colder than a car for travel in cold weather, Pa thought. And a horse is sure easier than a car to get started. He'd heated the oil and water that morning, having drained it from the car the evening before, and all night the car had rested under blankets with a light bulb blazing near its engine. What a misery. He really missed Toad.

Emma cruised in past the arborvitae. She climbed stiffly down from the Rambler and made her way into the kitchen, leaving Robert out in the cold where he struggled with the blankets, trying to corral the engine's fleeting heat. Even so, they knew they couldn't visit long with Clydis and Edith. Pa stamped his feet. He really missed Toad.

At the kitchen he was greeted by: "Thanksgiving at our house and Christmas dinner here." Pa smiled, but didn't speak. His teeth were chattering and he hunkered up beside the open oven door of the range. Grandma, Edith on her lap, turned her attention back to Clydis. "We have a turkey already," she said. "Sky Ferndin had two dozen shipped up from Grand Rapids. He said to Robert, 'You'd best get yours quick while there's a good choice,' so Robert picked out a nice plump hen turkey. It'll roast up nice. You might bring a can of cranberries if you have some." Morley had delivered cranberries to Emma and Robert earlier in the fall and Emma had canned them and brought two pints out to Clarence.

Clydis checked the pantry. "We've a pint."

"We're all set on that then."

Robert had warmed some and he slid back from the range, tuning his ears in disbelief to their new topic: A trip down to Tobertons! "You women are crazy," he admonished. "I want to stay inside." Pa continued his scold. "This is a day to drive horses, not cars."

"We'll stop at Chester Faygard's," Ma informed him. "Robert, we can't just stay inside."

Robert was delighted. He'd thought that to be a good idea, and he'd mentioned it to Emma, but she'd been cold to the idea. But now, by gosh, she has frozen her buns, he thought. So now she sees. Of course we need a horse for the winter. "Let's get going," Pa urged, much encouraged.

Chester Faygard was happy he could rent a horse and light buggy for the winter. Chester had too many horses. He could not stable them all. Twenty head of the heavy work horses were assigned to winter pasture, a large wooded field with a rill of fresh water; water which fed Faygard's swamp and, in the spring, the rill helped to make a quagmire of Faygard's dip. An aging former sheep barn located some distance from the other farm buildings sheltered the horses. The Tobertons were obliged to employ a similar arrangement with their idle horses, sixteen head of heavies. On the Toberton farm however, none of the horses were extras. All were needed during the spring, summer, and fall seasons, but Chester, unlike the Tobertons, knew he was hoarding an over burden of horses. Hoping for a sale, he led out a gentle mare named Peanut. "She sure looks good to me," Pa declared.

"She's one I was going to rent to the Leadford livery for the winter," Chester replied. "He's ordered six from us, all lights, for the winter. You could have rented her there, but I'm glad you stopped by. The reason," Chester explained, "is that Sid and I will each be stringing two. It would save us a cold walk back to the farm here if you could drive us back home."

"Be glad too. The women folks are on their way to Tobertons. I'll be going back to town as soon as Peanut is hitched to your buggy."

"Suits," Chester said, his face grinning. "We'll be at the livery."

Chapter Seven

Great grandmother Tillie Mae Toberton was in the yard as they pulled in. She was dressed head to toe in bear furs and her face, pinked by the cold air, crinkled into a smile as Emma pulled to a stop beside her. "Morning," Tillie Mae greeted. As she raised her hand a steaming milk bucket rose with it.

"It's good to see you," Emma said as she stopped the engine. A chill gripped her as she climbed stiffly down from the car. Emma, with chattering teeth, walked up to Tillie Mae.

"Going to feed a calf. Come along," Tillie Mae invited. Emma went with Tillie Mae while Clydis and Edith hurried into Red and Billie's portion of the huge much added on to Toberton house.

A short time later Billie greeted Grandma warmly, offering her a chair and a cup of tea as she came into the house. Emma kept her coat on and still she shivered while seated in a parlor rocker cooing to Clydene whom she held in her lap. "I'm sorry we can't stay long," Emma said. "If the car gets cold, I can't start it. That's why Robert is renting a horse and buggy from Chester Faygard. I'm agreed, a buggy would be warmer and a horse less trouble."

"You can go right on back," Clydis said seriously. "Billie and I have a project to accomplish then she's going to drive me back."

Emma was relieved. "I'll go right on home then."

Soon she was headed back along Jericho, expecting along the way to catch sight of Robert driving his new horse.

Quickly she caught up to Chester and Sid. They were riding bareback and each of them trailed two horses. All six of the horses were wearing harness. She eased on past them. Robert had made good time. She didn't overtake him, but she caught sight of him crossing Lead Bridge as she was entering town. At home she parked the car in the carriage barn behind the house. She felt dizzy and very fatigued as she climbed down from the Rambler. The cold, she realized, had really gotten to her. Her teeth chattered and her eyes were glassy.

46

Emma swooned. She plopped to the floor of the carriage barn. She lay on her side shivering and crying, very much afraid. She struggled to get up, but couldn't. Her head was swimming, she was weak and she hurt. Robert carried Chester and Sid home then cruised home himself, completely content behind Peanut. He fell into shock, his heart pounding, his face numbing, as he entered the carriage house and found her there.

He knelt beside her on the floor. "Emma, Emma," Robert pleaded. He held her close. "Oh, Emma, Emma," Robert held her, trying to catch his breath, trying to help her, thinking: Get hold. Get hold of yourself. Desperate for control, he held tight to Emma.

Gradually he composed and he carried Emma into the warm kitchen. "Robert, I'm so sorry," she said as he placed her in her chair beside the oil stove. He turned up the oil heater then lit the kitchen range, also fueled by coal oil, and placed a pan of water upon it to heat. Emma was shivering violently now. Robert hurried into the bedroom and dragged back a cot. He picked her up and placed her on the cot fully clothed, including her coat and hat and boots and mittens, and placed covers over her. At the head of the cot he raised each corner and placed a book to raise the head of the bed, this hopefully to deter coughing.

Emma rested quietly on the cot, tears running down her face. She sipped some of his warmed brandy, this also to ward off coughing. "Will you be all right a few minutes? I'm going for the doctor." She nodded. He kissed her forehead and squeezed her hand. Moments later he was on his way toward Dr. Laird's office.

"I'm sorry," she said through her tears as Dr. Laird began to examine her. "It's Edith," she sobbed. "I kissed her face. Oh, I'm so sorry. I hadn't cleaned my face. I didn't think. I picked her up. I love her and I kissed her." Emma shook violently, her eyes huge.

"Emma," he said, resting his hand on her forehead, "I'm taking usual precautions here. We'll check up on your whole family. Have them all come to my office. But I don't believe your problem is a recurrence of tuberculosis. Your symptoms, including your sudden attack, are consistent with the flu. We've treated several cases of the flu lately. Also, we haven't lately experienced new cases of active TB. I want you to rest for a few days. I mean, do nothing more than necessary. Will you do that?"

He'd been looking at Robert as he was directing Emma. Robert nodded, relief registering on his face. "Yes," Emma said, her tears dry now. "Believe me, I surely will."

Meanwhile at the Tobertons, Billie and Clydis worked their way through the book of children's bedtime stories. Billie then read the book through perfectly. She produced a pad of tablet paper in which she had printed 'Clydene' numerous times and 'Clydene Toberton' several times, but she didn't show the exercise to Clydis. Instead she opened the tablet to a blank page and printed 'Clydene

47

Toberton'. "Billie, this is wonderful," Clydis assured her.

"I want to learn. I am afraid to ask Jane or Satin or Molly or Helen or anyone. They would think I am stupid; they are right. I cannot even ask Red, I'm so ashamed."

"No more, you're not. You can read well already. And you'll become still better at it. Your handwriting will be beautiful when we're finished. And it won't be long, I assure you."

Tillie Mae looked after the little girls while Clydis took her lesson in horsemanship. Within an hour Clydis knew how to install and remove harness and she did a fine job of driving Junifer around the yard.

When it was time to leave, Clydis tied Junifer behind Billie's buggy. At home, Billie looked after the little girls while Clydis hitched Junifer to the buggy usually pulled by Bunny and drove her around the yard. Clevis Harold, when they'd asked him about it, had been delighted that his horse would be getting winter care in a nice warm barn. He longed for the day when they could see their way clear to building adequate quarters for their horses. The horses were cared for well enough with their winter pasture arrangement. Still, Clevis Harold was a farmer and a horse lover. He was pleased that Clydis wished to house the gentle little mare. Clydis drove once more around the yard and then steered her onto Jericho. She drove down to the corner and back, smiling radiantly as she cruised past the arborvitae. Gosh, she was proud.

Toad and old Jude had free run of a box stall and the horse paddock as well as to a pasture everyone called the High Ten. That arrangement accorded vacant stalls along beside Bunny's. Those vacant stalls Clarence liked to have available for guests. She stabled Junifer next to Bunny's stall, still leaving two stalls vacant for guests. Clydis chuckled to herself in imagining Clarence's surprise when he arrived home.

He'd be home within hours. The overburden of work at the mill was nearly completed. Red and Tom were finishing up while Clarence looked after the boiler room. Rik was due in anytime to relieve Red and Tom. John Purley had been sent home some eight hours earlier. Upon John Purley's return, Clarence would be free to return to his home on Jericho. Clarence and Red had caught snatches of sleep during the last five days and they'd eaten what food came their way; each man coming on duty had brought a bag of food in with him, but they were, none the less, nearing the end of their endurance. Red climbed into the buckboard that Rik had driven to the mill. He was asleep in the seat by the time Tom started the team. Clarence, seated on a crate near the boiler, fought off sleep as he awaited the arrival of John Purley.

It was fully dark by the time Clarence arrived home. He stabled Bunny by habit, without the aid of a light, but did notice the extra horse. Who could this be? A guest? Who? An overnight guest? We've not had one before. His foggy fatigued mind pondered futility.

He happened to notice Morley through the kitchen window. At the rear steps by that time, Clarence was relieved the puzzle was solved. He had in mind to congratulate Morley for his purchase of a fine horse when he entered the kitchen.

"I see you did it, Morley. You've made a fine choice," he greeted. Morley stood in confusion as Clarence walked on over to Clydis and kissed her. "Did you miss me?" Clydis murmured her reply, giving him an extra squeeze and a peck on the neck. Edith had a bear hug on his leg by that time and he knelt beside her. She pressed an oaken horse into his face.

"Orse."

"Horse. Nice horse." He sat a chair near the table with Edith on his lap.

"Pah, Pah," she placed a hand on his face.

"What did I do, you said?" Morley was confused. Just minutes before Clarence had arrived home, Morley'd come over on an errand that he dreaded. He'd just been to the side sink for a glass of water, hoping to calm himself. He had bad news. Seeing Clarence not present, he'd hesitated relating the news to Clydis, but now with Clarence home, he steeled himself and began. "It's about your mother," he looked forlornly at Clarence.

Clarence sobered at once. "Ma?" He stared at Morley.

"She's ill, fainted. They called a doctor." Worry lined Morley's face. Robert and Emma were among his best of friends. "She has chills and fever."

"Coughing?"

"He didn't say so." Morley was stepping foot to foot. "He did mention Thanksgiving, but I didn't get what he said. I was too worried about Emma and all." He didn't know more to report about Emma, but he was still confused about what Clarence'd mentioned that he'd done. "You were saying about me choosing fine?"

"I see your new horse in the stable. I thought we must be having an over night guest, but then when I saw you here. . ."

"I don't have a new horse. I walked over. I just came to tell you that your Pa called about your Ma."

Clarence stood agape. "Well, there's a horse."

"Her name is Junifer. She's going to be my Christmas present." Clarence looked at her in disbelief. Why she'd never before as much as touched a horse, let alone drive or ride one. He must not have heard her correctly. After all, five days at the mill. I must be loosing my mind. "Billie taught me to drive her. I meant her to be a surprise." Clarence smiled now, but wondered if he'd ever understand Clydis. "I'm sorry about Ma. I'll get Edith ready. We'll go in with you?"

"It could be a recurrence of TB."

"Oh, pray no."

"I'll be back as soon as I can. I don't like the sound of this. You and Edith had better stay here."

"It sure has me scared," Morley admitted.

"Thanks, Morley. We appreciate your coming over. If I see a light when I get back, I'll stop in."

Morley nodded. He began to button his coat. He saw himself out while Clarence was buttoning his. "God speed," Clydis said.

Clarence saddled Bunny, rode him hard into Leadford, reining in at his parent's where he tied him to a porch rail. He rushed into the kitchen.

They were surprised to see him. "Why, Clarence. Nice of you to drop in." Clarence could see that Pa'd been reading a book to Ma. Ma was tucked warmly into the cot. She smiled at Clarence.

"Morley came over." Pa smiled. Like Morley to get the message all diced up, he thought. "Ma, are you?"

"Sick, but not with TB," she answered. "Dr. Laird thinks an acute flu attack. We called Morley so you'd know the Thanksgiving plans are defunct. Your Ma and Pa just better be here by our selves for Thanksgiving. We want you to take the turkey home with you. Dr. Laird has confined me to bed right on through the holiday. I pray Edith doesn't get the flu."

Clarence bid his good night. He hurried out to Jericho. Morley's house was well alighted, a virtual beacon. Before Clarence could open the door, Morley opened it and peered out, his eyes questioning, his face a register of concern. Expecting bad news, he asked, "Is she unrelapsed?"

"Dr. Laird doesn't think it's TB. He thinks she has the flu." Morley was greatly relieved. "Thanks, Morley. You did good."

He entered the kitchen to find Clydis swaying on her feet, very ill. "Clydis, Ma's okay. Clydis!"

Clydis collapsed onto the floor! Flu? Clarence soon had her fixed up, much as he'd seen that his Pa had fixed up his Ma. Bed rest, wholesome food, and plenty of liquids. A difficult next few days were their due.

On Thanksgiving Day Robert and Emma Groner stayed home and they opened a can of venison to go with their cranberries and pumpkin pie. They were grateful, praising the Lord for their personal good fortune and well being. Their son, Clarence, for whom, along with his beautiful wife and child, they were also grateful, spent the day at home with his treasured wife, Clydis, and their darling bouncing daughter Edith. On this fateful Thanksgiving of 1906 they were thankful and ever so happy to be home.

***

Marvin Edward liked school more and more as his reading skill improved. He came to work with Roger every day and he studied with Jennifer Faygard for an hour then worked an hour for her, usually at washing clothes or folding them; sometimes at doing dishes or making butter. He mentioned one day that he was teaching Raymond Perkins to read, working with him every morning before they walked to school. Ray was trading his time at the Edward's woodpile.

Ray came in with Marvin on an afternoon shortly after Thanksgiving. "This is Raymond Perkins," he said. "His dad's a building mover."

Roger's eyebrows arched happily. "A what? House mover, did you say? Glad to meet you."

"He wrecks houses but instead of that, he'd rather move them to a new spot. We've moved quite a few in Grand Rapids, but Dad wanted to get out of the big city. He says that stringing electric wires all over the city has made his job near impossible; too many big problems. My grandfather is still there working in Grand Rapids. Dad's going to move the house we live in out to nearer the highway and he's going to start a lumber yard for used lumber."

Roger said, "Well, I'll be!" And with a sigh of relief, he clapped Ray's shoulder. "You may have him stop by. I know some folks who want to move a train car down the county roads to their farm.

"And Marvin here," he said to Ray, but winked at Marvin, "has spent so much time in school lately that there's not time enough here in the shop to have him working every day, what with his schooling."

"He's helping me, too," Ray said. "And your wife is helping him?"

"That she is. She helped me too." Ray looked surprised. "It's a good thing to know how to read. I'm glad I learned. But what I was saying about Marvin. And now Marvin you hear this. I'm taking back what I said. You don't owe me anything. Just work the hours that you want."

"Okay," Marvin said. "And honestly, sir, some days I'd just as soon not come. But I like the work. Monday, Friday, and Saturday are the heavy days?"

"They are indeed. That time would be about right. If you wish now, and don't let me push you into this. The Clout brothers are buying the Ford agency. They are good men. They tell me they're going to move the agency over onto the corner of Groner and Bridge. Better location, they said. Well, they're good men. They'll need mechanics because they'll reclaim the business the agency has lost to us and will expand from there. So the training you have here in my shop will not be wasted." Marvin looked at him questioningly. "It's because I want to cut back on automobile service." Marvin looked worried. "No, not right now. As a goal, I mean. I want to get myself converted into a machinery shop; building things people want me to build."

"Oh."

"Your job is secure here. Don't worry about it. You guys keep on with the reading studies, what ever else you do."

"Okay, we will." Marvin grinned ear to ear. "I'll be here Friday."

"I'll look for you."

Marvin hadn't wanted to let on to Roger the work had become a burden. But Roger had sensed it and had to think of a solution that he hoped would not hurt Marvin's feelings. He smiled seeing that Ray produced a baseball as they were leaving the shop. Posthaste, Front Street was transformed to an arena for a game of catch.

***

The flu had kept Clydis down for only a few days, and those days were lightened by Marsh Rockney. He stopped out to let them know there'd be no trial, Mr. Klinert had withdrawn all charges, but they owed Jason Plinkly for his services. The Groners were floating high with the news. The bill was but piffle compared to the emotional burden they'd been toting.

She decided to drive into town to let the folks know of their good fortune and to check on Ma. As she was passing through the intersection of Bridge and Front, Junifer turned her head at the same moment that Clydis caught sight of an object rolling toward them. Vision of a run away horse popped into her mind along with herself careening from the buggy. This being her first foray as a horse driver, she knew that Junifer must be controlled, but didn't know how!

Chapter Eight

"Whoa!" Desperately she pulled.

Junifer obediently stopped. Junifer calmly eyed the baseball bounding along the street. Clydis made ready to leap. Streaking under the buggy, the ball struck a hitch rail then bounced into the Ford agency display lot. "Sorry," some one said.

A boy ran in front of Junifer and on into the sales lot. Clydis had difficulty believing that she'd handled the situation correctly; yet, glancing about confirmed they were stationary. Her eye caught the approach of another boy. "Whoa," she stammered.

Marvin Edward slid to a stop. "My fault," he admitted. Seeing his concern, and with her confidence returning, Clydis broke into a smile.

"Perhaps you could play catch in that lot," Clydis said. "It's vacant."

"We can play here!" Marvin called to Ray who had by that time caught up to the ball.

***

It'd been a cold fall season without any snow, but on that day it was warm, near forty degrees, and dark puffy clouds filled the sky. Pa was hitching Peanut as Clydis pulled Junifer to a stop beside him. "Whoa, Junifer," she said nervously; and gratefully, as Junifer stopped at once and stood quietly.

Pa looked up, surprised to see that it was Clydis. "Why, hello," he greeted. "I was about to try out my side curtains." He stood proudly beside his newly enclosed buggy, expecting her approval.

"It should keep you warm as toast," Clydis said encouragingly. "Nice and cosy. How's Ma, by the way? And had you heard that Clarence is free? There's to be no trial."

"Fantastic! Good news of Clarence. We'd always thought that Marsh and

53

Jason had beaten um on those charges." He'd removed his hat and brushed his fingers through his sparse white hair as he spoke. Tears threatened his eyes. "Now Emma, oh, she's fine. It was only the flu." He noticed now that Edith was not with her. Worriedly, he asked, "How is Edith?"

"Clarence is minding her. She and Clarence didn't get the flu, yet. It's my first day since we came home to be without her. I miss her, but I was afraid to have her with me on my first trip with Junifer."

"Pretty name for a horse," Pa remarked. "I like Peanut, though I miss Toad. I hadn't heard that you folks had bought a new horse."

"I've borrowed her from Clevis Harold. Billie taught me to drive. I'd never before driven a horse. Billie said that a horse is better than a car."

"In the winter it sure is. I was about to take our buggy out to try it. We need a very tightly enclosed buggy. I'm not taking any chance on Emma getting cold again." Pa hated to admit that he too had suffered more from the cold in recent years. He wanted to be warm right along with Emma. "I wanted this thing better enclosed than what I'd seen from the wagon shops."

"Molly and Helen stopped by this morning with their new milk delivery wagon. It's heavy, pulled by two horses, and has ice inside. Molly calls it their rolling refrigerator. They don't have ice in it at present, of course. Chester Faygard and Sid built it for them. They could as well have built a tight buggy for you."

"I asked them. This community is growing by leaps and bounds. They come by train because the roads are so bad. Then once they get here they want light horses. Of course that leaves Chester with an over supply of heavies and he could use more lights. Folks aren't going into farming or logging or such. They're looking for factory or service jobs. Chester and Sid are good men, but we needed it closed in right away."

"Clarence has said there's no shortage of work around here, but a shortage of workmen. Outsiders must have heard him say it," she joked. "But today, Pa, I've come to town to buy staples at Sky's; and to see how Ma's doing."

"Oh, she's fine. Raring to go. I'm sure she'll think of a good reason to go with you to Sky's." He looked around at the weather. "Doc told her to stay indoors. But it's warmer today. I'll pretend Doc never told her that. And while you're gallivanting, I'll see how I've done with this buggy."

Emma couldn't think of a thing that she needed at the store so she went along with Clydis. She couldn't understand, however, why Edith wasn't with her mother.

"It's because I wasn't sure I could drive well enough. What do you think?" She was walking Junifer up the street toward the mercantile.

"I wouldn't have known you hadn't been doing it for years."

"Thanks. And, Ma, I'll surely have Edith along the next time. But really this is only my first try at driving to town and I did want to be careful."

Sky was pleased to see them. "Good morning good ladies. What may I help you with this fine day?" As usual, despite his gabby light talk, Sky was all business.

"A bag of flour and one of sugar," Clydis replied as she began to look about the store. More than a year had elapsed since she'd last been inside the mercantile.

"Have you tried our ice cream?" He could see their interest perk. "It actually tastes better, or as good, now as in the summer."

"Maybe a little dab," Emma said.

Sky seated them on his special springy iron chairs at a wrought iron table. Sugar and spice, Emma thought appreciatively. She passed her fingers along the lacy edge of the delicately pretty table spread that centered the table. Clydis too fingered the table spread. Sky had done beautifully here. "Will you join us, Sky? My treat," Clydis beckoned. In the past she'd not trusted Sky, but her life had changed greatly since fall and she'd decided to befriend him.

"Well, now, I don't normally do that," he replied, "but, Clydis, I especially wanted to talk with you. If you don't mind." He took a seat, sitting proudly in one of his dainty, but strong, springy chairs.

Mrs. Coats took their order; sundaes all around with crushed peanuts and chocolate syrup.

"It's about your parents, Clydis," Sky began. "And none of my business, I assure you. They've separated. I'm not sure you knew that." Clydis nodded, not surprised. "Your father has left town. Sold the business to the Clout brothers. But they're not going to operate it where it is. Seems Kroust bought it from them. Some deal he worked out with them on behalf of the town council. The agency building is going to become the power plant. That's so that folks out farther from town, you folks say, will have electricity. That'll get to you next summer. Telephone too. Man named Edward, that's his last name, no s on it, is starting a telephone company. This town has really started to grow. Even got ice cream," he finished, as Janet Coats had arrived with their order.

"This is Janet," he introduced. She's sold the Ellington store. She's working out real fine here. I need a good person, especially since Joe Marvin Benson's in school. Even when he isn't I need more help. I'm expanding again, you know. Putting in a meat locker now and a new main entrance to the store." Mrs. Coats had returned to the kitchen by that time. "Her husband has died, you know. She's doing very well here."

Clydis had enjoyed eating ice cream in ice cream parlors, and in many different cities and countries, and now as she remarked that Sky's parlor would rank high among any she'd ever enjoyed, Sky sat beaming, but as he listened, his eyes were on Emma. Emma had never before tasted parlor ice cream. Her eyes were alight and her face radiant. So engrossed was she in her treat, that her mind had shut out all else for the occasion. Sky was immeasurably pleased. Emma was ecstatic. She was nearing the bottom of the long stemmed dish. Sky had indeed done everything right, her tiny spoon scooped for every delicious morsel. She patted delicately with the lacy napkin Sky had provided. She looked over at Sky. "Sky, you devil," she joked. "Now I may not be able to stay away."

"Many folks make it a weekly occasion," he bragged. "Usually when they come in for groceries or supplies, but some come in just because they want to enjoy the treat. You come anytime." His attention now returned to Clydis. He looked at her.

"Clydis, it's about your mother. And I know you do not owe her anything and I'd be terrified if I knew she was anywhere near you or Edith and again I know this is none of my business, but I'm concerned about her. I know you cannot do anything about it, but maybe I can if I can figure out what's going on. She's there alone in the house. I didn't know it until yesterday. She called in for groceries and I delivered them. Living all alone, she is. Keeps her Franklin in that heated garage. Gastoff Kroust has bought the house. Likes that heated garage. He keeps his car in the garage under the agency, but he'll need a different place, like everyone else who parks there. The house would be an improvement for him because your parents had built the finest house in town so I'm glad to see he got it.

"She didn't say much to me when I was there to deliver the groceries, but I could see she'd packed some things into boxes and she'd written addresses on the boxes, but I wasn't close enough to read where the boxes were being sent. She paid me, with a generous tip, you know she was always good about a tip. Tipped big, generally. She drives the Franklin to the agency nearly every day and she drives in the back way, uses that alley, you know, and puts her car in the garage down cellar.

"She still has a key to the agency as others do who park their cars down there but she must also have keys for upstairs. We see her over there most every day looking out. Once, a time ago, maybe a few weeks, no, about a week ago, before Thanksgiving, I saw her come out and stand beside a car. The cars are all moved off the lot now. But that day, a few were there. It was a cold, cold day and she was out there with no coat or hat on. Then the first thing I knew I saw her hurrying back into the agency. Of course she's probably lonely, but she doesn't associate with anyone as far as I can see.

"But after she gets to the agency, around ten o'clock, then we see her just sitting over there. Then around noon, or a little after, we see her driving slowly around town, the south end mainly, as though she is looking for some one. That's why I got the idea she was lonely but I don't know whether she is or not but her behavior is not like the rest of us might behave, I'm sure of that. I believe it's as if she was looking for someone to . . . ."

The table crashed! A terrible scene flashed her mind, hurling her from the table.

Screaming, "Ma, hurry!" her movement was a blurred streak to the door.

Ma grabbed her things, buttoning her coat as she ran, hat and gloves tucked under an arm, her scarf whipping. Clydis had left her hat, gloves, and scarf and hadn't buttoned her coat by the time she'd untied Junifer and clambered aboard the buggy. Ma was barely seated when Clydis yelled to Junifer to "Get. Get up! Up Junifer!" Slapping the reins. Junifer broke into a full run headed for Lead Bridge.

The buggy slid around to near side ways as she hawed Junifer onto Summit west of Lead Bridge and the pace did not slacken as they careened onto Cross. Straight on Cross, slapping the reins, "Get. Get, Junifer!" her scream wailed over the loudly trilling wheels of the buggy. With the buggy bouncing and rocking, Ma held on for dear life, experiencing the fastest most terrifying ride of her life. Clydis seemed glued to her seat, at one with the precipitous buggy, urging Junifer still faster.

Junifer gave her best for her master. Valiantly she charged on, responding to the will of her master, taking the corner at Jericho at a full gallop. The buggy slid from the roadway at the corner and clattered down the ditch on two wheels past the burned out privet to the arborvitae where the left side airborne wheels slammed down and the right side wheels rose skyward. They spun an arc in the south lawn while Junifer slowed, ending at the rear steps.

Clydis shot for the kitchen. She rushed to Edith and picked her up, clutching Edith to her. She stood crying, kissing, and hugging her beautiful daughter. Little Edith clamped her legs around her mother's waist and she scooted upward until she had clasped her hands behind the neck of her mother. Her curly brown hair bounced to the cadence of her sobbing mother. She pressed her cheek to her mother's cheek. Oh, how Clydis did cry. She stood holding Edith. She held to her beautiful daughter, drawing strength from her and she from her and Clarence held them both in his arms.

Emma tied Junifer. She grabbed a carriage blanket and threw it over the foam streaked, panting magnificent horse, knowing that the horse needed to be cared for as soon as possible. Emma'd lost her hat along the way, and her gloves, and now her scarf slipped to the ground behind her as she rushed inside the house.

She stood a moment, watching; wondering how really awful it must have been for this courageous young woman. She knew she could never comprehend the hurt her son had felt, and that his wife had felt. She knew she could not understand the terror. She'd witnessed it, been a part of it, and had been frightened by it, but Clydis had felt it, lived it. Emma stood in the kitchen. She looked across to the middle of the room. She could never describe what she saw, she could never draw nor paint the scene before her, she could only hold in her soul an immense gratitude. She thanked God for allowing her to be even a small part of the little family on Jericho. Emma looked on for only a moment then she turned and went into the yard. She must care for Junifer.

She uncoupled the horse and led it around and around, perhaps ten times around the yard and then to water, ended at the barn where she stabled her next to Bunny. The horses nickered their recognition then settled down to chewing their oats and hay while she gave Junifer a rub down with a slip of burlap. Shivering now, Emma began to wonder what had become of her hat and gloves.

She entered the kitchen to find Clarence and Clydis seated at the table while Edith, at their feet, thumped persistently upon a wooden bowl with an oaken pig. "Pig eats," she said. "Pig eats water." Grandma knelt down beside her. "Pig." Edith thrust it at Grandma's face. "Pig."

"Pig. Yes, pig. Nice fat pig."

"Aat pig."

In her other hand she held her tin cup, much dented now, and at her feet her rag dolly rested, Dollie wearing a pretty green dress made of pretty feed sack yard goods. Edith wore much scuffed patent leather shoes that had once graced the feet of Naddy James and her cambric gown which had leaped from the pages of Sears, Roebuck and Co., spread softly around her, the gown enhancing the drab much trod upon throw rug upon which she rested. Grandma brushed her fingers gently through the curly soft brown hair then she rose painfully up from the floor, her joints not used to that posture. She took a seat at the table with the others. Old Sniffer rose stiffly up from his station beside the range. He stretched then wandered over and placed his head on Emma's lap. She scratched his ear. Old Sniffer let out a contented sigh then plopped down beside her chair.

"Ma," Clydis began. "I'm sorry, I . . ."

"No, no. It's okay. Everything's okay. You're okay, as am I."

"I was so frightened. I could feel her watching for the moment that Edith was not with me. I felt her coming for Edith. I couldn't believe that Edith was okay until I had her in my arms. I was afraid as well that she would shoot Clarence."

"I understand your love for Edith and I share your concern. You're a natural mother, Clydis, and," she looked now at Clarence but spoke still to Clydis, "you are one superlative buggy driver."

Clydis accepted the compliments, relieved that Emma hadn't been injured. "Can you stay a while, Ma? Generally, I feel safe enough because we have Sniffer, but Clarence will be leaving for work soon."

"Yes, it's my pleasure."

"I have hours yet."

"You have not been to bed since your shift last night. I'm going to stuff you full of food and tuck you in."

"I want to stay. And for as long as I can, but we must get word to Robert. He'll be about town, showing off his newly enclosed buggy. Probably at Sky's or

Haimmer's."

"I'll go over to Morley and Helgie's and use their phone," Clarence said.

Clarence reached Pa at the Haimmer's. "I'll be out directly."

"Pa, if you'd rather, you can send someone out from the livery. It has started to snow now."

"I'll hustle. Anything else?'

"If you would stop by the mercantile. Ma and Clydis may have left their hat and gloves there and she'd ordered some staples. Clydis and Ma also ran off without paying their bill. You might tell Sky that I'll be in tomorrow to settle up."

She had fried potatoes, eggs, and ground beef ready upon his return. They sat down to eat. Clarence was soon nodding, the heavy food doing wonders for his eyelids.

As soon as he'd settled in bed Edith climbed all over him. She could climb up on the bed now all by herself. He was a most contented dad as he drifted off to sleep.

An hour passed before Pa bustled into the kitchen carrying a large sack. He sat it down then rushed back out, this time returning with a sack of flour and one of sugar. "I'll be right back," he said.

While outside he stabled Peanut then bustled back into the kitchen, shaking snow on the floor. "Robert, what are you doing?"

As he was removing his coat, he looked up to see that Emma was putting hers on. "Didn't you look in the sack?" Robert nodded toward it. She looked at it. "Our nightshirts," he said.

"Pa, how wonderful," Clydis said. She walked up to him and pecked his cheek.

Chapter Nine

It was just about full dark when Clarence bid his farewell to the womenfolk. He with Pa and Sniffer went out to do chores. Soon, with a pail of eggs in his hand, Pa waved as Clarence mounted Bunny. His lunch bag bumped against the saddle as he began his journey to the mill.

He'd assigned himself permanently to the night shift, believing that Mrs. Klinert would be less apt to trouble them during the night and besides, and of no small measure, he enjoyed being home during daytime with Edith and Clydis. Bunny rose to a smooth lope, not mindful of the snowy air or of the inch or so of snow that covered the road.

Bunny's head lifted after a time and he snorted. Clarence pulled gently with the reins. In a moment he recognized the huge horse approaching from the gloom as Shotgun.

Their horses halted: "Evening, Clarence." Marsh, at well over six foot, sitting a horse several hands taller than Bunny, gave Clarence the impression of God calling down to Moses as he spoke.

Clarence looked up at him. "Marsh, how goes it?"

"Well enough." Marsh leaned toward him from the saddle. "Keep an ear open for me, will you? I want to know about anyone interested in buying or shipping horses. I've just been to the Tobertons and Faygards. No one's approached them although Faygard has extra heavies he'd sell, he said, if they did."

"You might ask Clifford James. His brother, Charley James, is involved in a big operation further north, around Bruin City. A power company there is having a vast area logged off. They're building dams on the river. Charley says that his and another outfits are logging like mad because when the dams are finished they'll flood, logs felled or not. He said they need horses up there."

"I'd heard about that, deputy." He knew Clarence would have perked up his ears at the mention of 'deputy'. "You are still deputized, you recall?"

Clarence frowned at him.

"I need you, son. I've deputized Ed Benson and Tulip Board as well. I'm concerned about what your mother-in-law might do. You can keep your eye on that situation. Get any ideas, let me know. I'm also concerned about the possibility of horse thieving."

"I'm honored, Marsh, that you should rely on me," but I wish you wouldn't, he thought, "and I know whose ears should hear me if I should hear anything."

"You have any idea about Mrs. Klinert?"

"No. Clydis either. We'd sure like to know why she hasn't left the area, having sold both the business and the house. We're keeping Edith close to us. Did you know her mother carries a gun?"

"No. Where?"

"Clydis figured out that she carries it strapped to the inside of her left thigh about half way up from the knee so it doesn't show. A double barreled derringer with barrels about an inch long."

"Deadly at six to ten feet. Could kill a man."

"Today she charged home from town. She'd had a vision of her mother shooting me to get to Edith. Scared the bejillies out of us."

"Keep alert. As an official deputy you have the authority to arrest her if necessary."

"Oh." He hoped Marsh couldn't see him shudder.

"Have a good night, Clarence," he said, nudging Shotgun.

"Same," Clarence called as he'd started Bunny.

A train was just leaving the station southbound as Rockney was crossing Lead Bridge. He waited impatiently, drumming his fingers on the pommel. Finally able to proceed, he nearly touched the caboose as he crossed the tracks in his determination to reach the station. His mind was on the telegraph message he wanted to send. He was thus flabbergasted when a tall man turned and said to him as he entered the station, "How goes it, Marsh?"

He was relieved and grateful to see Herm Dinning standing there. He and Herm had trained together in St. Louis some thirty years before. Herm had become a railroad detective, just the sort of help Marsh had in mind as he entered the station seeking the telegrapher. "Herm, if you've retired, I'll shoot you," Marsh greeted.

Herm chuckled as they shook hands. "They've talked on it, believing a bald head and stiff joints equates to inadequacy. I'm here for your help, you old rascal. There are horse thieves using our railroad."

"I've been working on that, Herm. Can't figure it out yet."

"Me either. If we could wrap around a coffee pot someplace, I'll go over with you what I know; though it isn't much."

"I have a room in the rear of the haberdashery. It's yours. I don't use it. I generally sleep in my office."

"I'm obliged. Let's sling my kit in there." He hoisted his battered case.

Marsh led Shotgun to the livery then proceeded to the apartment, Herm in tow. Upon entering the office, Marsh introduced him to Deputy Ed Benson.

"Ed's been working with me on this case," Marsh explained. "I have two other deputies. One's at work now, works the night shift. My other deputy operates the coffee pot." Herm looked surprised, his mouth forming an 'o', but he didn't comment as he pulled a chair over to a table. "Ed, can you hold here a while? I'm going to fetch Tulip Board." Ed nodded his affirmative. Anticipating Marsh, he'd begun to clear the table as soon as Marsh and Herm walked in. Marsh placed a folder on the table. "Herm, Ed can show you our report so far. I'll be right back with deputy Board."

Ed wondered, smiling to himself about the 'right back'. Lately Marsh had taken an hour or two to get 'right back'. Ed delighted in sharing their secret. He'd lately noted an obvious difference in their relationship. He knew love when he saw it. Marsh had recently received authorization to pay his deputies a few cents per each hour they were actively in his employ. Ed was at last, to his great relief, contributing to his family's income, even to planning a big Christmas for them. He said, "Take your time, Marsh," as he and Herm began their scrutiny of the file.

It was a warm evening, around thirty degrees. Snow fell in huge wet flakes that had by then accumulated to four or more inches of soggy clinging snow. He took small steps, beating a path through the miasma to her door at the rear of the restaurant. She answered his knock.

Overjoyed to see him, she pulled him inside and laid a firm kiss to his lips. Rockney pushed her off, regretting that he must do so, desiring as much as she to be close. "Later," he promised. "I've a guest. Herm Dinning, railroad detective, friend of mine." He held her at arm's length. "If we could all get together, maybe we could make some headway. There is indeed, just as we've been thinking, horse theft mixed up with those mysterious train cars."

Her look was of disappointment, her attitude of duty, as she reached for her cape and boots. "I haven't seen a soul around them," she said while struggling with a boot. Marsh steadied her, she leaning back against him as she tugged on the boots. His lips brushed her cheek. "You'd better marry me, Rockman. Let's get this show on the road."

From Rockney's file Herm learned that Marsh knew about there being more than one location involved. "You're correct here," he said. "As a matter of fact there are eleven sites altogether. They're parked into sidings all the way from Comstock Park to Reed City. The cars at Comstock Park, Leadford, and Bruin City are too obvious to concern me. I believe they're decoys. Locally, I'd bet on the cars parked at Ellington to be the ones they'd use. I've set a man to keep watch of them. The cars are parked into the stockyard where they bring in slaughter horses. With the slaughter operation continuous, extra horses would be easily overlooked by anybody not in the know."

"I'm agreed on the potential of Ellington being the site. There're three horse herds nearby. That's Toberton, Faygard, and Jonnicks. Jonnicks is closest to Ellington. He deals in saddle horses. I've warned him to be on the alert. A horse drive from either of the other two farms would be six to eight miles; rather an easy night's work."

"We must do more than just catch the rustlers, as you know, Marsh. My plan would be to follow them until we've caught the whole gang; especially we want the mastermind, and I'm admitting to their being a mastermind involved. We have reports form Branch and Hillsdale counties; old reports, several years old, and many reports have come in all the way from Detroit to Chicago over the last several years. The operational set up here on the Pennsylvania is characteristic. We hope to nab the whole gang this time."

"We'll stay out of sight. But if seen, by chance, we'll try for capturing all we can then sweat some cooperation from them," Marsh said emphatically.

Their meeting broke up finally around ten o'clock. Ed was glad to be headed home. Herm too was tired. He headed gratefully for Marsh's room in the rear of the haberdashery. Tulip, yawning, had left a little ahead of Ed. Marsh set about the process of battering down for the night.

Marsh's lock up area had four cells positioned along one side to hold men prisoners. Across the alley from the men's cells was a bathroom that the men entered from the alley. Next to the bathroom was the women's cell, its wall solid to the bathroom. The women's cell included a closed in bathroom and the cell was twice as large as a men's cell. With no women in residence, Marsh used the women's cell as his sleeping quarters. His last step was to hang a 'Ring Bell' notice on the outside of the office door. No sooner had he entered the lockup headed for the women's cell than the bell rang.

"Darn," he remarked. He hurried to the office door and swung it open. As the door swung inward she stepped inside with it.

"What . . . er, Tulip! Gosh," his eyes were bugged, "am I thinking this right?"

She turned to the door and locked it then turned to him. "You're going to keep me warm, Rockman."

***

The morning dawned cloudy and as the air was colder, the snow would be staying a while. Old Sniffer stood out in it seemly discouraged because it'd dulled all of the beautiful smells he'd left familiar. It's a wonder he didn't run out of marking fluid so busy was he at marking out the key components of his territory. He stood eyeing the arborvitae now, finally deciding that it deserved a squirt. He'd just raised his marking machine when his ears caught familiar wavelengths from down the road. Clydis and Edith were in the kitchen preparing to do the washing. Clarence had gone to bed. All three of the Groners heard Sniffer remark that a friendly was nearing. Clarence listened carefully wondering if he should get up. Edith and Clydis, watching from the kitchen window near the side sink, were elated upon identifying the impending visitors as Billie and Clydene, yet Clydis frowned, not recognizing the third party aboard the buggy.

Billie pulled in past the arborvitae while Sniffer hurried along beside a buggy wheel attempting to mark it. He would no sooner raise his machine than the buggy would pass him and he'd be unbalanced a moment before hurrying to catch up. On his third attempt the buggy stopped and at last the vigilant hero watered the wheel. His eyes now strained to bring the third party unknown into view and his machinery also stood ready.

"It's Billie," Clydis called and Clarence, having heard her, instantly fell asleep.

Billie and Clydene and Mayfeather climbed from the buggy. Sniffer sniffed them and he poked his nose against Billie. He looked up at Clydene, ready to give her a welcome lap with his tongue, but was halted in mid motion by a hand which moved toward him. Sniffer froze, watching the hand.

"This is Mayfeather," Billie said, and he allowed her to touch his nose. Still wary, Sniffer went along with them as they went inside.

"This is Mayfeather," Billie introduced, "My mother. We're here because I know you will help us. My father is dead."

Mayfeather smelled of wood smoke and the forest. She exhibited the gentle innocence of a fawn and her eyes were bright like a chickadee. Her obvious oneness with the natural world attracted Clydis, rendering into her a wholesome sensation of belonging, as though through Mayfeather she was a part of the earth and the water and the sky. "I'm delighted to know you," Clydis said in awestruck understatement as they were shaking hands, and hugging. "I'm sorry to hear about your husband," Clydis murmured. But she then brightened as she told Mayfeather, "Billie and I are great friends. It'll be my esteemed pleasure to assist you in any way."

Mayfeather smiled, but looked confused. "She understands primarily our language," Billie explained as they were seating around the kitchen table. "Potawatomie. It is the language of our people. We need you to help her learn to speak and to read and write the English words."

Clydis had trouble believing at first. How could anyone living in America all of their life not speak its language? Clydis placed an arm on Mayfeather's shoulder. "Say words that you know." Mayfeather responded with a dozen and more English words all scrambled in with her native language. "I'll be able to help you. We'll begin with the words that you know."

Her last name is Allen, as is my nee name. Red and I were wed as

64

Raymond R. Toberton and Billie May Allen. We were married first at powwow, but later a reverend came to a store in Belmont and married us in a Christian ceremony. Indians do not usually have last names. A Captain Moses Allen was a friend of our family long ago so my grandfather chose Allen as his last name when he joined the Army.

"Grandfather served as a scout after your civil war and is still in the army out west. My brother is also a soldier. He tends horses at a post in San Antonio. He hopes to join our grandfather in the horse cavalry out west. Many of our people stayed behind when most of them were removed from southern Michigan. My family stayed in the woods and lived by the rivers. We raised horses. My grandfather spoke English so he could go to towns to get supplies and to stockyards to sell horses, but he wanted to fight in the war.

"My father, William Allen, did my grandfather's work, but he did not like to speak English. My brother Bill would have taken over the work, but he wanted to fight too in the army. Now my father has died of a disease called TB. He is buried beside a river near Athens, Michigan. Our ogeman, Baw Beese, from Hillsdale, met an ogeman named Roughwater on a reservation in Iowa. Ogeman is our word for chief. I will use some Indian words at first so that Mayfeather can follow what we're discussing. Later in life, many years later, chief Roughwater, also a shaman, came to find us. He told us about the Leadford powwow. So we came here and I met Red. So now you know more of our story. My mother is alone now and she wishes to live with me. She has never been to a town."

Edith had been all of this time standing either at her mother's knee or at Billie's, dashing between them while looking wondrously at Mayfeather. At Billie's knee she handed an oaken horse and a pig up to Clydene. Clydene, asleep in her mother's lap, didn't respond. Edith again studied Mayfeather, peering with bugged eyes at the strange bright dress and soft leather doeskin moccasins, and at the necklace of beads and teeth and claws. She was attracted as well by the long glistening black hair with its braid ends bound by leather bands decorated with beads and feathers. Suddenly, Edith ran over to Mayfeather. "Horsh," Edith explained, holding it for Mayfeather to see.

"Horse," Mayfeather agreed, smiling down at the beautiful child.

"Aat Pig."

"Fat Pig," Clydis explained.

"Pig," Mayfeather repeated. Her schooling had begun.

***

The next day the town of Leadford awakened under a mantle of snow. The sun rose as a huge orange ball, its fiery light glistening from tiny snowflakes a spatter of which still graced the air. A mantle of snow, especially the season's first, mellows the attitude of people as it mantles and softens the contours of habitation; contours of horse dung and debris, of starkness, of memory and of hate and of insult and fear. The people stayed inside as though being blanketed warmly impeded their desire to uncover. This until their discipline prompted them to sally into a world of mellowed reality. One hates to disturb that. One hesitates to trod upon it for each footfall, each hoof beat, wheel rut or runner track resumes the harshness of reality, laying bare the fact of man's relentless proclivity for assaulting the status quo, altering it to the wiles of his need for progress. Thus the school children ventured forth to arrive at school on schedule and Mrs. Klinert had arose in a snit seeing that the snow had mantled and squelched her scheduled plan for the day. At present she sat grieving her thwart, seeing that Naddy had begun her scheduled walk along Bridge.

Naddy delighted in the footprints she was leaving. The day had warmed slightly, just warm enough to make the snow pack easily. She paused to pack a snowball and to toss it ahead of her. She ran up to it and kicked it, making the snow fly. Above her rosy cheeks her eyes sparkled with glee as she paused at the alley between the marshal's office and Meads. Proudly she stood on the boardwalk awaiting the passage of a Franklin that was halted down the alley. The driver of the Franklin, a middle aged lady, well clad in furs and with a black hat tied beneath her chin, motioned Naddy to move on. Naddy looked the other way then back toward the Franklin then hurried across to arrive at Meads only one minute behind schedule.

As usual Claire greeted her warmly. Both Claire and Clifford had complete confidence in her ability to progress safely about town now, even to Clifford's not always going with her to her starting point near Faygard's garage. Instead, Naddy watched the clock in the freight office each morning to determine the moment to resume her odyssey. Claire, confident as she was in Naddy's ability, had ceased the need to crane her neck each day in her look to where Naddy would come into view, resting assured that her daughter would be there on time as expected.

Mrs. Klinert had planned well. No longer was she even Mrs. Klinert. Her identification card bore the name of Clydis Marie Groner. Her apartment in Bruin City was let to Clydis Marie Groner and her daughter, Elisabeth Marie Groner. Elisabeth's birth certificate placed her birthday on December 8, 1902, nearly Naddy's correct age. She had but to post a request to an acquaintance in New York to make those arrangements and to procure passports. She loathed the man, having paid for his promptness with a previous loan of her body. A tutor had arrived early one day, unforgivable in itself but of ever greater condemnation he had overheard Clydis screaming. She alone understood the need for and the extent to which physical abuse administered by electrical shock and pounding was required pursuant to complete obedience from her reluctant daughter. The man in New York had obtained the derringer for her and she had soon after in an obscure

Manhattan apartment ended the threat resident in the recalcitrant tutor. But the man in New York did not wish to be paid in money. She regretted his domination yet the promise of an impending visit to New York on her way to Europe had quickly provided the requisite paperwork.

From Bruin City she'd arranged overland transportation to Saginaw. They would then sail the Great Lakes and the Atlantic to arrive in Austria in the early spring. Elisabeth's training was scheduled to begin in March, sufficient time she deemed for the child to come to her senses. As Naddy had passed from her view, Mrs. Klinert sat fuming, her fingers tapping the steering wheel. If not for this filthy snow, she thought. And her thoughts sunk deeper, taking on a general hate of the world's propensity for blanketing certain of the lecherous wanton creatures of mankind. Her thought slid from the lecherous creature in New York to that of Sky Ferndin. It would be easy and she could in safety and without serious repercussion kill Sky Ferndin, ending forever his wanton lust of her. Beneath her fog of hate there kindled a renewed spark of Naddy, propelling her mind in slow ascension back to present reality.

She needed skid boots for the Franklin, an oversight that had that day been her thwart. But she'd be ready on the next attempt, no matter the weather. And she, in transference of her hate of Sky Ferndin back to that of her man in New York, knew that she and Elisabeth would indeed end his domination. Her promised impending visit to New York on her way to Europe would render payment the likes of which mister lecherous was not imagining.

Chapter Ten

By mid afternoon the clouds had disbursed and the sun's radiance bathed the town. The snow had grown sodden and slippery and Roger'd laced studded leather skid boots to Marsh's Oldsmobile. At the farm the Groners were at table in preparation for his departure for work. In Grand Rapids a man had just finished fitting skid boots to a Franklin. The Franklin had ditched twice in getting there, but now was ready for its safe clamorous return to its heated garage in the northeast section of Leadford. By the time of its return Clarence would have ridden Bunny to Moppit and be hard at work at the mill. At present Clarence was reaching for a second scoop of mashed potatoes. "She could use some more, too," Clydis said.

Clarence placed a small plop on her plate. "Would you like gravy, sweetheart?"

"Ohweeohgin."

"He spread oleomargarine over her potatoes and his own. He reached for the pepper."

"Not for her," she said.

"Okay," he agreed. They settled into the job, both with forks. Clarence was careful to set a good example. He took small bites, did not cram his mouth; to no avail, she packed in each mouthful of the delicious potatoes. Clydis returned the conversation to Mayfeather.

"She's taken the name, officially, of May F. Allen. Tomorrow, Claire and Lorraine are going to cut her hair and style it. Then she will be presented with appropriate saganash clothing; that's their word for white people. We're all contributing clothes. Then we'll go to Sky's for an ice cream sundae. Do you think that will be too much for May all in one day?"

"Probably," he chuckled. "But she'll know she's wanted and is welcome to our society. It'll be a high point of her life. You ladies amaze me."

"May also wishes to learn to drive a car." Clarence's eyebrows popped upward. She smiled. "But we'll wait until summer for that."

"There'll be others buying cars next summer. The Clout brothers are right about that. It's because of Faygard's dip. After it's filled people'll be able to drive the back way all the way from Leadford to Grand Rapids any time of the year; barring generalized mud or deep snow, of course, but they could do it much of the time."

"Then May and I can visit the Herpolsheimer." Now what sort of Indian term is this, he thought. Seeing that his eyebrows were raised, she continued: "Herpolsheimer is the largest department store in the city." His expression telegraphed 'Oh, my!' "When will they fill it?" she asked, leaving at hang his worry over the Herpolsheimer as she'd returned the discussion to the dip.

"When keeps changing. First they talked of bridging it, a summer job. Now they're leaning toward putting a big concrete tube across the road, the tube extending way out on each side. They can do that during winter. Then bury the tube in crushed rock, raising the level of the road up about six feet. We will be able to drive over that with horses, but the sharp rocks would likely ruin car tires." He paused, a thought bringing a grin to his face. "So you'll not be able to cross it to get to the Herpolsheimer. But then next summer they'll cut some dirt from the hills on each side of the dip and put the dirt on top of the crushed stones. You likely will not be able to drive through that loose dirt," he joked. "Sorry, no Herpolsheimer. But they'll end up with a nice gravel surface to the road. By then, of course, you and May will've forgotten all about the Herpolsheimer."

"I hope you've not told all of that road prattle to the Tobertons."

"They told it to me. The road, they judged, was hard enough last week for them to drag the refrigerator car home, but they weren't yet ready. Now it's warm and the road's too soft, too soft even for the wheels. They're on wheels now instead of a plank road, their first idea, because of Sal Perkins, Ray's dad. He's called Sal; Raymond Salsam Perkins; no relation to Morley. Well, Sal is a house mover. He's gone in with the Tobertons. So the refrigerator car'll be moved on wheels. Nonetheless, the road needs to be firm. Besides that, other train cars are at present parked in their way. They would rather the dip be left alone because they know they can cross it when it's cold enough. So they're hoping for frigid weather. Morley says they'll get it. Morley goes by squirrel nests. That's why he dissected my woodpiles. Studying nests, he was. The squirrels pack sycamore fuzz balls into the woodpiles. The bigger the mess, the colder the winter, Morley thinks. So they're main concern now is to have Morley's prediction come true before the county road department begins their assault on the dip." Edith giggled, drawing their attention to her, and to Sniffer! He with his nose on her plate. "No, Sniffer! Sniffer, go lay down." Sniffer backed away, disappointment obvious on his face. Edith, aware of their disapproval, began to pucker. "It's okay, dear. We love Sniffer."

"Sninififer," she looked over at him as she stood up in her chair.

"We love you, too." Clydis began to clean her with a washcloth. Clarence carried Edith's plate over and scraped the orts of Edith's repast into Sniffer's bowl. Sniffer commenced gobbling, his tail at wag, and Clarence gave him a few firm loving pats adding additional rpm to his tail. "See," Clydis encouraged her. Sniffer wants to eat over there."

"Sniffer's hungry." Edith was happy now as she climbed down from her chair. She rushed over to Sniffer and stood near him, watching him eat.

***

By late afternoon clouds had again blanketed the community and intermittent rain ensued. With the sunset the rain had ceased yet the air was made pregnant by humidity. Clarence shivered as he mounted Bunny. He was dressed warmly, but the air was moist and the zephyr cool, a combination which drove the thirty degree air into every pore of his body, seemingly cooling his body more than it cooled his hands and face. He urged Bunny to a bone-jarring gallop, serving to warm both himself and Bunny and held the gallop for nearly a mile along Jericho. Nearing Faygards, he pulled Bunny into a walk. Bunny fought the walk, wanting to move faster, but then snorted and stopped. Clarence, a bit annoyed, nudged him. The horse stepped ahead a pace or two before stopping, stopping as though he was expected to stop. "Darn it, Bunny. What's gotten into you?" Bunny's ears leaned forward as though listening, and then he nickered, warning his master that another horse, as Clarence could see now, was nearby. Marsh approached, walking Shotgun slowly, much slower than his normal pace; this difference was perhaps the reason for Bunny's capricious behavior. Bunny and Shotgun touched noses.

"I don't like the feel of this night," Marsh quietly said. "Your horse tell you anything?"

"He didn't need to tell me it's cold. Damp cold, runs right through a man. But Bunny did act up just now, came to a stop. But then you came into view. But it isn't like him to just up and stop, however."

"Shotgun didn't stop, but I'd given him his head. Surprised me that he slowed so." The horses turned their heads to an easterly direction, their ears pointing. "We've company," Marsh whispered. What's the lay of the trails into the tracks?"

"One's behind me at the big white rock. Go around two bushes then it's a straight shot of eight hundred feet or so to the tracks. Another trail, a lot harder to find, but Bunny knows the way, takes off along the dip. It leads to the railroad bridge that crosses the dip."

Marsh reached into his saddlebag, pulled forth a pistol and holster. "Take this. Start at the bridge. Work your way up the rails. If you see anyone, yell halt, shoot in the air if necessary. Unless they shoot at you, then shoot them."

Clarence strapped it on, hoping that he wouldn't be called upon to use it; hoping too, that John Purley wouldn't be overwrought at his tardiness. He knew Marsh's concern. He appreciated Marsh's confidence in him, but right now he'd rather about anybody but himself be Marsh's deputy. But then, why wish this hazard onto anybody else? "This sure in heck isn't my kind of work," he whispered to Bunny as he turned him off Jericho. Bunny made his way along the dimly marked trail to where they heaved onto the railway.

Marsh hung Shotgun's reins under the chin of his well-trained horse. Shotgun would stand quietly by the bush until Marsh called him. Marsh drew his big sidearm before moving silently onto the tracks. Standing quietly, faint sounds reached his ears. Some one was walking toward him. The furtive character made no sound as long as he stepped firmly on each cross tie, but shifting stones sent a clear rattle with each errant step. The shadowy figure made his way along the ties to within ten feet of Marsh before being jolted into a palsied wreck by "Hold!" Marsh's demand was a harsh whisper. "Move nothing but your hands. Grab sky! You move and I'll drill you."

"Wha. . . what d. . . do you wha. . . ?"

"I'm Marshal Rockney out of Leadford. Turn around." The man obeyed. "Bring your left hand down behind you." Marsh soon had him in cuffs. Patting him down produced a shouldered pistol and from his belt, a knife."

"Can't a man even take a w . . . walk?"

"Shut your mouth. Don't make a sound. We're just going to stand here."

Clarence, soaked in sweat, moved slowly, steadily along the rails. Ten very long minutes elapsed before Marsh picked up their sound. The man was sweating by then, and visibly shaking. Marsh hadn't said a word nor moved a foot during the harassing ten long minutes, hoping that he may detect the presence of other visitors, if any were around. Clarence came into view finally, not seeing them until Bunny halted not five feet from them. Marsh stabbed the man in the back with his pistol. "You alone?" The man didn't answer.

"We'll string him up," he said to Clarence. "I'm sure he's a horse thief."

"No. Wait!"

"There're trees over there along the right of way that'll do."

"We didn't take no horses."

"You've taken your share of them up and down this railroad." The man shuddered in disbelief. The man can't just hang me, he thought. Marsh called Shotgun in.

Marsh dropped a loop of rope around the man's sweaty neck then coiled the rope and pushed it into the man's cuffed hands. "Hold onto this."

The man obeyed, a believer now. "But, M . . . Marshal, you just can't hang a man."

"Move!" Marsh jabbed him with the pistol. Clarence, thinking that Marsh's actions had been a ruse, hadn't worried until that moment. Now, he was inclined to believe it.

"Marsh," Clarence stammered, "maybe he knows something."

"He hangs now," Marsh retorted, stabbing once more with the pistol. "Move." Trees came to view dimly against the skyline. "Head for those trees."

"But I do know something. I'm not alone in this. We're horse buyers. We weren't rustling. There's been a mistake."

"Keep talking," Marsh said. "I'll listen as long as it's interesting. But keep moving toward those trees." He jabbed him again.

"We buy saddle horses in cities then sell them to out communities. I just came from Faygards. We sold him stock from a police department. My partner's in Belmont with those horses, all mares. I rode on out to complete the deal with Faygard. But my horse took lame so Faygard's keeping him. So my job also was to find a route to drive Faygard's heavies to Leadford. We use railways whenever possible to drive because there's less chance for them to be scared by somebody. It got dark quicker than I thought, but I was hurrying along the tracks thinking to find shelter in Leadford. Then I heard a horse snort and I got scared so I was real quiet. Then you came onto me."

"What do you think, Clarence? Horse dung?"

"Better string him up, Marsh."

"No! No. Take me to Faygards. He'll tell you."

The three separated at Faygards, Clarence going on to work.

Rain drizzled.

Chester confirmed much of the man's story, even to his horse being lamed. Marsh borrowed a horse from Chester and took his man, one Simon Doty, into town and bedded him down, much to Simon's dismay, in a cell of Marsh's lock up. Simon's tale, ironclad to the average listener, was a sieve to the fertile mind of Marsh Rockney. He'd sweat him all night alone in a securely locked cell. In the morning Simon would be invited to occupy the seat of utter intimidation before Marsh's desk and Marsh would sweat more from him.

Clarence thought that John Purley was due an explanation for his being two hours late. "Thanks, John Purley. I knew you'd be wanting to get on home, but I had some trouble getting here."

"Edith, okay?"

"She's great. No problem there, but we knock on wood. I met the marshal on the road. You may know, I'm deputized."

"Dad too, I know, and Tulip Board. I don't see how she could get to Edith with all of you involved. Dad and Tulip have guns and I see you have."

"Forgot I had it," Clarence explained as he began to unbuckle it. Marsh had me wearing it tonight. He was suspicious that we'd encountered a horse thief." He looked hard at John Purley. "I shouldn't have mentioned what we were doing. Keeping my mouth shut is a part of deputy duty. Sorry."

"No problem. Dad's the same way. But I can't help but catch little bits. I know it's about those train cars. And everybody's wary of Mrs. Klinert."

"I'm proud to be helping Marsh, John Purley, but its nerve racking being a deputy. I don't recommend it."

"I hear you. But, you know, I believe dad likes it."

He can have it, Clarence thought, but decided the prudence of changing the subject. "How is everything here?"

"No problems, except for that squeak in the forward flutter wheel. Red wants to shut it down and realign the bearings. He's waited for you. I just stoked an hour ago, so that'll hold. He's down at the wheel. I'd rather not stay to help. I'm due at the depot restaurant."

"What's going on there?"

"They have four telegraphers now. Just hired one," he explained, enjoying Clarence's confusion.

"So?"

"She came with them, the Wainwrights, name's Emily. She works in the restaurant."

"Oh, oh, oh, I see," Clarence chuckled. "Well, good luck, John Purley." He smiled seeing John Purley rein greedily into the dark and drizzly night.

John Purley's rosy thoughts abandoning the drizzle to those less in love as he rode Strawflower along the railway to Leadford.

The dreary night would linger long and be a thwart for Red and Clarence but would be in duration all too short for John Purley.

***

Night passed into early predawn morning. The day shift started. Within minutes after Tom and Pal arrived, the Power Wagon cranked awake, the heat of its exhaust shimmering the morning air and its silver blue exhaust gases drifted upward to caress the naked branches of the maples. Pal was soon crossing the steel girded bridge on his way into the box plant at Grand Rapids. They'd ridden in on saddle horses, foregoing the buggy in deference to the mud. Work was scheduled to begin at the dip during the day as well. Tom and Clarence stood talking on the loading dock while they watched Pal pull away.

"Those big concrete tubes came in at Leadford siding yesterday afternoon, shipped clear from Hannibal, Missouri, Pal said. And a shovel crew's coming today from the county road commission in Grand Rapids to dig out the dip. Each tube is a wagon's load. Clifford James is one of the teamsters, pulling with a four-horse hitch. And they've hired Sid to drive a four-hitch and freight wagon of Chester's. The tubes'll be set today, they think, but the crushed rock isn't due till tomorrow. The rock crusher's located along the highway about three miles below Leadford.

It's a steam-powered outfit. Sid says the rock will all come through here. It'll be a sight seeing them climb old Moppit hill there," he concluded, nodding his head at the hill.

As they looked toward the hill the morning sun was just bringing it awake. The distant ruts on its crest glistened syrupy and flashed their warning in the morning light. Don't try me today, the hill was saying, while below Leadford a mighty steam powered crusher pulverized the rock which on the morrow would be mired to the axles in the brown mud of Jericho.

Chapter Eleven

Clifford's four Clydesdales made child's play of the heavily loaded freight wagon as they pulled onto Bridge from the freight siding. They stamped their impatience, jetting the cool moist air with their breaths as they plopped used timothy and oats onto the street. Nearby Sid's heavy wagon was settling beneath the weight of the huge concrete cylinder being rolled onto it. Finally loaded, Sid started his Percherons, pulling in behind Clifford. "Yeaah, Hooo!" Clifford yelled and the mighty dales muscled into their harnesses. The wagon crunched across the concrete surface of Lead Bridge gaining momentum for the up slope turn toward Cross. The first quarter mile of Cross was surfaced in crushed rock; treacherous stuff when pitted against automobile tires, sharp unyielding stuff as Clydis had discovered in her plunge into it some eight weeks past, but welcome support for the weighted wagons. "Eeeeyaaaa! Get. Get." Clifford strained them into still greater momentum as they took to the muddy way beyond the crushed rocks. The wheels plunged, the dales dug in invincibly. "Eeeeyyaaaaa!" Muscles bulging, they plunged onto Jericho. Hard on their tails drove the mighty Percherons.

Tiny Sid Toberton sat the high seat of his wagon, his feet braced to the foot rail in front, his arms corded. Four separate sets of reins threaded his fingers, controlling the Percherons individually. "Haaaa! Haaaa!" His stentorian bellow contrasting the high-pitched banshee howl of Clifford. "Haaa! Get. Get Haaaayaaaah!" Sid bellowed.

The Percherons pressed their collars. Five feet four-inch Sid Toberton, spring steel wrapped in rawhide, his stentorian roar cracked the air as he brought the Percherons down Jericho. Near Roughwater's gate on the only firm section of Jericho, Clifford swung his hitch to the right shoulder and stilled his heavy team of invincibles. Sid hauled to a stop beside Clifford, their rigs now fully blocking all passage along Jericho. The horses rested, the men rested. "Will your leads follow?" Sid wanted to know.

"No, I'm afraid not. Though I see your point. We'll need to pull with six

75

the next trip if they expect them all delivered today."

"That's what I was thinking. This road is softer than I expected; and it sure won't get firmer. My follows swing, I believe. We get these unloaded we'd best pull into Chester's to hitch six."

"Gotcha, pard," Clifford acknowledged. He slapped his reins. "Eeee Yaaaa!" The dales dug their hooves into the mud as they resumed their trek for the dip.

In Leadford Roger had just finished polishing the marshal's car. A good coat of wax under the mud helped in mud removal. He'd polished the car repeatedly over the weeks and as many times had rinsed the mud from it. Marsh rode Shotgun on trips outside the town but within the town he drove the Oldsmobile. On so warm a day the car would be parked in front of the marshal's office. On cooler days Roger kept it in his heated garage. Never more than one turn of the crank was needed to start it. Roger took special pride in his attention to the car. He'd paused his labor but briefly since before dawn, this to watch the heavy freight wagons rolling across Lead Bridge.

Workers at the dip had planked the road near it and Clifford swung his four smoothly into position for unloading. The workmen soon had the first cylinder positioned in the bottom of the ditch. Clifford pulled away, headed for Faygards. Taking Clifford's swing into Faygards as signal, Sid started his willing Percherons. Mud flew up from their hooves spattering the wagon, spattering the large concrete cylinder, spattering Sid. His eyes squinted and his stentorian bellow urged the mighty Percherons to the dip.

"Chester," Clifford called down to him.

"Yoh!" He sat his oat bucket near the door of the stable. "Be right up. Get unhitched."

Clifford unhitched Ruth and Ruby and was leading them to one side as Chester approached, his six-rein assemblage draping his shoulder. "I figured you'd be back for six," he chuckled. "Are you a six driver?"

"Never have. Has Sid?"

"Some."

"Think you'd better take it?"

"I'll ride drag. Keep watch of things. That Sid is tough. He'd not forgive us if we took the honor from him."

Pick and Slim were already hitched in their usual positions as wheel horses as Sid, having off loaded the cylinder, pulled into the farmyard. His four were moved into position with Blaze and Hawk at swing. The leads were Gander and Goose. The reins of all of the horses were threaded into his hands in a manner prescribed to afford control of each separate horse. Additionally horses, like dogs, know their names and would respond when addressed individually. Sid spoke to each horse, touching each rein as he did so as they started out, reminding each of them of their responsibility. "Up, Goose! Get in, Gander! Blaze, you move! Hawk!

Hawk!"

He did not personally know Clifford's Clydesdales, Pick and Slim. "Pick," jiggling his reins, "you listen. Slim, you pull! Slim!" Slim wiggled his ears. The team pulled at a steady fast walk toward Leadford through the deepening mud of Jericho. Chester rode a big bay charger behind Sid and Clifford tailed the caravan with Ruth and Ruby struggling to keep pace with their empty wagon. The day was yet warmer and the mud deepening.

Sid's was the first six-horse hitch that anyone, including Roger, had seen in Leadford. Roger eyed it as he delivered the Oldsmobile, parking it in front of the office handy to any quick departure required of Marsh. Then he hurried back down the street to marvel at the magnificent aberration, taking his position amid a throng of gawking onlookers, believing, with the others, that his eyes were befalling the day's acme of excitement.

Meanwhile, across town, Mrs. Klinert had removed the skid boots from her Franklin. She'd carefully topped off the fuel tank from a can kept in her heated garage. Now she adjusted the straps that she would draw around Elisabeth making her one with the passenger seat. Luggage for herself and Elisabeth was strapped into the tonneau seat. She checked her Fahys Moutauk watch, fuming at herself for being too early. She hadn't slept during the night. Now dreading that the thoughts which had kept her awake would return to vex her, she scanned futilely around the garage seeking a task to occupy her mind, finding it in checking the oil level in the crankcase, a task she'd already completed a dozen times. Still flustered, she went into the kitchen to make tea.

She felt lost at sea with but one remaining hope for survival. Abetted by her carnal compatriot Clydis had mutinied, taking Edith with her as unwilling baggage, ruining every chance that Edith may have become, under the careful deliberate tutorial of a true lady, a respected, envied, successful lady in her own right. Her remaining hope lay in Elisabeth. In Elisabeth she'd instill a profound hatred of men, thus staving any carnal intervention the likes of which had ruined eighteen years of careful, thoughtful, deliberate preparation of Clydis. Elisabeth would appreciate the fine art of using men when it came time for her conception but she would not for a single moment suffer cohabitation. Men are livestock and Elisabeth will see that the culls demand eradication. Groner deserved eradication, and Ferndin. Regretfully she would be leaving the miserable burg with those tasks unfulfilled, yet in her mind she could visualize a later return of Elisabeth, completing that work. All remaining hope lay in Elisabeth. She sipped her tea from her china cup imported from India then she started the Franklin.

Clifford sat behind his tired team of Clydesdales. Naddy warmed him with her departing kiss. His was an expression of total contentment and pride as Naddy climbed down from the high seat. He'd wanted her beside him on this morning safe from the heightened frenzy that emanated within the freight yard. Naddy was safely started and had made her way two blocks up the street before his view of her became blocked by Sid's proud stepping six. They made child's play of the heavily laden freight wagon as they clopped onto Bridge from the freight yard.

Naddy James, dressed too warmly, moved sedately along Bridge. Her woolen collar itched and her brow beaded sweat in the forty-degree heat of a sunny day in December. She removed her hat and mittens and her scarf and jammed them into the coat pockets. Now she paused to unbutton her coat, daring herself to remove it entirely, knowing that her long flannel underwear and woolen dress would be warm enough, but worried still that a scolding could consequent the action. Feeling better now, she held the coat open to the gentle breeze that rode the sunbeams into town and the breeze lifted the coat like a kite. She spun around, the coat floating with her, she giggled and her merry eyes sparkled. She ran and she spun and she flapped the coat reveling in the sunshine and the gentle breeze until Mrs. Klinert suddenly grabbed her!

Naddy yelled, "No! No!" as Mrs. Klinert slammed her into the seat. She struggled under the weight of Mrs. Klinert who reached across her clawing for the retaining straps. In stark terror Naddy reared upward nearly thrusting her assailant from the car. Mrs. Klinert screaming her rage pummeled Naddy viciously with slap after searing slap until she'd shocked her into a mouth-gaped silent scream.

All of the town's eyes save one were on the six-horse. Banker Leevy, at work since dawn, was just leaving the Farmers bank. He was on his way to Tulip's for a tad of breakfast. His eyes had at first turned toward the six, but his ears had protracted a commotion from the alley across the street. He saw her stretched across Naddy, again straining for the straps their distal ends having now fallen from the car into the street. He could see enough of Naddy to fathom at once her peril. He screamed, "Marshal! Marshal! Help! Help!" He waved madly but fear and disbelief had immobilized his feet.

Hearing his yell, her rage distorted face turned in that direction. Seeing his mouth gaped and his arms swinging, pointing, her decision was made in an instant. She delivered a series of bone shattering chops to Naddy's face with her elbow then, foregoing the straps, plunged herself into the driver's seat. Her movements served to loose Leevy's feet and as he moved into the street his voice rose to a howl. "Marshal! Marshal!" His howl was answered by a pitiless rev of the engine and by the grinding of gears as she ripped the Franklin into motion.

Marsh rushed from his office and was galvanized into instant action by the scene unfolding. In a wink the Olds was started, twin rooster tails of slimy mud pelted Leevy head to toe as Marsh floored the Olds.

Little more than a block in lead of him mud filled the air as she hadn't shifted from low gear but kept the throttle in full. Careening, her rear wheels threw the mud skyward. She clung to the wheel, her foot embedding the accelerator with Naddy turned in the seat, her bloodied face turned toward Marsh, gripping the seat in desperation, in terror, her mouth wide open, her scream pitched above the roaring Franklin. Marsh was gaining, closing the gap.

The Franklin slithered onto Groner Street, offering a broadside to Marsh and he took it, slamming his right front wheel into the churning left rear of the Franklin. Claire James, alerted by the noisome clamor outside Meads shop poked her head from the door and was confronted by mud spattered Leevy. "Naddy," Leevy wailed, beginning a lunge up the street. "Naddy. She took Naddy!" Claire in turning his indicated direction saw the impact and within its cosmos of hurtling debris caught a glimpse of Naddy's coat just as the coat and Naddy disappeared, crumpling against the dashboard. Claire mindful not of the mud, eyes only to her stricken child, run the fastest run of her life up Bridge, her tears streaming.

Marsh's axle had driving deep within the Franklin where it tore loose the drive train and plowed the rear axle assembly from her car while a part of her car neatly holed his radiator. The wreckage slid to a stop, blocking Groner Street. Robert Groner, at work out front, decorating a pine tree, began running at once toward the wreck. He saw Marsh leap his hood landing in the Franklin. The debris had not settled before Marsh had Naddy in his arms. As he plopped into the passenger seat holding Naddy, a tiny, barely audible whimper rose from her.

Robert rushed up. "Marsh, Marsh. Oh, my gosh!"

Marsh raised his tear filled eyes to Robert Groner, "Get a doctor," he pleaded. "Oh, please, get a doctor."

Claire blazed into the scene, at once grasping for Naddy. Marsh released her to Claire tumbling Claire in a rearward plop to the mud. Claire cuddled her, kissed her, showered kisses on her, her grief driven sobs bewailing a relentless beseeching of God for the survival of her blood spattered beautiful child. Naddy remained motionless, not responding at all but for a tiny pain filled whimper rising from deep within her battered soul.

By that time Mrs. Klinert had walked away from the wreck. Robert had seen her walk away, had met her, and passed her, had paid her no mind, she being at the moment of no consequence, his thrust driving arrow straight for Marsh, his friend, and Naddy.

Word spread through town in a wave action, heads turning with each call of "Wreck!" then new heads turned and shouted, "Wreck!" Sky heard the word at the same instant he espied Mrs. Klinert crossing the lots between Groner and Front. He hollered "Wreck!" and darted into the store, thinking to help her.

Chester, Roger, Sid, and Clifford were in conversation around the six-hitch. Sid from his high perch looked toward Sky, sighted the wreck and told Roger. "Car wreck up the street." Just then "Naddy" waved through to them jarring Clifford instantly into action.

"Lord, God!" he shouted, and reached the high seat behind his Clydesdales in a single bound. "EeeeeeYaaaaah!" his banshee command sent them in full gallop up Bridge.

Mrs. Klinert reached up under her skirt popping the deadly derringer into her hand. She knew all hope was lost. She would go to prison if they caught her. She'd lost Clydis, Edith, and now she'd lost Elisabeth. Hate shared space with despair in her mind. The hate drove her.

Going too fast, the Clydesdales couldn't stop at the wreck. Clifford pulled the hand brake and yelled "Whoa!" as he pitched from the seat. They traveled on as he plunged his knees to the mud near his family. He clung to them bewildered, knowing not what had transpired, seeing only that his daughter was injured. He held them close. The horses were a half block in stopping.

Doc Nealy rushed into the pandemonium, oblivious to the presence of mud as he knelt to examine Naddy. "Let me see," he said gently. He reached for her, white cotton gauze in his hand.

"No!" she twisted away from him. "Oh, no."

"Claire, it's Dr. Nealy. Please let me help. Naddy needs help."

His eyes met Clifford's, beseeching. Clifford lifted Claire and Naddy as a unit from the mud. Cradling them, he headed for Nealy's office. Claire sobbed uncontrollably, her body shaking, lending a cadence to Naddy's faint whimper.

Sky had hurried through his store and out through his residence to stand upon his rear stoop, arriving just as Mrs. Klinert neared. "Ma'am," he addressed her, sincerely wishing to help. "Wait. Please wait. I'll help you."

She didn't slow her step. Her expression bewildered him. Wanting only to help, he was met with a steely hard stare striking at him from beneath lowered eyebrows. Her teeth were tightly clamped. Her lips opened slightly, her slight smile creasing the rigorous hatred molded in her face. She did not aim the derringer. She merely pointed it toward the lecherous antagonist and pulled the trigger.

Sky'd seen an object in her hand, too small to be a gun. He'd seen two tiny flashes and a whiff of smoke. His shoulder felt suddenly heavy. Too heavy to hold up and it pulled him downward. He twisted with it as he fell, ending on his knees turned away from her, facing his stoop. She didn't look back.

Robert Groner walked up the street to where the Clydesdales stood blowing. He spoke to them and he patted on them before grasping the bridle of Ruth, the off lead horse. Having walked the team to the freight yard, he left the wagon to be loaded with the next concrete tube. At the livery, he watered them and ordered a rub down and an offer of timothy and oats. His thoughts were on Toad as he worked. He could not suffer Peanut to carry him to Toad through the mud. He knew Morley would take care of Toad along with old Jude even to rubbing the liniment into Toad's pain filled shoulder. Still, he missed Toad.

Rockney waited near the wreck for Roger to pull up with his wrecker. Roger had built up the wrecker beginning with a Cadillac purchased from a thoroughly disgruntled man who'd tried to cross Faygard's dip one rosy day in the spring of

1905. The front seat remained and the hood, beyond which little resemblance to Cadillac was retained. He dragged the Franklin off the street and into a nearby lot and would leave it there. The battered 1905 twenty four hundred pound two-cylinder Olds touring car soon dangled from his derrick. His rear wheels bit into the mud, beginning a restoration process on which Roger would labor incessantly through the night. During reconstruction Roger would replace the engine with the more powerful four-cylinder model now in production.

Clifford placed Claire on the examination table in Nealy's treatment room. Her left leg remained folded under Naddy. Naddy rested on the leg and Claire clutched her close, her head bent forward, her cheek resting in Naddy's hair. Claire's right leg draped from the side of the treatment table. Clifford stood much perplexed at himself for thinking about it. The dress was pulled upward exposing her shoe and several inches of her leg. The heavy woolen stocking stretched over the cotton long john could not hide, but only emphasize the shapely delicious composition of the leg. Without preamble save the warning, "Hold her still, Claire," Nealy reached in and pulled her nose straight. Naddy struggled and moaned. Sweat popped from Claire's face and she began shaking. She stared daggers at the doctor, wanting to hurt him. "She's going to be all right," Nealy crooned soothingly. "That was a good response." He taped her nose into position. "Let's remove her coat." Claire consented, relaxing her hold, but the action hurt Naddy and Naddy moaned and struggled.

"Please," her look was a warning for him to desist.

Nealy prepared a basin of warm water to which he added a pinch of Epsom salts. He began to clean Naddy's face. She took the cloth from him. Gently she washed the blood spatters from the face and hair of her beautiful child. Clifford still standing behind her gently rubbed her back and patted on it. Nealy began the cutting of her clothes, needing to examine thoroughly her entire body looking for broken bones, bruises, and abrasions, recording each discovery in the medical report. "Help me, Clifford."

Clifford eased the pieces of her clothing away as Nealy snipped ending with Naddy attired solely by the tattered remains of her johns. From this position the leg was exposed nearly to her garter and Clifford even more perplexed scolded himself: at a time like this, you idiot. But he couldn't divert his attention from it. He loved Naddy no less for thinking about it and his concern for her welfare, he knew in his soul, was eminent, yet he wanted Claire. He wanted to slap himself. So intense was his inner turmoil that he failed to respond to Nealy's next imperative. He caught only ". . . flat . . . Cliff?"

"Huh?"

"She needs to lie flat with her feet elevated. Help with Claire. She'll need a chair."

Clifford snapped out of it; embarrassed, ashamed, but able to conceal those emotions in his rush to move a chair next to the examination table and to assist Claire, one leg numbed, momentarily useless from its support of Naddy, into it. Claire held Naddy's hand and she fussed insistently with Naddy's hair and she talked of her love for her. Naddy seemed to be peacefully asleep now.

"Her vital signs are good. She's been in shock, driven there by terror and pain and misery. The terror is gone. I'll check her vital signs again shortly, but my guess is that she'll awaken soon. As soon as you wish, you may move her to the bed in the recovery room."

"Thank you." Claire nodded her assent. "Clifford, your work?"

"I can't do any of it because of mud. I'll catch up later. This is a good time for me to go get Harold from school, do you think, Doc?"

"Certainly. It's a good idea."

The streets were firm beneath an inch or more of slimy mud. Clifford slogged his way home where he hitched horses to a carriage. The horses stepped out, their hooves sinking an inch into the road surface and skidding with each surging step. His mind was not on their problems, but upon his family's. His pistol was strapped to his waist, an accouterment of his job, there having once been a robbery of a freight wagon. Had he chanced to turn his head to his left while he was slogging home to get the horses he would have seen Mrs. Klinert hiding behind the gristmill. Now the horses' path as he drove along Groner Street would pass within sight of where she was hiding. Fate alone protected her. But for the narrowed focus of his mind he would have seen her and shot her.

Chapter Twelve

The mud that morning crimped progress at the dairy. May'd just returned from Faygards where she'd delivered their milk order on foot. Molly and Helen were saddled upon May's return. The three waited for Billie. Red had staggered in from the mill, his legs in agony's citadel, fighting the pain, struggling to prevent pain bringing tears from his eyes. Billie doled eight Upjohn pain pills for him that he downed with milk before retiring. Billie alone had ever seen him cry. They were ready then for departure. Helen and Molly each trailed a packhorse loaded with twenty gallons of milk, the burden to be eased at the mercantile. Billie and May had milk orders for Perkins and Groner packed into saddle bags along with the four customer orders on Cross, the farthest being the Bailey farm a half mile out. The ladies by gentle commands started their horses toward the railway.

May and Billie split from the others behind Morley and Helgie's, negotiating the woods and fields with ease to arrive on Jericho. Clydis had been worried, seeing not how their planned day with May could unfold, but now was delighted by the ingenuity of Billie and May as they rode in past the arborvitae. Sniffer pranced beside them. May rode on across the fields to the customers on Cross. Billie tied Spirit to the hitch post.

"Clyeeeen!" Edith, agog with excitement, strained against her mother's firm grip on her sleeve, wanting to run out in the wet to greet her friend. "Clyeeen." Edith hopped and waved her arms. Her eyes were big and round and her curly brown hair bounced as she hopped and she held her little hands together in front of herself and wriggled and giggled: "Clyeeen."

Edith was soon charging around the house with Clydene in the baby carriage. Clarence had replaced the Bessemer steel carriage frame with a wooden structure that lowered the China rattan basket of the carriage to rest between the wheel tops ending with a height of carriage handier to Edith. She'd placed her doll, that day attired in a red dress, in with Clydene who nestled upon the pomegranate-colored Bedford liner of the basket with a pillow on either side of her, and then she'd heaped Clydene with oaken animals. Meanwhile, Billie and Clydis were seated at the table over coffee and Billie's reading lesson while waiting the return of May.

By that time Molly and Helen had arrived in Leadford. To their relief they'd completed the journey ahead of the southbound local which would have blocked their progress across Lower Lead Bridge. Edith now halted her tour in front of her toy bin under the side sink where she industriously removed most of the wooden animals from the carriage replacing them with her tin cup, a wooden bowl and her spoon. The mothers looked on, contentment and pride their register, as delighted as was Edith to see Clydene grasp firmly to the spoon and begin to wave it. "Clyeen likes it," Edith giggled and squirmed, nearly climbing in with Clydene in her enthusiasm to please her.

***

Mrs. Klinert had paused her flight at the north end of the gristmill. Patches of snow remained in the shade of the mill and her feet plunged through to the mud beneath. Each of her footprints filled rapidly with water. She stood a minute to gaze at them, shocked at their starkness and precision, stating to all that she'd passed here though no one had witnessed her passage. She felt exposed, as though now all was known of her, that she had no secrets.

Ridiculous! They could only erroneously think that knew her! They would think of her as evil when in truth her mission had been to better the world if not more than by one person, one perfect lady. She alone understood the importance of that. They'd all been against her, slobbering their mediocrity, unwilling to sacrifice leniency to success. She'd murdered Sky Ferndin. They would think that act to be brutal, heartless, when in fact she'd acted of necessity. Those of lecherous ilk anchor in wanton pit the moral standard of society, necessitating the removal of all such throwbacks as impediments to social enlightenment. She stamped her feet, emphasizing that commitment as she glared down at the derringer still clasped tightly in her right hand. All was lost now but the derringer and she'd use it. She'd go to New York and she'd use it. And if necessary, she'd use it to get to New York!

***

It wasn't until Roger was hauling away the Oldsmobile that Marsh's attention had returned to Mrs. Klinert, wondering now where she'd gone. Likely she would've run to her home or to the agency seeing one of them as haven. He didn't feel rushed to seek for her, wanting instead to check on Naddy, but he could be of no service there, he knew. He began unwillingly in the roadway looking for tracks, experiencing distaste in his thinking about her, wanting not to meet her again, anticipating only trouble from her, but he would do his job. Robert's was the first face he'd seen after the wreck. He started for the Groner residence, intending to question him.

"Hey, Marsh!" Robert, on his way cross lots from the livery, had seen Marsh standing alone on Groner Street. Seeing Marsh wave, Robert hurried toward him, taking a path but yards and inches from the way she'd gone before. They'd no sooner found her tracks and began to follow them when Janet Coats rushed up to them, her neck red from yelling something about Sky.

Sky had remained in place on his rear stoop a moment wondering what force had felled him. He could not think of what happened to him. Finally he'd turned around and sat on his stoop and looked inquisitively at his shoulder. He felt with his fingers where a small patch of blood darkened his shirt. Shot? Could I be shot?

He entered the store from his quarters and walked toward Janet. "Janet." She'd not seen her love this way before, shaken and pale, holding his shoulder. "Janet, I think I've been shot!"

Ed Benson earlier that morning had eaten his oatmeal mush and toast before moseying into Marsh's office, thinking to relieve him so that he could breakfast at Tulip's. Marsh had introduced him to Simon Doty. "I don't believe he's hungry," Marsh said. "But I do believe he'd like to chat with me after I return from breakfast."

Marsh winked an eye during that revelation, Ed taking cue that more would unfold.

Upon the marshal's return, Ed let Doty out of his cell, but hadn't seated him in front of Marsh's desk before the commotion in the street outside occurred. He placed Doty back into his cell and had remained on duty since, wondering all the while what in the world was going on out there; getting quite frustrated really, until suddenly Janet Coats burst into the office with news of Sky, frantically in quest of the marshal.

Ed had sent her in a correct direction, he guessed, to find the marshal and he telephoned Dr. Nealy.

***

Mrs. Klinert had stepped out from behind the gristmill. She could see the railway and beyond that she glimpsed a large concrete structure which she knew to be the dam and waterworks. Her thought was to go up the railway in the direction she believed would lead her eventually to Bruin City, but hadn't taken a second step before a yell reached her from an unknown direction. She resumed behind the mill from where she peeked toward Lead Bridge and the train station.

She could see two horses and beyond them, over nearer to the Lower Lead

Bridge, but coming toward the horses, two riders whom she watched intently. She was appalled in recognizing what they were: Women dressed in canvas men's trousers sitting straddle their horses in total abandon of any semblance of decency and leading horses to which were attached milk cans. Sluts! Sluts! And one slut was obviously pregnant. That one waving shamelessly and calling "Hello, good morning," drawing the attention of any nearby innocents who in turning to interrogate would have their eyes stunned by this wanton carnal aberration.

Just then the horses moved forward, forward, until not two but six horses hitched together hid her view from the awful wanton sluts. As she watched, two men, in obvious abandon of civil decency, were engaging in conversation, though she could no longer see the sluts, now shielded from her scathing view by the wagon, in conversation no less, she could tell, with the sluts.

The large hitch of horses having thrust forward, she saw the huge concrete tube. She could no longer see the sluts, nor did she try to see them. Her attention was drawn instead to the clamor of a train as it entered town from the north. She decided to stay behind the gristmill. When she flattened against the building she could see little of the town. Looking across the alley in which she was secluded she could see only bushes. And nobody, after all, thus far had sought her in that place. The place had grown familiar to her. She felt secure. The horrible monstrous stinking train hove into the station not thirty feet from her. And now her feelings concerning the place had abruptly changed. Trapped now! She pressed her back to the building.

***

Their first clue that May had returned was the whinny of horses outside the farm house entry. Looking from the window, Clydis' eyes suddenly rounded and her forehead creased. To this moment her thought had been to a buggy ride into town. May, in deference to the mud on Jericho, had saddled Junifer, expecting Clydis to ride with them, not recalling that Clydis had never before ridden a horse. She blamed herself for May's misunderstanding. May, Clydis understood, was to teach her to ride in the spring while Clydis, in turn, would teach May to drive a car, but here was May behaving in complete opposition to their belabored plan. "Billie," Clydis beckoned without taking her eyes from the dreaded scene before her. Billie joined her at the window.

"Oh good, she's ready."

"Billie," Clydis whispered nervously, "I've never ridden a horse."

Billie giggled, poking her friend with her elbow. "May will show you."

Billie hurried after Edith, now deep into the bedroom where she had pushed the carriage with Clydene in it. Now, having off loaded the tin cup and wooden bowl, she was in the process of loading her mother's hairbrush and comb and mirror in for Clydene's inspection. "Come," Billie said. "We'll put on our coats. We're going to ride a horse."

"Horse," Edith repeated. "Clyeen, too?"

"Yes, Clydene, too; and your Momma."

"Momma, too," Edith wriggled with delight as she ran to find her coat. On the way she grabbed her diaper bag to which she stuffed in her doll and several oaken animals.

Outside the ladies were greeted by a cacophonous din punctuated by loud stentorian commands erupting from the swollen throats of the teamsters. Sid and Chester were affording no quarter to the horses, demanding their steady advance through the Jericho mud. Mud flew from their hooves, plastering the teamsters who, seemingly oblivious to the pester, kept up their stentorian urge, moving the wagon with its awesome burden smoothly through the brown mud of Jericho.

May sprang to the bare back of Acorn whose saddle she'd placed on Junifer. Clydis stood holding Clydene. Edith was at her side with her tiny mitten-clad hand clasped with that of her mother. Clydis watched acutely as Billie with two firmly loaded diaper bags draping her shoulders, placed her left foot in a stirrup and swung gracefully into the saddle. Spirit stood calmly as Billie leaned down to receive Clydene whom she promptly inserted into a sling affair, rather like a hammock, which hung from her neck, placing Clydene securely before her while allowing her hands free to control the horse. Clydis, having made no such preparation, stood perplexed, her hand still clasped with Edith's. Billie smiled down at her. "She'll ride with May," she said, nodding toward May, her smile lending little assurance to Clydis.

May, a broad smile on her face, reached for Edith, swinging her deftly into a straddling perch before her on the bare back of Acorn, leaving Clydis to, in her mind, make a total fool of herself in her effort to mount and ride Junifer.

Billie was not surprised but May was astonished at seeing Clydis' skit split full length, hem to thigh, as she heaved onto Junifer. Nearly pitching off the far side, her hand fairly strangled the pommel until finally she gained the other stirrup and pushed herself into a posture somewhat resembling an accomplished equestrienne.

Clydis had designed the pant skirt herself, intending that it would ease the awkward process required of women in mounting or dismounting travel conveyances. That operation was made easy by the accepted attire of men. Said attire was, however, not generally deemed suitable for women. Thinking to stifle such nonsense, Clydis, beginning with the new slenderizing fashions illustrated in the Sears, Roebuck, Co. catalog, had with Billie's assistance in carefully pinning the hem of each leg preparatory to stitching by Singer, constructed a daring new form of feminine apparel. The idea for the outfit was not new, there being full skirted versions on the market, but application of the concept to the new skirt styles, had been the sole inspiration of Clydis who sat now reveling May's astonishment; but steeling herself, nonetheless, in dread of impending embarrassment.

They crossed the front yard, slanting to the corner of it where they passed through a burned out privet hedge intending to make a straight across transect of Jericho, spending as little time as possible in the mud. Having crossed the road the others looked back finding that Clydis hadn't crossed but was floundering, riding this way and that all around the front yard. Junifer was trained to neck rein wherein a gentle pressure from a rein on the left side of her neck would turn her to the right. Intending to turn right, Clydis pulled the right rein and nearly fell from the horse when she'd turned left, the horse being in total confusion as to what her rider desired of her. Clydis was off balance at each turn, the saddle shifting side to side as though attached to the horse by grease. "Whoa, Junifer," May gently commanded as she rode to the struggling, frustrated Clydis. "Do not use," May directed, taking the reins from Clydis. "Just cling to saddle, Junifer will follow." So Clydis was feeling a bit more secure as they crossed Jericho. Here they turned south along the charred sumac margin of the wheat field, Clydis the while studying the riding techniques of her companions.

May was controlling by pressure from her legs against the sides of her horse, not using the reins at all. She noticed that Billie didn't pull a rein in making the turn required of them in aligning their passage along the north edge of the field past the naked black thornapple which stood defiantly along Cross. The field and events pertinacious stirred fearful memory in Clydis and she felt no release of tension until they finally exited by way of the farm lane onto Cross. Now on the roadway, she felt her tension abate and her confidence to struggle upwards. She resumed her grip on the reins, copying Billie. Suddenly she was a rider, having graduated at least to kindergarten status as an equestrienne.

***

Earlier that day, before daylight, Red had left the mill at the end of his shift, leaving Clarence, at Clarence's insistence, to finish up. They'd endured a cruel night at war with a flutter wheel's bearings. Red's crippled legs, Clarence knew were a well of discomfort by the time the wheel was returned to service. Another few hours had elapsed before Clarence was free to be on his own way home. In riding along the railway in full daylight, he was able to see Toberton's heavy horses. They snorted their greetings as he and Bunny were passing the winter pasture. Red's horse had earlier snorted at this location and Red had wondered about it but could see nothing in the black of night nor concentrate long on the mystery due to his overwhelming pain.

The horses, Clarence saw, were located in a hollow near the railway margin of the pasture. He couldn't see into the hollow from his location, but they seemed to be grazing, a situation incongruent to the season there being little if any succulent grass abounding at that time of the year. Nearing the off trail to Roughwater's gate, his attention was diverted by the clamorous passage of the six-hitch down Jericho.

No sooner had the clamor subsided than he was surprised to see fresh horse tracks at the junction with Roughwater's path. He studied them a moment before deciding that the ladies must have made their way along this route on their way as planned to visit Clydis. He followed the hoof prints.

Within a mile he arrived to where two sets of the hoof prints left the railway and he followed them into a woods, lost them in the woods, but gave Bunny his head, Bunny leading him uneventfully through the trees, delivery him finally into the Perkins' back yard. He smiled now in realizing that Billie and May had led him home. In another minute he reached the barn where he intended to stable Bunny.

In passing he'd seen the buggy resting in its shed next to the barn. The situation had him perplexed. The buggy still here? He knew that Clydis hadn't learned to ride a horse but now saw that Junifer was missing from the stable. Toad and old Jude were still there. They with free run of much of the barn had stabled themselves and now waited for a doling of oats and timothy. He obliged them but didn't stable Bunny, instead leading him up to the rear stoop of the house where he tied him to the hitching post.

She'd left breakfast for him in the warming oven. He saw it there and was appreciative, but couldn't eat. A strong sense that something was wrong had taken him. The trouble was not at the farm as evidenced by Sniffer's attitude, seemingly content even to his usual look to Clarence for sustenance as his only salvation from mortal hunger. On impulse, knowing that indeed Sniffer couldn't be famished, likely as not even overfed by this time of day, Sniffer being expert at food acquisition, he nonetheless swept his breakfast into Sniffer's bowl. He retained only a clasp of bacon to munch on his way into Leadford.

He picked up their trail quickly and set Bunny to a lope, easily and quickly following Junifer, Spirit, and Acorn's tracks to where they exited the field onto Cross. From there he could see across to Lead Bridge. His heart beat quickened when he caught sight of Clydis with the others crossing the bridge. He shifted position in the saddle, easing a binding discomfort that had arisen in his clothing. Bunny continued his lope into town.

He rode briskly up to the women who were gathered at the depot, their ranks swollen by Molly and Helen whom they'd joined.

Molly and Helen filled them in on events which over the last hour had unfolded in the town, leaving all of them fearful for Edith's safety. May still had Edith in front of her on Acorn. Clydis tucked Junifer in beside them. The other riders boxed in the pair and they made their way to Meads. Once the womenfolk were safely inside, Clarence removed the pistol, loaned to him by Marsh, from his saddlebag and strapped it on.

Chapter Thirteen

Tulip emerged from the cellblock just as he entered the building. She'd been removing Marsh's belongings and photographic equipment from the women's cell and bathroom, tidying the area in anticipation of a female prisoner, namely Mrs. Klinert. Seeing Clarence, she asked, her voice stammered by nervous tension: "Did you hear that Sky's been shot?"

"Yes. How bad is it?" Clarence too was apprehensive, wondering what peril they were to face.

"I'd think not too bad. He walked to the doctor's office. Marsh is over there talking to him. Ed'll stay on duty here. Marsh wants us to meet with him to organize the hunt. We're to assume she's armed and dangerous." Her eyes were rounded, her forehead slightly furrowed. Light glinted from the shiny new deputy marshal badge pinned to her coat. Determination lined her face as she strapped on her pistol.

"I'm going to kill her, Clarence, if need be, without regret, I assure you," she declared in steeling herself. "I know it's the wrong attitude for me, but I can't help it. She nearly beat little Naddy James to death."

"I don't blame you," he replied, relieved to see that she was also on edge yet equal in determination with him. "I feel the same way. We're the wrong two people to be in on this. But, believe me I'll do my job to the utmost, if necessary."

"Now wait, you two. Calm down," Ed warned them. "You listen to Marsh. Do what he tells you. I'm sure your job will be to find her, I repeat, find her, not to blow her away." Ed was himself upset, struggling to remain calm, wanting to go in their stead, but exertion, except that of exceedingly short duration, brought numbness to his face. His heart was acting up again. He worried about it, but had told no one. Instead, he volunteered for any task he estimated to be within the range of his physical limitations. He wanted to do all that he could for Marsh. "Likely Marsh'll be the only one to actually confront her, anyway," he advised them. "So keep calm."

Clarence and Tulip turned now, Tulip reaching for the door, ready to find Marsh and get the business underway, but the door opened before she'd reached it. Pa Groner stepped inside, his eyes bugging at the sight of Clarence and Tulip. "Oh, uh," he stammered in collecting the scattered fragments of the message he was to give Ed. "Er, Ed," but he again halted and now looked at Clarence. "Marsh and I found her trail. She left tracks in the soft ground. We started to follow them, but Janet Coats rushed up to us to say that Sky'd been shot. Now Marsh will not let me help to find her; wouldn't deputize me either and," looking at Ed, "Ed, he said I couldn't relieve you either. But Tulip, he said, because he didn't know you were here yet, Clarence, but I'm sure he means you too. He said to meet him at Dr. Nealy's office. And Ed, I'm supposed to go get a breakfast for your prisoner then you're supposed to release him, but to try to get him to talk on his own volition first so maybe he'll say something Marsh wants to know. Those tracks," he said now to Clarence, "lead off toward the gristmill. And, Tulip, you are supposed to bring the camera bag and the plaster bag and stuff and an evidence bag or two."

***

Mrs. Klinert felt trapped behind the mill. She looked across the alley to the bushes, desperation compelling her to dive into them, but as she took a step from the building her eyes glimpsed Robert Groner and Marshal Rockney already onto her trail. Flattened once more against the building, she'd viewed her situation with extreme trepidation, seeing only the horrible monstrous stinking train before her. The train horrified her, yet her mind's eye revealed a picture of Clydis and Edith diving beneath a train. She'd lost them forever that day because she couldn't get past the train. She dashed the thirty feet and dived under the first car to loom before her, smashing her knee against a rail as she did so.

Her knee hurt and then her hand hurt, having bashed it against the opposite rail. She scrambled to her feet and took several steps from the train where she paused to look around. Depressed instantly in seeing herself wide open, fully vulnerable, standing in plain sight of anyone on Lead Bridge or along the west side of the train or from across the way beyond the dam, her eyes darted. North along the railway were two layers of nearly empty rail siding and in the distance some widely scattered trees that she imagined were standing along the river. She was naked now save for the derringer. She raised her hand toward her face; and her eyes popped; glowering at her pain filled empty hand!

Yanking her skirt upwards, she saw only the bullet pouch attached to the holster. She started back toward the train realizing the derringer must've been driven from her hand, that it was under the train. Suddenly the train moved, backing a line of cars into the siding. Moving close to the train she could see the derringer between the rails, but dared not reach for it. The train slowly clattered before her. Hating the train, she turned and ran from it and ran the nearest route which remained open to her.

The dam!

The Black Sucker arises from a myriad of widely spread icy cool springs and tiny lakes in the upper reaches of Kent County. Tiny clear rivulets coalescing broaden it to the size a man could easily jump across until Duke and Cedar creeks near Ryanton double the width of it. At Ellington the icy trout laden waters of Stebbens creek become one with the river on its meander down county to the dam at Leadford. Along the meandering turns where the river's healthy current hammered the banks deep pools are formed and the black suckers lie there in their element. In many sites between the turns the bottom is rocky and deep and swift and this is element to the chub and the trout and to the crawfish, darter, and sculpin. In those rocky places Indians waded the water aching their feet in the icy swift current and the pioneers in their turn also waded the waters until chance found them at a wider place of shallow swift water. And the bottom was firm and they forded it to commence the town of Leadford. And they dammed it above the ford and the millpond became element to pike, bullhead, and bluegill and the sluices powered the mill wheels of sawmill, gristmill, and factory.

At Ellington a slaughterhouse was built and its offal joined the river. And at Leadford a tannery was built and its offal joined the river. And unseen in the river the little things live; the microbe, the fungus, and protista, whose function is to cleanse the river. Offal is food to those things as they are food to the others. And at Leadford in a mighty roar the icy water cascaded over the dam to pound the rocks below. On the walkway over the dam she hurried, her head at sway, her eyes darting. She'd lost Clydis. She'd lost Edith. She'd lost Elisabeth. She'd lost the derringer. She had nothing. The Black Sucker cared not when she joined it. All is food to the river.

***

By the time Clifford and Harold had arrived back at Dr. Nealy's office Naddy was awake. She smiled when her dad kissed her forehead but began to cry when she saw that Harold was crying. Claire assured him that his sister was going to be all right and that he could help take care of her; even he could if he wished instead of going to school. They were in the adjoining room with Naddy when Sky Ferndin arrived at the doctor's. Hearing of still more trouble, they grew apprehensive, deciding without further delay to journey home. They nestled Naddy in blankets and she rested on Claire's lap with Harold sitting close beside his sister. Clifford drove a block out of the way going home to avoid any of them suffering to view the ruins of the Franklin. The car was still ditched where Roger had made a derelict of it and was destined to remain there until a court order made junk of it. Soon the James' team of light horses began to forge ahead in recognizing their neighborhood, knowing their stable stood nearby. Horses like people like to come home.

***

Marsh, Clarence, and Tulip soon discovered where she'd paused behind the gristmill. As they progressed with the search he took photographs and he made a plaster cast of a print found near where she'd shot Sky. Beyond the railway a few prints were found near a concrete apron which bordered the dam. During their examination of the area, they discovered the derringer. Marsh noted that it'd been fired and that its cylinders now housed spent shells. "She could've gone any one of several places; even to plunging over the dam. Or, she may have jumped the train!" He rushed to the depot to place a hold order on the train, preventing its stopping anywhere short of Grand Rapids where officials there could search it. While Marsh was in the depot Clarence and Tulip searched the area for additional sign of her passing, but found nothing.

The buildings along the west side of Front Street were essentially one building in that all were interconnected by passageways. Clarence began his search at the depot, looking upstairs and down and all through it before passing through an archway into the restaurant. The telegraph was clicking as he neared the restaurant and he'd barely arrived there when the telegrapher caught up with him. "We were too late, Clarence, the train had time to stop at Moppit. We did manage to have it skip Belmont and Comstock Park. It'll be pulling into Grand Rapids pretty soon." Clarence hurried through to the gristmill where Marsh and Tulip were at work, knowing that Marsh would want the information right away. The bullet ripped into a support beam not inches from his head as he entered the gristmill! He crashed to the floor and lay shaking.

Within moments Marsh and Tulip burst into the scene. "Hold," Marsh bellowed, surprised that she still had a gun.

"It's me, Marshal, Clifford. I think I shot her."

"It's me you shot at!" Clarence shouted, weaving to his feet.

"Clifford, come out of there," Marsh bellowed.

Clifford emerged from behind a stack of feed sacks. "I'm going to find her, Marshal, and I'm going to kill her."

"Nobody's going to kill her unless in self defense," Marsh admonished. "And we don't think she has a gun. We found hers already."

"The train stopped at Moppit."

Marsh nodded, his eyes still boring Clifford. "How long have you been in here? Where have you searched?"

"I'm sorry, Clarence, but I am going to kill her. Marshal, I've been all through the depot and this floor."

"Get this straight, Clifford. She does not have a gun. If you shoot her it's murder. Do you get me?"

Clifford plopped down on a sack of feed, frightened now that he'd nearly killed Clarence. He looked forlornly up at the marshal. "I got to do something. I just got to do something."

"Clifford, I've something you can do. Are you listening?" Clifford nodded. "There's a possibility she may have gone into the river. We need someone to ride both banks as far down as Moppit pond while we investigate other possibilities. You game?"

"I'll get right at it."

"And, Clifford, I suggest you unload your gun. Take it with you, but don't have it loaded or leave it with me."

Clifford began to unload his pistol. "I'm really sorry about what I did, Marsh."

"You'll calm down shortly. Just take it easy. Try not to get too excited. I know we're going slower than you'd like on this. But it's necessary to cover all of the bases. Riding the river is necessary and will be a big help. If you see any sign of her, hurry back, or call back, to my office. Tulip will be on duty there. She'll always know how to contact me. You clear on all of it?"

"Yes. Thanks, Marshal." Clifford hurried from the mill and across the street to the livery where Boliver was stabled. Minutes later he began to search along the river.

"Clarence, I'm sending your dad and Ed Benson down to Moppit by handcar, watching all the way for tracks; especially for any sign of her around the Moppit area. I want you to get them started on their way. Then come back to the restaurant here," indicating the depot restaurant. "I'm afraid you and I'll need to do a door to door search down around this end of town."

"Tulip, when you get to the office, call Robert Groner and then send him and Ed to me. Have Ed bring a badge for Robert. Likely I'll be with the telegrapher, but if I'm not, I'll be in this restaurant."

In short order, Robert and Ed arrived at the depot. Marsh was still working with the telegrapher, and with the stationmaster, arranging the use of the handcar and two men to pump it along the rails. Pa soon had his shiny deputy marshal badge pinned on his coat. Clarence took them around to show them what her footprints looked like. "You see how pointed the heels are? You're not likely to find any other woman with a print like that in Leadford."

"Really narrow and pointed, aren't they?"

"They're real high society, all right."

Having sent them on their way, Clarence returned to the depot restaurant. He called Meads to bring Clydis and the others up to date. They decided to remain in haven at Meads until her location was known. "You're right, dear. It's a secure place. And I'll be along as soon as I can, as soon as we believe it's safe, and see you and Edith home. It may be an hour or more yet."

As he was hanging the phone, Emily Wainwright walked up to him. She carried a pot of coffee. "You must be Clarence Groner, boss of John Purley." Clarence nodded and his mouth gaped. She was astonishingly pretty, instantly setting a whirl to his head.

"I've no wonder John Purley eats here," Clarence managed to remark as he seated himself at a table.

"Coffee?"

"Huh?" He peered at her, trying to figure it. Clydis is beautiful. This woman is pretty. "Oh, oh, yes. Coffee, cream and sugar," he managed to say. Now he noticed Mabel. Mabel looked painted, not pretty, but painted boldly. Now this one is pretty, he decided, as a third woman entered the room from the kitchen. Must be her mother. Looks like her, a lot. Emily began pouring his coffee. He could stand it no longer. "What's going on?" he blurted. "I just cannot understand what's going on."

"I'm training to be a beautician," she said as she pushed cream and sugar closer to him. "I have my mother's makeup just right, don't you think? But I still need to work on Mabel. She isn't yet just right, is she?"

"Remarkable," Clarence interjected. "Will wonders never cease?" She began to turn from him as other customers had entered the restaurant. "You're very skillful, very talented," he said after her.

She turned and smiled at him. "Thank you, Mr. Groner."

Clarence carried his cup of coffee up to the counter. He sat upon a stool close to where Mabel was working. "We're going to start a beauty parlor through there," she motioned toward her storage room as she approached. Clarence waved her closer. When Marsh entered the restaurant moments later, he saw that Mabel and Clarence were whispering together. Marsh and Clarence began a meticulous door to door, room to room search. From a window of the former Ford agency on Bridge, Clarence managed to catch a glimpse of Emily hurrying up the street toward Meads.

***

Chyle and Jimmy pumped the little repair car. Chyle'd worked on the repair crew with Robert Groner before Robert's retirement from railroad work. A strong man was required for the work and as Robert had begun to show his age he'd felt increasingly guilty. One day he had gone to the swinery north of Leadford to buy a pig which they would dress out for him and smoke the hams and bacon and make the delicious, as they alone knew how to do, sausage, and while he was there he found Jimmy. He was one of twelve boys in the family of sixteen children. Harvey and Princep had begun the enterprise many years previous and he'd died leaving four children so she married again. But later he died, leaving six additional children. Then she again married but she died before having more children. Then he married but later died leaving three children then she married again bringing the present family to sixteen children. They all worked hard to make a living, but there were too many. The older children'd looked elsewhere for their livelihood, Jimmy finding his way onto the railroad repair crew. This was an easy pump for Chyle and Jimmy as slow and easy had been their orders.

Ed and Robert sat one to each side of the little pumper. Their eyes were straining. They were almost afraid to blink lest they miss something. "Can't you go slower?" Ed requested. This was an easy pump for Chyle and Jimmy. They allowed the car a short coast before they resumed their slow delightful leisurely pump down the Pennsylvania.

They found no trace of her. No women were employed at the Moppit mill so her tracks would be obvious. None were found. Chyle and Jimmy began the pump toward Leadford, a little harder now as the rails leading from Moppit traced a gentle upgrade. Slow steady powerful pumping kept them rolling. Robert Groner looked on. He looked on as long as he could. He tapped Jimmy.

Robert pushed down on his handles. Chyle looked over at him. Chyle smiled, kept pumping, with apparent ease. Robert struggled to keep his end of the bargain, pushing with all his might. All were smiling now, except Robert. Robert felt himself tiring, tiring fast. Wanting to make good he reached high, his arms raised high, his back and legs braced, but as he started down a terrible low pitched chatter emerged that rose in pitch to a screech before finishing in a delicate whoosh!

Chyle and Ed and Jimmy could not contain themselves. The little car coasted back toward Moppit as they laughed. They couldn't stop. They tried to stop, but a glance at Robert prevented their doing so. The car began to pick up speed. Robert alone noticed the enhanced momentum. Suddenly he jumped on the brake pedal lurching the others nearly off the car. He set the brake. They all sat back down on the car. Jimmy reached over and patted Robert on the back. Robert smiled then and his smile grew into a chuckle and the chuckle chorused with their final triumphant round of glee. Ed was the first to cease laughing. His face'd grown numb and had they looked they would have seen him pale and drawn. Ed was very much afraid as he sat with them on the little repair car.

But after less than a minute of time Ed felt okay again. He knew his trouble to be a malfunctioning heart, made so by a bullet in Cuba. He declined to mention his problem to anyone, especially not to Lorraine. She had enough to think about, he was sure, in carrying the baby, now in its eighth month of gestation. His worry was against that one time where his numbness would go deep, too deep, and he would leave her. Of that he was very much afraid.

The pumper had slid to a stop at the south edge of Faygard's dip, having lost a hundred yards or so of its journey before Robert set the brake. Chyle and Jimmy resumed their position at the handles. "Wait," Robert said, holding his palm toward them. "Wait."

Looking at Chyle, Robert touched his nose and he sniffed upwards. Chyle did likewise then shook his head, no. Robert dismounted the pumper and walked up the tracks toward Leadford. Chyle walked slowly toward Moppit. "Robert," Chyle said, his voice barely reaching. Robert walked down to where Chyle stood.

Chyle said, "Wood smoke?" as Robert neared him.

"Wood smoke," Robert confirmed, sniffing. "We'd better hurry in and tell the marshal."

***

They were the Nelson brothers. For some time now, each morning as day was breaking they'd been with the Toberton horses. Early on they'd gained the confidence of Boot, the lead horse, as every horse herd does have a lead horse as they well knew. Having befriended Boot the others soon had fallen into line. The horses relished the oats delivered to them in the little hollow near the rail line every morning. They were ready now, ready to halter each horse and then to string them together for their lead to the train cars parked in the siding near the Lower Lead Bridge in Leadford. Ray and Tom spent the lighted portion of each day hunkered down in a hollow south of Faygard's dip. They waited heaped in blankets under a canvas cover with brush pitched atop it and they slept long hours each day, but of late they'd become antsy, tired of the game, daily cursing Slim Jones and Simon Doty, unforgiving of their tardiness in moving the herd.

Slim Jones, too, was frustrated. He sat in the unpretentious Belmont Inn while his charge of light horses waited in a corral nearby. Meanwhile Simon Doty occupied the Leadford lock up. Doty'd had a good breakfast and later had hollered for someone to let him to the can but nobody'd answered. He'd been obliged to use the pail and now it stunk there. Doty was himself much frustrated.

Each day as the southbound local passed on the rails nearby, the Nelson's built a small fire and they boiled water. With this they made tea and they made cornmeal mush with nuts in it and on other days they made oatmeal mush with raisins in it. Their meal, their sole luxury in any given day, had begun to promote linger in them. That linger had grown proportionate to their boredom and frustration and they'd now been smelt. Chyle and Jimmy pumped with firm steady strokes propelling the repair car ever closer to Leadford.

Chapter Fourteen

In Leadford as Emily Wainwright entered the dress shop, her eyes fell upon Lorraine who was seated heavily upon a chair along one side of the room.

Lorraine's dulled eyes did not lift at Emily's entrance. She had fit May in appropriate attire and was pleased with May's transformation, but was highly depressed no less. Claire, occupied, of course, as she should be and that she had every right to be with her injured daughter, would not be in to help Lorraine do May's hair, but her depression stemmed not from that but from her own painful disapprobation. Her carry had developed into a difficult carry. Her sciatic nerve was sending jolting discomfort down her left leg while the small of her back screamed eternal excruciation.

Emily didn't know to who she was to administer aid. She looked to Clydis and Billy, seeing them as presentable, but the poor dear suffering in that chair was in obvious ruin. Trella, whom she noticed, but did not know her name, or any of their names for that matter, was presentable but made up too severely, adding uncalled for harshness to her demeanor. And the slim black haired beauty before her she saw as the most appropriately made up of them all, her clear unadorned face matching perfectly her brilliant long black hair. To change anything about her would create a different person. She had taken them in and evaluated them in a moment's time and she wondered: Who am I sent to help?

"I'm Emily Wainwright," she introduced. "Mr. Groner sent me to help."

They hadn't before met Emily. "Pleased to meet you," Clydis returned. Promptly all were introduced and Emily's profession revealed.

"No," Emily said. "Not May. Oh, yes, May, but not May first." She walked over to Lorraine and kissed her forehead. "Please," she said to Lorraine. "I'll be honored to help you."

Helgie bustled in as Emily was working on Lorraine. Trella had called her earlier because she'd been concerned for Lorraine. Helgie had shouldered her med bag and walked into town. With but a glance at Lorraine, Helgie opened her med bag drawing forth a bag. "Make tea," she ordered, handing the bag to Clydis.

Of all of the teas, powders and potions that she and Morley knew about, and sincerely believed to be beneficial, the sumac tea was the only concoction the doctors freely allowed Helgie to administer to pregnant ladies, but the tea had caught on, becoming a ritual. It was a 'for women only' ritual which they enjoyed with Helgie.

The sumac fruits were collected each fall and packed into double thickness bags fabricated from feed sacks. A bag was lowered into a pot of water and boiled until the water became a coppery red at which time Helgie dropped in a single drop of vanilla and a pinch of cinnamon. Lorraine sipped the tea while Emily styled her hair.

Unnoticed, Edith walked over to where Clydene lay sleeping on her pile of dress making material. Edith carried a pair of giraffes with her and a horse and a pig. Without ceremony and with intent only on being nice to Clydene, she dropped them onto her, two striking her face. Clydene awoke with a howl. Edith jumped back, herself nearly in tears and ran to her mother. "Clyeen wakt," she said to her mother, tears forming in her eyes. In shock, Clydis held to her and rubbed her back, questing to assure her that it was all right. "Clyeen crying," Edith looked over to Clydene.

Billie comforted Clydene by putting her to breast. Suckling now in perfect contentment, Edith walked over to her. She reached out her hand and patted on Clydene. "Clyeen wet?" Clydene continued in her repast, completely ignoring Edith. "Clyeen hungry," Edith observed. "Edith wet."

Claire and Naddy entered the shop as Edith was being refreshed. "She's been asking for Edith," Claire said, placing Naddy gently on the floor near where Edith lay on a table. Claire looked very tired, as tired as she would've looked having just birthed the child, and her clothing was muddied and soiled by blood. Naddy's face was bruised and swollen, her eyes, especially the left eye, swollen nearly shut. A large adhesive plaster held her nose. Edith, now freshly diapered, looked down at Naddy from her position on the tabletop. She came to her hands and knees with her eyes still upon Naddy. She backed off of the table onto a chair and presently came to her feet beside her friend. She reached out and touched Naddy's face and Naddy placed her arms around Edith. The girls went hand in hand over to where Edith had left her doll. The doll was today dressed in yellow, the dress looking a perfect match for her grandma's bathroom curtains, and she pressed her precious doll into the arms of Naddy. "Dowee wike you, Naddy." Naddy giggled for the first time since Mrs. Klinert had grabbed her. Watching them, Claire's expression registered relief as she sat upon the chair offered her by Clydis. "I'm sorry to come like this," she began to explain.

"We're so glad you've come," Clydis said. "We've been worried."

"Our men have deserted us," Claire said, not in anger, but as a matter of fact. "Clifford wouldn't stay home since he saw that Naddy was going to be okay. He went out after her. I'm sorry, Clydis, I hope he finds her. I hate her." Claire began to cry. Clydis held her. "Oh, Clydis, I'm so sorry. I hate her so."

"I understand, dear. I cannot forgive her either." She continued to hold Claire.

"Naddy sat on the couch with Harold until she wished to lie down. Then Harold got up from the couch as though his job was finished. He said he wanted to go and help Mr. Ferndin and he began to put on his coat. Sky'd come into the doctor's office while we were in the recovery room. That's how Harold knew about Sky's trouble, but I wanted Harold to stay with us, not go to Sky. But Harold wanted to go so I kissed him and told him to go ahead, that Mr. Ferndin would be pleased. Harold is over there now at the store. I just couldn't stay home. I hoped you'd be here. I just couldn't be home."

"We're so glad you've come."

Claire looked away now to the voices, the activity nearby. She couldn't understand at first what was taking place. She knew not the two ladies busy before her, but she recognized Helgie Perkins. "Remember meat," Helgie was emphasizing. "Frozen steaks. Don't unwrap them. Just use them until they're thawed then send them back to Sky's freezer. You can use them over and over. And get yourself into any position that gives you the most comfort. To heck with posture or decency. You are in for a difficult carry, Lorraine, but you'll manage. Mark my word now, you hear?"

"Yes, Helgie," Lorraine mumbled as Emily was working on her face. "Thank you ever so much, Helgie." During her face make over Lorraine was putting to memory Helgie's instructions for alleviating pain. Suddenly Claire recognized her.

"Oh, Lorraine," she cried, rushing to her. You're so beautiful."

Lorraine sighed; with contentment, not with pain and she nearly cried; wanting to jump with joy as she watched the final steps in her transformation in the skillful hands of Emily.

"This is Emily Wainwright, new in town," Clydis introduced. Emily is a beautician, as we can see."

"Claire James," Lorraine completed the introduction as she stood from the chair. "Emily is Mrs. Santa Clause. No. No, not that. Emily is . . . Emily is dearer than that. Eros? No. Better yet. Emily is my, our, friend."

Emily was very pleased. "Thank you," she said, and returned the compliment. "I'm so happy to've met such nice people."

May now approached Claire and directed her into the seat just vacated by Lorraine. "I'm May," she introduced.

"Oh, I'm sorry," Billie called from her station. She'd shifted Clydene now, settling her at the other breast. Clydene suckled loudly. "May's my mother." Billie smiled over at them, herself a much-contented mother. "May Allen. She's come to live with us."

May worked side by side with Emily in washing Claire's hair and to prepare her face for make up. Emily braided the hair and drew the braids up along each side of the head. A beautiful large roll was brought down over the ends of the braids and fastened by combs.

Realizing by now that she was to transform May into a different person, Emily took a deep breath then promptly lopped off eight inches of her hair in back, ending with it at her neckline. She clipped the hair upwards much as a man might have it except that the angle was held longer. Then, taking advantage of the natural thickness and body of May's hair, she projected it slightly forward of her scalp and curled it at its borders. May was herself, but taller, emphasizing her native stateliness. May, though astonished, as were all of them, was greatly pleased.

The day had turned out rather well for Lorraine, May, and Claire despite it having been severely tragic in its beginning. Melancholy had been set aside, kindness had reigned and although the wounds were deep and would heal slowly, they were soothed and would continue to be soothed by kindness for kindness is personal, reaching each one individually.

By late in the afternoon the east wind tempo had picked up and swung more northerly where it acquired icy teeth. It cut into Clarence's face as he braved his sorrowful trek to Meads. It was clear by now what must have happened. Clifford found no trace of her, nor had Ed and Robert. Clarence and Marsh had searched exhaustively, leaving but one conclusion; her tracks had approached the dam. Likely the Black Sucker had her. Clarence entered the shop, fear lining his face, his wind reddened face pitiful in its anguish, knowing not how to tell Clydis, but Clydis knew the moment she saw him. She knew her mother had departed.

She looked at Clarence. She walked to him and held him at arm's length. She looked into his pleading eyes. "I know," she said. "I'll always love her, but only God can forgive her."

He didn't tell her that a special crew was on its way by train from Grand Rapids. The Kent County sheriff's posse headquartered there would drag the river, knowing not but what they would find her; but they would not. She was food to the river. Finally, the river sated, it would disgorge what it had chosen not to ingest and they would find it there in the spring. It would be a skeleton wearing rings on its fingers and on a golden chain a Fahys Moutauk watch, the whole wrapped in ermine, for the little things of the river may have found this flavor despicable. The ermine would be grasped in the spiny talons of a massive oak that had fallen into the river, the oak the victim of a relentless course which was the river.

***

"You might think me capricious, Emma, and you're probably correct, but if you could've seen the outfit you would surely concur with me. Stunning, daring perhaps, and I'm sure that short of any other explication, liberating would describe it, but I want to try and I'll take full responsibility, but I need your help." Emma listened attentively, trying to comprehend Trella's concern. Perhaps on a different day rather than the evening of the very day the town had suffered upheaval to the extreme, maybe at some other time Emma could put her mind to it. For now, as much as she was glad for Trella's visit and as much as she would like to help her, she could not divorce from her mind the overwhelming events of the day.

"I'm sorry, Trella. I cannot comprehend my role in this."

"It would be just cut and fit, using your artistic perception, until we get it right."

"But putting seats in dresses?"

"And legs."

"But, 'Ladies' legs', you said."

"Men's legs won't do. You should see how Molly and Helen look wearing men's legs. Men's legs will not fit most women. Billie wears men's legs without condescending, but she's lucky. For most women, to wear men's trousers is to advertise inferiority to men; as much as to admit that trousers have no place on a mere woman. Clydis has destroyed that ill begotten concept by designing stunning apparel; trousers, designed to fit women exclusively. If you could just see the garment she came up with, I'm sure you'd agree."

"Robert." He looked to her from his station of bewilderment across the table from her, looking as lost as was she. "If we could just get out there, we could see it," Emma said.

He shrugged his shoulders. "Maybe I could ride out there on Peanut, not take the buggy." His forehead crinkled in thought. "Or, if we call Morley, maybe he could ask her to ride on in here to town so that you could see it. But it would be, as you know, a lot to ask of her so soon after the awful day in town she just went through, so I'd rather go out there on Peanut. Maybe I could borrow it and bring it back to town."

"I'd like to go."

"Now, you can't. We can't have you sick again. It's a muddy mess and the wind's cold."

So it'd been decided. Robert would leave before daybreak riding bareback on Peanut. He owned no saddle, Toad never having been subjected to one.

***

Edith had been soundly asleep by the time her dad returned for them at Meads. Clarence and Clydis, with Edith positioned ahead of her dad on Bunny,

103

made their way back to the farm on Jericho by traveling the perimeter of the wheat field. Home at last, Clydis immediately tucked in with Clarence, offering comfort in lieu of the short rest he deserved before his return to work at the mill. She clung to him fiercely, as though seeking oneness that would defray all past and future invasions of their matrimonial rights. Later she hated to wake him to send him off to work. He arose willingly, however, and was soon on his way along the railroad tracks toward Moppit. He munched his supper of boiled potatoes, boiled eggs and pork sandwich as he rode.

Chapter Fifteen

The day was just dawning as Pa began his ride out to the farm. He decided his best bet was to give Peanut her head through the mud and was at first panicked as she disdained the road, seeking in lieu a farm lane leading into a wheat field. Trusting his horse, Pa hung on and was promptly rewarded seeing that she knew an alternate route along the wheat field. Emerging from the field at a passage in the charred sumac that led to crossing straight across Jericho, he was surprised to see that Clarence, barely visible in the dawning light, was just emerging from the Perkins yard. "Morning, Clarence," Pa greeted. "Where you been?"

"Through the woods," he answered. "These horses know more routes than we do. I guess they like to avoid the mud."

"Seems like it."

"They tried bringing in the crushed stone during the night. Both loads are mired on Moppit Hill. They were trying to drag them back down off the hill, back down into the mill yard where it's graveled, as I was leaving. The mill apron is firm where it's graveled."

"Gravel's what your road needs. Nobody never did gravel it except Chester's little stretch."

"His he graveled so that folks would not get discouraged and turn back. When they strike his graveled stretch, they speed up thinking that at last they're breaking free of the mud. Seconds later, of course, they're mired to their lights in Faygard's dip. It's been a money maker for Chester." They rode side by side across the yard and were approaching the stable. "What brings you out so early?"

"I've been sent out to see Clydis. Talk to her, I mean. And don't worry its not about yesterday. No wait, it is about yesterday. But it isn't about awful stuff; least I don't think so. Trella and Emma wanted me to bring in Clydis' pants."

"Her what? Pants?" Clarence was shocked. "I don't know as she'd allow that, you carrying her pants to town. And I'd object myself."

"No, not them. I couldn't do that. I can't even think of how to ask her about the others, let alone them. Those, I mean. No, it's them I mean I'm to ask about."

"What them?" Clarence was feinting alarm.

"Her new ones. Darn it Clarence, you aren't helpful," he complained, much in dismay. "I'd hoped you'd help."

"Help? Help you be scandalous? No, not me, Pa. You're on your own with this one," his tone emphasized his disgust of Pa's wanton mannerism. It was with considerable worry then that Pa entered the kitchen to confront Clydis.

Sniffer'd warned of a visitor, a friend, and she'd glimpsed him as he and Clarence passed in view of the kitchen window. Edith was on a tour of the house with her doll along with her tin cup and a wooden dog stuffed into the baby carriage. She'd already changed her doll's dress from the yellow pattern of yesterday to today's flouting pink. Clydis added a setting to the table and placed four additional thick slices of bread on the range top and sliced an extra helping of ham into the spider ending with breakfast ready to serve as the men entered the kitchen.

"Pa, welcome," she greeted.

"Pa's reason for being here, I can't even mention; least not till after we've eaten; lest you won't let him eat."

A statement so stupid, of course, warned Clydis that a joke was on. She'd wait and see, letting Clarence have some fun with his Pa. At least their banter signified there was no trouble; except that which he was causing Pa, that is. "I've lost my appetite," she wailed. "I cannot eat with all this suspense hanging over me. Pa, you will expose yourself at once!"

"He's come to expose you!"

"Indeed."

"Now, Clarence, this could've been easier. But, no. My own son chooses to defile me." Edith was standing at his knee by that time. She held her dolly for him to see and she looked up at him as if expecting a hug and a lap seat, but now stared up at him, her face a beacon of concern, her eyes shadowed by indecision, worried in detecting a difference in adult behavior. Finally, as though in desperation, she grabbed onto Grandpa's leg. His hand moved down and ruffled her curly bouncing brown hair. He was raising her to his lap in the same motion used to seat himself and stating as he did so: "Aren't you going to ask her?" throwing the next move onto Clarence.

"I'll have no part in this," Clarence replied adamantly. He folded his arms and sat back in his chair. "The very idea; and my own father."

"It's about your pants, Clydis," Pa decided to say.

"My?" She looked shocked.

"No, not those. Them others."

"Others? Turn in your toast, Pa." She reached for it.

He clutched the toast to him. "Clarence, this could've been much easier.

Now, please tell her."

"He wants to carry your pants into town."

She glared at Pa. "You'll never hear the end of this," she warned him. Grabbing his toast away, she gave it to Edith then stomped from the room.

"You've done it now, Pa," Clarence admonished.

Pa could see that Clarence had been funning with him, but could as clearly see that Clydis was dead serious. He sat fiddling with his breakfast, not eating any. Clarence, meantime, was enjoying his toasted ham sandwich. "You'd better eat, Pa. She could be coming back. No telling what she has a mind to do now. I'm siding with her, as you'd know. As surprised as she that you'd do such a thing."

Clydis returned presently wearing her new pant skirt. A lavender blouse blossomed from the top of it and she'd placed riding boots on her feet. "Lord in heaven," Pa interjected. "I sure do see!"

"I'm riding in to Trella's," she announced. "I've decided to help Pa with the pants."

"Good idea," Clarence concurred.

"Thanks," Pa said.

They finished breakfast and were soon packed up to leave. Clarence decided to postpone sleeping and go into town with them. He could hold Edith in front of his saddle. Clydis had the diaper bag stuffed with changes for Edith. Her doll and her tin cup and a wooden horse were also crammed into the bag. The diaper bag along with a second bulky parcel, containing along with its other accouterments, a Singer, was tied across behind Junifer's saddle. Pa would ride bareback but would be burdened by a backpack stuffed with patterns and cloth. Just ready to leave the house, they were interrupted by a terrible roar that accosted their ears from out by the arborvitae.

The roar settled into a steady groan, barely audible over Sniffer's report, his report a mixture of friend and foe, much confused was he by the enigma, not as yet having decided on which message to bark. He stood his ground at the kitchen door. Clarence opened it. Sniffer rushed outside.

Charley James emerged from the mud caked Packard. Sniffer sniffed carefully over him then walked over and watered a wheel, barely denting the mud of it, and then stayed right beside Charley while Charley made his way to the rear stoop.

Charley hopped up onto the stoop beside Clarence. "Charley," Clarence greeted. "Good to see you." Charley walked on into the house.

"I got over a hundred logs down," he said, looking at Clydis.

"My wife, Clydis," Clarence introduced. Charley nodded.

"Jeramiah Coffee has near to over two hundred. They're flooding the backwater. You're gonna have electric power through here next summer. We couldn't get them out. It was too muddy."

107

"And my dad, Robert Groner." Charley nodded.

"Well they said we could cut and brand our logs then haul them out as they floated up so we're doing that."

"Pleased to meet you."

"Well I came to finish Clifford's house. He doesn't know I'm here. Drove all night. Terrible trip. Worse road though is here. My crew is left up there now at Croton along with Jeremiah's crew to drag them out as soon as the water rises to high enough ground; it's really been a muddy mess up there lately, but not worse than the mud in your road."

"It's had heavy traffic that drove the mud down to even deeper."

"So I see I need to work from here with horses. School's out up there for Christmas. Albert was going to come with me, but I thought it might me a difficult trip, maybe even to being out all night. It was. Florie and Rylus, that's our newborn," he said, looking at Clydis. Clydis nodded. She smiled at him. "They're coming down today by train. Clifford doesn't know about it. Wanted to surprise him. Want to get the fire going and the house warmed up before they get here. Can I cut a tree on yours? I thought we'd even get up a tree. Course I'd know they already had a tree but we don't. Thought it would be fun to spend Christmas right here in the new house while we work on it then they could come out later on Christmas day after they'd had Christmas at home and we had Christmas here to eat an evening meal with us in their new house. Florie is bringing along a goose I shot, but I'll need a pair of horses and a buckboard. Yours is the worst road. And I'd like to borrow a catch of firewood too if you can spare," Charley paused to catch his breath.

"Nothing until after you've eaten breakfast," Clydis interjected. "Sit down here. Clarence will pour coffee."

Charley seated. "I brought their present with me you ought to see it. It's a Waterbury mantel clock. Chimes, you know. Real pretty." He reached his coffee. Took a sip. "Good. Been up all night. Real hard trip. But it's the best time. As soon as I could I planned to get back here. I told that to Clifford. He'll be surprised, but I didn't want him to know yet so now I guess I'll have to tell him because I'd need to borrow his team. Does he have a buckboard or wagon, do you know?"

"I have a light wagon which Bunny pulls when the road is firm.

"Good. I'll use Clifford's team then." He bit into his mustard ham sandwich. "Real good," he mumbled around a large bite of the delicious sandwich.

They harnessed Bunny and Junifer to the wagon, the first time they'd ever pulled as a team; and they did very well, no problem for Clarence who drove them. The saddles and all other needed paraphernalia were piled on the wagon along with the people. Peanut was tied on behind. Clydis and Clarence filled Charley in on the recent happenings in town, assuring him that his coming would be just the therapy needed to offset their minds. Clydis herself, she told him, had arisen that morning with the intention of going into town, hopefully to help Trella, but any wholesome activity was therapy to a mind trying to forget horrid recent events. She was sure that Claire would be seeking such therapy as well and would likely also show up at Trella's. So Charley was feeling pretty good about being on hand with just the diversion the Jameses needed.

Trella, Emma, Clydis, and Claire worked very hard but enjoyably all the day long, using Trella's three White sewing machines and the Singer, finishing their day with pant skirts for Billie, May, Molly, and Helen. Helen's was a special problem, and truly taxed their imagination and skill not just to fit her now, but as she expanded. But Trella wanted to meet the needs of any and all women who may desire such apparel no matter expecting or not; and indeed she did so, and beautifully.

While the ladies were setting to work in the Mead shop, Charley ran on out to the unfinished house to get it warmed. Clifford, a short while later, waited with his Clydesdales at the depot, perplexed the while as to whether or not he could remember what Flora looked like. Fortunately Albert hopped off the train first carrying a diaper bag and just behind him was Flora, Rylus in her arms. He'd seen her but seldom since her marriage to Charley, not seeing her in fact until Albert was a year old. She lived wherever Charley found a place. The place would be near one or another of his projects and she would make a home of it however temporary. No matter the place, she preferred to be near Charley whom she loved. Flora's was a hard life, Clifford imagined, yet he didn't see her distraught but cheerful as she was detraining.

Flora was a stocky lady with dark brown hair pulled into a bun. She didn't notice Clifford at first, her eyes being busy in their feast of the Christmas decorations about the depot; not like at home. At home she hadn't decorated because they'd planned on spending Christmas in Leadford. That is, Charley planned on it. She didn't doubt but what Charley had worked out the arrangements with Clifford and hadn't realized differently until when they were packing. Charley would stop ever so often during the ordeal of packing to stand there and smile, sometimes even breaking into a chuckle. "Clifford is sure going to be surprised," Charley had finally voiced his glee.

"You loon," she'd chastised him. "You should've let her know!"

"That'd spoil the surprise!" he returned to her, and indeed it would have.

"But ladies do plan things, Charley. And it is important."

His leather apron and his pistol aided her recognition of Clifford. "Little Jesse," she greeted, for she'd first know him by that name.

"Clifford," he said. He hadn't heard the nickname for some time, having outgrown it locally; and he would just as soon not have it rear up again. The Jameses were related to Jesse and Frank. The unfortunate "Little Jesse" had been laid on him because of the pistol he was obliged to pack in connection with his work.

She had numerous crates and boxes with her, and did not describe their contents to him except for one on them; "Goose. Charley shot it. It's for supper on Christmas day."

"Sounds good to me."

"Can you get Claire and me together sometime today so we can plan things? Charley just goes ahead as though everybody already knows the plans or as if plans aren't needed. I'd bet she doesn't even know we're here."

"I'll get you to town during noon hour. She's working today at Meads. Harold's caring for Naddy. They're over at Sky's mercantile. Supposedly to help Sky, but I know he'll stuff them with ice cream cones or chocolate sundaes; just the thing they need. Likely Claire will want to eat in there with them. We'll order sandwiches and soup from the depot to eat at Sky's so please, you folks plan to eat lunch with us."

"That'll be good. I want Charley to hear the plans."

Charley had loaded his tools and supplies at the farm where he'd abandoned his powerful Packard. Remaining spaces on the wagon were stuffed with oak, hickory, pine, sycamore, and maple chunks from Clarence's ample collection of firewood, hardly denting his supply as he had toiled mindlessly in seasons now past to vent his frustration through the relentless production of firewood chunks. Charley'd dug deep enough into one of the stacks to reveal a messy squirrel's nest constructed of downy sycamore fruits, laying bare and confirming Morley's prediction of a cold, cold winter. This winter is going to get cold, Charley thought. Morley's prediction was indeed bearing fruition as frigid air crammed with snow now assailed Charley, impeding his lust for efficiency, daunting his quest to have the house warm as toast and to be hard at it by the hour of Flora's arrival.

Flora, Rylus, and Albert arrived before the Acme airtight stove had more than marginally mellowed the numbing air of the house. Clifford had selected the stove, constructed of a double layer of 26 gauge steel, because Sears, Roebuck, Co. had advertised it as burning wood chunks or chips, straw, hay, corn, or corn cobs and et cetera, but not coal. The heater was located in the living room and Charley'd crammed it with wood chunks. It would do the job, he was sure, but his impatience had led him to the kitchen.

They'd chosen a coal oil fueled kitchen range and Charley placed a match to it. Pretty blue flame curved around the base of a kettle of water he'd placed there, rapidly warming it toward coffee and tea and cereal mush.

Feeling the warmth as he made his way into the kitchen with Rylus in his arms, Clifford was duly proud of their forethought regarding the range. He placed Rylus in his basket on a chair near the cheery little appliance and Albert stood by him ever mindful of his self-assigned task as protectorate.

***

Meantime at the mercantile much cutting and fitting and sewing was going on. Janet's Burdick machine with its Clark's O.N.T. spool cotton thread was busy transforming Harold into an elf. Sky had ordered a Santa Clause suit, planning to wear it at the school on a day during the last week before Christmas, and to wear it around the store as well. No doubt his would be the tallest Santa Clause in history and little doubt it would be the broadest, requiring numerous pillows to fill out the enormous suit, but he'd moaned his frustration to Janet. His shoulder was very tender. One of the .32 bullets had lodged in his shoulder joint while the other had scored a shoulder muscle leaving him in lament because Santa could not lift his bag of gifts. Harold's arrival the previous day, his mission to help Sky, had given Sky the idea. Harold would be an elf and would pass out the presents. Janet would be Mrs. Clause and would carry the bag of gifts.

Janet had spent nearly the whole night sewing for the elf; luckily she needn't sew a dress for Naddy. Trella Mead displayed dresses in her shop window. By the morrow she would have an entirely new type of apparel displayed. She made a substantial living by manufacturing and marketing dresses, coats, and other household cloth items of interest to women. She preferred selling patterns and materials for most items, except for the dresses and coats, and now the pants. Hals Bingsley's haberdashery sold goods for men and boys. Although most men and boy's apparel was sewn at home, a substantial business had developed for finished goods as well. Old Bingsley was doing well with his store. But Sky had noted, clever entrepreneur was he, a gap in the apparel scheme and had added to his inventory a line of baby and little lady's apparel. He'd lost money so far this season, but was sure his idea would catch on. Thus while Harold was transforming into an elf, Naddy'd been transformed into a calico emblazoned Miss Contrary, as his plan was to represent the nursery rhyme characters as sales promotion.

No time of year is snow more desired than at Christmas. Whereas the east wind had brought chilly air to the community, the following north wind had turned frigid. Now the wind had shifted northwest and snowflakes swirled onto the land. The people were greatly rejoiced and a chirrup had rejoined their whistle for now the Christmas season descended.

Chapter Sixteen

Clifford loaded his wagon for local delivery, holding back on his country side deliveries in hope that the roads would firm consequent to the chilling air. He, for one, had not been pleased to see snow that day; for Christmas, surely, but snow now would insulate the mud rendering the roads even more treacherous. He'd tasted that menace an hour ago when he'd conveyed Flora and the kids out to the place. The temperature, he prayed, would rapidly fall and showed signs of doing so. The snow fell in huge flakes, soon weighting the tarp protecting his load of parcels. Among the wares was a pair of Acme bicycles pined for by Marvin and Ray. There were skates too on the wagon and sleds and a beautiful walnut box held a set of Roger's Brothers Berkshire silverware. The silverware was the first whole set of anything domestic Lorraine would own, and was a gift from her husband with money saved from his few cents per hour duty as Deputy Ed. In keeping with his atmospheric contribution each season, Clifford had attached sleigh bells to his Clydesdales. They jingled merrily as the Clydesdales made jocular their mission through the swirling downfall, confirming for all that the season was here, His birthday neared, Santa was on his way, all were rejoicing.

Sky was much pleased at the gathering in the mercantile at noon. Nearly every place in his little parlor was occupied. They brought a kettle of soup with them and their spoons and bowls. He supplied the crackers gratis, anticipating that all would be topping their repast with chocolate sundaes, which they did. His polished brass bell ringing National cash register chimed deliciously.

Charley and Flora hadn't before eaten commercially prepared ice cream nor had they ever thrilled at being seated in a real ice cream parlor. Watching them eat, Sky was reminded of Emma at her first encounter with this stupendous treat. How she'd dug into it making lightening fast digs with her tiny spoon, thinking not of the world's duress in her voyage to the last eeny morsel of the chocolate-smothered concoction, much as he was at the moment witnessing the James family's grandiose pursuit; especially Albert. Albert could not make his spoon hold enough or his arm move fast enough. He leaned low over his bowl, his spoon a blur, his concentration complete. Sky'd winked and nodded to Janet. No sooner had Albert arisen from his task than she placed a second bowl before him. Albert beamed his smile, not realizing that Santa Clause himself had privileged him. Finally, stuffed as kittens, they returned to their work.

Charley had painted the kitchen ceiling before coming to town at noon. He'd yet to hang the wallpaper and paint the woodwork and lay the linoleum to finish that room. Flora meanwhile was painting the plaster walls of the living room, wishing it to dry as soon as possible to make the room presentable to the tree which lay thawing in a bedroom. Albert busied himself pulling Rylus around in a wagon. In with Rylus he had tools, a coffee jug, and various sizes of nails in keeping with his commitment to be a gofer his family could appreciate.

***

That evening Clarence left early for work. At Marsh's request, in addition to his lunch sack, he'd slung two canvas bags behind his saddle. One bag contained a revolver. He'd never fired the gun and had confessed the fact to Marsh. Marsh, alarmed in finding his deputy inept, had provided him with a Parker twelve gauge shotgun which along with a dozen shells containing buck shot, occupied the other canvas bag. Marsh did know that Clarence had fired the shotgun once at a deer. Regretfully however, he'd missed it. Clarence didn't profess any aptitude as a hunter nor exhibit a modicum of interest in guns but, at least, Marsh thought, he could make lots of noise with the shotgun and, if Marsh's plan went concordant to his thinking, even noise production would not be required of Clarence.

Marsh expected the rustling to occur that very night. Simon Doty'd as much as said so. Before releasing Doty, Ed Benson had questioned him, learning only that the mares that Chester Faygard had ordered would be delivered in the evening and would be in trade for Faygard's heavies. Doty, in thinking his statement would but confirm his role as a legitimate horse dealer, had set Marsh's plan in motion. They'd let the rustle unfold, believing that the mastermind behind the rustling scheme could only be discovered by following a rustler, in particular, Simon Doty, to his chief. Herm Dinning was stationed at Ellington store overlooking the Ellington stockyard three miles north of Leadford. It wasn't clear to Marsh and Dinning which rail cars, the ones parked in Leadford or those at Ellington would be used. Marsh was setting up as though the Leadford cars were the ones while in Ellington Dinning was doing the same. Not Clarence with his shotgun nor Marsh, Tulip, or Ed would need to fire a shot if Marsh's plan worked. His plan depended, above all else, that the rustlers believe themselves unobserved in they heinous act should they choose to commit at Leadford.

Bunny's hooves sunk into mud beneath six inches of new fallen snow as he made his way to Chester Faygard's place. The snow had stopped falling but with the temperature dipped into the twenties, it would remain for a time. Clarence stopped at Faygard's to pay for Peanut and the buggy, planning to place the receipts for them into an envelope as a Christmas present for Pa. While at Faygard's he through casual conversation with Chester confirmed that a horse deal was indeed to take place. Upon his arrival to his job at Moppit mill he would telephone the information to Marsh. As he rode on toward work his mind was not on the mission he was to perform for Marsh, his thoughts being directed toward Pa's other present, a Chautauqua Lake split bamboo fly rod. He'd teamed with Marsh on that, Marsh adding in a box of hand tied flies, and his mind also winged to include his gift for Ma, an elegant thirty-six piece set of burgundy imitation cut glass dishes which Sears had promised could not be distinguished from real cut glass. He could visualize the set gleaming brightly from the new china cabinet that Pa was building for her with the help of Ben and Hanna Haimmer. So engrossed was he in the spirit of Christmas that he over ran Toberton's. He turned Bunny and headed back.

At the Tobertons, he paid for Junifer. Clydis would receive the receipt in her Christmas envelope. He'd also purchased an elaborate toiletry set for her in addition to a silky nightdress. He could now add in when he phoned Marsh that Tobertons hadn't lately been approached by any horse buyers.

At that time in Belmont twelve handsome fillies were leaving the stockyard on a tramp to Faygards to be traded, even up, for eight of Faygard's heavies. Simon Doty'd walked the railway to Belmont after his release from Rockney's lock up. Slim Jones was nervous wreck by then. Shepherding the stolen mares had been a heavy assignment made sorely more acute by Simon's tardiness. Slim'd been drinking to pass the time. He wasn't as yet fully drunk, but was obviously wide on judgement and balance as Simon could plainly see upon his arrival. Praying that the walk would sober him, Simon'd directed their departure from Belmont.

Meanwhile Ray and Tom Nelson waited impatiently near their hideout along the south edge of Faygard's dip. The passage of the mares along the railway nearby would be their signal to begin their trek with ten of the Toberton heavies. Around midnight Clarence observed the mares being herded through Moppit. He recognized Simon Doty but not his partner, Slim Jones. He reported by phone to Marsh that he'd seen the men and that as far as he could see, they were unarmed.

Simon and Slim passed through Roughwater's gate then herded down Jericho to the Faygard farm. Under cover of their arrival Tom and Ray Nelson, each leading a string of five Toberton horses, headed up the rails toward Leadford.

Chester was pleased to see the mares. "They seem alright," he commented as he looked them over with long practiced scrutiny. "Yes, sir. They're just as you said. Nary a bad one."

"I pride myself that way," Simon assured him. "And I couldn't do better than trade with you, of that I'm also sure. Chester, you're a premier horseman."

Rope halters were installed on the horses to be led by Simon and Slim. Slim stayed with the haltered, stamping impatient horses while Simon and Chester went inside to conclude the deal.

Simon removed his coat and placed it over the back of a chair. Sitting now in a business suit at Chester's table, he remarked of three additional horses they were buying that night from Jonnicks, a herder near Ellington. The horses were to be shipped from Ellington. His comments were designed to leave Chester with an avenue of doubt as to which station his heavies were headed.

"Didn't think he'd sell a one," Chester said. "I tried to buy mares from him before I made contact with you. He wouldn't sell any."

"Mares, yes. He would not. I approached him myself. Best I could do is to talk him out of three geldings," he replied. "But, I say now. I should tell you that he mentioned his looking for a stallion. Do you have one to go?"

"Could. I'll see what he wants."

"I'll be seeing him," Simon lied, "and will drop back in here tomorrow to let you know."

"Good of you," Chester said.

"Well say, a slug of coffee might go good about now before we start our walk," Simon said.

"Coming at you," Chester returned. He went into the kitchen to get the coffeepot and cups. While he was out Simon placed a one next to the eight on the bill of sale. The bill of sale now read eighteen horses purchased from Chester Faygard.

"Here's looking at you," Simon toasted as he raised his cup.

"Yours," Chester returned.

Slim waited impatiently near the horses. Beneath his heavy parka he wore two gun belts. Each of four holsters held a Smith and Wesson .38 caliber six-shot revolver. They were heavy. Additionally his feet were tired and he wanted a drink. That scamp Simon had tried to make sure he was packing no alcohol and Slim damned him for that. Now he stood shuffling his feet damning him still longer for his sitting in there sipping coffee while he was out in the cold wearing out his arms holding eight horses.

Finally, they were on their way. They didn't turn in at Roughwater's gate. Chester, if watching, would've seen them pass by the gate and would've thought they'd headed on up Jericho to where? Leadford? Ellington? No concern of mine, Chester would conclude. He'd made a good bargain. Of that he was sure.

Simon and Slim led their charges off of Jericho within sight, were it daytime, and sound of the James house where Charley and family lay abed. Blazed by the Nelson brothers some time previous, the trail was known only to the rustlers. Flora and Charley were sleeping on cots, or rather Charley was; as his steady, window jarring snore attested, but she'd responded to a whimper from Rylus, drawing him in with her from his blanket cushioned card board box crib. Flora was dozing contentedly. Rylus suckled. Albert snored sweetly from his bedroll near the Acme heater, between it and the freshly decorated Christmas tree which he, in high hopes that Santa Clause had noted their change in residence, had helped to decorate. Flora roused at the sound of horses blowing their slobbery commands to one another, recognizing at once that they were horses, not threatening beast nor menacing ogre. She cruised back to contented slumber. Rylus continued his suckle. Each of the Nelsons led a string of five heavies quietly along the right of way toward Lower Lead Bridge. Their timing was superb. Slim and Simon's passing muffling the passage of the ten Toberton heavies.

Slim cursed softly into an ear of Prince, whom Chester had identified as lead horse, warning him to keep his darn slobber to himself; that Slim would handle the herd, needing no help from a loud mouth horse.

Slim was an unparalleled expert at handling horses. His patience with them was profound in comparison to his impatience with humans. He drank too much and his opinion of humans degenerated proportionate to his imbibitions. He was nearly full drunk now, having secreted a small flask in the groin of his pants. Thus his pausing, his reaching in, his pulling out, and his delivery were but camouflage of his need to appease a deeply ingrained hunger. Nearing the railway, the lead horse paused and let loose. Most horses in the string would also let loose, he knew, because the lead horse had done so. He reached also, but not to let loose. His neck cricked a little as he tipped back draining, to his consternation, the last drop from the flask.

Simon waited patiently with his string of four horses, sapiently admitting his meager horse sense, letting Slim decide their rate of progress. Hearing now the reason they'd paused, he loosed with the others, grateful for Slim's insight, yet finding Slim's horse sense to be his sole ingratiating quality. They'd plenty of time to reach the station, planning that the loading be completed just before daybreak, leaving but a short interval before the northbound local would attach the cars for their transfer to Bruin City.

Marsh knew the cars were to be attached that morning. The knowledge, however, didn't confirm the locale for the rustle because stock cars all along the Pennsylvania had orders to move that morning. Dinning had sent word down to Marsh confirming it. The messenger, disguised as a traveling salesman, had urged Marsh to concentrate his thinking on the Ellington cars, stating that Dinning had a strong hunch as to its being the focus for the rustling, but Marsh'd disdained, trusting his own strong hunch delineating Leadford as the correct location.

Tulip was awakened by the sound of horses. The sound was but a murmuring of gentle snorts as though horses were recognizing one another and the snorts were punctuated by an occasional low whinny offered in exhortation by a wary leader amid the throng. She heard no human voices. She'd only time enough for one word; "Horses," before Marsh'd hung the receiver. In moments he was at the rear door of the restaurant, arriving just as the rustlers were preparing to flee the scene. One of them saw Marsh and motioned the others to immobility and silence behind a rail car. They were trapped, their only clear escape route, and the route they had planned on using, led back across Lower Lead Bridge; now in clear view of the marshal.

Marsh imagined there being three or more men hidden behind the loads of horses. They hadn't shown themselves except for the lower legs and feet of one of them glimpsed by Marsh as he was arriving at Tulip's. He and Tulip stayed outside her doorway in full view as they looked now from the rear of the restaurant. Realizing that his plan of allowing them to leave town unopposed was thwarted because they probably knew they'd been detected, his mind struggled to adapt his alternate plan to the situation. Blaming himself for having blundered into the scene, his mind having been more keenly poised to seeing Tulip scantly attired than to the business at hand, he poured energy into formulation, willing the puzzle pieces into harmony, ending with a risky, but workable, he believed, solution. He stood with Tulip in his arms. His eyes bored the train cars, while he whispered the plan into her ear. Releasing her, feeling her warming comfort retreat, he remained in clear view while she went into the restaurant.

She phoned Ed Benson. She phoned the mill asking for Clarence Groner. She then phoned Roger Faygard, asking him to bring the marshal's car around to the front of the restaurant. Lastly she phoned Malice Lee at the swinery, he being the closest to Ellington whom she could reach by phone, asking that he rush to Ellington to inform Dinning.

Clarence instantly started on his way, pushing Bunny at a full gallop up the right of way, arrowing straight into a job of which he was terrified, wondering why in the world he was doing it. Why had he not told Marsh that he didn't want the job? His thoughts were to his family, to Edith and Clydis, to his obligation to them, to his desire and his right to be with them and to grow with them and to be alive with them. The canvas bags slapped against Bunny. The bag banging his left flank held a double-barreled Parker 12 gauge. Through its sparkling clean and lightly oiled twin Damascus barrels he was to send buck shot against a rail car, his assignment being to scare the assailants, to hold them against their flight from Marsh Rockney. Or, if necessary, he was to slam the lethal shot into the fragile body of a human being!

How had he come to be in this fix? He'd been deputized originally because the safety of his friend, Red Toberton, had been at risk and, as well, the capture of Simon E. Lowgo had been in the offing. Both were issues of personal interest to him, though strictly not his personal business. Later, in view of continuous peril resident in his mother-in-law, his deputy duty was extended. And he understood this; was proud, even, that Marsh had placed such confidence in him and as proud; no, more so, to realize that his deputy's role was in direct benefit to his family; but now this?

Marsh being unmarried, Clarence assumed wouldn't be hampered by the injustice which he was suffering having been ordered to abandon his family. As he rode toward Leadford, indeed into battle he rode, but whose battle? Why am I doing this? Clarence chided himself for not fathoming a mere inkling of an answer to his plight, not realizing that Marsh too was afraid.

Tulip? He recalled their mutual sharing of fear before braving their quest of Mrs. Klinert, but she'd do the job. He knew she would, imagining that she would because of her love for Marsh. Ed Benson? Would he be afraid? Likely not. Ed was a soldier and had suffered the pangs of battle, pangs far in excess of the mere, as Ed would regard the situation, confrontation that was impending.

But Clarence was wrong about all of this. Marsh's family was too large for Clarence to see. His family, the folks to whom he owed personal obligation, numbered in size no smaller than all people on earth who chose to live within the compass of legal and natural law. And Tulip stood beside him in this, not fully comprehending it, but feeling it; feeling she and Marsh through God's help must be there always for all the families, always and forever.

Ed Benson had once felt as Clarence was feeling. He'd been called to battle, called to fight a battle that wasn't his. It wasn't his, he'd thought, because his wife and the boys were elsewhere. They weren't in Cuba. No, they rested safe in a small town in Alabama and he should be there with them, not here! What was he doing here? But Ed had found some of the answers. Through blood and gore and fear and death the answers had found him, cried at him, pummeled him, pierced him, laying bare the truth of a larger cause, a bigger family, a family called Country of which he and his were a part and so now he'd answered again. He would give again for his Country. He hurried to the restaurant.

As instructed, Ed entered the restaurant from the front and stayed out of sight in the kitchen as Marsh explained the role he would play in the upcoming saga of capture; God willing, not of battle.

Ed's role was to remain low along west of the railway and to move up to within a few yards of the railroad cars. The cars were located to the east of the main rails and rested on rails some five feet below the level of the through tracks. On signal from Marsh, Ed was to fire against the sides of the rail cars. He would not expose himself. His role was to scare the bejillies out of them. Ed would have plenty of time to get into position because the action was not to commence until Marsh had detected the presence of Clarence on his way into the scene from Moppit.

Ed Benson was a soldier wounded nine times in Cuba while leading his men against a small village. The first of the bullets had lifted and spun his body such that a later one had torn its way up through his abdominal muscles before lodging in his chest. In the fly infested gore embellished battlefield hospital the blood spattered surgeons had removed bullets from him and had covered his wounds except for the one bullet in his chest. They feared its removal would surely kill him while leaving it in could keep him alive to gain strength so that its removal could occur later, under better conditions. He'd told no one about the bullet, fearing that its removal would separate him forever from Lorraine, but he could die of it no less. The bullet was strangling his heart, killing it, killing him, but to the end he would give for them, for his family, for his Country.

Tulip's chore was to remain in the restaurant on alert for any of the villains who may deem an escape to the east. She would pepper her side of the cars with bullets from her .32 caliber six-shot Smith and Wesson revolver as she saw the need. She watched now, nervously awaiting the signal that would call her to action.

Clarence drove Bunny up the Pennsylvania, making his fastest time ever from Moppit to Leadford. Soon, however, he sensed that Bunny was tiring and he ceased urging him. Bunny slowed to his favorite pace, a smooth lope that drew them swiftly toward Lower Lead Bridge. Marsh, listening carefully, managed to hear his approach. He headed for his Oldsmobile.

All was quiet behind the train cars. The men whispered their talk. "It's our only chance," Slim insisted, but Simon disagreed. The water would numb anyone trying to cross the river, quickly making a log of him and the icy current would draw all life from the log. "We can't stay here," Slim insisted. "I'm going across the bridge. I'll shot my way if I have to." Simon chastised him for thinking only of himself, for his being cowardly, and for not affording him time to think. Simon schemed for a chance to use his strongest weapon, his time proven salvation, his mouth, the mouth that he'd used successfully more times than he could count. Given time to contemplate, he would come up with something, some way to talk himself, hang the others, out of this. He wore a business suit. At the first sign of trouble he'd placed his gun and gun belt into the willing hands of Tom Nelson, stating that Tom, being a much better shot, would be their best hope. Tom had proudly taken them just as had that fool on a day in St. Louis, the day when he the innocent business man had been held hostage, so he led them to believe, by those roughly clad gangsters. If Slim would shut his mouth, he could get them out of this, he told Slim. And in his mind the decision was made. If they did get out of this, a nod from him to the Nelsons would be enough. Slim would never reach his home in Detroit.

Marsh turned the Oldsmobile onto the tracks. In doing so he could see that Ed, hunkered down along the railway, had perfectly achieved his position. Not realizing that Ed was unconscious, Marsh gunned the Oldsmobile.

The Olds would carry him to near the loads of horses where he would beep his siren, signally Clarence, Ed, and Tulip to begin firing upon the cars. He would himself cut his ignition and leap from the moving Olds with his gun drawn. During his hurdle across to the head end of the horse laden cars, he would shoot against the same side of the cars as was Ed, scaring them further as he scurried to the relative safety at the front of the lead car. He would then yell at them, convincing them of their being surrounded, of it being prudent they surrender. Slim didn't hesitate. Before Marsh had but bumped the siren switch, Slim's bullet found him.

Tulip saw his hat fly off in a pink mist as his body tipped from the moving car. His body slid down the railway embankment to come to rest within the field of fire of the rustlers. She fired her gun at the corner of the car nearest him, the corner she must pull him past to get him out of danger. She rushed to Marsh and grabbed him but could not lift or drag him with her free hand. She saw them looking at her, raising their guns. It was point blank, she and them. She fired at them.

She holstered her pistol and grabbed her love with both hands and heaved, moving Marsh some several inches before a bullet grazed her cheek. She again blasted at them. She grabbed Marsh and dragged him to momentary safety beyond the corner of the car. She poked shells into her warm pistol. They would have to pop out now to shoot at her. Several bullets whizzed past her. What saved them was that she was in a different position each time an assailant popped out to fire. They could not see the three railroad ties stacked beside the siding twenty feet behind her and as many feet to the north. Safety lay behind them. The gunmen expected her to seek safety behind the car, not away from it, toward the ties, because they could not see the ties. So intent was she that she didn't hear Clarence open fire with the shotgun.

Ed did hear him, though vaguely, during his struggle back toward consciousness.

Clarence, hearing gunshots, had dismounted. He could not imagine himself going toward the gunfire. He hadn't expected to hear gunfire. Only a fool would go toward gunfire. But they were not shooting at him. Maybe he should go across the bridge. He was about to make his way across Lower Lead Bridge when he was startled and wondrous at seeing Marsh's Oldsmobile being driven across it. He moved Bunny aside as the car passed, not until then noticing that the car had no driver, recognizing as well that something was desperately amiss.

His shotgun was disassembled and stored in the canvas bag along with a dozen shells loaded with buckshot. His weapon quickly reassembled and loaded, he stuffed the spare shells in his pockets and on his hands and knees began to scurry across the bridge. The shooting continued up ahead out of his view; first a shot or two, then a short gap followed by a few more shots. He caught sight of Tulip then, backing away dragging someth . . . ! Marsh! She was dragging Marsh. Tulip fired.

She grabbed Marsh's shoulders and heaved for all she was worth. Bullets tore past her as she gained another yard in her determined quest for haven. Clarence caught a glimpse of a figure located between two train cars and drawing a bead on Tulip and Marsh. He fired both barrels, one after the other. The furtive bushwhacker jerked back out of sight, leaving a blue of curses in the air. Clarence reloaded.

He continued his crawl across the bridge, his sight on the north east corner of it where he deemed he could get shots at those behind the cars. He had no thought now for his safety. No thought now that he should be home with his family. Fear drove him. He felt nothing. He only knew fear and he watched himself crossing Lower Lead Bridge where he ducked down off the north east corner of it.

Ed's face had grown numb before he'd crawled a hundred feet down the side of the railway embankment. He'd rested, trying to clear his head, trying to feel his face, and as they rectified he'd crawled closer to his goal. Finally in position, he'd passed out completely, his heart simply not able to send sufficient oxygenated blood to his brain. Gradually he came awake, sorting out the gunfire as he did so. He could see the trouble Marsh and Tulip were in, but could also see that she was nearing safety.

She fired again, and then heaved with all her strength, bullets ripping past her, one bullet entering beneath her arm, tearing arm and chest simultaneously. At last she pulled her Rockman to safety behind the ties.

"Don't you dare die on me, Rockman. You hear. I love you, Rockman. We're having your baby. Don't you dare die on me." She tore loose her petticoat and pressed it against the cratered skull, forcing bone fragment, hair, and blood clot into it. Tears streamed her face. "I love you, Rockman. Don't die. Oh, God, please don't die!"

The shotgun fired twice. A man jumped and limped, cursing. Clarence having gained position was now able to shoot at their legs as they were exposed under the cars, but the soldier listening knew that Clarence was doomed.

He has a pattern. He fires twice then reloads. They will rush him as soon as he fires twice. Ed's big Colt was loaded with hollowed out soft point bullets. He'd shot a rabbit once with the gun, destroying it, mixing gut and hair and bone and muscle into a gruesome inedible tangle. That pistol, he deemed, could drop a deer. He wanted to provide deer meat for his family and carrying a rifle had proven too hard for him. Watching the men, he could see they were about to rush Clarence.

Ed's first shot entered the back of Ray Nelson's head, splattering it against a stock car. Slim Jones turned in time to receive lead above his ear, jerking his head back, his mouth gaping as the mess of him settled earthward. Tom Nelson turned in rage to face his doom head on. His forehead disintegrated carrying the top of his head along with it. Simon Doty had fallen flat on the ground. He held his hands over his head and lay screaming. "Don't shoot! Don't shoot! I'm not armed! Don't shoot!" The soldier didn't hear the plea. He'd slunk to the rails from where he'd laid firing. His gun had fallen from his hand and was silent.

Clarence could see that Tulip and Marsh were in safety. He'd heard shots, but didn't know Ed's location. He wasn't sure even whether Ed had joined into the fracas. He could hear the pleas of Simon Doty. Listening, he expected Ed to say something to Doty. Hearing silence, Clarence again emptied his barrels under the train cars. "Please! Please!" came the response. "Stop! Don't shoot! I'm not one of them!"

"Come out of there!" Clarence heard himself yell it, yet looked around him in awe of anyone having nerve enough to yell it. "All of you come out," he heard the brave man say, though he himself lay shaking.

"I'm alone. The others are dead! Don't shoot at me. I'm not armed!"

He could see Doty crawling out, crawling under a load of horses. Roger had arrived now and kneeling next to Marsh had retrieved his handcuffs. Roger, as scared as Clarence, still managed to hear a voice, more like an echo, emanating from all around him, spoken by some one who appeared to be inside his head. He heard the echo say, "Keep him covered. I'll cuff him," and he noticed himself walking over to Simon Doty.

John and Henry Clout came running. Someone yelled at them, "Get a doctor! Get a doctor!" John ran toward Dr. Nealy's office.

Clarence and Roger and Henry, Clarence in the lead with the shotgun, moved cautiously to where they could see behind the train cars, seeing at once as their eyes fell upon them, that all were dead, their skulls all but nonexistent. Roger looked at Clarence and at the shotgun wondrously. Clarence too looked at it, hardly believing that he could have done this, surely, not wanting to believe it. He handed the gun to Roger.

Roger pushed it away. He didn't want it. Henry took it from Clarence and broke it, looked inside. "It's not loaded," he said.

Once more Ed was crawling. He could moan. He could not speak. He wanted to live for them, for Lorraine, for the kids, for his family. The bullet must come out. He may die when they took it out but leaving it in would kill him. His face was too numbed to feel himself form the words; "Bullet. Chest." He moaned incoherently and lay silent.

Chapter Seventeen

Henry stabbed the shotgun down into the bloodstained snow, burrowing the beautiful Damascus barrels through six inches of snow and deep into the sucking mud. He turned and ran as fast as he could toward Dr. Laird's office.

Unseen by the men, Doty had raised his body upwards and was struggling to regain his feet. "I'll kill you!" Tulip shouted, snapping Clarence and Roger back to heightened reality.

"Get down!" Clarence yelled at him.

His eyes popped large as he looked down the barrel of Marsh's big revolver. He plopped to the ground and lay shaking, struggling to hold his bladder. "Move!" she yelled. "Move! I want to kill you!" But she'd dropped the gun. She clung to Marsh, cradling him in her blood smeared arms, her tears wetting the blood oozing from her torn cheek, blending hers with his as she held him to her. "Don't die, Rockman. Oh, please, God, help him!" she screamed. Her body shook mercilessly. She held her petticoat to his head and she held to him and she held to him. She held her Rockman. Tears streaming, she held her Rockman.

Bunny, driven by curiosity walked up to Lower Lead Bridge but he decided not to cross it. He turned from it and wandered off into the brush heading west along the river. He wandered along sniffing at stuff and he chewed some twigs from a willow. Finally he found himself on Summit Street from where he recognized Lead Bridge and walked toward it.

Dr. Nealy examined Marsh. "He'll need to be in surgery as soon as possible. His skull is pressed against his brain." The doctor, the Clout brothers, and Tulip began to carry him toward Nealy's office. A buckboard loaded with grist clattered up. Rockney and Tulip were hoisted aboard.

Dr. Laird rushed into the scene with his medical bag. He began his examination of Ed; looking perplexed. "You say he was shot in the chest?" Laird was looking up at Clarence, wonderingly.

"Yes."

"Old wound here," the doctor said, just as Lorraine knelt beside them.

Lorraine, from their apartment over the mercantile had heard the shooting. Knowing Ed would be in it, she hurried from the mercantile in time to see John Clout running toward Dr. Nealy's office. Soon after, she saw Henry Clout also running away, probably to get a doctor. As she came into the scene her eyes beheld the blood spattered Tulip and Marsh being transported. In her rush toward them she saw Laird, Roger and Clarence, and Ed! "He was wounded in Cuba," she said as she drew him into her arms. "His heart is bad." Her chin quivered, tears began to stream her face. She held him, her tears splashing his pallid face.

"Find transportation for him," Laird directed. "Get him to my office."

By that time Marsh's Oldsmobile had arrived in Moppit. Pal Toberton was surprised to see it there, let alone it being there without a driver and that it had come into the mill yard by rail. In wonder he rushed to it, leaped aboard it and stopped it. Seeing not an obvious solution to the mystery, he turned the car around and began to drive back along the tracks toward Leadford.

A dozen and more townspeople were on the shooting scene by then. Of them Hals Bingsley heard that transportation was needed. He turned, stating he would get it. He ran toward the agency to get his Franklin.

Herm Dinning with his three men were just entering town. Malice Lee had ridden hard to get them, but could not stay with them on the return. His horse tired, and he was tired. So nearing home he left them and rode into his yard at the swinery. He returned to his bed and was soon sleeping.

Bunny saw the horses from Ellington trotting down the tracks and decided to join them. They stopped near the shotgun that stuck up from the mud and snow. Bunny crowded past them to where he could sniff at its polished butt. It smelled of Clarence. He decided to stand by it.

Dinning took charge. "Secure that man," he ordered the traveling salesman. The salesman, badge shining from his chest, ordered Simon to his feet. They moved off toward the lock up.

Clarence filled him in. "There was a fight. The marshal and deputy Board are shot. Deputy Benson is lying over there. They've sent for transportation. Marsh and Tulip, deputy Board, have been taken to a doctor. Marsh is head shot. It's real bad."

"Who shot these men?" He viewed them in disbelief, thinking them exploded, yet knowing the conclusion to be ridiculous."

"I don't know. I was shooting with a shotgun. Marsh and Tulip had pistols. Ed, I think, also was shooting." Clarence was a pallid wreck stammering through the explanation.

"Just take it easy, deputy. You did good." He had a hand on Clarence's shoulder. "You rest now. Let us take over for a while, okay?"

Clarence in thinking to rest, thought of home, thought of Bunny and was saddened in his recall that he'd not tied Bunny. The fool horse would have walked away, he just knew it.

Railroad deputy Cramer, badge shining from his farmer's bib overalls, asked about the shotgun, wondrous as to it sticking from the mud, regretful that anyone would so miss use a valuable arm. "It's mine . . ." Clarence started to explain, but just then he saw Bunny. "Bunny, you old dumb head, horse," he exclaimed proudly, walking up to him, "you didn't walk away." He patted on Bunny.

Several folks had gathered to load Ed into the Franklin. Lorraine struggled to get up, wanting to go with him. Sciatic pain screamed down her leg, paralyzing her. She whimpered softly. Someone supported her, helping her in beside Ed. "Send for Helgie Perkins," Laird directed. "Tell her to get to Lorraine Benson." The car moved off toward his office.

The coroner, Dr. Betz, retired now from medical practice but still functioning as coroner, arrived with a buckboard, pressed into service as a hearse. Dr. Betz and two railroad deputies began to care for the bodies. Just then Pal arrived on the scene driving Marsh's Oldsmobile. At the crossing on Bridge he pulled from the rail bed. Seeing Clarence, he drove up to him.

"I found this in Moppit," he called, stopping the engine. "You'd better get things out of the way. The local is behind me heading in from Moppit." He looked curiously at Clarence. "What the heck happened here, Clarence?"

Clarence, holding tightly to Bunny's bridle, clinging to it as though sanity and security dwelt only in Bunny, began in a confused, mind boggled manner, to explain the situation to Pal. Beside them the buckboard was leaving with the bodies. One of the railroad deputies sat on the seat with the coroner. The other deputy walked toward Pal and Clarence.

Railroad deputy David Weed, his badge glinting from his denim, walked up to Clarence and Pal. He grabbed the shotgun as he passed it, jerking it from the mud. "It's the marshal's," Clarence said. Weed tossed it to his shoulder. He walked off toward the lock up.

"Clarence, I'll need to get right back to the mill," Pal explained. "Nobody even knows I've left; or at least don't know where I'm at. Can I borrow Bunny? I'll stop at the farm to send Tom in to relieve John Purley. Tom and Rik will double shift until you and John Purley get back."

"Thanks." Clarence handed the reins to him. Pal galloped out onto Bridge Street, heading for Jericho Road. Tight behind his departure, the local lurched across Lower Lead Bridge.

"Right on schedule," the engineer told himself proudly, for by this time to him the town looked normal.

***

125

Janet's family had been grocery wholesalers headquartered in Cincinnati, Ohio. She'd met Chris Coats on the job. They married and the couple decided to try retailing. The Ellington store was advertised for sale. Soon they were established, and doing well, at Ellington. Life was rosy. She ordered a Burdick sewer from Sears. She ordered the works; a full cabinet model of handsome carved antique oak, and with attachments; foot hemmer, tucker, thread cutter, quilter, ruffler, gatherer, and binder, wanting to sew for her family, her child, but she was still without child when Chris died. Almost before they realized he had TB it hemorrhaged and Chris died before she'd sewn a single stitch for a child.

She hadn't liked Sky at first, finding him nosy and assuming, but she wished to be out of the Ellington store. The store was a shattered dream and at age thirty-seven she lamented yet another shattered dream. She would never sew for her child. She sold out at Ellington and came to work for Sky, occupying spare rooms, one for storage and one as residence, which he provided within the mercantile. Her Blue Willow, her Rogers Brothers, her Burdick, other treasures, shared residence with her until later when she began to share residence with Sky. Now Santa Clause had been shot and he needed a Mrs. Clause and an elf and she owned a Burdick.

Little Harold became the long yearned for child and the Burdick turned fabric to splendor as she poured her love into each stitch of it. The brown denim spats fastened under the foot and snapped to the slender green cotton legs of the trousers. The little red vest was ruffled at the hem and sequins glistened at the v-neck. The white cambric blouse ruffled at the collar and cuffs and the little pointed hat wore a bright red rooster feather. Lastly a beard and mustache were fashioned from a theatrical beard from Sky's collection of Halloween getups. And there stood an elf, her creation, her love; and she was more than Mrs. Clause. Standing now as proud and happy as the hen in springtime, as the ewe in March, she was woman.

Ed'd come down that morning from their apartment above the mercantile. He'd taken frozen steaks back up with him to serve as cold packs to ease Lorraine's sciatica. The pain had just eased sufficiently for her to limp to the bathroom when the phone rang; Tulip calling, summoning Ed to the restaurant. The elf and Mr. and Mrs. Clause greeted him as he was passing out through the mercantile. "Morning," he answered, and this surprised them for it was his habit to chat a moment on the way to his work as deputy. His laconic response had afforded them no opportunity to show off their outfits. Indeed, he seemed not to notice them as he rushed through the store.

"Something awful's going to happen," Santa said, speaking as though doom was befalling, yet not able to state the reason for his comment.

"Not for elves to hear about," she'd said though she also was edgy. "Perhaps we're too excited," she suggested. "But we must be patient. We've time on our hands before leaving for the school." But in her mind she rued that Sky was correct. There'd been enough trouble in town. The past day involving Mrs. Klinert had been tragic. She wanted no more. She, like Sky, had felt ominous air descend as Ed rushed from the store. A thought came to her: "Why don't we go get the sleigh? We'll load it then cruise around town. We'll celebrate Noel on the way to the school."

The livery supplied the sleigh and had hung bells on it and red and green ribbons. Boliver had bells dinging as well and stepped out sprightly along Front Street toward the Ford agency on Bridge. They turned onto Bridge and were nearly back up it to the mercantile when shots rang out from the rail yard behind Tulip's restaurant. Janet's only thought was to get out of there! She wanted to get as far away as they could, to let distance shield their elf. The elf'd had enough for one week. He'd enough tragedy indeed for a lifetime and whereas the elf had graced them with his offer to help after Sky'd been shot, the elf too had benefited by an abrupt change in venue; and now gunshots. Can't they leave him alone? She urged Boliver to a faster pace, outdistancing the disturbing melee as they turned onto Groner. Up ahead they could see school children on their way to school. Mrs. Clause pulled to a stop beside them. "Merry Christmas," her cheery greeting stirred their spirits and bugged their eyes. They gaped in wondrous disbelief to find themselves standing face to face with Santa Clause!

"Climb in," Santa invited and two of them with eyes still bugged squeezed in beside Santa while the third, a little girl named Nellie Platt, snuggled in up front with the elf.

The elf and Santa and Mrs. Clause had a lovely time of it. Nearly every child in town was found in time to ride to the school that morning side by side with Santa Clause. Just as they were passing through town with their last load of children, Santa espied Betz with the buckboard and seeing it, his "Ho, Ho" took on a saddened note. Mrs. Clause too had seen it. She urged Boliver on toward the school. In the distance behind them the northbound local was hooting Lower Lead Bridge and nearby, but unknown to them, Marsh Rockney lay comatose in Nealy's office while Tulip stood beside him, refusing her own treatment. "Help my Rockman," she'd said, and now washed his face as Nealy probed the wound. Nor were they aware that a block from Rockney Ed lay on Laird's treatment table, Lorraine by his side. Surely, of the injured, the dead, the dying, the elf and Mr. and Mrs. Clause were oblivious for they were immersed in the spirit of Christmas; as were twenty-seven bright-eyed kids.

***

Now long past the time that Clarence should be home from work, Clydis, much worried, had bundled Edith and arrived at the arborvitae on her way to the Perkins' telephone. Hearing a rider, she was shocked to see Pal Toberton gallop before her riding Bunny. She yelled, but he, not hearing her, kept his press upon Bunny, riding like the Pony Express, heedless of the snow covered mud of Jericho, bent on his self imposed mission. Helgie was speaking on the phone as she entered the kitchen and Morley, as she could see, had pulled on his hat and coat and held her med bag in a gloved hand. "We're on our way," she said into the receiver. Then hanging it, she said to Clydis: "He's in town. Trouble in town. You can come with me."

"Is Clarence . . ."

"He's okay, I guess. Others have been shot!"

Morley climbed in behind the wheel. He worked throttle, spark, and ignition as she cranked the little Ford awake. He hopped out, yielding the wheel to her. "The call was from Leevy," she said, climbing in. "Lorraine and Ed are in Laird's office." The car was moving now onto Jericho. She gunned the engine. Bounding, slipping, and sliding, Clydis hung tightly to the dash, Edith bundled to her. Helgie plowed onto Cross. They splattered into Leadford only to be halted by the northbound that blocked Lead Bridge. Clifford was halted also at the bridge.

"Good morning," Clifford called. "I see we both had good timing."

Helgie didn't respond to his joke. She surprised him by asking: "How many are hurt?"

"Hurt?" Immediately his face registered concern. "In town?"

"There has been trouble: shooting."

"That bitch!" Clifford shouted, jumping to an erroneous conclusion. "Is Naddy all right?"

"It isn't Naddy. It wasn't her. Not Mrs. Klinert," Clydis hastened to explain. "We're sure my mother is dead."

"I'm sorry, Clydis. I shouldn't have jumped to it. It's just that . . . Well, I." He peered at her.

"I know," Clydis said. "But the trouble is about . . . I don't know, really."

"We hoped you would know," Helgie explained. "There's been shooting. The Marshal's hurt as is Ed Benson. We're on our way to Dr. Laird's. Leevy called me. Lorraine and Ed are over at Laird's office. I didn't hear but what your family is okay."

"That's sure a relief," Clifford remarked with a sigh. "I've been out of town since about six delivering parcels to the farms. Been way behind at it because of the roads, but they've much improved already with this cold. I'll be pulling a sleigh the next time out. Roads are good for it now, I see. Naddy is with her mother at Meads. Harold is with Sky and Janet. They're dressing him up as an elf. Last night he was telling us all about it. I can't think of a better way to get his mind diverted from what happened to Naddy. We owe a lot to Janet and Sky. Sky's shoulder hurts too much, he said, to pass out the gifts at the school so elf Harold is going to help with that. We're real pleased. Naddy looks real bad, as you'd know, but, she was in good spirits this morning. Real excited about helping her ma. Claire said that, among other things, they're going to make new dresses for her doll. Those other things, Clydis knows about."

"Other things? Like what?" Helgie wanted to know.

"Ladies' pants," Clydis answered. "Like those I was wearing the other day. Trella is starting a new, and daring, she says, line of women's apparel. You might stop in there and look."

"I hope I have time," she said, "but: Tally Ho!" she let in the clutch. The train was departing. She drove on toward Laird's office.

***

Not even the teacher recognized the elf. Joe Marvin Benson recognized Sky and Janet at once. It is doubtful that any of the other children recognized Sky. Perhaps half of them recognized Janet Coats, she being the least in disguise, nor did anybody give either of them but modest attention. Elf captivated them, young and old, seeming to know them one and all. Mrs. Clause held the bright red cotton bag open handy for the elf to reach into and as his hand drew forth a gift, his eyes lit up and he danced around with it while Mr. and Mrs. Clause kept up a "Merry Christmas. Merry Christmas," and Santa frequented a melodious lusty "Ho, Ho, Ho" and the elf often jumped off his feet in his dancing and he laughed and giggled ending unerringly to the intended recipient of each gift.

The three older boys found that Santa had honored them each with a three bladed ivory handled pocket knife which the boys, one and all, needed, or soon would need, as boys are prone to lose such. Nine smaller boys were delighted to find rubber bulb powered jumping rabbits in their brightly adorned packages and the ten smaller girls squealed with glee to discover that Santa had brought each of them a musical rubber doll attired in a brightly colored worsted dress. The elf now danced on one foot then on the other as he circled Mrs. Clause.

The dark green package he presented to black-haired Rita Burns and the red packages he placed in the laps of Jill Faygard and Sandra Gillis. The light green packages ended in the laps of Fern Wills and Wilma Gillis. How could the elf know that braided wire hair rolls were to match the color of the wearer's hair? And how had Santa guessed the rolls were in vogue and were much desired, needed in producing the popular pompadour hairstyle or that a lacy edged pastel dimity handkerchief spelled the difference between a girl and a young women?

Two gifts remained. One was large and was exquisitely wrapped and tied with a satin-green ribbon. The little elf hopped and spun and giggled. All eyes were on teacher Nancy Like. She nearly cried in sighting the elegant china tea set. "Oh, thank you darling little elf. And thank you Santa and Mrs. Clause from all of us. The students chorused their thank you as well, but then teacher said to Santa;

"Santa, we have a student missing today. He's a darling little boy. He's home today helping his sister who has been injured."

Mrs. Clause looked deep down into the red cotton bag. "There is a gift, Santa. It's for a little boy. We must take it to him. He is helping his brave sister."

All grew quiet now while the teacher read the Christmas story from a book. Following the reading, punch and cookies and Christmas carols rounded out the morning. An hour early, for school was to resume until noon, she dismissed. By that time Sky and Janet and Harold had returned to the mercantile. A little elf played there. With each squeeze of the rubber bulb the little rabbit hopped forward and he hopped and dance along with it.

***

Outside the mercantile and walking toward it was a young woman of nineteen years. A little girl clutched her hand and she walked along on strong little legs and she held a rag dolly in her arm, pressing the doll protectively against her blue woolen coat. The bangs of the woman's brown hair bounced from beneath the brim of her Sears and Roebuck hat. She wore the bangs a bit long, masking a roughened reddish scar on her forehead. Her eyes were sad, her forehead in frown. It'd been a different morning for her, not one of elf and Santa and Mrs. Clause, for she'd seen a man, a good man torn. His head was fractured and his brain in coma. His woman was beside him, holding him, herself torn of body of soul of mind and oh so greatly in love with her man. And beside him also in the rear of the Oldsmobile was a second man, her man, her love, father of Edith, holding Marsh against his falling from the seat as Roger began the drive to Grand Rapids.

In a different building she'd seen a man, pallid, near death lying on a table while Laird probed into his chest by x-ray. And nearby was his son and beside him his mother, Lorraine, with frozen beef steak tucked at her waist against sciatica. Then on the way to the mercantile she'd seen a little girl at Meads. Her face was a swollen mass of purple, yellow and brown, her eyes nearly shut, and beside her a woman who hurt for her, with her, who would soon be happily their neighbor, but whom now knew only sadness and grief and sleeplessness. The distraught young woman thought not of Christmas day, of rejoicing His birthday, for she like Claire, like Lorraine, Tulip, Clarence, Roger, many others that day knew anxiety, worry, regret. Those emotions were the press, the lid, clamping down the spirit of Christmas.

She climbed the steps to the covered porch of the mercantile. A bench rested there, a hewn bench shaped of a derelict log by a lonely pioneer so long ago, the bench the haven now for the weary, the thoughtful, the lover, and the sad. She sat on the bench. The little girl, wishing no help, big girl she was, pulled herself up onto the bench "Sanny Caus!" she shrieked. She stamped her tiny feet, she waved her arms, she giggled, eyes merry beneath the bouncing bangs of her curly brown hair: "Sanny Caus! Momma, Sanny Caus!"

It was as though Christ himself stood there. Come rejoice be merry it is My birthday and Clydis knew then who had sent Santa Clause, who had sent Santa Clause with an elf to help him and a wife to be at his side, to love him, to be there, to say all is well. "It's Christmas! Rejoice," Santa encouraged. "It's Christmas and for this we're grateful."

Clydis was at once merry, so petty her problems, so disgraceful her melancholy when her friends needed cheer. "Come," she said to Santa Clause, "a little girl needs you."

"We were just on our way," Santa chuckled.

"Mrs. Santa handed a large parcel to the elf. The elf danced and laughed merrily for he was on his way to Meads to cheer his Naddy, his sister, his friend. Roger had reached the highway by that time where slowly, smoothly, he pressed the accelerator and the Oldsmobile swept into rapidly gaining momentum, its siren wailing. The car was as a sleigh smoothly soaring to the rooftops, trying to reach there in time, for time was the issue, time their denominator of Christmas.

Roger'd worked all night to rebuild the Oldsmobile following its altercation with the Mrs. Klinert's Franklin. The car had a new front axle, wheel assembly, steering arm, and radiator and, as an upgrade for the car, he'd installed a new engine; this one nearly twice the horsepower, but he'd had no opportunity to road test the car before Marsh had taken it down the rail bed. He knew as well that the car had bounded along on the ties all the way to Moppit and home again, thus he eased the car to higher and higher speed carefully feeling it out, but soon greatly exceeded the sixty miles per hour boastfully heralded by Oldsmobile.

Tops and windscreens were available for the Oldsmobile, but Marsh preferred to ride in the open wearing goggles and a leather hat. Roger was that way attired but with the addition of a scarf which covered his face and neck. It was nonetheless very cold with only the energy that fueled his determination to warm him. In the rear Tulip and Clarence fought to keep themselves and Marsh, especially Marsh, covered by blankets head to toe and to keep him upright in the seat with his head and neck supported. The Oldsmobile screamed down the graveled surface of the highway, Roger aiming for the spots he deemed to be less slippery, aiming also to miss drifts from the last snow fall which the county road commission was struggling to clear away.

A horse drawn road plow loomed ahead. The plowman, busy trying to remove a large drift three miles below Leadford, was working in the passing lane, frantic to clear it, while the lane Roger tore down was blocked by the drift. He backed off the throttle but fearing a skid dared not slam the brakes but aimed for the center of the drift, striking it with explosive force.

The plowman didn't know what happened. There'd been a catamount's howl and an explosion of snow. He didn't see the car. The car had hurtled through the air to land fifty feet down the highway. It landed straight with the road. Roger rested his nerves for but a moment before he was again flooring the accelerator. In the rear the three occupants had been shaken but had managed to keep Marsh securely pressed in position against the seat. Clarence and Tulip riding with Marsh with their heads and his completely covered by blankets had seen nothing. They'd felt a crunch and an eerie airborne sensation then a spine jarring reconnect with the road.

They screamed onward toward the city of Grand Rapids. In the city, and outward from it, police cars and horses streamed out to clear the road or block the road of traffic whether oat or gasoline powered, having been alerted by telephone and telegraph that the Oldsmobile was on its way. Knowing only that the car hurtling toward them carried Marsh Rockney, injured, critical, needing the hospital immediately, was knowledge enough for them. A police officer was down! They charged to the aid of their fellow, rendering all assistance possible, willing to give their ultimate in respect of an officer, a man who'd put his life on the line for his Family, his life now dangling from eternity by a shred.

Streaming out from Grand Rapids, the lead car spotted him way up the road, closing fast, but how fast they could not have imagined or now can imagine. A bobbing distant speck suddenly became a full sized car that in a blast of wind and sound rocked their car as of a tornado before receding to a bobbing speck behind them. Roger brought the Oldsmobile in at a speed greater than anyone had before in the history of the world ever imagined possible, reaching the city from Leadford in less than ten minutes. Marsh was briskly wheeled into an operating room.

Chapter Eighteen

Landsteiner had a few years previously determined the human blood types. "He'll need blood," the orderly said, and the three willingly submitted to their blood being drawn and tested, finding that Roger's type A matched Rockney's.

Roger was wheeled into the operating room where his bloodstream was made conduit to Marsh. Roger pumped his fist until he fell asleep, was then awakened to pump his fist until he again fell asleep, soon losing all concept of actual time, surviving in a fog distant from the fervor of the operating room. Roger knew not when the ordeal had terminated but slept on and on, oblivious to Marsh having been wheeled into recovery.

Clarence had dosed then awakened repeatedly since being sent to a waiting room to wait, feeling ashamed with each awakening, knowing that Tulip had remained stalwart, refusing sleep until sure that Marsh wouldn't die. Clarence hadn't been asleep more than two hours of the past twenty-four, but the dozing had partially restored him. He could see Tulip at Marsh's side in a hospital room, herself as yet having disallowed any treatment of her own wounds, standing over him kissing him, begging him, begging God. "Please, God. Let my Rockman live." He went in the room to be with her.

"Tulip, he's in the hands of God. He would want you well, Tulip. Please let me be with him while you get your wounds treated." She glared at him.

"Go away, Clarence."

"No. I will not go away. Darn it, Tulip, we need you to stay well. Marsh needs you well. You need to be well to take care of Marsh. Now you get out of here and get help." She stared at him agape, tears suddenly flooding her eyes.

"Okay, but at the least sign."

"Exactly. At the least sign, I'll get you."

***

133

Back at Leadford Clydis was on her way home driving Morley's Ford. Helgie'd stayed in town to assist in Ed's surgery.

Morley'd finished chores at the Jericho farm by the time Clydis returned and he was in the Groner kitchen bagging orders for root crops. Morley had two root cellars, one under the kitchen at the farm, the other across the road at his place under the kitchen. He was behind his promises on deliveries; now when old Jude was able, he would not be behind, he told himself; fool cars, anyway; yet the car is nice, weather permitting, and today, "Lord willing, I'll catch up." Clydis and Edith helped him carry packages out to the Ford. He planned to make his deliveries around town and to conclude at the doctor's where he would wait for Helgie.

The three doctors met in Laird's office. It was agreed that Dr. Betz would be stationed at Nealy's office to tend those needing general assistance. Betz had viewed the x-rays of Ed's chest along with the other doctors and was amazed at the detail one could discern by that means, but knew his aged hands and eyes to be wanting in the task confronting them. Despite high quality x-rays, as fine as any he'd before accomplished, clarity was still far less than Laird wished for. Laird would be cutting into the outer lining of Ed's beating heart and would accomplish the miracle by feel, not actually being able to see precisely where he was cutting. Helgie functioned as anesthesiologist. Nealy stood ready to restore a collapsed lung, as the left one almost certainly would collapse as Laird entered the chest. Nealy would also serve as surgical nurse to Laird.

Laird opened Ed's abdomen then pressed a scalpel through the diaphragm into Ed's chest, pushing inward until he could feel each heart beat touch the sharp point of the scalpel. He moved the point around until he could feel a hardness bopping the point of it. The beating heart was actually doing the cutting as it pushed the bullet and its enclosing jacket of flesh against the point of the scalpel. He continued, sweat pouring down his face, his breathing slow and steady, his hands seeming to not move at all, letting the beating heart be the motive force in releasing the bullet, until finally he felt the bullet move. Leaving his scalpel in position, now using it as a guide, he pushed his forceps into the wound and grasped the bullet.

All breathed a sigh of relief as the wayward bullet clanked into a pan. "It's out," Laird said softly, but hoped that Lorraine and the boys sitting worriedly in the waiting room would hear.

"Thank you, God," they heard Lorraine murmur.

"I believe he'll be okay now," Laird said as Nealy closed the wound and restored function to the lung. "You can move some chairs on into the recovery room," he directed, looking at John Purley who had just entered the room. "We'll have him in there in a few minutes."

"His heart is okay now?"

"We still have infection to worry about, but his heart is doing better

134

already. Merry Christmas."

It was well after dark that Christmas Eve, before Ed was able to go home. They used a carriage for the short trip to the mercantile, where with a son under each arm they labored slowly, painfully up the stairway to his bed. Lorraine sat beside him, held his hand, just generally fussed over him, she with frozen beef steaks tucked to her lower back, her sciatica just barely at bay, her eyes moist, and reflecting a blend of tears, hope, and love. In the living room John Purley and Joe Marvin were reading aloud to the delight of their parents. They read from Horatio Alger first, their favorite author. Then Joe read the Christmas story from the same book he'd taken to school that morning, now seemingly days ago, that the teacher had read so beautifully. The story had a dual impact in the Benson household for while they could rejoice Christ's birthday, they also rejoiced the rebirth of a man. A man snatched from death, a man whom they loved, a man who would remain with them and love them and would be with them and the baby yet unborn, but kicking it's readiness to be so, into the distance of time.

On Christmas Eve at the Jameses, Clifford and Claire set out egg sandwiches and milk for Santa. Naddy and Harold were soon tucked in and asleep although Harold went to sleep wondering as to the true identity of Santa Clause. As for the elf, Naddy hadn't been fooled. She'd recognized Harold at once despite his get up. She'd laughed delightedly when he handed her the large package from Santa. Her new teddy bear was tucked in warmly beside her as she lay sleeping.

Albert too was asleep this Christmas Eve, but Rylus fussed with colic. Charley sat up with him. Flora was more than a little annoyed with Charley. "It's the goose broth," she'd complained. "Charley, he just isn't ready for goose broth."

Charley was feeling a bit guilty, but resolved no less that his decision had been correct. After all he'd boiled the goose giblets and neck on the kitchen oil heater for the expressed purpose of providing them with internal warmth, which he assumed the fat would provide, and he darn sure wasn't about to exclude little Rylus from such protection. Now he paced the floor with Rylus until suddenly the little fellow filled his diaper and one leg of his pajamas. Still feeling guilty and not wanting to wake Flora, he set about the cleanup chore. Meantime sleeping Flora had cracked an eyelid and lay watching with a tiny smug smile on her face. Rylus nodded to sleep and all was well at the new house.

Morley and Helgie'd had a hard day. He'd finished his vegetable deliveries in time to be on hand as Ed was awakening from surgery. Helgie was tired. She was groggy from ether fumes and the whole top of her head ached. Morley drove them home. He prepared a willow bark tea. He drank of it himself although not for headache. It, they believed, also thinned the blood, staving off a stroke. Besides, with the brew laced with brandy, it served its function as the toddy they craved on this Christmas Eve. Additionally, the terminus of two days of trouble and woe deserved to be toasted.

At the mercantile Santa and Mrs. Clause were cuddled, he rather clumsily for his shoulder throbbed. But their close togetherness soon dulled the ache, superceded, as it were, by a greater one and then with the chime of sleigh bells and the gleeful revelry of children dancing their heads the grand couple settled into slumber leaving the night to the real Clause.

At the swinery Malice Lee had gone with his stepdaughter Wilma Gillis out to a shed to gather arm loads of pine boughs. In the shed he pushed her down onto the boughs and was there with her. She cried softly while on the boughs and when she arose from them to lift her armload of the boughs she cried still for she did not wish to be with him. Fifteen-year-old Wilma longed for the day school would end in the spring. Then she would go away and leave the swinery and start anew. That would be her Christmas, but for now Malice Lee would have his.

Christmas Eve for Jennifer Faygard and for Jill, Johnny, Meggy, and Fred was one of loneliness. They missed Roger, it being their tradition to eat a large meal late on Christmas Eve and to say prayers and to snuggle into their beds where slumber would soften their anticipation of Santa's visit. They ate the delicious repast with Johnny; their eldest son at age nine, doing the honor of slicing and serving the hickory cured candied and spiced Christmas ham, which she had roasted to perfection. Their prayers that night included well wishes for Tulip and Marsh and for Ed and Clarence along with those for Roger, their dad. And for Roger, the husband, her love, she sent a special plea that he would be home for Christmas for the children, for her, for him. "Please, God, let him come home."

"Jeeus, Jeeus, babee Jeeus," Edith grabbed at the pages to the Christmas story.

"Yes, baby Jesus. Christmas is baby Jesus' birthday," she explained, tickling her tummy. Edith giggled. "And Christmas is when Santa Clause comes."

"Sanny Caus," Edith pushed away the Christmas story, replacing it with the book from which Santa jumped brightly. "Sanny Caus, Sanny Caus."

They were seated in the wide armed chair. To their left a fire popped merrily in the potbelly and on their right stood a-much-pulled-upon Christmas tree. Its bottom branches were nude of ornaments where she'd pulled them down for a closer look at the irresistible eye-bogglers. Pine needles too were strewed about and somehow a pretty bow had found its way from one of the packages to Sniffer's blanket next to the kitchen range and a candy cane had ended up in his dish. He'd made short work of the cane, but stood a long while in awe of the bow before he'd turned around twice then plopped down beside it. Edith'd then commenced bringing him decorations from the window ledge located next to the tree. "Oh, I think just one bow is enough for Sniffer," she'd said, and Edith sat down beside him and patted on him and placed the bow on his ear.

"Sniffer pretty," Edith declared and this, and so many little things, which they would have hoped to share with Clarence that Christmas Eve had passed by and were gone forever and Edith would not remember them nor perhaps would Clydis. Clydis would remember the Eve as one of loneliness and worry and would always recall the vapidity, but she would never blame him. A man so good she knew could not belong solely to them. She and Edith must share him; and she did so proudly, believing in him, loving him, but wanting him home.

Edith began to nod. They'd eaten a supper of mashed potatoes, green beans, fried pork, pork gravy made with corn starch because it shined that way, much as though it were made of marble; her favorite, and his. Then before she'd but turned around to draw water to do dishes, Edith'd found a candy cane for each of her supple little hands and had begun earnestly and adroitly the process of getting sticky herself, Sniffer, her dolly, and umpteen else. Clydis had postponed the dishes, filling instead a No.3 tub. They'd bathed Dollie too by wiping her with a damp wash cloth that Edith had handy and Clydis'd placed Dollie in the warming oven to dry. The doll was still there but Edith hadn't missed her before drifting to deep slumber. Clydis tucked her in and she kissed her and she moved her fingers through her curly bouncy brown hair and brushed her finger lightly along her cheek as her dad would have done. Then, with her eyes near to tearing, she hurried to the kitchen, much work still, and her heart pleaded as she set to work: "Please, God, let him come home."

***

As if hearing her plea, Clarence at the hospital was getting anxious. As far as he could see things were more or less in order and would remain so with no help from him. He'd sure rather be home as, he was sure, Roger would also rather be, but Roger lay sleeping.

Roger'd been fatigued to near exhaustion before he'd begun his pump for Marsh. Now he lay in sleep not far from death's door. "What he needs is rest and plenty, I mean it, plenty of fluids and lots of wholesome food," the doctor said, staving Clarence's concern. "If you could get him home, it would be best."

It would be just himself and Roger for the trip home. The hospital had admitted Tulip and she lay in a bed next to Marsh. The head nurse had merely wheeled her in. The doctor had turned and looked at her, his eyes questioning. "Special case," she said, and he smiled. Tulip smiled back at him, determination lines on her face. "She's as good a nurse as I for what he needs now," she continued. "Merry Christmas, Doctor."

The doctor soon after began his journey home, his horse stepping out briskly for its feeble mind sensed that oats waited, and as they clopped merrily along the deserted streets of Grand Rapids, the doctor was elated. Marsh, he believed, would be all right and wouldn't need him until sometime tomorrow, and deserted streets meant that folks were home. If they would stay there and stay sober, and he had faith they would do just that, he could look forward to an entire Christmas Eve with his family. He jiggled the reins. The horse cantered.

Clarence puffing like a train engine carried blanket-wrapped Roger in his arms like a huge baby out to the car and plopped him onto a blanket in the front seat. He would draw the seat blanket across Roger's lap and sit on the end of it to keep Roger from falling out. Clarence knew nearly nothing of cars, least of all this one, but had seen Roger start it more than once. It's bursting to a powerful idling at the first quarter turn of the crank startled him. He stood out in front of it a moment with his hand on the radiator cowling, but it kept chugging and he, feeling a bit foolish, but pleased, stepped proudly around to the driver's seat and heaved himself up to take the wheel.

The route home was simple; merely follow Plainfield; can't miss Plainfield; big street off to your left. You can't miss it, the orderly had said. Large snowflakes began to descend as he eased the Oldsmobile into the street that bordered the hospital. Over to the left someplace, huh? By the time he'd crossed Plainfield several times looking for the big street, one of more than one big one he soon discovered, he was ready to declare stiff penalty on anyone removing or turning any street sign. To worsen matters, by the time he'd reached Plainfield and was sure he was on it, and feeling much better now, and confident, the snow flake populace had trebled, filling the air with awesome splendor.

The snowflakes were large in size and they fascinated him. Not one of them fell straight down. Each flake careened to and fro as if seeking a landing site most in need of beautification, yet the flakes all seemed to curve away from the car. Still, no, they all didn't. Some landed on it, in it, but he couldn't tell which ones were going to. And all were so absolutely beautiful! The headlights turned them golden and they sparkled and spun, cavorting in their mission of beautification as he drove on toward the bridge on Plainfield where he would cross the Grand River.

The street lamps as well as the light shining from numerous homes and businesses and the striking splendor of Christmas lights guided him and he purred along smoothly, contentedly, but then he crossed the Plainfield Bridge. Instantly his field of vision became limited to a tiny world of swirling snow dancing in the beam of his headlights. He could see no other lights to either side of the gliding car. Indeed, he was not sure where the road was located. He slowed, but then the engine faltered! "Shift! Shift!" He clutched then grated the rears and tried the new ratio. The engine noise was louder, but now the car kept smoothly on.

He had a feeling that was he on Bunny he would be going faster. But each time he attempted to go faster a ditch suddenly loomed within the snowy world of his light beams and he would slam to a stop or turn sharply, or both, to try to get back out into the center of the road. At least we're moving. If I just keep moving we'll get home, he thought.

He didn't feel the cold. He didn't know when he'd removed the goggles because snow stuck to them impeding his vision. He didn't know when or where he had lost his gloves. The snow was mesmerizing. Minutes became fuzzy hours or fleeting seconds. Passing blindly into the snowy white and golden swirling field before him, he wished he could see his watch. With about ten miles to drive and assuming his speed at ten miles an hour, he would be home by? What time did we leave? What time is it? He stopped the car and walked around to the front of it. "Twelve-thirty. By about a quarter after one, I should be at Leadford." He drove on through the blinding snow.

In lieu of a ready timepiece, he started to count. "One thousand one, one thousand two;" at a thousand and six hundred he planned to consult his watch, but somehow after a while he imagined that he'd counted the one thousand and two hundreds twice, or the three hundreds twice, or had skipped the three hundreds? He drove a while longer, his anxiety building with every inch of progress through the swirling golden beauty before him until he could stand it no longer. He stopped. "Ten minutes," he mumbled, standing out in front of the car. At least I haven't driven right on past Leadford. From where he stood he could see nothing but snow ahead of him. Warily, he climbed back into the car. Bunny could have found and followed the road. "Am I stupider than Bunny?"

The rear tires of the Oldsmobile spun as he let in the clutch and the car swerved from side to side. The six inches of sodden heavy snow were beginning to test the Oldsmobile. Now Clarence dared not stop unless he felt they were going down hill. He wished Roger or Marsh was driving. "But . . . I am!"

The powerful Oldsmobile engine began to labor. This may be the second of the big hills, he thought, but he hadn't noticed the curve! The first big hill was located immediately beyond Plainfield Bridge. On that hill his world had suddenly shrunk to the size of his headlight beams, but he'd shifted and the Olds pulled the hill without difficulty. This second big hill was preceded by a large sweeping curve that he didn't realize he'd traversed; yet he must have. The car was certainly laboring, but he wasn't adroit at shifting the car. The car chugged. His foot rested on the clutch, ready to keep the engine from dying. He didn't feel the cold. Didn't know he was sweating. He didn't think of Clydis or Edith, of home, only ahead. Don't lose the way through the blinding golden swirling snow. Elation revved his heart. Engine speeding up? "Yes, yes!" We've made it over the second big hill! He resumed counting, finally stopping the car at one thousand one hundred to consult his watch.

The car moved slowly ahead, its engine racing. There were many small hills to climb and then he must make it over a big, big one. After having crested the real big one, there would be but a mile to go before reaching the turnoff road into Leadford. Roger slept on, snoring peacefully beside him. He worried about Roger, expecting him to have awakened by now, but he hadn't roused a wink.

The Oldsmobile roared on through its tiny world of swirling golden snow, finally cresting the last big hill. Main lay a mile ahead. "I gotta find Main!"

He counted, "One thousand one, one thousand two . . . but couldn't see far ahead, couldn't see Main. Suddenly out of the corner of his eye a light glowed behind him to his left. He stopped the car. He stared back over his shoulder. Light over there. Shining from? He backed slowly to where the light appeared directly beside him. He might be at Main but he could see no road. He walked toward the light.

Plunging into a ditch, from his hands and knees he again saw the light glowing faintly through the falling snow. He made his way toward it, nearly running now, the light a beacon from heaven drawing him. Finally he stood before it, but below it. He craned his head back and looked up at it, straining to see, for his eyes to inform his brain, for his brain to mull over it . . . "Church! Heaven's sake! It's the church out on the highway; the Methodist church; and its parking lot borders Main!"

He stumbled onto Main and turned back toward the car. Listened. Do I hear it? As he waded out Main, sure enough, he heard the powerful idling engine of the Oldsmobile. He ran. Out of breath when he reached it, coughing and wheezing he clung to the car. Finally, he could talk. Triumphantly: "We found Main, Roger! Roger, we found Main!"

Still in low gear, he made his way down Main to where it cornered with Front. To the right this intersection led to a school while straight ahead it would carry him to where Mrs. Klinert had hidden behind the gristmill. Fortunately his lights glinted from the corner of the mill, else he may have joined his mother-in-law, so he made the turn cleanly onto Front. Easy going now. He could see a light ahead on his right, no doubt left on for Roger. Moments later he pulled up to the door of Roger's repair shop.

He rushed up to the door to reach its handle, but was knocked on his rump as the door unexpectedly swung open.

"Roger! Roger!" she yelled.

"As if I didn't have enough to think about," Clarence said, slowly regaining his feet. "He's in the car."

Chapter Nineteen

She rushed to him, grabbed his shoulder. "Roger, Roger!" She tugged.

"He's asleep. He was awful tired then he gave a blood transfusion to Marsh. His is the same blood type as Marsh." She pulled at Roger, trying to bring him from the car. "Here, let me help." He tugged the blankets from him. "The doc said he would be okay. He needs rest and lots of fluids, any kind you can get in him; and he needs lots of food, the doc said; when he wakes up."

With Clarence lifting at one shoulder and Jennifer at the other and with Jill lifting his feet, they lugged him up the stairway like as if he were a sack of potatoes and into the kitchen. "Oh, Daddy! Daddy!" Meggy wailed.

She went into uncontrolled sobbing, clinging and pulling at her dad. "Oh, Daddy, Daddy!"

They carried Roger into the bedroom, their task made immeasurably more difficult by Meggy who keep pulling at her dad and sobbing. "Daddy sick, Daddy sick," herself being tripped over by Jennifer and Jill.

"No, he isn't sick," Jennifer finally could tend to her three year old. "He's only very tired and he's sleeping."

Meggy climbed right up on her dad and would not get down, but at least she was no longer out of control. Jennifer tossed a blanket over both Meggy and her dad. Clarence meantime had made his way back to the car.

Clydis, as well as had Morley and Helgie across the road from the arborvitae, had a light burning in every window. With great relief and gratitude, Clarence made his way toward them. As he pulled in past the arborvitae, the Perkins' lights suddenly all began to go out showing Clarence how much they cared, having waited up for him, wanting him to find his way home in the storm. At the rear stoop, he cut the ignition and extinguished the headlights. Clydis was there. Oh, praise God, she was there. They stood in the snow in the yard. They clung together. Oh, how they did cling, so glad to be home. Oh, so glad to be home.

She was bare footed, clad in a thin cotton night dress, and was rapidly being covered by falling snow and drenched by melting snow from his coat and hat, but she yet clung to him; hugging, kissing him. He lifted her into his arms and carried her into the kitchen. "Merry Christmas," she breathed as he placed her feet on the floor. She began with unbuttoning his coat. He helped with the removal of his clothes. Soon he was wearing only his damp johns. He was unshaven, uncombed, needing a bath and smelling of it, but he was home. She would feed him and warm him and give him rest. The clock was ticking at three o'clock when she'd accomplished those things. Then, cuddled together, they slept.

***

Edith awoke at six-thirty. Immediately she felt around in her bed for Dollie. Worried, she pulled all of the blankets off the bed and tipped her mattress to look under it. Where is Dollie? She flung the bed covers a last time then scampered toward the bathroom. It wasn't clear in her mind just what she was supposed to do in the bathroom, but Edith abhorred wet clothes. Having made her way up to the bathroom, she removed the damp pajama bottoms and her diaper. Now clad only in her top, she was getting cold. In the early morning the warm places in the house did not include the bathroom. Near Sniffer, the sage who wisely had chosen his bedstead to be near the kitchen range that they banked each night, the air was warmer. Typically, she found comfort by associating with Sniffer while playing with Dollie and her other friendly toys.

But she hadn't found Dollie!

It came to her mind that something truly evil and onerous had befallen Dollie. "Doollieeeee!" she howled and she howled it repeatedly on her way down the stairs to the kitchen.

Sniffer was by her side on the instant she'd called out and together they charged into the bedroom with Sniffer barking his alarm bark and with Edith yelling "Dooollieeeee! And with tears streaming down her face and both of them climbed onto the bed.

Edith, totally distraught, yanked at the bed cover, dragging it from Clydis. "Dooollieee! Momma, Doollieeeeeeeee!" she shrieked, yanking at the bed covers while at the same time Sniffer'd gone to work on Clarence, mopping his face then burrowing his nose along next to Clarence's neck. Sniffer shoved on Clarence's neck and whined pitifully.

Awaking with a jerk, he pushed at Sniffer. "What's the matter? What's the matter?"

Clydis slid out of bed, catching Edith in her arms as she did so. "Doolliee, Dolliee," Edith sobbed. "Momma, Dollie's gone!"

"There, there, dear. We'll find Dollie," she promised, reaching for a robe,

142

the robe of special necessity that morning because she and Clarence had fallen asleep naked. Edith nearly ended up inside the robe with her in that she would not release her hold on her mother's leg nor relent her plea for Dollie. Clydis' mind raced to resolve the calamity. Seeing Edith's sleeping area a mess of wadded and strewn about bed covers, she reached for them hoping that Dollie may have secreted within.

"No, Mom-mom-Momma!" Edith yelled through her sobs. "Dollie not there."

Suddenly it dawned on Clydis. "Her Dollie's in the oven," she said to Clarence.

"Oven? Oh, my gosh!" Thinking that Edith had somehow cooked Dollie, Clarence scrambled from the bed, tangling Sniffer in the bed covers then into his robe as he pulled it on. He rushed from the bedroom while still struggling to tie his robe, the robe now free of Sniffer as he'd torn on ahead to join Edith and Clydis.

"Here she is," Clydis cooed, removing Dollie from the warming oven as Clarence entered the kitchen.

Edith grabbed Dollie, clutched her firmly to her chest and accused "Momma hurt Dollie," anger registered obvious on her face as she glared at her mother.

"No, darling," Clydis was assuring as she knelt down beside her. "Dollie was too wet. We gave her a bath, remember?"

Edith didn't remember; or she chose to ignore the fact of the bath. "Momma hurt Dollie."

"Come, Edith, let's get Dollie dressed," she cooed, reaching for Dollie, and placing her arm around her distraught child.

Edith jerked away from her. "No," she said as she turned away, stamping her little feet, her curly brown hair bouncing, her strong little arms holding firmly to Dollie. "Momma hurt Dollie." She stood defiantly away from her mother.

"Now you listen, you little dickens. I love you. I like Dollie. I will not hurt Dollie. Do you hear?" she spoke firmly. "Now go and get a diaper and bring it to me. And get Dollie a clean dress. It's time to get breakfast."

Clarence was shaking down the stove as Clydis turned to him. "Clarence, what shall we do?"

"Her tantrum? I'm shook up too," he admitted as he began stuffing the firebox with kindling, "but I think you did just beautifully." He stuck a match to the kindling. "Maybe if we just went about normal routine," he suggested as the kindling flared. He replaced the stove lid, reaching for the spider with his free hand. She was beside him by now and he placed an arm around her. "You did good," he assured her.

"Clarence, I'm really worried."

"Dear, I don't think this is a big problem."

"But, her gift!"

"Her new doll?"

"What will we do when she opens it?"

"Let's go see," he replied with assurance. But inside he was much less assured of himself as he called to Edith. "Oh, what a pretty dress Dollie has," he said, trying to act natural. Edith looked at him; almost smiling as Clarence slipped the fresh dress onto Dollie. "Edith, we're not going to eat just yet," he said. "Momma tells me that Santa Clause came during the night. Shall we go and see?"

Edith brushed past her parents. Her eyes bugged as she espied the tree in the living room. She ran to the tree and knelt down beside it. The first brightly wrapped parcel she grabbed had her dad's name on it. Clydis picked up a gift she knew to be Edith's. "Here," she said. "Santa brought this for you." Edith grabbed her gift and began an immediate assault on the wrapping, tearing merrily away until there rested before her a large box with a picture of a doll displayed on it. She pulled the box open.

"Momma, Momma," she cried. "A dolly! Oh, a new dolly." She hugged the doll to her and began to dance around with it. Clydis had tears in her eyes, realizing how much she loved her bright little daughter and realizing that the human heart held boundless love. Love enough for all of them and for a doll or two besides and that she and Clarence had somehow out of the bungling maze of parentage of which they were learning, had managed to express their love in just the right way; and had made a little girl happy. It was enough. It was Christmas, the birthday of Jesus Christ. She sat next to her husband on the couch, her head on his shoulder, his arm around her. "Thank you," she murmured, and Clarence understood that she wasn't thanking him.

"Praise God," he said.

He began to unwrap his Empire State camera and home developing kit that she'd ordered from Sears. He'd purchased an elaborate toiletry set for her and a silky nightdress. He most wanted to see her in the nightdress and so handed that package first. She opened it with oohs and aahs and decided at once she would wear it around the kitchen while they prepared their breakfast of fried ham and eggs and oleo laden bread of which they would make sandwiches. Clarence could hardly keep his mind on his food, as she well knew, and was pleased. She sat right on his lap while he drank his coffee. Edith meantime had placed her dolls together in the baby carriage.

Her dolls found comfort in the carriage, sharing it with her wooden bowl, tin cup, and a horse, cow, pig, dog, giraffe and her big spoon. All were becoming acquainted.

"And she can close her eyes to go to sleep," she explained. Speaking in her language, of course, but her proud parents thought they were following the conversation as Edith continued: "and she likes pigs and dogs and she squeaks when you pat her back and her name is Emma and she likes Sniffer too." Sniffer cocked an ear.

Never failing to hear his name mentioned, he looked expectantly at her wondering where his special treats were concealed; as though his eyes could ask her where the candy canes were hidden. She continued her discussion at the baby carriage, ignoring Sniffer.

Sniffer could stand it no longer. He padded over to the carriage and stretched his neck to see inside. Then he rested his chin on the rim of it. Still getting no response, his whine almost said candy cane and as if she'd understood him, she explained to Emma: "Sniffer is going to eat a candy cane, Emma dear, but you are not to get all sticky." Sniffer didn't hear the end of the conversation. She'd handed two of the irresistible canes down to him. Before she'd had time to finish her explanation to Emma, he'd rushed over to his blanket with the canes. He began to make short work of them as she held Emma up above the rim of the carriage. "See, I tell you Emma dear," she said as the doll's eyes popped open. "Sniffer likes candy canes for Christmas."

The eastern sky glowed faintly, lending a pale pink cast to the thinning clouds. Clarence received a sprinkling of snow on his way out to start the Alamo and to do his chores but could not clearly see the day. He could only guess the portent of it yet his hopes were for a good one. At least the day would not be bitterly cold and it would be nice to have it remain windless and with, he hoped, but a few scattered snowflakes to grace the air. After a while he was emerging from the hen house with more than a dozen eggs in a basket and would conclude his chores by shutting down the Alamo. With the storage batteries recharged the lights would shed their dimness and the pump motor could be turned on. In the void of silence left by the Alamo his ears began to differentiate a din coming from deep down Jericho. Presently he could discern the distinctive booming voice of Sid Toberton who'd been out since the wee hours plowing snow from the road.

Sniffer whined.

"It's okay, Sniffer," he patted the dog. "It's only old Sid out plowing." But old Sniffer's whine hadn't been voiced to bring attention to the plowman, no indeed. Old Sniffer'd not missed the possibility of his enjoying a second breakfast. Cold enough for that, he seemed to be telling Clarence as he pressed his nose against the cloth lined egg basket. Then, nervously, Sniffer backed away. "Sure, there'll be some, old Sniffer. Don't go away mad. Likely all of these are frozen. Likely you'll have them for breakfast." Sniffer wagged his tail. Dog and man made their way into the kitchen. At the door Sniffer darted past Clarence. He rushed to his blanket and sat upon it then looked forlornly at Clarence.

They'd each polished off ample breakfasts before he'd gone up to bathe and shave. It'd been but an hour since, yet, along with Sniffer, his thoughts were firmly to food as upon entering the kitchen his nasal acuity was quickened by the lingering aroma of recent repast. Sniffer whined from his blanket. Clarence hurried with the cooking. "Don't worry, old Sniffer. They're cooking."

Outside, the stentorian roar of Sid drew closer, attracting the attention of Clydis who was seated in the wide armed chair with Edith and Emma and Dollie. Clydis, looking out the front window, suddenly called: "Clarence, come and look," and Clarence, his teeth just in the first sever of a toasted egg sandwich, placed it hurriedly out of reach of Sniffer and rushed into the living room.

"What?" he asked.

"Her arborvitae."

Taken aback an instant, his thoughts having been to commenting on Sid and his four hitch hauling an ungainly looking snow plow, he looked long at the arborvitae. The lengthy duration of his scan however was caused not by inability to see at once what she wished him to see, but by his desire to savor the scene a moment before commenting: "Beautiful, the view could not be more pleasant." Snowflakes were swirling down around the snow-laden branches of the arborvitae. The Perkins house across the way with its tall dark snow draped balsams formed a backdrop for the arborvitae. The scene fueled their revelry until suddenly Sid burrowed through with snow curling relentlessly from his snow blade as he shouted the Percherons into speedy progression through the foot deep snow.

"He and Chester built that," Clarence explained. "Sid designed it. He thought they'd need it this winter if they were to bring the refrigerator car home from the freight yard. Of course, his first concern was of Helen, wanting to be sure a doctor could get to her or that she could get to a doctor despite deep snows. And then they have the dairy business to run. So construction of the plow made good sense to Sid. These points are all well and good for Chester too, but mainly, and as usual, his view is to dollar signs. That could come about if enough pressure is put on the county board. They voted in the tax increase, you know, with the understanding that roads would be improved; including snow removal, but they own little snow removal equipment save shovels and a dozen weary backs. Chester figures to sell snow and gravel graders, the same machine good for each, like the one we just saw go past. Looks like a winner to me."

In her mother's lap Edith'd explained Emma's exciting features. Momma oohed and aahed when Emma closed her eyes and she'd oohed and aahed when Emma spoke in her squeaky voice in response to a pat on the back. But Momma'd had less than her typical duration of sleep and by the time Clarence had completed his lengthy recital and turned about looking for her comment, his gorgeous, charming wife had taken on the very pose of Emma. But unlike Emma, in her slumber Momma snored faintly and sweetly.

One of his Christmas gifts was a small vial of powerful cologne, which she said he needed, and he'd splashed on a reeking proportion of it after his shave and bath before going out to chore. Now Edith wriggled her nose as her dad lifted her gently from Momma's lap. Edith fingered her nose as Clarence carried her into the kitchen. He sat her down adjacent to her play cupboard from where she looked over at him wondrously. Sniffer, as Clarence had come into the kitchen from his bath on his way to doing the chores, had rushed over to him; and sneezed. The horses had all reacted nervously to him while he cared for them and now, some hour and more since he'd applied the stuff, Edith fingered her nose as she sat over by her pile of oaken animals. Clarence's nose, fortunately, had by this time become overwhelmed by pungency, allowing the invigorating essence of a fried egg sandwich to enliven his constitution. He reached for the sandwich.

***

Five horses made their way up Jericho following the way that Sid had plowed. At the arborvitae Billie and May hopped the horses, May had Bunny on lead, over the cord of snow made by the plow and rode through the pristine snow of the driveway to the Groner rear steps. May dismounted and came into the house with the milk order and her saddlebag. She set them inside the kitchen door. "I'll be right back," she said in greeting. Outside, May directed Acorn toward the home of Helgie Perkins.

Billie, riding Spirit, rode on over the fields to make the deliveries on Cross. Molly and Satin, their horses burdened by ten gallon milk cans, rode on toward town.

Those who lived along township roads were expected to keep the road in good condition along their properties, and they did, more or less, yet funding for clearing and maintaining the roads was sorely needed. Taxes had been raised for that purpose. But present wisdom was that Sid should plow all the way into the doctor's office. He was worried. Helen shouldn't be in labor yet she thought she was. His bellow cracked the air behind his charging four-hitch. The mighty Percherons dug for Leadford, leaving a cleared lane in their wake.

Clarence watching from a window, said, "Something's wrong. She's gone for Helgie." He began pulling on his heavy mackinaw. "They brought Bunny with them. I'll need both Bunny and Junifer on the sleigh."

No sooner had he readied the sleigh than Helgie and Morley were there, she with her med bag. Helgie slapped the reins and the team started down Jericho.

The doctor would wait while Sid plowed his way back home, thus widening the cleared area sufficiently to accommodate most vehicles. Later Sid would make two more passes along the roads, widening them more still, and Clevis Harold would drag planking alone the road to smooth and pack it. It would freeze solid and would be a good surface for moving the train car. Predicting her labor to be a slow process, as typically labor was, and knowing that Helgie would be attending, Dr. Nealy settled down to enjoy a few hours of Christmas with his family.

May came into the kitchen. "Helen's baby will be early," she said. "We're concerned." She was seating at the table when Clarence arrived with a cup of coffee for her. Suddenly, May reared back, struggling to catch her breath. She sneezed. Clydis zeroed in on the scent at the same moment.

"Clarence, how much did you use?"

Clarence looked embarrassed. "Why, I splashed . . ."

"Splashed? Dear, that is not witch hazel! Just a dot here and there is all one needs."

"How long will it last?"

"Too long. Bath time, my dearest. Even Sniffer's avoiding you."

Sniffer didn't bother to arise upon hearing his name. His tail thumped his blanket lethargically, his sigh long and weary. May laughed merrily. In frustration, Clarence mounted the stairs to the bathroom, wondering what the cologne was for anyhow. "As if I didn't have enough to think about," he mumbled as he ran water into the tub.

"She's at least a month early," May said, her voice slightly elevated, projecting over the sound of his pouring bath water. "We've beseeched our Manitou and your Jesus. Will you also ask your Jesus?"

"Oh, yes. My prayers go to him now. He'll be beside Helgie and Helen and Dr. Nealy."

"I'm pleased. We're much concerned." She'd retrieved her saddle bag from near the kitchen door where she'd placed it along with the milk order. "We're reading Little Women by Louisa May Alcott. We read to each other. I wish you to hear us. Billie will be back soon."

"It's a very good book. I'd love to hear it."

"We're reading The Red Badge of Courage as well, by Stephen Crane. Grandma Tillie Mae's reading it with us. Then she's reading it to Grandpa Job Franklin. I thank you for teaching us to read."

"I do appreciate your thanks, but really, I thank you. It's my esteem pleasure to read with you. I enjoy it very much."

Chapter Twenty

May opened the book to where she'd placed a ribbon as a page marker and began to read. The passage was about Meg and Amy discussing proper dress and good manners. At the word 'elegant' she faltered and Clydis pronounced it for her. "It means 'very good'." May repeated it then continued with the reading. Edith came to May's knee while she was reading and handed Emma up to her. May held the doll and smiled down at Edith as she read, the distraction of Edith and Emma having but little impact on the reading. She read to the end of a paragraph then turned her attention to Edith.

"You're very sweet. You have a nice dolly."

"Emma," Edith said, and she went on to explain, in her language, how Emma could close her eyes when she sleeps and that Emma could cry out when patted on the back. May listened with keen interest, trying to comprehend the little girl's serious jubilant conversation, smiling broadly as Clydis interpreted for her.

"Emma's very nice, Edith. You have a nice dolly."

Edith grabbed Emma and went dancing away with her. May returned to the reading, but hadn't finished the next page before Edith returned, this time with the baby carriage loaded with splendor that she proceeded to show to May.

"I'm sorry, May," Clydis said. "You read beautifully."

"It's my pleasure," May was assuring. "I like to be with Edith. We'll know more as Clydene grows." Clydis smiled at this, remembering a time not so long past when she was frightened thinking about the awesome task of rearing Edith properly. Clarence said they would learn by observing others. Clydis had learned a lot by their acquaintance with the Jameses and the Faygards who were rearing youngsters and she was grateful. How gratifying to know someone who actually wished to emulate the Groners!

Elated, she remarked in understatement, for no statement could match her elation: "Thank you, May." She spoke softly, from the heart for on that Christmas day Clydis knew she'd received from May a most precious gift, a gift greater than gold or frankincense. She'd been regarded a mother, a good one. She sat with her hands around a warm cup of coffee. She looked across at May who was now in deep contemplation with Edith and in silent prayer Clydis thanked God for sending May to them on Christmas.

"Have I missed any of the story?" Billie wanted to know as she rushed into the kitchen.

"I would like to hear those pages over again," May replied. "Elegant. Very good."

"Oh, very good. Elegant," Billie repeated as she removed her wraps. Clad now in her fancy pant skirt, stocking feet, and lavender blouse, she looked fully as people thought of her; princess, one could not pardon the expression from one's mind upon seeing Billie. "Oh, want pretty aroma do I smell?" she wanted to know as she took a place at the table.

"Clarence," Clydis informed her, "put on too much cologne. Now he's upstairs in the tub."

"I think I'll buy Red some," Billie giggled. "It tickles my nose."

"Please, now listen little princess," May joked, "let Clydis and Clarence experiment until they discover the correct dosage before you offer any! to Red."

That brought more giggles from Billie, near guffaw from Clydis, and a gentle smile from May. It was into this atmosphere that Clarence entered the kitchen. Seeing Clarence, the ladies heightened their glee.

Clarence stood agape. Worried, he began to look himself over. Have I not buttoned? His actions generating yet further glee from the women. A bit riled now, he stood in defiance as his beautiful wife approached him.

"This is what it's for," she breathed in his ear. She kissed his neck. "You have it just right now," she whispered. "Wear it often."

"Wow," Clarence said. "Merry Christmas."

Edith was by this time hugging his leg. "Emma can close her eyes." Papa picked her up.

"Emma's very nice," Papa said. "Did you show her to May and Billie?"

"Clyeeen," Edith struggling now to get down. She ran off to get her Dolly.

"I'm going out to shovel snow," Clarence declared, to no one, really, as Edith had again taken the stage.

"May I see your dolly?" Billie asked, catching up to Edith. "Clydene didn't come today. She'll come tomorrow."

"Kissmus tree," Edith explained pointing it out. "Sanny Caus gift Emma. Sniffer likes to eat canny canes. My dolly can close her eyes when she goes to sleep," she continued, in her language; which Billie was able to discern the gist of, as busily she placed Emma in the carriage with Dollie and her wooden bowl and tin cup. They were back in the kitchen in a moment, arriving just as Clarence was leaving with the snow shovel in hand.

Clarence shoveled a path from the rear steps to the road, skirting Marsh's snow laden Oldsmobile in the process, then continued on across the road shoveling paths and parking space for Morley and Helgie. He'd just finished his own driveway to a depth of perhaps seventeen feet when Ma and Pa arrived by a rental sleigh.

They were a sight to behold. Peanut stepping proudly, Ma with her rosy cheeks peeking from beneath her muffler, her eyes dancing while beside her Pa sat proudly erect, his reddened face bare to the chilly still air, his face radiant and wrinkled deeply by his proud grin. Peanut struggled on past the Oldsmobile, drawing the sleigh to a halt at the steps. Sniffer, who'd been down to the barn to visit with Toad and old Jude, came loping through the snow, arriving in time to label the sleigh just as it stopped.

Ma was obliged to pat his head before dismounting as Sniffer'd rushed up to her and placed his head firmly in her lap from where his heart pulling eyes ogled up to her. Pa'd managed to dismount from his side of the sleigh before Sniffer had time to properly greet him, but now Sniffer ignored Pa completely, his nose having detected the waft of a roast of beef rising from a cloth covered wicker basket.

There were other parcels as well. In a moment Clarence had arrived at the sleigh to carry the food basket. Ma and Pa Groner scampered on into the kitchen, she carrying a bag of gifts, he with a bag of baked goods. Clarence lugged the food basket with Sniffer twisted amidst his legs. Sniffer's effort to stay close by his discovery resulted in his being tripped over, plunging Clarence across the kitchen where he managed to slam the basket precariously upon the edge of the table before crashing head and shoulders under Billie's chair, rocking her nearly out of it.

"Jimminy, the man has collapsed," Pa said.

"Darn it, Sniffer!"

"I thought we were just friends," Billie joked.

"Strange way to enter a kitchen," May remarked.

Ma in her rush to him, collided with Clydis, she on a like mission, and they both nearly trod upon Edith! Edith, squealing gleefully, had rushed in to climb onto her dad's back in readiness to ride horse. "Orsie, orsie!" She bounced upon him.

"Goodness, Clarence," Clydis said, as Edith gleefully rode the bronco, now on its hands and knees.

"Orsie! Orsie!"

"Most interesting household indeed," May said.

"Orsie! Orsie!" The bronco's knees were hurting and its back had arched to nag status. The bronco ceased its futile efforts to dislodge its Calamity Jane and rose unsteadily to man stature, Calamity in its arms; and kissing Calamity. Edith giggled, her bouncing brown hair brushing his cheek and he hugged her and placed her in grandma's lap.

"Emma," Edith said, struggling to get down from grandma. "Emma."

151

"Emma?" grandma asked, shocked that the child would address her as such. Her face registered disappointment in her glance toward Clydis.

"Her new doll," Clydis quickly explained. "She has, and now believe this, she with no prompting from us, named her doll Emma. Just right out of the blue, Ma, really, right from the first time she laid eyes on the doll, she's called her Emma."

"Really?" Ma's eyes were large.

"We're very proud," Clydis continued," that the name means so much to her."

"Merry Christmas, Ma," Clarence added his approval. He'd retrieved his hat from under the stove by that time and was putting it on.

"Thank you," Ma said serenely, in obvious pride of the little family on Jericho. "I'm so pleased." Tears sparkled in her eyes as she held her arms out to Edith who'd returned to her grandma's knee with Emma.

Pa, his composure a mix of pride and impatience, stood at the kitchen door with a snow shovel in hand, his body English urging Clarence to hurry along with it, much snow needing to be shoveled, and Clarence joined him, both men eager to sling the pristine accumulation. They began by widening a path to the Oldsmobile.

"I'd guess you drove the car here," Pa said inquiringly.

Clarence filled him in a little on events that occurred at the hospital and of the trip home.

"About one thirty or two, you think. It's a wonder you didn't see our lights. Your mother was up by that time baking pies and getting the roast ready. We got the roast from Sky's. His freezer is proving out to be a good investment, he says. Well, Sky says that Herm Dinning stayed on as temporary marshal. He's living right there in the women's cell like Marsh does. Now Ed seems to be alright. His heart is beating real good. Amazing isn't it, his carrying that bullet all that time. Stuck right in his heart it was, I hear."

"Merry Christmas," Billie and May saluted as they were leaving the yard.

"Merry Christmas," Pa and Clarence returned. They watched as the ladies enjoyed the easy going out past the arborvitae, itself still beautiful under its burden of snow.

"There's trouble down their way," Clarence averred. It's Helen. In labor today, they think. She's way early, May said. Helgie and Morley are down there."

"She's in good hands then."

They shoveled a while, their minds in contemplation until Clarence said, "Red said they were glad to get back their horses. A few were grazed, but none serious. But, now old Chester, he's complaining. Instead of selling heavies, he still has them, and along with the mares he got from Doty, he's tight for space and feed."

"Herm Dinning is looking into all that, Sky says, trying to decide who gets the horses. The guy up a Bruin City ordered and paid part in advance on eighteen heavy horses. Sky says they got Doty dead to rights on the theft. Shows clearly on his bill of sale where he put a one in front of the eight on it after he bought Chester's horses. Course, that's because he had stolen ten from Tobertons. Got him dead to right, Sky says. Imagine that Simon claiming to be innocent; kidnapped even. But that bill of sale being altered, well that's nailed him, Sky said."

Pa'd been shoveling along ahead of Clarence. He'd cleared a path directly to the hen house, the power shed, wood shed and barn, and Clarence, following behind, had widened each path into an expanse the breadth of which could accommodate a team of horses with appropriately situated turn around space. Pa seemed not to notice that his wearying son was doing nine tenths of the work. As he gleefully slung aside the pristine snow, Pa's efforts were in cadence with his chatter. Finally he called a halt, looking around then at Clarence. "Tiring you, is it?"

Pa acted as though it were hard to believe. "Don't seem to tire me at all," Pa proclaimed. "I really like shoveling snow. Course, if you need to rest," he quipped as he stepped toward his aching son, "well, I'll just joi . . . Well, what is it I smell?" he expounded, interrupting his own joke, thinking now that one even better was at hand. "I declare," he raised his nose, sniffed at the cool crisp air, "I can't discern the origin of it." He moved around in circles sniffing the miasma as he went, but moved as well closer and closer to Clarence. Clarence waited, wondering how he might parry Pa's assault. Not for a moment was Clarence fooled. He knew he was in for it. Pa moved up close. Suddenly he reared back, bracing himself with his shovel. "Why, Clarence, it's from you," he said as in disbelief. "What in the world is it?"

"Cologne. Clydis said I needed it."

"What for?" Clarence reddened.

"Well . . ." but he couldn't complete the statement before Pa continued his relentless belittlement.

"Why, son, you don't smell right, she must think you don't act right."

"No. Darn it, Pa." Pa bore ahead.

"Then what's it for?" He acted serious, his face feinting genuine concern. "Why, if you got a trouble, you just go on and explain it in detail to me right now. This is serious. Now, what is it for?" He turned then to his shovel, acting as if his son may tell him if a face to face confrontation was deterred. Pa thrust his shovel deep into the snow. His knees bent, his arms strained in getting the shovel thrust deeply. He commenced to pour power into his lift. The explosion began at a high whooshing pitch that developed quickly into a low pitched pants jarring growl and finished with a gentle protraction of quietly rushing wind as through from the mouth of a tunnel before an oncoming train. Pa was shocked, Clarence in seventh

153

heaven.

"That's what it's for," Clarence declared, jubilantly. "She figured I'd be working behind you."

The tide had turned so unexpectedly! Now Pa held the short end.

"Now, Clarence."

"I'm going to tell her right now how right she was. Let's go inside."

"Darn it, Clarence. Wait a minute. I've a problem here. Been happening to me about a year now. I ordered cathartic pills from Sears. I'm glad this happened today. Getting so I don't dare to exert myself around nobody. I don't think the pills work at all, though I don't blame Sears. Their pills didn't say specific for this problem. What we need is a retail druggist here in town; or, I've a notion to go to Grand Rapids to consult one. What do you think?"

"A lot of noise but not much stink."

"Now what in the world do I make of that?" Pa was disgusted, let alone embarrassed. "I already know that."

"Morley. He'd had it."

"You expect me to ask Morley? Why, this is personal."

"He looked it up in his herbal book. Says he cured his. You know he helped the horses. Though in part he borrowed Clevis Harold's book for that."

"They didn't have this problem," Pa insisted.

"Age is the problem. Morley changed their diets. Changed his too."

"What stuff is he eating now?" Pa was worried, imagining that he may have to give up his favorites; roast beef for instance, and red cherry pie; the very menu for that Christmas day."

"He just drinks something and he puts something in with his vegetables. Says it makes the vegetables better. Says he eats a little less meat too."

"Sure, there would be a catch to it."

"As you please, but you should do something. You go around scaring people and horses with all of that noise."

"Well, it's as though you didn't have a problem, but you do. You know you do. My problem folks will sooner or later hear about. Can't help it. But anybody can whiff you got a problem you won't talk about. They'll get so they'll worry about you. That medicine she gave you makes you smell darn odd, Clarence. What's it for, anyway?"

Clarence knew that Pa was joking. He nonetheless decided to be more discrete in the future as to when he would apply any of the stuff. As to Pa's problem, he was sure it sounded like the same problem Morley had mentioned to him, saying he'd cured it. That both of their problems were trivial was made clear in the next moment.

Doctor Nealy came past behind his dappled mare. His face set by concern, he only nodded and waved a hand but slightly in response to their calls of "Merry

Christmas!" Three miles on down Jericho lay Helen Toberton. All were praying a merry Christmas for her.

The men had finished with their snow shoveling and were headed in. Their stomachs had told them they would be called at any moment. Still, Clydis was surprised to meet them nose to nose as she was opening the door to call them. "My," she expounded, in confirming the power of mental telepathy. "Dinner's ready."

***

They were seated around the bounteous table and had begun to eat. Sniffer'd just managed to down his first ort ejected to him by Edith, when he was obliged to go to the door and to tell them a friendly was nearing. Having fulfilled his mission, Sniffer returned to his station near Edith. By that time Charley James was tapping the door.

Charley came right on in. "Merry Christmas. Sorry to bother you. We ate breakfast and we're going to eat later when Clifford's family gets here. We already opened except some of Albert's weren't wrapped. Sure had trouble hiding his presents. Got him a bicycle and a sled. Warm clothes too. Well we knew he couldn't very well ride the bike today, but he's trying anyway out in the road. It's sure plowed nice. Who was that? But the sled we thought he could use. So I went into the woods between yours and them thinking snow don't get so deep in the woods and knowing there was a hill in there. But there is not. No, there's no hill in there. Did you know?" Giving no one time to answer, he continued. "Now I know trees and they're virgins. There isn't no hill in there. Looks like a hill but did you ever go in there?

"Why, it's tall trees you're seeing. Virgin! Come and see. I'll show you." His eyes were bugged and he'd waved his arms excitedly while describing the trees, but now he dropped his arms as though wind had forsaken his sail. "Not till later though," he looked disappointed. "Didn't come to see about trees. But I thought you'd want to know about them. Thinking trees I'm caused to recall a fellow name of Harvey Sykes, the preacher up at the Croton construction. Said he used to live around here, but today I've come to see about your hill back there," he explained, gesturing toward the High Ten. "It's a nice hill there. It'd make Albert a good sledding hill. Florie likes to coast too. We brought her toboggan and I brought my one runner for me. Did you ever see a one runner sled? You'd like it. Surprises you, how good it goes. I'd pack the hill a little with snowshoes then we could start. Thought you'd think it all right."

"Sure." They peered wondrously at Charley.

"Come and join in when you see us out there."

"Sure." But Charley'd popped back out the door, leaving in his wake a

155

disbelief that he'd even been there.

Pa and Clarence looked at the door a moment, until Pa shrugged his shoulders signaling he could wait. Clarence concurred, lifting his fork. Big trees could wait, virgin or not, but Christmas repast was cooling. They bent to their rejoice. Sniffer by this time had pushed his nose right up next to Edith. He'd in his mind not to miss out on single moment of Christmas.

As dinner was closing Clarence reached into his pocket for two envelopes. Clydis opened hers to find a receipt for Junifer across which Clevis Harold had scrawled 'Paid in full.' Pa's 'paid in full' was for Peanut and a buggy. Clydis had expected hers, even to wishing it aloud for Christmas so that Clarence could hear, but Clarence had made no response at the time, causing her to wonder until now whether he'd understood. He had and she kissed him.

Pa's surprise was genuine. Elation fumbled his tongue. "Why, Clarence," Pa stammered, his eyes close to tearing. Pa's thought had been to giving up Peanut come spring. He'd spent all of his savings before Emma came home from the Battle Creek sanatorium in getting the house fixed up and modernized for her, for them, but they'd been obliged to live hand to mouth since, living primarily on Emma's small wages earned from Trella. A small measure of their meager sustenance also garnering from his rags and paper shed.

"I . . . I love you . . . son." He displayed his gift for Emma to read.

Ma ran around the table to her son's chair where she planted a moist one firmly to his forehead.

Clarence reddened. "Darn cologne water," he grumbled. "Attracts women like flies to sumps. Meaning no offence, Ma," he corrected, patting her shoulder. "I hope you get many miles and years out of Peanut. Austin Bailey tells me that he has hay in excess and will deliver same to fill your loft along with oats for your bin. You can expect him any day soon."

Chapter Twenty-one

"Thank you, Clarence," Ma murmured. She'd been working four to six hours a day for Trella Mead, taking materials as part of her pay. With those goods, along with printed feed sacks, she'd fashioned her gifts, shirts for Pa and Clarence, a quilted carriage blanket for Clydis and a crocheted bright red afghan for Edith.

Edith tore open her gift. "Blankee, blankee," she babbled as she stuffed it into the baby carriage as comfort for Emma and Dollie and her tin cup.

Pa'd dreamed, but had never mentioned, his desire for a fly rod. His old casting rod and reel he had "stolen" at an auction sale for seven cents and it had served him well over twenty years. The number of times he'd snarled the reel were uncountable, as were the fish he was certain he'd missed through the years while unsnarling the fool thing. The little box from Marsh contained hand tied flies and a note. "Robert, Good fishing. Merry Christmas, 1906, Marsh." Pa's hand shook when he read it and his heart palpitated stuttering his murmured response: "God be with you, old friend."

Marsh lay still in coma in Grand Rapids, Tulip at his side. "I'd like to see Marsh," Pa said dreamily, but directing his comment to no one in particular.

Pa's comment, however, immediately roused a plan in Clarence. "Tulip will need clothes," he said. "I can't get down there until tomorrow because I'll need to be at work tonight. Would you want to take things to her? Marsh too, for that matter? You could take the train. Stay in a hotel. I have the money for that." Robert and Emma jumped at the chance. Clarence would drive them home and return to the farm with Peanut. He may need Peanut to get to his job at the paper mill, Junifer and Bunny being tied up at Tobertons. It was a relief to Clarence. Marsh and Tulip had been burdening his mind all morning.

"By all means," Clydis concurred, rising from the table. "And I'd like to know how Helen's doing," she said as she was walking over to the south window near the side sink, looking toward Tobertons. "Somehow I feel my place is to stay in proximity to her. I'm torn actually," she confessed in turning to look at Emma.

157

"Tulip and Marsh mean a lot to us. It would please me to have you go."

Ma joined Clydis over by the sink. "Clydis," she asked seriously, "have you ever gone sledding?"

"Why . . . no." The abrupt change of subject had surprised her.

"I love sledding," Ma explained. "I see the Jameses approaching. "No one seems to realize what a person goes through while they're waiting and can do nothing but wait." Clydis cocked her head, wondering the point. "Last night you waited the worst kind of waiting for Clarence and today you wait, you worry, you pace for Helen and Marsh and Tulip. Tell Flora to send little Rylus in here to me. Go sledding Clydis. Take Edith with you."

***

Sid, Rik, and Red were, meantime, suffering their own kind of waiting. Rik and Red would be leaving for work soon and would have else to do but then Tom would join Sid and the two of them would wait in the kitchen along beside Morley.

Crowded into Helen's sitting room, Billie, Satin, Jane and Molly waited. All were ready on an instant to be needed. And in Prissy Momma's kitchen the older folks waited around their cups of coffee. Prissy'd been over there a while previous and had returned shaky and pale. "He's going to cut open her belly," she'd said, plopping into a chair. "Going to cut her plumb open. He says it's a breach baby and can't get out natural."

***

Charley, with his one runner sled draping his shoulder by a tote strap, tamped the hill with his snowshoes while Flora and Clydis with Edith between them were poised at the High Ten's acme. They willed slow Charley to give way. He stepped aside and the ladies pushed off. Faster and faster down the hill. The toboggan bumped pleasantly beneath them. A powder of snow streamed at them while further out from the toboggan their eyes were treated to landscape flashing their view. Giggling and laughing, the ladies plunged on past Charley some twenty feet before stopping. Albert coasted to a stop just behind them. In the wintertime Clydis had seen children pulling sleds, going about activity of which she could not attend, beneath her dignity her mother had tutored, but now she'd partaken and was thrilled, grabbing greedily in restoration of a fragment of the childhood denied her.

Eagerly she pulled the toboggan up the hill. Edith held on tightly. Flora trooped behind in position to lend a push as needed as Charley veered around them, snow arcing away from the well-polished runner. "Whoopeee!" he called, thrilling Clydis to goose bumps. She was out sledding. Coasting down hill. Thinking of

Helen, of little Naddy, Marsh or Tulip? Yes. Way back there. Way back on the back burner from where they could heal. They'd be okay. She was sledding for them, for Edith, for herself. Oh, gosh! Sledding. Coasting down hill! Wonderful. I really, really am out sledding.

***

The baby emerged pink and soiled and it wailed not at all as the doctor held it aloft. "Girl." He passed her to Helgie. Helgie sat with her on a chair by the kitchen stove. On the kitchen table Helen lay oblivious to the cesarean, not able to know the plight of her first born, her child, not aware the child was dying, turning blue while Helgie rubbed her and pleaded with her. "Breathe, darling, breathe."

Bluer still grew the baby.

Helgie placed her mouth over the baby's face and puffed a tiny puff of breath into her. Her little chest bounced. Again she did it. God alone may answer why she did so. Never before had she seen it done or ever heard of it, yet she did it. Nealy, busy with his stitches, glanced her way. The baby was dead, this he knew, so could it hurt, this that Helgie was doing? This barbarity born of desperation, anguish, pain? Helgie must try. Try with all the heart she had in her. This he knew, but when should he stop her? When is it the moment to say enough, Helgie, enough. She is with Jesus?

Helgie gently, ever so gently puffed and Helgie gently rubbed as though trying to squeeze out a breath. A tiny wail crept from deep within the valiant tiny chest. Tears gushed from Helgie's eyes. Bernice, pinking, struggled on, her tiny desperate wail screaming for life due her, for the mom that would hold her, for the dad who would read to her, for parents who would help her grow. Born this Christmas day, 1906, Bernice Clydis Toberton, five pounds, one ounce, her limbs waving, her voice growing lustier, she the tiniest baby Helgie had ever seen, she the most precious child on earth, she the daughter of Sid and Helen Toberton.

Doctor Nealy drove up Jericho on his way back to his office. Seeing Clydis in the yard, he paused briefly. "Girl," he called out. He waved merrily as he upped the horse. Clarence, having left Pa and Ma at the train, met the doctor at the corner of Cross and Jericho. "Girl," Nealy called. Clarence smiled and waved. Moments later he pulled in past the arborvitae.

"Girl," he called as Clydis hurried up to the sleigh.

"I heard." She was nearly dancing in the snow. "It's so wonderful. Did you hear, are they alright?"

Charley and Flora had moved up to the sleigh as well. "Oh, I do hope to see you again before you must go home," Clydis said, reaching out to touch Rylus' rosy cheek.

Flora smiled. "Well, the way we're working, it won't be long, I'm afraid.

159

Charley thinks a week."

"Week'll do her. Including their moving in," Charley confirmed. Charley took off then on a brisk walk toward his brother's unfinished house; no hope that Flora could keep up, but she didn't mind. Charley would have the Alamo running before she could reach the house and would have added wood to the living room heater and a fire under the potatoes in the kitchen. Albert walked along with his mom, pulling both his new sled that really slid well, like a rocket even, along with his mother's faithful toboggan.

"Come again," Clydis called after. "We had a wonderful time." Flora waved her farewell; much pleased the day had been so fun.

Clydis turned to Clarence and said, "Edith and I'll go with you when you leave for work. I want to see Helen and Bernice."

In a few minutes his lunch was packed and the family snuggled into the sleigh. He set Peanut to a lope down the smooth surface of Jericho.

***

In town, Clifford, Claire, and Naddy and Harold had just finished packing their sleigh. Clifford knew his nephew would be receiving a sled for Christmas. A day previous he'd delivered a bicycle and sled and Charley'd hidden them in the attic of the power shed. Now, upon his recommendation, a pair of skis, a sled and a toboggan protruded from the rear of his family's sleigh. They were tied in place by heavy string. The Jameses had opened gifts at dawn, after Harold and Naddy'd waited by the tree for hours, it seemed to them, for their parents to awaken and see what Santa Clause had delivered during the night. He'd been there they were certain because the egg sandwiches and cool milk had indeed been consumed and obviously he'd left the gifts.

Naddy and Harold were aware that in addition to the surprises left by Santa, it was customary for others to present gifts to one another in honor of Christmas much as baby Jesus had received gifts. Their minds kept easily separate the Jesus inspired gifts from the Santa wrought gifts. That there was a Mr. and Mrs. Clause and elves there was no doubt. After all, their very role Harold had been honored to emote, fooling all but Naddy, and now his elf suit lay in a paper sack right next to the sack which held the pies. The elf would perform again after dinner; after which there would be sledding on the hill in the woods between their new house and the Groners.

Albert saw them coming in time to be out in the road with his new Acme bike. Its wheels sunk into the smooth surface of the road. Nonetheless he was able to present a fair demonstration. Puffing now, he pushed the bike along behind the sleigh as it progressed up the drive to the rear stoop. "Merry Christmas," Albert hollered as the sleigh was stopping, and Harold and Naddy hurried over to him to

160

see the new bike.

Inside, Charley greeted them, but directed his oration primarily to Clifford. "Be about a week until you're moved in. We'll help. There's no hill in those woods. No sir, there isn't. Virgin timber so tall you thought it was a hill in there. Can't sled in there because there's no hill so we got a hill ready over at Groners. I'm confounded as to his not knowing there's no hill in there. Did you know it?"

Clifford had taken a seat near the Acme sheet iron heater and wanted to be a part of the conversation, but to no avail, Charley kept going right on without pause. "Your Alamo works fine and your well is a good one, didn't I tell you it would be when I witched it? And you've plenty of electricity stored in the batteries why I pumped your upstairs tank full without need to turn the Alamo back on and we heated the water. Your charcoal heater up there works good and we all took good hot bathes, wish we could do that so easily at home. Those trees were probably a little too small to cut when this area was logged off before but now they have grown up, my, I guess so, near to five foot boles, they have, of good quality white pine, makes my mouth water. Did you bring pies? The hill over to Groners is a good one. Saw them go past a while ago. Been a doctor down there. Lady had a baby. Suspect she's going down there to help but I'm sure we can sled their hill, she sledded with us this afternoon, nice lady, their little girl had fun, she did too, so did we, you'll like the hill. Doesn't that goose smell good? I cooked the giblets and neck a day or so back. Made goose broth. The rest she roasted. I'm going to carve it directly she says to. Then we'll eat."

***

Edith, burdened with Emma and Dollie and her wooden spoon, struggled along beside Billie, joining her as she carried Clydene home to their parlor. Once inside, Clydene paid little attention to Edith's explanation of Emma's being able to close her eyes to go to sleep, but she perked up with a start at the sound of Emma's squeaky voice. She laughed and waved her arms each time Edith clapped Emma's back and she was able to get a firm grip on the big wooden spoon, which she waved, delighting Edith.

Meantime, Clydis was seated beside Helen's bed. She fussed with Helen's hair and spoke softly with her. Bernice, the very tiniest babe any of them had ever seen, oh so very, very beautiful, wrapped in a soft cotton coverlet, snuggled next to Helen. To the other side of the bed, Sid sat, saying nothing, seemingly in a daze, holding her hand.

In the sitting room Clevis Harold was in a low voiced, though heated, discussion with Helgie. "Yes colostrum!" he expounded. "It's high in protein, vitamins, and minerals, and it contains antibodies a baby needs against disease. I have it right here." He held his copy of Morrison, Feed and Feeding, 5th Edition,

161

open for her to read.

"It does not mention human babies," she complained. She was fearful of any help or advice offered by the male members of any household at a birthing; especially that offered by the bungling, well meaning, ignorant father, but had by now begun conceding the point with grandfather Clevis Harold. Reluctantly, she concurred: "Mixed one half with boiled, and cooled water," making sure he wouldn't give boiling water to the babe; knowing he wouldn't, but one can't tell, men being typically more zealous than smart at a time such as this. "And every second feeding. Each fourth hour that will be. Do I make myself clear, Clevis Harold? And at the first sign of distress, you contact me."

"Get you, yes. By all means." Clevis Harold rushed from the room.

A huge Holstein cow had freshened and May sat beside her pulling the colostrum laden milk from her swollen udder. The calf'd had its fill yet May could see her bucket was nearly full. Clevis Harold tapped her shoulder, startling May; as the milker milked with thoughts far off from milking. Her thoughts were of a baby birthed in a thicket beside a river in St. Joe County. How she'd loved her and reared her the Indian way that she be pure and good and that she be a worthy credible Potawatomie; worthy credible human being, and wife and mother. Thus, his tap on her shoulder had startled her, snapping her back to "Huh?" as she looked back and up to him over her shoulder.

"I need the colostrum for the baby, don't feed any of it. I'll freeze it," he directed, handing her a fresh empty bucket.

"Mare's milk is better," she advised, recalling the Indian way. But he didn't hear her in his rush away with the life sustaining colostrum. She guessed that he hadn't heard her, and no matter, Mayfeather, you loon, she thought, and a smile sweetened her face, any colostrum from any new mother, Helen's foremost, would be good and Clevis Harold has grained this cow heavily during her dry spell. There are many gallons of colostrum from this cow.

From her supply of nursing bottles that she routinely ordered from Sears, Roebuck and Co., Helgie selected her smallest graduated flask to which she attached the rubber hose and her smallest size of rubber nipple. Clevis Harold strained the colostrum and diluted it with boiled, cooled, water as she'd directed. She demonstrated the temperature it must be on the bottom of his wrist. Proudly he entered the bedroom, Helgie at his side, and handed the unit to Clydis, but Bernice Clydis would not suckle it.

Clydis tried, Helgie tried, Helen tried. Bernice would not suckle. Helen began crying in lament, "I'm no good. I have no milk." Tears streaked her face. She felt her stitches but vaguely, her total concern being to her child, her tiny child, her Bernie. "Oh please, God," she sobbed, holding Bernice to her bosom. "Oh, please. Sid, Sid. Oh, Sid, what can we do?"

Sid held to her, kissed her, looked toward Clydis, toward Helgie, his eyes pleading; help us, help us, please, we will not let her die.

"Get Billie," Helgie ordered. Sid's eyes snapped to her. As he began to rise up from beside Helen, his eyes grazed the thought filled frown of Clydis, seeing her eyes brighten.

"Get Billie." Sid ran from the room.

"Hurry! Hurry!" Sid screamed, grabbing Billie by the arm, dragging her toward the door. "The baby! The baby!" Billie's heart pounded.

She grabbed little Edith and ran, little Edith with her legs around her, her arms around Billie's neck, her soft curly brown hair brushing her cheek; Edith in instinctive recollection of another time when a woman had ran with her, whose spirited carry had thrilled her. But in a moment she was placing Edith at her mother's side and Edith looked up at her mom and she scanned the others with her eyes, wondering why the game had stopped, or, what she'd done. Her eyes fell upon Clydene in Sid's arms. "Clyeen," she said, pointing.

"The baby won't eat." Billie understood at once.

Sid suddenly also understood. Clydene still in his arms, he walked over and held his hand for Edith. She took his hand, wondering what this was about, what fun they might have. "Come, grandpa," he nudged the shoulder of Clevis Harold, glancing to Billie as he did so.

"Thank God," Clevis Harold now also understood, but lamented in doubt. The men hurried outside, Clevis Harold was needed, he knew, at the barn where milk was to be carried.

"I'll get to the separator directly," Sid called after as his father was nearing the barn.

He would do Billie's job. She and Clydene strained the milk as it came into the dairy then ran the milk through a separator, dividing the cream from the milk. Cream and milk were then stored in five and ten gallon cans. The milk would be carried to Sky's, the cream to Jennifer Faygard, in the morning, but Billie's function that afternoon far out ranked any enterprise of the Toberton dairy.

Bernice was tiny, barely a double hand full. So sweet and pink and soft and so very tiny the ample breast loomed over her as a mountain. Billie had come to them a maiden of fourteen years whom Red fetched from a wood. She could speak little but Potawatomie, she having been of the woods and the Indian way since her birth along beside the St. Joe River. As she began to speak English it became obvious, to their shock and dismay, that her god was a different god, someone unconventional, inferior, whom she and her people called Manitou. Shunned by the Toberton women, she was dirt.

By and by the dirt had transformed to a daffodil thence to a splendid peony and iris and rose and aster and they were she. No longer dirt save in the eyes of Prissy Momma whose narrowed eyes saw only the pagan never the princess. The princess held tiny Bernice and as though her pounding heart pumped it forth, milk ejected from her throbbing breasts, wetting the little darling's face, her soul, her hunger as gently she held Bernie's tiny lips to the nipple; and Bernie suckled.

"She wouldn't drink it," he said sadly to May, referring to the colostrum, knowing that she knew of his plan to feed it. "Billie's gonna try," he said as he hefted two pails of milk and started for the barn door. Milk poured from the cows. May and Satin and Jane, Molly, Prissy Myra, and Tillie Mae pulled milk from the cows. No other sound filled the barn. The breasts of the women ached as did their hearts, wanting to help. "Sid's handling the straining," he reported on his next trip in.

"We have to know," Jane declared, getting up from her cow. "Here, finish here."

Clevis Harold sat on the milk stool and reached the taps. "No hope, is there?" he asked, his voice sad, barely audible. He could see no way. He pulled at the teats caring not that the precious golden streams were missing his bucket. Jane, herself six months along, rushed from the barn, ran toward the house. "No hope," he bemoaned after her. The others sat quietly crying, pulling the golden precious milk from the udders, each herself in personal communion, heart and soul rooting for Helen, for Bernice, for a little Indian princess whom they had grown to love, to care about, to cherish. God be with her. Let there be Christmas.

Jane was yelling before she'd returned half way to the barn. "She's drinking! She's drinking!" She swooped into the barn. "She's suckling Billie," she breathed triumphantly. "Billie has done it."

All was quiet in the barn. The ladies in silent personal grateful communion pulled the precious golden streams from their felicitous cows. In the house a smile graced the composure of Helen's tired and drawn face. Her eyes slowly closed as relief and fatigue drew her into sleep. She slept. Bernie suckled. Billie held her to a breast while her other breast dribbled her garments, the dampened garments adding misery to her chafed bosom and upper body. Tears of elation and pride and gratitude dampened Billie's cheeks.

Soon after Bernie had fallen asleep Clydis eased her from Billie's embrace, replacing her with Clydene who had entered the house with Sid and Edith. Helgie draped Billie and Clydene with a receiving blanket. Sid entered the room and seeing that all was well he sat in the chair across the bed from Billie and Clydene. Over the pleasant smacking of Clydene's cornucopia and with his precious daughter cuddled, Sid nodded into sleep. Clydis eased Bernice from him, nestling her with Helen.

Outside the house, she advised Morley, "We'll wait for Clarence."

"Sure," Morley replied as he and Helgie were mounting the sleigh, meaning that he would keep the fires going at the farm and that he'd gather the eggs and would care for Toad and old Jude and Bunny and Junifer until their return, such was the goodness in Morley.

Chapter Twenty-two

Sky Ferndin was a kind man whom one would think had chosen his life as bachelor, but his feelings had ever been contrary to that assumption. Of women, any woman, a woman, the woman, he dreamed but fear restrained him, muted him, kept him an unwilling bachelor trapped by his trepidation; but on that one night around the time of Thanksgiving, after he'd bid her good night and she him and he'd in frustration climbed into his bed and she in hers . . . No! Not she in hers! He couldn't believe it! He lay cringing in awesome fear, clutching his blankets as she, carrying her pillow, swooped into his room.

Now on a bright cold winter day late in December he'd bedecked the store with tidings. On that day and the next a grand sale would occur. Lucky he'd been, so he said, to have found this stock at such bargain he could pass significant savings on to his customers. And he hoped to empty his storeroom of goods he'd bought in excess of demand or for which demand had forsaken. But she'd said to Sky on that cold clear winter morn: "We must go to Grand Rapids. I've reserved a special suite at the Pantlind."

"Huh?"

"Hurry. Get ready. We'll go on this morning's train."

"But."

"We are to seek legal assistance in this matter," she tapped her tummy, smiled proudly.

"Gollleeeeeey!" Sky yelled, slapping his knee; grabbing her, kissing her.

Joe Marvin looked on in wonder of such jocularity. Oh, not that he hadn't immediately guessed the reason. No, not that. He was not as naive as his age may imply. No indeed. He had eyes and ears and he knew Wilma Gillis to be no toad. Many were the hours he'd dreamed of her. Oh the passion, the passion he ached to release on her, in her, reaching her very soul, transforming her into an animal not unlike Janet. But she was far away. She with her eyes so sad. She whom he loved so that he could not speak to her lest he lose her, lest she go away from the school where he could see her not. No, he dare not talk with her. But how had Sky talked with Janet? He recalled the day he went to her store, leaving him at this store, and how when she'd come to this store he'd talked to her, with her; of business, they'd talked of business not of love. And now this. Now they would go away a few days to Grand Rapids. He wanted to know, but was afraid to ask, how one comes to make the arrangements.

***

At the swinery Wilma Gillis lay bleeding. She knew the worst had happened to her. That which had occurred with regularity these several years had not occurred and she knew and was terrified that her mother would find out, all would find out; blame her, outcast her; know of her guilt. He'd come for her, needing help to sort pigs, he'd said, but she knew and she ran away from him. He'd grabbed a heavy stick along the way in pursuit of her and had used it behind the fence row behind the farthest farrowing abode where a sow laid birthing. He'd beat her long then taken his pleasure and now she lay bleeding behind the fence row without solace save the sow's grunting.

She knew she must die.

She heard the southbound local on its way into the station. Sky and Janet heard it as well and their hearts beat faster and they held hands at the station, their grips beside them, waiting for the train. Joe Marvin also heard it. He was glad for them, but wondered how his day would fare; already there was a rush of customers. Wilma rose painfully, body, mind, and soul in mortal pain, and she pulled her clothes together around her and followed after the train. The day was clear, windless, and bright, but cold. She didn't feel the cold, saw not the day; misery and fear drove her legs, and shame drove her mind as she followed the train.

To her right as she struggled along the rails she saw that the Black Sucker, frozen shore to shore, ran beside the rails. The sounds of hoots and blasting reached her ears and tapped upon her brain, but the brain dulled to all but misery and purpose made no sense of those distractions. Her reddened tear filled eyes looking from swollen lids saw not that the train was leaving but that it was farther away, still farther, farther still the more she drove her legs to reach it. In a daze now, she drove her legs after the train.

Weaving and stumbling, her vision blurred, one eye swollen closed, she found herself now staring at the station, realization dawning that she would not reach the train, but her purpose hadn't wavered. If not the train? Her mind pondered in recollection of a woman said to have joined the Black Sucker. She could hear the dam, its roar pleasant to her ears. Yes, of course, the troubled mind said pleasantly, the river. She wobbled toward it. Falling, she got up again and staggered toward it. Sounding pleasant and peaceful to her numbing brain, its rushing water called a welcome to her anguished soul, and its depths would cleanse her of shame. Mr. Wainwright grabbed her.

She struggled against him, her purpose not altered nor slackened by his thwart. He would not let loose of her, but dragged her, screaming, backwards from the brink towards the station. Nearing it she grew limp in his grasp. A moan from deep within her beaten soul ended her struggle and she slipped from his grasp, falling to the rails. Whimpering, she lay at his feet. He screamed, "Help! Help!"

"Help! Help!"

A rush of people from the restaurant and depot converged upon them. "What happened?"

"She must have fallen from the train!"

"Get a doctor. Get a doctor."

"Carry her into the station."

"Here, let me help."

"Did anyone go for the doctor?"

"My, Lord. What happened?"

"She fell from the train."

"The poor dear. The poor dear."

"Oh, the poor dear."

Wilma moaned a terrible heart-rendering moan and Wainwright grabbed her up in his arms and ran with her up the street.

Joe Marvin saw them in the street. He recognized her coat and her pompadour hairdo and he saw that Doctor Laird was there and he watched in compassionate alarm as they carried her up the street.

Henry Clout, in the store in response to the signs out front which promised great reductions, was admiring a suit of red long johns which he imagined he just might could get cut down to his size, and for only twenty five cents, why . . . Joe grabbed him. "Take over, Hank. Mind the store. I'll be back as soon as I can." He ran from the store, leaving dumbfounded Hank in his wake.

Dr. Laird heard Wainwright, amidst his wheezing and panting as they carried her, attempt to explain that she had fallen from the train, but a glance at the battering was enough for him to decide contrarily.

"Did you see her fall?"

"No." he panted.

"I don't believe she did," Laird gasped, fighting for breath. It was hard to walk backwards. "She's been beaten nearly to death."

"Lord, God," he panted.

"In here." Laird said. "On the table." He began to examine her, speaking to Wainwright. "Mr. Wainwright. Let them think what they wish for now. Falling from a train is good. Will you do that?"

"Yes, sir."

"What happened?" Joe Marvin had burst into the treatment room.

"Get out!" Laird responded; much annoyed.

"She fell from the train."

"It's Wilma," Joe said, standing fast. "I don't believe she would have been on a train."

"You know her?"

"Wilma Gillis."

"Mr. Wainwright, I'll need a woman here to help. Your wife, if you can. And, Mr. Wainwright, I want you to get a message to Clarence and Clydis Groner. Say only that I need them, that I need both of them. Hurry."

Joe Marvin helped to remove her coat and her hair roll. Laird started him on cleaning her face and head with warm water. Cuts and lumps were in profusion through her hair, an eyebrow had been severed to the bone and a tooth had torn through her lip. He stitched her lip then began restoration of her eyebrow. Mrs. Wainwright entered the room. "My husband said that you needed my help."

"Yes. Thank you. Joe, you must leave now, but please remain out in the waiting room. Watch for Clarence and Clydis. When they get here, send Clydis right in, but have Clarence wait out there with you."

Clarence lay sleeping. They'd eaten a hardy breakfast of pancakes, fried ground meat, eggs and maple syrup. A heavy load, she'd found, would help him get to sleep. Edith climbed onto the bed and was sitting on her dad and watching Emma whom she had placed by his ear. Emma, her eyes closed, was nevertheless hearing about the sleeping man who had worked all night and about Sniffer who likes to eat eggs and pancakes. Clydis entered the room. "You may wake Papa," she said, pulling on her coat. Edith began to bounce up and down on her dad. "I'm going out to hitch Junifer and Bunny."

Clarence heard a fragment of " . . . hitch Bun . . . d Junifer".

"What?" He wanted to know, tumbling Edith as he pushed back his covers coming awake, "Where?" but Clydis'd already left the room.

"Morwy," Edith explained.

"So Morley's been here," he said ruffling her bouncy brown hair. "We're going bye-bye," he hugged her. Finding her wet, he changed her then stuffed her into her warm leggings and coat. He was pulling his coat on when Clydis returned from the barn.

"Morley said only that Dr. Laird wanted both of us at his office as soon as possible." They both knew it had to be bad news of Marsh.

"Oh, Lord, help us. And Tulip. We just cannot do without Marsh," he lamented, reaching for Edith's diaper bag. He momentarily lost his balance trying to lift it. "What's in this thing?"

She'd decided to pack her new cast iron milk delivery wagon replete with attached horse and driver, ten pounds shipping. He peered down into the bag at it. Edith with Dollie and Emma embraced danced over to the door, so pleased was she to have thought of everything important to bring. Clarence stuffed extra diapers in the bag, filling it. Clydis grabbed a paper sack for her bottles and extra clothing.

They'd removed the hair from her head and he was stitching the last of seven rents as Clydis entered the treatment room. Upon entering the office, Joe'd told them about Wilma. Relieved that Marsh was likely still with them, they were yet appalled upon hearing of Wilma, thus her heart thumped and her hands quivered as she approached the doctor.

Wilma lay naked under the blanket. They carried her into the recovery room. Mrs. Wainwright stayed with her while Laird spoke with Clydis. "She says she wants to die," he whispered. "She's been beaten and raped. She's also pregnant. Clydis, we've got to know who did this."

For an hour Clydis sat beside her, held her hand. She told her of a beating. A rubber hose had pounded her body and electricity had shocked and burned her genitals. "I felt that I was guilty and somehow deserved such punishment, that I was no good; too guilty to live and I wanted to die. I know differently now, Wilma. Wilma, you are not guilty of anything. You've done nothing wrong. You did not deserve this beating. My mother did it to me. Who has beaten you? Your mother? Has your mother beaten you?"

"Malice."

"Malice has caused your pregnancy?"

"Yes."

They talked longer, until Wilma lay sleeping. Clydis and Clarence retired to Laird's office. Joe went in to sit with Wilma.

Later, as Clarence stopped in at the marshal's office for his badge and pistol, he was surprised to see that a woman occupied Marsh's desk. "Hello," she greeted. And answering his unspoken query, she added, "Callie. I'm Herm's wife."

"Callie," Herm introduced, emerging from the back, "you've no doubt heard of Deputy Clarence Groner."

"My pleasure," she said, but worry clouded her face. Herm had retired, his retirement was his Christmas present to her. He would be home soon, he'd said, but wanting to be sure, she'd boarded the next train departing Pittsburgh. He had only to wait here until Marsh Rockney, or his replacement, returned. They were to begin a retirement of peace and safety and good health in Pittsburgh, but now this. She fought to control her shaking hands, to fight back her tears. This rotten stinking little town. Once again they would ask him. They would ask him to walk into hell and he'd go.

"I'm to bring in one Malice Lee," he was pinning on his badge.

"That girl?"

169

"Wilma. His stepdaughter. Beating and rape this morning. She's also a month or more pregnant by him."

Herm clapped on his Stetson and reached for his coat. "No, Herm! No! Don't go!"

"He likely will not be dangerous," he said in calming her. "I've known him a long time. Always kind. Hard worker. Gone batty now, but I believe he should be reasonable. This should not be a big adventure. You need not go, Herm."

"We'll need to rent a livery horse for me. He can ride back on one of his own horses," he said, pulling on his coat; and he drew a Winchester from the gun rack.

***

In the mercantile Clydis and Edith were met by Henry Clout; and a host of bargain shoppers who by now had made a shambles of the store. "Afternoon, Ma'am," he was ringing up an order. "Saw you go by. That girl okay?"

"She's better. I wondered who was working here. Joe's over there. He's her friend."

"Thought as much. He left here in a rush." He counted change into Mabel's hand."

"Good afternoon, Clydis."

Clydis smiled. "Happy New Year." Mabel started away. "Mabel, wait. I need to buy clothes for the injured girl, Wilma." Mabel cocked her head. "I believe she's the same size as Emily. Could I meet her at Meads?"

"Sure, I'll send her."

"There sure was a rush this morning," Henry said. "Good sale. I'm sorry he and Janet had to miss it."

"Miss it? What happened?"

"They went to Grand Rapids. Then Joe had to go so he collared me. It's been a long morning, but I've enjoyed it. John came over too. Wanted to see why I wasn't back yet. I sold him a huge pair of red flannels; way too big, but for only twenty five cents, he thought he could cut them to size."

Clydis smiled remembering that she'd seen the johns that Sky had ordered for himself but had not clearly specified the diameter. John would have to do plenty of cutting. She began a scan of the store, looking for undergarments and stockings.

Emily and her mother came into the store. "Lucky we saw you in here," she greeted.

"I've never seen wares so mixed up," Clydis complained. "But there are bargains galore," she averred, sweeping her arm. "And I'm glad you stopped. Look at these shoes. Will you try them on?"

"I'd better," Mrs. Wainwright said. "My feet are a little bigger; darn it."

"Why, thank you, Mrs. Wainwright."

"Vera."

"Vera. A pretty name. What do you think, Vera? Style, I mean."

"Iceem. Iceem." Edith had wandered into the ice cream parlor, closed for the day. Henry had closed it, having neither time or help to run it. "Iceem, Iceeem."

Vera obliged the sundae while Clydis and Emily trooped over to Meads.

***

The swinery lay in a vale about a mile beyond the northwest corner of town. Hill and forest, and friendly breezes, were the towns protection from it. It was a valued enterprise despite an occasional reek reaching the town. Garbage from homes and businesses went to it and pork came from it; its smoked hams, sausages and bacon finding equal nowhere in the world. Malice was out by the scalding vat placing wood under it in preparation for scalding and scraping the hair from pigs; a twice weekly ritual in cold weather. They rode up to him, their badges flashing. They made no show of concealing their weapons.

"Malice Lee."

"Mal."

"I'm asking you to come with us."

"You've no cause," he accused. He'd gone back out there and had seen that she was missing. Her tracks led off toward the rails into town. "She'd been cattin' around. Caught her at it. Beat her," he admitted, looking the innocent wounded parent. "I know I hurt her and I see she went to town. No business doing that. She's a run away and I hate to do it, but she'll need more tanning."

"We'll need you in town to answer some questions. Her injuries are severe."

"It's none of your affair."

"You're coming with us," Clarence dismounted and stepped toward him with the handcuffs. Herm nudged Boliver a step forward.

"Man's got a right to discipline his own."

Clarence reached with the cuffs.

"You've no right," Mal hissed. His iron fist blazed at Clarence, landing in the same instant that Herm brought the Winchester barrel down on Mal's head.

Malice and Clarence were both on the ground; Clarence dazed, Mal unconscious. Herm waited, his Winchester aimed at Mal's head. "Cuff him, Clarence." Clarence pushed himself to his knees, walked on his knees the two steps to Malice; and cuffed him.

"My gosh," Clarence declared, shaking his head, that guy is strong!" He looked up at Herm. "How would Marsh have done this?"

"Likely would have asked him to cuff one wrist himself then place both hands behind him, maybe; or would have clobbered him; or shot him, more than likely."

"This certainly isn't my line of work," Clarence declared, shaking his head. "I don't see why Marsh depends on me for it."

"Seems you're the only deputy still standing."

"Just barely." He rose to his feet, shaking his head side to side to clear his daze. His left hand rubbed his cheekbone that felt crushed; numbed anyway, and his right hand lingered over the butt of his pistol. "I'd better find him a horse."

"Use the black," she said, startling both officers. "It's his."

Clarence looked at her: "Ma'am, I'm sorry."

She knelt beside her husband and smoothed his hair with her hand, looked up at Clarence. "He said he'd disciplined Wilma. She didn't come in to lunch and I sent Sandra and Lillian out to find her, but she didn't answer their calls. Mal said she'd run off and he told me he had beaten her because she admitted to catting around."

"She's in town, Ma'am. At Dr. Laird's office."

"Is that a reason to arrest him?"

"We were to take him in for questioning. Wilma is hurt severely."

Mal moaned and rolled over, coming to his hands and knees, his hands cuffed in front of him. He broke wind. She looked away.

"I'll come in. I have never punished a child for telling the truth; no matter what they'd done. I think Wilma knows that. She'll tell me the truth."

Herm'd gone to the stable for the black. Mal, with Herm supporting, rose dazedly to the saddle and teetered there glaring at Clarence. "You've no cause. A man's got a right."

"This could have been easy," Herm remarked for Mal's benefit. "Lead out, Clarence."

Deputy Ed Benson greeted them, to their surprise, as Mal was being marched into the office. "Cell's ready."

"Ed, you okay?"

"Laird says so." He stood rock solid and with a grin on his face. "I believe him. I'm doing more every day. Your wife's over at the mercantile, Clarence."

Returning from the lock up, Clarence asked how Lorraine was doing. "Fine. She hurts a lot, but those frozen beef packs certainly help. Clydis has gone on up to see her. Your little girl is quite a talker isn't she?"

"Yes, right now!" They heard voices rising from the lock up.

"But, Callie. I can't."

"Put on your suit. I bought you a new shirt and a bow tie at the sale."

"But, I just can't."

"We're going to Pittsburgh."

Their voices quieted. "She sure wants to get out of here. But no problem, Clarence. I'm all right and had you heard, Marsh woke up?"

Clarence breathed a sigh of relief. "Great news, but are you sure you'll be alright?"

"Certain," he answered confidently.

Again voices rose from the lockup. "But it's ruffled!"

"It's beautiful."

"It's ruffled, darn it. Callie, I can't wear this!"

"You'll like the admiring glances. Herm, please put it on and try the new black tie with it."

Mal sat in his cell, hearing all and being amazed to discover that law people have a domestic existence. Somehow he, like many people, had never thought they had. He sat wondering how their role as law enforcers could be so in utter contrast to their domestic lives, not realizing that his own actions, those which had led to his being in jail, were radically different from his role of loving husband and breadwinner. Herm was tough he knew that, yet, amazingly, bamboozled by his wife. Suddenly he shivered; but then smiled slyly, sure that his own wife would believe him. Or . . . Well?

Finally they emerged. Herm looked very stylish in his black suit, shined boots, ruffle-fronted shirt, and black bow tie. Hers was a burgundy outfit topped by an enormous flower and feathered hat. "Don't laugh, you two," he warned them.

"She's right Herm. You look great."

She took my badge and put it in her purse; where it'll never be found again, dressed me like a dude, and now she says we're boarding posthaste for Pittsburgh. Sorry to leave you guys with a lap full."

"No trouble," Ed assured him. "Marsh is awake."

"Great news. I'll stop by there and fill him in."

"No, you are not! Get it in your head, darling. You're going direct to Pittsburgh."

"Yes, dear," he replied feinting lamb-like obedience. "I've written a report for Marsh, Ed."

"I'll add mine to it. Get it to Marsh."

"Come on, Herm." She grabbed his arm.

"I'll be back for Doty's trail. It's in the report. Trial will be in Grand Rapids."

"Herm, I swear, I'm going to drag you." She yanked at him.

"See you," he waved, a huge smile on his face. "We're bound for Pittsburgh."

Chapter Twenty-three

Upon arriving at the mercantile Clydis and Edith had gone directly upstairs to visit Lorraine. Vera had dressed Edith in a fresh outfit, made necessary by Edith's gleeful assault on the chocolate syrup covered ice cream. Edith placed Dollie and Emma to rest on John Purley's bed, but in a moment her stuffed tummy pulled her to sleep beside them. Clydis tossed a blanket over her, and then sat down to chat with Lorraine, her hands around a steaming cup of creamy coffee.

Joe had announced that Wilma would be staying in the spare room at the mercantile. He'd returned to it and went about ordering it while Wilma was dressing in her new clothes. Of course, Sky and Janet had no knowledge of those arrangements. Clydis was sure that Sky would relish the draw of customers, her presence in any room of the mercantile would assure a good draw of customers, yet she was leery that Joe's rash decision may lead to trouble. Lorraine, believing in Joe Marvin, saw it differently. "Wilma will be a welcome addition to this household, Clydis. And it's not just because my Ed has returned to work leaving me to fend for myself hours at a time. Joseph Marvin truly wants to help her and Wilma and I'll be handy to help each other." Clydis, even though still leery of Joe's plan, decided it best she change the subject. Her sure tack, she decided because she knew of Lorraine's interest in the matter, was to update activities at the Tobertons.

" . . . I go down there nearly every day. The women have their hands full with the dairy. Especially they're busy now that Billie has two babies to feed, and with one of them on a two hour schedule. Helen finally did make milk, after three days, but scanty. Dr. Laird tells them it's not enough milk for Bernice and that Billie could continue as needed. The cow colostrum seems to be a good idea, but the funny part is that Bernice wouldn't drink it. It just dribbled out. And all were sure that tiny Bernie needed colostrum. Bernie refused to swallow it. The other day Red and Sid were there as were Tillie Mae, Jane, and Pricilla Myra.

"'Why doesn't she like it?' Billie asked, nearly in tears.

"'Yours is sweeter,'" Red said, and immediately Red turned Red, bringing

174

a smile to those looking at him. Then as they looked at one another and back to Red, they all burst into laughter, save Tillie Mae; who apparently didn't catch the significance of Red's comment.

"Immediately Jane, still in a giggle, began looking around in Helen's cupboards while Pricilla Myra and Tillie Mae ran from the house; all on a quest for corn syrup.

"Tillie Mae, because Job Franklin loved to eat it on pancakes, which he ate every morning, was the first to return with corn syrup, beating Pricilla Myra's return by more than a foot.

"They began stirring the syrup into the colostrum formula and Red tasted each batch.

"'That's it,'" he finally said.

"Little Bernie drank it greedily.

"'That Red,' Tillie Mae said proudly, 'I wonder how he knew.'

"Her comment rose peals of laughter. Red, getting redder and redder, edged toward the door. Sid, the new and inexperienced father, was laughing too, but at Red's behavior, missing the real situation as had Tillie Mae. Suddenly recollection fueled the mind of Tillie Mae. 'Oh, I see,' she said, smiling now. Red dashed out the door."

A story such as that had truly brightened Lorraine's day. Handing Clydis a book, she lay back against her pillows, her meat packs pressing. But after a few pages, Lorraine fell asleep.

Clarence, with his cupped hand soothing his face, didn't know how long they could keep Malice without formally charging him. Ed said he'd call Judge Barley for advice. They would sweat Mal as long as possible.

Clydis sat reading as Clarence lightly tapped the door. He could barely hear her whispered response. Serenity warned him that some were resting. Edith typically went at hard charge until her sudden impulse to slumber. Except at bedtime, it was fruitless to put her down for a nap before she was ready. He tip toed over and kissed his beautiful wife's forehead. "Please give up the badge," she said.

"As soon as Marsh returns," he whispered. He wanted to get shed of the badge as much as she did. "He's awake. It won't be long. Ed seems stronger. I believe he'll soon be in top fiddle. Herm and Callie have departed for Pittsburgh and into retirement. We don't know how long we can keep Malice locked up."

"Papa! Papa!" Edith began jumping on the bed, each jump landing her nearer to the edge of it. She spun around and grabbed an edge of the blanket. Her next jump carried her off the bed with the blanket dragging. Clarence caught her, with a sigh of relief, and lifted her to his lap for a hug. "Dollie and Emma," she explained, "like to sleep on John Purley's bed."

"We're going home now with Dollie and Emma. You can put on your coat."

"Wet." she lifted her skirt. Clydis was already rummaging the diaper bag.

On their way home a call from Roger stopped them at the corner with Front. The Faygards were just loading into a sleigh. "Did you hear Marsh's awake?" Roger asked. "We're on our way to your place to get the Oldsmobile back to town."

"I heard he is. I'm sure glad to hear it, but I don't think there's any rush about the car."

Roger had ridden a livery horse out to see about the car on the day after Christmas. They'd cleaned it of snow and Roger made certain it would start readily and run smoothly then covered it securely in tarps. Leaving the car at the farm rendered less congestion at his shop. The automobile business had slowed handsomely for the winter giving him time for other projects. Jennifer, with four months old Fred tucked against her bosom with one arm, had in her other hand a paper sack as she walked over to Clydis.

Expecting an opportunity to hold Fred, she held her arms for him, but Jennifer thrust the sack rather than Fred into her arms. "Look in. Roger just finished the molds."

Clydis peeked upon a half pound of butter, "How lovely," pressed into shape by a butter press. Each lump of butter not only had its whey thoroughly pressed out of it but had the letter F surrounded by a design of maple leaves pressed in. "It's truly a compliment to your exquisite butter. Have you sent one to Clarence's mom?"

"Johnny delivered their pound earlier. She sort of 'Oohed over it' he said." She handed Fred up now.

He was awake and making cooing sounds as he fixed his eyes on her. "Baby," Edith remarked. She was standing on the seat between her parents from where she reached to pat his face. "Baby."

"Fred."

"Fed."

Edith noticed Meggy trying to climb up beside Clydis and she crowded past her mom dragging Emma and Dollie with her to get to Meggy. Clydis reached for her, thinking to help her alight but Edith squirted past landing in a heap at Meggy's feet. The girls sat giggling in the snowy street as the adults fell to conversation.

A grand shuffling of personnel occurred before long such that Jennifer ended up driving Bunny and Junifer with Fred, Meggy and Edith crowded into the seat with herself and Clydis. Of the two sleighs, this was the noisy one; the little girls in perpetual giggle and with the ladies obliged to pitch their tones above their reveling, enabling them to continue a discussion of potty training. In the other sleigh Clarence drove with Roger beside him in the front seat. The men were discussing the trip home, which Roger had slept through, from the hospital on that snow blinded Christmas Eve while Johnny and Jill, with the whole rear seat to themselves, looked forward to sledding with Harold and Albert.

The sleighs flowed into the James yard. "There's wet paint inside," Charley said. "We just finished the last window frame. Can't hang the curtain yet. It's too wet. They can do it tomorrow. Naddy already got paint on her. Cream colored paint. Good enamel, Dutch Boy. The kind I always use. The sledding is good. Clifford, couldn't we close off that room?" he asked, eyeing Meggy, but gave him no time to answer. "Did Clarence tell you about there being no hill in the woods? Well, there isn't. There's trees in there. Virgins, I'm sure so tall they look like there is a hill in there but there isn't. They're virgins. So we've been sledding the yonder hill over to Groners. Good hill. Real good hill. You can build a fire. Albert and Harold are already over there," he said, turning his attention to unloading the toboggan from the rear of the sleigh where Jill had lashed it.

"Come in. Come in." Clifford wedged in his greeting while Charley busied himself at the knot he'd created by pulling the wrong string.

Charley'd given the string a firm tug and now strained his fingernails in extrication. "You'd aught to know half hitching," he complained, but was not heeded. The others, his would be audience, had vaporized while he worked, leaving him to test his nails against the heavy string. Winning at last he continued his explanation of the utility of half hitching to Sniffer who had at once seen the need to enlarge his circumference of responsibility.

Sniffer'd had a hard time of it marking the trees around the woods as his. He'd begun the work on Christmas day when he'd whiffed that Naddy and Harold were to abide over beyond the woods. They were to be treated as equals with Edith as far as he was concerned. He was a tired out dog as he sat down upon the hard packed snow of the driveway next to Charley's leg. His eyes wearily scanned a sleigh as Charley reached down to gently twist his ear. He looked expectantly up at Charley. His tail wagged the driveway and he whined as if asking advice. Seemingly, Charley understood. "This one's temporary." So advised, Sniffer stretched out upon the drive resting his chin on his outstretched paws where he drifted into wary sleep.

Jill and Johnny charged out of the house presently and began following the path through the woods toward Groners. Jill had a toboggan in tow.

Charley went to the shed where he stored his turpentine. Grabbing his can of it and some rags, he moved toward the house, a knowing glint in his eye.

"Edith! No!" He heard the mournful wail. His lips responded in a knowing grin as he quickened his pace toward the rear stoop.

Her immediate response to wet hands was to dry them on her bright blue woolen coat. "I'm so sorry," Claire apologized as she and Clydis dabbed at it. Promptly Flora had shooed Naddy and Meggy from the parlor and began opening the can of cream colored enamel. She would again repair damage. Charley joined

Clifford, Clarence, and Roger in the kitchen.

Her comment directed to Clarence, Clydis said over her shoulder: "Gather up everything dirty." He and Clifford jumped to the task leaving Charley and Roger at the kitchen table with their cups of coffee.

". . .that's why I bought the Packard," Charley was saying. "It's a heavy hauler and a good mud car."

"I was lucky to get the Cadillac," Roger said. "It's been a fine service vehicle."

"I'll stop on my way past," Charley said "to study your derrick arrangement. Clifford says it's real slick. We're leaving in a few days. All finished here but the move in. They like the house. Ours is at Bruin City where the mill is. Smaller than this, but Flora wanted to be near me so we located her right at the mill. Hauled in the building. We have electricity and running water, but no bathroom. Did you see how this bathroom and water system works? Groners have the same arrangement. Saw theirs and knew right away what Clifford would need. If we had an upstairs at Bruin, Florie could have this arrangement but she doesn't mind the outhouse to use. It's good and tight, and the range heats enough water if she washes twice a week. Sure will be glad to get back home. My crew's up there working at Croton. I'll say we'll have enough work to do now that we can get in there again with this snow and the ground will be frozen up firm so we can transport our logs to Bruin."

Clarence and Clifford trooped through with heaped cardboard boxes of dirties. Clydis had invited them over to use the washer. Flora was especially grateful. "Here, put these on, Charley."

"No need," he complained.

"Do it!"

Charley, looking sheepish, began to climb the stairway to the bathroom. A grumble escaped him as he disappeared up the steps, not seeing the need at all for a skin out change into fresh clothing.

The washer was ready to go at the Jameses but the paint wasn't, as Edith, and Naddy before her, had testified. And it would be good to visit in Groner's big kitchen while the children played and the ladies chatted, cared for Rylus and Fred, and worked their way through the wash while at the same time preparing a help yourself supper of dump soup.

***

At the Pantlind in Grand Rapids Sky and Janet rested in their suite, each trying unsuccessfully to conceal their boredom from the other. Closeness can lead to fatigue, to their surprise, and now yet early evening, they were bushed. "We could go and see how Tulip and Marsh are doing," she suggested.

He perked up. "Prima!" he agreed, reaching for his clothes. They walked to the hospital, arriving just as Marsh was having his first try at standing.

Sitting up had been terribly painful. She'd cranked the bed up as far as it would go, placing him almost upright. A full five minutes of agony followed through which he wondered if not his head was still on the pillow, the heavy head somehow dragging behind his efforts to further arise. She'd supported him, her arms aching, her side stitches pulling, hurting. They were tough, the two of them, and finally he'd sat rigidly on the bed with his feet dangling over the side. Slowly his head cleared and the pain somewhat subsided. "Ready," he'd said, recommencing the ordeal, this time with a bent on standing erect. He stood swaying, agony his sole being save for Tulip's comforting support as he clung to her. "Whooee," he managed to say. His body was reeling; Tulip struggling, failing, she knew it. Gravity was winning the battle as Sky dashed to their aid.

"I got you, Marsh." He lifted Marsh into an upright stance by pulling Marsh's arm over his shoulder and heaving upward. Janet elbowed Tulip aside to take her place under his other arm.

"Who?" Marsh managed.

"Sky. Me and Janet."

Marsh forced his eyes open, focusing them at once in search of Tulip. Finding her: "Sorry. Are you hurt?" he asked.

"Not a bit," she lied. Her side hurt and her fear was that she had torn stitches.

"Guess we should've waited," his comment an understatement.

"I'm glad we happened in," Sky said. He could feel Marsh steadying, gaining strength. "I believe you're going to make it," Sky was encouraging. "I'm glad we decided to stop in."

"I sure don't want to lie back down again," Marsh declared defiantly. "Get that Melba in here. Get the darn tube out."

The flashing six light startled Nurse Melba Pruin. Her mind raced ahead of her down the hallway. "Oh, no." Entered the room on running steps her feet slid to an inch of Marsh, her face pressed to his chest. Slowly her head tilted back and she looked up, still up at him only to find yet another head, this one a stranger, towering over Marsh's! She stepped back. "Why, Mr. Rockney."

"Get this tube out."

For an instant too shocked to speak, she stared up at him. Then she said, "The doctor will likely remove the tube in the morning."

"Get him in here now, please."

But she refused, explaining that the doctor's day had begun with a broken arm, a man had slid down his rear steps, and that the entire day'd been a hazard including a ruptured appendix, which had concluded not an hour ago. "Can't you give him a break? He has family."

Marsh mellowed some at her recital, but insisted he wouldn't return to bed. "Make what ever arrangements suit you," she said. "My duty day has terminated. I'll send food in for you before I go."

They ended up with a chair wedged between his bed and hers, the chair pressed to within a few inches of the wall and topped by a stack of pillows. Tulip had by this time also pulled a second gown onto him, this one applied backward in response to Janet's reddened face. The behind bulged beautifully, to Tulip's mind, but Janet, shocked, had turned quickly away. Tulip with a grand smile on her face had given him a pat back there as she was fitting the gown. He eased into the chair, and his urine bag dragged with him. He began chatting with Sky who'd seated himself on Tulip's bed.

Tulip and Janet drew up chairs along the foot of the beds which positioned them to be an active part of the conversation, yet in apparent disregard of the men's presence, Janet directly addressed Tulip: "We're here to get married."

"Me too," Tulip said.

"Really? You sure?"

"A month."

"Same for me."

"Does he know?"

"It's the first news he heard about when he woke up."

"I told Sky this morning. Do you think a double wedding right here in this room would be fun?"

***

At the mercantile in Leadford wedding vows were unspoken, but Lorraine knew. She'd taken her boys to a town in Florida where she nursed a soldier at the Army hospital. She'd held to him not through pity or sorrow, no, another factor had ruled: Commitment. She'd stayed steadfast beside Ed Raymond as Joe was beside Wilma. Without sleep or food, naught but drink, applying ice to her lips, pressing cool compresses gently to her shattered scalp and to her shredded eyebrow. They were in love.

***

At the base of the High Ten a fire roared, attracting the interest of Toad and old Jude as much as did the sledding. Firelight glinted from their eyes as they looked up the hill to see which gleeful chattering contrivance would sweep into their view; and on past them, drawing their heads again down slope beyond the fire to arrest near the cattails beside the paddock. The horses lightened their front quarters, tensed their rear, ready to turn and hurry away as the contrivance coming toward them was noisier than any before.

Their nostrils flared, their eyes grew large and shined in the light as the toboggan load of three women zipped past them in a curl and bath of snow. Theirs was the first vehicle to have reached the cattails and to smash through them to coast out onto the icy bog surface where it slowed to a stop. Flora, Jennifer and Clydis sprang gleefully up from it. Snow and shattered cattail leaves and down and sticks stuck to their coats, hung from their bangs, itched their necks. Roger rushed past on Charley's one runner and close on his track Albert, Johnny, and Harold flowed past, their toboggan sending delightful jars and jiggles through their bodies.

Now light glinted once more from the eyes of Toad and old Jude. Their vision strained, their legs tensed as side by side two apparitions appeared. On one there rode, his belly to the boards, a howling banshee "Whooooeeeeee!" and off Clifford's port Charley whoooeeed! He came down the slope sitting on his sled steering with his feet, his gloved hands each firmly holding to a sled rail as he slid past to the cattails.

In joyful climax to their exciting stint on the hill the men and boys headed in to dump soup. Dump soup, however, but weakly called to the ladies. The snowy High Ten held them strongly through several more rounds before they resumed their delight in the house with the babies and Edith, Meggy, and Naddy.

In the house meantime the three little girls were going strong. Edith had started them out that afternoon with a tour of the house pushing the baby carriage loaded with oaken animals, her tin cup, wooden spoon and bowl along with Dollie and Emma and her cast iron milk delivery wagon with attached horse. The cast iron rig soon became a battering ram for disbursement of neatly stacked wooden blocks. Each block was decorated with a number or a letter, a gift from grandma Groner, and the blocks took a nice beating for nearly half an hour before the delicate little imps were enticed to the table for dump soup and chocolate milk.

As the imps were finishing the men and boys moved in. They employed oversized spoons. A big spoon was challenging for a gape the size of Johnny's and Harold's, but Albert, being older, managed rather well. They were just settled into rhythmic efficient spooning when they heard a titter from the bathroom upstairs. The three little girls were up there. Apparently, something magnificent had occurred.

Chapter Twenty-four

It had begun to unfold right after their soup and chocolate milk. The three trooped up there and Meggy took her pants off and climbed up on the stool and wet there. Then Naddy removed her pants and climbed up on the stool and wet there and by this time Edith had removed her diaper. Edith had before climbed up on the stool. As a matter of fact she had lately done so as one of her first chores in the early predawn mornings, but this time it happened! At last she'd discovered the reason for climbing up on the stool with her diaper off. Her little tinkle splashed the water of the stool. Its merry trilling had raised the titter heard down at the table. The men all glanced up that way; quiet now, all ears listening. "Edith did it!" they heard Naddy exclaim. Edith climbed down off the stool and then she placed her hands on the seat of the stool and leaned way over the brink to see down inside the amazing chamber, looking for what she'd placed there. Seeing it not, she looked inquisitively at first Naddy then Meggy.

"My wet?" she asked, setting free a high decibel giggle from the older girls.

"It's in there. It's in there!" they managed to declare amidst giggles. "Now we have to flush it."

Their discussion was greeted by no less than snickers and knowing smiles by the boys at the table. They could visualize the three of them gathered around the bowl, all looking inside, ready to be thrilled half out of their minds at the pull of the handle, which they were. "There it goes!" The swirling splashing water cascaded down the pipe, its gurgle in concert with shrieks and giggles from the little girls. The boys burst into uproarious rapture. The men sat with pleasant placating smiles.

Jill and Claire were as proud as peacocks as they met the girls at the base of the stairs. "Wonderful," Claire expounded. "Edith, Momma will be pleased."

Momma heard about the earth-shaking event when she returned from the hill but could not congratulate her; nor even hug her. Edith was under a card table fast asleep. She had Emma beside her and her head rested on Naddy's abdomen. Squeezed up next to her was Meggy with one leg thrown over Edith's and with Dollie resting in the crook of her arm. They'd constructed a home by sliding two card tables together. Blankets were dragged off her parents' bed and draped over the tables to wall their abode. They'd dragged pillows in there too. Naddy had a foot on one of the pillows and Meggy's head rested beside the other.

The kitchen range felt good. Nine o'clock was past their bedtime. Roger yawned and glanced at Jennifer then went in and pulled Meggy from her domicile and wrapped a blanket around her. Jennifer with Fred tucked beside her and with nodding Johnny holding to her other side, pulled out with the sleigh. Roger eased the Oldsmobile into the starry night. He and Jill with sleeping Meggy followed some distance behind the sleigh. Jill felt that her role that day had been as a grown up and her thoughts were of a day hopefully near when she too would find him. Meanwhile, Roger's thinking centered on the one runner sled of Charley's. "Well, what if that runner was a few inches longer and grooved like a skate?"

Clydis proudly tucked Edith in. As she'd entered the kitchen, Claire awarded her with the news. Her first potty wherein she, as Claire believed having heard the excitement knew why she was upon the stool. Clydis was low on diapers. As many as she dared of Edith's she'd cut into fours and hemmed them having found they were just the right size for Bernice. She'd purchased soft cotton, planning to construct replacement diapers for Edith and to produce diapers for Lorraine's baby. Now perhaps she could begin to plan a new use for the cotton. Bloomers?

At Bernice's birthing, Helgie had used her professional scale that she'd purchased from Sears for thirty cents. Helgie also carried with her a second professional scale that would weigh up to twenty pounds, but Bernice hardly tested the smaller scale let alone the larger. Weighing Bernie on the Toberton's kitchen scale had been discouraging; the scales would a gain or lose of an ounce or two from moment to moment. But now Bernie was definitely and consistently tipped the kitchen scales at nearly five and a half pounds. A combination of the colostrum formula along with Billie's ample filler in addition to Helen's nutritious though less than ample banquet was filling out the tiny tyke. And her little kicks now had strength with their movement. As tired as Clydis was she sat a while that evening cutting diapers and hemming them, but not for Edith. My little girl, she thought; and oh how proud she was; wait until Clarence hears about this.

***

Harvey Winfield Sykes rode down from Croton. On lead behind him strode his packhorse. The horses were loaded with his meager collection of worldly goods. In front of him, across in front of the pommel, lay a dog with two splinted legs. In addition to the splints a large white bandage covered the stitching used to close her rented side. A log had been skidded over her. She moaned and he compassionately raised her into his lap and held her there. He scratched her ear and she blinked an eye. She'd been the camp dog. "Shoot her," the boss'd ordered. "A logging camp is no place for a dog. Especially it's no place for a friendly dog. Always under foot, now you see what has happened." Harvey spent hours working over the dog. Two days now they'd been on the trail. By now their route bordered the Black Sucker. Downstream lay Leadford.

In Leadford a small white church stood on a bluff beside a cattail bog which edged the Black Sucker. He'd preached there. He'd had some parishioners; staunch ones, but not many for his message had been stale. Sticking strictly to the Word, foregoing life's reality, speaking not to the people, but at them with threats and damnation, few had missed that he'd gone away. One Right Reverend Simon E. Lowgo had driven him out and had taken his church and Sykes had in sadness rode the train east to the Finger Lakes region of New York, his home, but he couldn't stay there. His heart had been heavy. No, not that he'd lost his church, but that he'd lost the people; or had never reached them. He'd known himself to be a failure, an unwanted man. In determination he'd ridden the train back through Leadford, closing his eyes as he passed it and had detrained at Bruin City.

Workers were needed in clearing land and in building a dam across the Muskegon River which would provide electrical power for a vast area of people and towns and he'd signed on as common labor. He worked hard and he listened. He heard what the men said about their lives, of their good times, their bad, their sorrows, their woes, their fears, their loves and he began to answer; and gradually he'd learned to be a preacher for, and of, the people. In addition, he knew horses and by and by he came to care for them at headquarters and so it was that the boss had sent him to Leadford to see into the location and fate of the horses he'd ordered.

Dr. Laird consented to examining the dog and to caring for it in his home until Sykes could return for it. Harvey Sykes' immediate assignment in the town, and his last job for the dam building company, was to track down those eighteen heavy horses.

Nearing Lower Lead Bridge, he paused along the rails and turned and looked across the bog of cattails to the church on the bluff and it shined to him on the evening sun. His heart leaped for now he would be a preacher for the, of the, people. He would fish the Black Sucker. He and Tawny would live in the church basement. They would be home. His church was to be called The Family Gospel Church.

So profound was his thinking as he rode along the rails that he rode right on past Faygard's and was obliged to turn off at the railroad bridge over Faygard's dip and to make his way along the brink of the dip until he was on Jericho. To his right he could see that the dip had been filled with crushed rock over a large cement culvert and to his right was the Faygard farm.

At his arrival Hillary Faygard was pitching hay to their overstock of horses. Hillary was a quiet faithful person who seldom was off the farm. Hers was to live there and to work there and thereon be ever cordial to any who would visit the Faygard enterprises and she was generally happy, but was a little begrudged at present. Not quick to judge Simon Doty, the law and God would do that, she, as a result of Doty's actions had more mouths to feed now and despite her better judgement, she couldn't help but feel a dispassion for him as she forked the bright timothy. The timothy store was dwindling rapidly. They may need to buy hay, also oats, likely before spring because she would not scrimp no matter when feeding horses or her own. "Hello, up there," she heard someone say. "Hillary?"

She didn't recognize him. "Chester's in the shop," she advised, looking from the loft. She searched her brain seeking remembrance of him. He did know her name. She watched through a knothole in the loft wall as her visitor approached the shop, hoping the while that he may be a horse buyer, yet knowing he wouldn't be as fortune had not lately shined on them.

Chester and Sid were all smiles when they came in to eat supper. "This will fatten the jar," Chester beamed, handing her a wad of greenbacks. "We're to ship eighteen on the morning train."

"He was a buyer?" She need not have asked.

"Preacher. Name of Sykes. Wants to run that vacant church. He's been preaching at Croton where the horses are going to, but now he is staying in Leadford, he said."

He watched as she counted. "That fruit jar behind the beans has enough in it for your hay baler," she said.

"Sure it does. This is for you. What with electricity and phone service due us this summer, I thought you'd modernize with a bathroom and such, and central heat. I'd think coal oil, but it's your choice." Smiling, she reached for the Sears, Roebuck and Co. catalog.

"You'll take in this order when you go with the horses."

"It could go more than fifty dollars for the well."

"So, buy a smaller baler," she joked.

"Our well came in at sixty three feet," Sid remarked. "Morley witch for yours?"

"Sal Perkins did. No relation to Morley. Same guy that's helping you move the train car. He said our well will come second after Groner. Clarence tell you their cistern's near dry?"

"Said so. It's no wonder. Modernization leads to heavier use of water, but we're all going for it next summer. Us with babies first. I'm looking forward to it."

"Us too," Chester replied dreamily.

***

In the early morning Edith climbed the stairs to the bathroom. She dragged her red afghan behind her and she clutched Dollie under her arm. She'd turned on all of the lights on the way and now stood beside the stool in the glistening interior of the bath room where she rested Dollie on the afghan and removed her pajama bottoms and her diaper. She climbed up onto the stool and sat a moment before she knew it was going. She giggled. She waited until it was gone! "Momma! Momma!" she yelled as she clambered down the stairway dragging her red afghan, Dollie having tumbled onto the bathroom floor. "Momma! Momma!" She climbed onto the bed and bounced on Clydis. "In there! In there!"

"What?" Clydis noticed the nude bottom. "Oh, how nice. Show Momma."

Abandoning her afghan in the bedroom, she held to her mother's sleeve. "In there. Momma, in there." She pulled Clydis along as fast as she could; pulled her right up to the stool where she rested her hands on the rim of it and peered down inside. "Wet in there," she said, wondrously.

Clydis hugged her. "Shall we pull the handle?" Edith pulled it.

They watched the water swirl down and they watched until the water in the bowl had stilled. "Come," Clydis said. "Today you'll wear big girl bloomers."

Meantime Tom drove the sleigh up Moppit hill. Beside him Red was suffering. By the end of his shift his legs had become completely pain filled and tremulous. At home he'd take pain pills and get into bed. There he would grit his teeth while Billie elevated his feet. After resting an hour or two he would be able to arise and eat before resuming his slumber. Astride Bunny, Clarence caught up to them just shy of their driveway where he bid them good day. I'm going to talk to him sometime today, Tom thought, about Red. I must.

Clarence's mind had long focused Red's duress and he'd discussed the case with Overmire. "You arrange it," Overmire had thundered into the phone. All would willingly work extra shifts as required to cover Red's absence, Clarence knew. They knew Red was afraid. The surgery would be risky, with no promise of complete success. He worried that time lost from work and the extra work for Billie, and the others, would be wasted. Clarence must convince his friend, but how? He was deeply ponderous as he opened the kitchen door, where a beaming Clydis impinged his thinking.

"She did it," she heralded from her position by the range where she'd just placed six slices of bread to brown.

"Once last night and again this morning," she continued as she reached for eggs to be poached. "Look at her, Papa. She's not wearing a diaper."

186

His mind unable to shrug Red, he was not sure that he had caught the gist of her splendiferous comments. He stammered: "Well, er . . . Red . . . What'd she do?"

"Used the potty," she beamed over at him. Big deal, Clarence thought; and he almost said so, but caught himself in time.

"Upstairs? Really?"

"All by herself."

"Why, that's marvelous," he agreed. "Isn't she kind of young for that? I mean . . . Well, I've heard that near three isn't bad and here she's near two." He walked over to her, ruffled her curly bouncing brown hair and kissed her forehead. "You did good. We're very pleased."

"Oh, I know she's young. But, who knows? I surely am full of hope. I've given away too many of her diapers, I fear, unless she exhibits less demand on those remaining."

Sniffer's mind wasn't to diapers, bloomers, or potty training as they sat down to eat. Edith was happily situated in her high chair. Sniffer's eyes followed her every move. He saw the milk dribble down her arm. She'd not learned to hold her spoon level on its elevation to her mouth. The milk dribbled out the back of the spoon and down her arm to drip at her elbow, to his frustration. The drops of milk that reached the floor served only as a means of cleaning the floor, but he stayed alert, not missing her slightest motion. Now her spoon was not working well in the dig. She tried a few times anyway before picking up a lump of the oatmeal and placing it on her spoon. His eyes fixed intently to the lump as she elevated it. The lump slid rearward on the spoon. The milk spilled off the back of the spoon and down her elbow, splashing in tiny discouraging splatters at his feet, but the lump survived its journey to her eager lips and she downed it. Now some one had addressed her. "We're very proud of you, Edith. You're a good little girl."

She waved her spoon that time and the lump couldn't survive such turbulence. It took to the air. In one fleeting gnash in mid air he had it. His tail thumped the floor. He looked about ready to jump out of his skin now as again she plunged the spoon. "Would you like some toast, dear, with oleomargarine?"

She had lavishly applied oleomargarine to hot toast and it melted in deep and lustrously and she cut the toast corner wise and handing a pointed chunk of the hilariously delicious morsel to Edith.

"Oweogin," she reached eagerly for it, bringing him to full expectation, every muscle tense as he followed the slice of toast. She bit into the soft middle of it, going for the gold. Following three bites to the soft toast belly she tossed it, reaching for its better half. The center-cratered ort didn't reach the floor. His tail thumped. He licked his lips; whined, giving full attention to his repast as she elevated the next exquisite morsel.

Clevis Harold had eaten his hardy breakfast long ago and by this time was harnessing his teams of four. It was a cold morning. Crisp and clear. A just-orbed sun glowed on the horizon. Its brilliant golden rays sparkled off the puffy billowing clouds overhead. That day he would bring a train car to the farm. He was anxious and impatient, but vigilant, checking every inch of the harness, every inch of the horses. He looked up at the sound of an approaching rider.

Clarence rode into the yard. He rode up to Red's door and knocked and Billie opened it and Clarence went inside. Red was at breakfast. Promptly Clarence promoted Red to boss of his shift then laid him off. "No sooner than two months, no later than six," Clarence said. "And if you report for work tomorrow you're fired."

Red sat dumbfounded, his fork paused in mid air. "But, Clarence."

"It's all arranged."

Clarence waved a hello to Clevis Harold. He then rode back home and climbed into bed.

Meanwhile, Harvey Sykes had arrived at the Faygard farm. He took breakfast with Chester and Hillary and they hurried out to the horse paddock.

Sid opened the gate.

"Move them out," Chester said.

Harvey Sykes knew horses. He liked the looks of them strung out ahead of him. Chester rode point. Satin Toberton, astride Rubin, rode on the right of the horses while Sid rode on the left, herding their massive charges toward Leadford. To Sid's delight, the road was hard packed, smooth and solid under them. The road would soon suffer heavy tonnage, but it would hold. Sid was sure of it.

The stock cars were still parked in front of the Toberton refrigerator car on the south siding at Leadford. The snow had been bloodied here and the horses knew it, some shying back, wanting to return home, but the drovers knew horses and their voices where reassuring to them while giving them no quarter, no options but to load aboard. The last horse scampered nervously into a car, its tail barely escaping the sliding door as Sid briskly closed it. They'd wait now for the arrival of Sal Perkins. Already by that time the northbound was hooting Lower Lead Bridge.

Along Jericho behind the eighteen heavies Clevis Harold rode perched bareback atop his lead of four and behind him came Tom on his lead of four. Behind them Molly and May brought the milk wagon and would make milk deliveries on their way into town.

"Horsie, horsie!" Edith jabbered, jumping on him. Clarence had slept not an hour. "Horsie, horsie."

From the kitchen he heard Clydis softly calling: "Edith, come here."

"Orsie, horsie," she now sat quietly on her dad but was determined to explain to him about the horses.

He could hear that May and Molly were in the kitchen, having arrived to deliver the milk and partake a reading lesson. Listening, he caught "refrige . . . car . . . day," and he hugged Edith. Leaping from his bed, he carried Edith to the window.

"What did you see? Did you see horses?"

"Big orsie. Oooh more." She spread her arms and fingers. Her eyes were bugged and she shook her head, her curly brown hair bouncing against his cheek.

"A lot of big horses, huh? Get your coat. We'll go see." He hated to put her down. Gosh, he did love her. She ran to get her coat and to pack her bag. He hurried to get dressed, arriving at the kitchen just as Clydis was pulling on her coat.

"I saw the horses, but was hoping to give you a few hours sleep."

"Thanks. I could use it. But we can't miss this. Why, the whole town could be out!"

"Did you notice her diaper?"

"Huh? Oh, yes, she's not wet."

"She doesn't have any on."

"Oh?"

"I want to see how it goes. I've packed several extra changes of clothes in addition to a few of her diapers, just in case."

She upped Junifer "Get, you, miss," and tuned Bunny with a lusty: "Bunny, you behave." In wonder he looked over at her.

Their sprightly pace overtook the milk wagon and she cruised on past. Ahead they heard slamming and saw smoke rising in billowing black puffs as the heavily laden northbound began its pull for the Ellington grade. Hidden from them by the train, Ma and Pa Groner waited.

***

"We'll wed soon," Tulip said on that Christmas when Marsh lay in coma. "I'll let you know when," and she'd asked them to return with special clothing and Marsh's camera and camera case. "Marsh will want Robert as best man and, Emma, I'd be honored were you beside me." Now having received a phone call in the night, they'd taken a leisurely breakfast in the station restaurant. The northbound local would make stops at Ellington and Ryanton before pulling into the siding at Bruin City, allowing passage of the southbound which Robert and Emma would catch. They'd have a two hour wait, but cared not. Two weddings were to occur.

Pa's body English pushed the northbound from the station and as it cleared they were amazed to see Clevis Harold with his four-hitch waiting on Lead Bridge

189

and behind him Tom stood waiting with his hitch of four. "There's days when it pays to be early." Robert said, "Gosh, what a day!" Emma cuddled close to him on the station bench.

Sal Perkins had engineered a framework of six by eight timbers that were constructed under the refrigerator car to raise it three inches above the rails, the whole resting upon the axles of eight steel rimmed wooden wheels. Each wheel carried a brake lever and each wore a socket that would accommodate a turning lever. Each of the wheels could be levered two inches out of line which made it possible, with some fore and rearward jockeying, to turn corners. During the trek there would be numerous weak turns to make as well as the negotiation of six ninety-degree turns. The first sharp turn would occur on Bridge and would transition the car from its railroad environment to one far different.

Robert and Emma, along with Clarence, Clydis and Edith watched from the station bench. Dozens of townspeople were on hand to see the car move sideways at the crossing. Clevis Harold's four-hitch of gentle, powerful Percherons easily pulled the car from the railway. His method with horses was the opposite of most horsemen in that Clevis Harold, and those whom he taught, was ever quiet and gentle with a team, the team responding through willingness rather than trepidation. He pulled as far as he could onto Lead Bridge where a softly uttered command from him halted the team.

The wheels were turned opposite then Tom spoke to his hitch of four and the car moved rearward, coming nearly straight with the way of the street. Reversing the process, Clevis Harold pulled the car straight onto Lead Bridge. They were on their way. Sal Perkins was everywhere for his design was in operation, his honor on the line to be judged by the dozens. The car moved farther out onto Lead Bridge. The southbound hooted its urgency.

People ran across the rails. They ran out onto the walkway over the dam. They crowded onto Lead Bridge. They surged across the dam and across Lead Bridge to gather on Summit. Those not crossing the tracks climbed to upstairs windows. Robert and Emma sat on the bench, their eyes hungry. Molly and May crowded across with the others, their milk wagon a bully. Clarence and family wedged into the Lead Bridge crowd. Robert and Emma sat on the bench, their eyes straining to see, their sight suddenly blocked by the passing train. "Shoot," Pa Groner said.

Jake Farmer Peterson eased the big Mikado through the station. His eyes strained ahead for the stop signal beyond Lower Lead Bridge. Steam hissed and wheels creaked. The monster was in. Its passenger cars bordered the apron. Already the conductor had opened the door and stood ready. Behind him a man stood with his family. Down from the north were they, seeking milder winters, the promise of higher pay, a good school, a church. Pa Groner caught the man's eye. Their evaluations were mutual, good people. Jake Farmer Peterson looked to the west from his cab. He saw the commotion first, but then the reason behind it occurred to him and he pined to leave the train, to go and see, to be a part of the adventure, to see a train car on the road, not the rails, on the road and moving out! "Lordy, Lordy, take a look," he said to his brakeman. The man and his family had by now stepped from the Pullman and were walking toward Robert and Emma Groner. Pa stood up, his hand extended.

"Elroy Stokley," grasping Pa's hand. "Here to set poles."

"Robert Groner."

"I need to locate Clifford James."

Pa pointed the way to the freight depot. "Or he might be across the bridge," Pa indicated beyond the parked train, "but he'll be right back."

Pa and Emma boarded the train. They rushed to a window seat. His nose pressed the glass, his nose bent, Emma crowded close. They were jockeying the car around the corner of Bridge and Summit. They saw Clevis Harold's hitch of four mighty Percherons lower into the pull. The southbound hooted its release of the station just as the refrigerator car hove onto Summit.

Chapter Twenty-five

Marion Shirley Rockney and Tulipina Princep Board were married shortly after noon on the twenty-ninth day of December 1906. Robert Groner stood proudly beside him and Emma, her tiny best hanky touching away tears of joy, stood beside her. Calvin Theodore Ferndin towered over Robert in their turn and Janet Wadsworth Coats held to Emma's hand. Mr. and Mrs. Ferndins' kiss was long and tender, he with his back acutely bend, his knees flexed, she tiptoed.

Mrs. Rockney stood on a chair, her back acutely bent, her knees flexed, he on tiptoes weaving slightly, and they'd met with a long and tender exploration of lips. Afterward they ate a catered lunch topped by a delicate lavishly frosted three-layer cake. Nurse Melba came in just as the Ferndins and Groners were leaving. She carried a DO NOT DISTURB sign. "Until four," and hung it on the doorknob.

***

The refrigerator car arrived at the brink of Faygard's dip. Few among the workers toiling around the car had voted for the tax increase, but it being a countywide vote, the voting in Grand Rapids, Leadford, and other towns had taken the lead. They could hope now for improved roads but none were willing to bet on immediate compliance. Still, as they looked from the brink of the dip, they could see that mire didn't cover its bottom and that the roadway leading down into it was a full two lanes in width, the width extending up the far side of the dip to crest near Toberton's driveway. The way down Jericho had been wide and smooth and firm, the condition creditable to Sid and to Clevis Harold, yet the dreamers among them saw its condition as harbinger to fulfilled expectation and were wondering the wisdom of automobile ownership. The wheel brakes screeched piteously as eight people tugged at the brake levers, stopping the car with the Percherons standing on the flat and with the car slanting down into the base of the dip. Tom moved his team to around in front of Clevis Harold's.

Satin and Tom took over the lead team of four. The team was chained to the tongue behind them and would be handled primarily by voice command. At a hand signal from Clevis Harold, Satin spoke to Boot, bringing the lead pair taut then at a low murmur of urgings the eight Percherons lowered into the pull. Freshly shod for the occasion of this very hill, the horses dug sharpened hooves into the roadbed and slowly, steadily, the car moved up the far side of the dip. No other eight horses could have done it. They were sure of that. No line of automobiles, no matter their length could have done it, they were sure of that and anyone harboring a thought that the age of the automobile had arisen soon shucked it as the mighty team pulled the grade.

Winded finally at the top of it, they rested the teams. The horses were rubbed down and watered and each given the enjoyment of an oat bag. Tillie Mae, Job Franklin, and Pricilla Myra had met the team at the crest with needed comfort for the horses and now the others were stuffing in sandwiches and slurping cream laden coffee, taking lunch on their feet near the magnificent animals. The worse was over. They'd crested the dip and could anticipate the car's being at the dairy by early afternoon. Their hearts rejoiced.

***

In Grand Rapids Robert and Emma sat reading magazines in the lobby of the Pantlind. They'd decided to stay in town for the night, advantaging the offer of free lodging put forth by the newly weds. Around six that evening they dined with Sky and Janet, taking this opportunity to relate recent events to them of the town; in particular, they talked of Wilma Gillis and Joe Benson.

"We'd better return posthaste," Sky said. She didn't immediately respond. He looked at her as though he expected her to jump to her packing. He'd risen half way from his seat, his napkin in route to the table.

"Now just a minute here," she firmly said. "What I heard was that everything's under control even to the Clout brothers running the store."

"Yes, but."

"But, they don't need us. After all, according to Robert they've turned the mercantile sale into a promotion campaign for their own grand opening." Sky cocked his head, amazement on his face. "We must not be rude," Janet advised. "Let's give them a few more days. We, both of us, all of us, surely want their grand opening to be a resounding success, do we not?"

"But Joe and Wilma."

"Do not need us," she said. "And that Mr. Lee will likely be under control a while even if, as Robert said, they'll likely not be able to hold him in jail. However, with Ed Benson on his feet, I don't think he'd dare try anything." A

193

vision of Ed Benson had arisen in her mind and a knowing confident smile graced her face as she recalled the recent breakup of the rustling. Three of the rustlers were nearly decapitated; the situation now quite universally credited to Deputy Benson although some still thought it must've been due to the deadly accurate shooting of Clarence Groner. No one of the officers had said who shot who, and no one dared ask, yet her guess was, and she could see that Sky was mellowing into agreeing that Mr. Malice Lee would be walking very softly.

"Still, we're missing out on a lot that's going on there," Sky replied. "Why they even shipped the horses. And they moved the train car. We could've made good on those events with our sale."

"We did, I'm sure. So what is left pending?" Sky began thinking his answer to her question.

"Ed Benson might need a deputy," she offered. Sky blanched. He'd had all he wanted of being a deputy.

"Perhaps we should go on to Chicago," he offered.

"Now we pack," she said.

***

In Leadford Doctor Laird had carefully examined Tawny and he removed the splints from her legs. "They're strong enough now, Reverend. They were badly bruised but not broken. You've done well with this dog. Laird provided a salve to be rubbed gently into the tender flesh of the dog's rib cage and provided liniment for the legs.

Out in the waiting room Naddy, Harold and Claire were reading magazines, waiting Naddy's turn with the doctor. It was to be, hopefully, the final checkup on her nose, wherein he would pronounce her full recovery from the beating she'd taken from Mrs. Klinert. Suddenly a tawny colored dog entered the waiting room from Laird's living quarters. The tawny ran directly to where Naddy and Harold were seated. She placed her head between them on the bench. Simultaneously their hands sought her soft inviting fur. Their fingers moved through the tawny fur. They patted the dog on the back. Her tail waving wriggled her back and danced her legs and brought passion flowing from her eyes.

Reverend Sykes rushed into the room. "Oh, my. I'm sorry," he apologized. "Dr. Laird was treating her in his quarters. He did not, of course, wish to have the dog in here. I'm sorry."

"Is she your dog?"

"I'm caring for her. She'd been injured."

"What's her name?" Claire asked.

"Tawny, I've been calling her."

"Pretty name. Don't you think, Harold and Naddy."

They were speechless. They petted the dog. They hugged the dog. Harvey Winfield Sykes said, "She was to live with me in the basement of the church. I really like Tawny, but I do believe that she'd rather live with children in a house."

***

Red, Billie and Clydene along with Helen and Bernice boarded the southbound the next forenoon. It would be a tough ordeal for Red. They intended to break his left leg below the knee and place it in traction to heal, wanting to lengthen it. They were to reroute a tendon in his right leg in an effort to make it stronger. Lastly, after affording time for the legs to heal, they would reconstruct his left knee. The bear had bitten into the knee crushing bone and rearranging cartilage. Red, now that he'd received but little option was glad to get on with it. They rented rooms at the Pantlind and the ladies and babies moved in. As Billie was the food supply for the babes, Helen had no choice but to go with the food supply, but didn't begrudge the arrangement. Already, however, she was lonely and was looking forward to Sid's coming to town. Sid would come in on each afternoon train then catch the early morning northbound each day for his return to work at the Faygards.

May and Molly filled Clydis in on all of the details the following morning when they stopped in to deliver milk and butter. Jennifer Faygard had sold her butter churning enterprise to the Tobertons. Jennifer was expecting their fifth to be born in the fall and her thriving butter business, she could see, would be a burden she could ill afford. The Toberton dairy was glad for the chance to buy the business. Excess cream had become a burden to them as taste for skimmed milk had increased with their customers.

Grandma and grandpa Groner, drawn to the out of doors by the bright calm cloudless cold, cold day, drove Peanut in past the arborvitae to tie up next to the milk wagon. Sniffer was at the door and vigorously wagging his tail as the grand folks entered the kitchen.

Emma joined greedily into conversation with Clydis, May and Molly. Edith and Grandpa were soon busy with the wooden blocks building as tall a stack as they could. The cast iron horse and delivery unit stood ready near the stairway. Grandpa thought he heard "Herpolsheimer" just as a mighty crash was giving disordered flight to the blocks. He looked over at the ladies. ". . . has a 1906 Packard," May was saying. "John Clout will have it at the mercantile, if you want to see it."

The ladies and Edith all piled into the milk wagon and left for town. Pa stood beside Peanut. He patted on Peanut. "They can have their cars," he told Peanut. "And you just wait, you and me. We'll see the day they come begging. The first day the car won't start or the day it's buried in snow or mired to its lights in mud, they'll be begging. Don't feel so bad good horse. Don't despair. Be ready to laugh with me when they come begging. We'll show them." He patted on Peanut and Peanut whinnied, sealing her secret pact with Pa. By that time at the mercantile John Clout had Clydis seated behind the wheel of the big Packard.

"I know a fellow who has a Packard," El Stokley said. He'd been admiring the car at the time the ladies arrived with the milk wagon.

"We know him," May replied, "Charley James. He does brag on his Packard."

"I'm wondering how many good cows, and food for them, twenty five hundred dollars might buy," Molly commented, as ever practical. She would rather they invest in the dairy or, if extravagance need be their bent, in home modernization.

"Mr. Clout says this has twenty four horses under the hood," May was musing. "What do you think, Clydis?"

"Charley has said this is the best car. I will say however that a modern house is a blessing."

"Molly, I have four thousand dollars," May said, "and a good job. I want this car. The remaining dollars are for Billie and Red to modernize. Cut my commission pay on the dairy in half, please, and invest the half into the dairy; okay?"

"All of this suffering for a car?"

"You'll learn to drive it, of course; as will the others. Sid can learn to drive it on our way home from the Herpolsheimer. That is, if you can take a little time off today. Molly, you need some time away."

"Herpolsheimer?"

"We leave at once! Clydis will teach us to drive on the way to there."

Pa knew they would buy it. "Darn cars!" He stood in the yard near the barn. He'd rubbed and curried Toad and old Jude and fed oats to them along with Peanut, Junifer, and Bunny and walked forlornly back out into the yard. "They'll ruin everything. People want them, but they are nuisance and pest. Won't start, get stuck, break down. A constant drain, yet they want them." Pa and Emma had essentially no money. The rags and paper shed was meager pittance and Emma earned very little at Meads. He knew he would need to sell Peanut. "She would surely rather have the car even if, as at this very moment, it sits in the barn crowding Peanut because it cannot be relied upon in bad weather; and bad weather is the norm, for gosh sake; yet she'll want me to keep it in deference to Peanut." A sad man was Pa as he wandered off toward the woods that stood between the Groner farm and the Jameses.

John Clout took a turn around the block with Clydis at the wheel. Clydis took a turn around the block with May at the wheel. "Climb up there," May said to Molly. "I'll see you at the farm."

Molly took her place behind the wheel. May drove the milk wagon with Edith and Grandma Emma up beside her, leaving Molly but little choice. And at home, at once, she knew she must get Clevis Harold behind the wheel. Her mind raced, seeking a plan that would capture Clevis Harold.

Pa walked slowly into the woods. He expected to climb a hill once inside the woods even if Charley'd said there was no hill to climb. Everyone had always known the woods contained a hill; and Charley was not averse to exaggeration. He walked along slowly, conserving his energy for climbing the hill. He'd walked perhaps a hundred yards when suddenly the way darkened before him. In wonder he stopped with his nose to a wall of wood! Pa leaned way back, trying to see the top of it.

Beyond the woods, along Jericho, the Packard cruised past with Molly behind the wheel. In town she'd made a wide turn onto Bridge and ran her far side wheels down the boardwalk in front of the bank. Clydis had grabbed the steering wheel in the nick of time to miss a hitching post. Sweat had popped out on Molly's forehead and Clydis had been strongly inclined to stop the car, but she couldn't. She could see May's logic. At all costs practical Molly must be sold the merits of owning a car. At present Clydis could see no reason for owning a car except many, she included, wanted to own a car; not sufficient reason for Molly to want one, she was sure. Lead Bridge was coming on fast. She braced herself. Molly careened across the bridge then edged ditches at the corners of Summit and Cross before executing a skidding heart thumping careen onto Jericho. Jericho was smooth as glass and the Packard flowed along it. Suddenly she yelled so loud that Pa heard her from where he stood within the woods. "Yaaahooo!"

From where Pa stood Molly's high soprano came to him as a scream. The same sound stabbed the ears of Clydis in the same instant that it brought sweat to her brow and a pounding in her chest and throat. "Yaaahooo!" But that next blast Clydis understood.

"Yaaahooo! Clydis yelled. Total rapture had consumed both ladies and they couldn't contain their glee. "Yaaahooo! Yaaaaahooooo!" The sound trailed behind them. Pa stood in stark terror. He recognized the screams as Clydis'.

He knew not where to go, but following after the receding sounds he found himself scratched and bloody and with his clothing torn, staggering into the rear yard of Jameses. Thoroughly winded he leaned against their porch and grabbed a hold on a porch rail post. The Jameses would all be in town to work or at school. No horse nickered to welcome him. Both teams must be in town. He would check the stable anyway. Perhaps a horse would be there after all.

A glance inside confirmed his estimation but a gleam did catch his eye and investigation disclosed a bright new bicycle with sunlight sparkling from its handlebars. Suddenly his heart nearly left his chest as a dog, a strange dog, a dog he'd never before seen, rushed past him and out the door of the stable. Quaking, he pulled the bike into the yard. He scrambled aboard the wiggling thing and began firm pumps on the pedals. Away to the south along Jericho he'd heard the screams receding. He pumped for all he was worth.

She must've got Edith! The clever witch was not resident in the Black Sucker. She had escaped and now she has Edith. Pa pumped as hard as he could. A large black car approached him as he neared Faygards and Pa slid to a stop in the middle of Jericho. He could remain on his feet only by clinging to the bicycle. The car stopped before him and his eyes rose to meet those of Clevis Harold.

"Robert?"

"Help," Pa croaked. "Edith!"

May bounded from the car and ran to Pa. She placed her arm around him. "Edith. Oh, my gosh, oh my gosh," he moaned.

Leaning on her, he allowed the bike to fall in the road. "South," his voice raspy. "Hurry." He pulled toward the car, May at his side. She opened a rear door and pushed him in. She ran to the bike, grabbed it and climbed in, holding it to the running board.

Clevis Harold backed the car into Faygard's driveway. He gunned the car sliding onto Jericho where its churning rear wheels sent it on a weave down the road where it dashed down into Faygard's dip.

They bottomed the dip then Clevis Harold floored the accelerator shooting the shiny Packard up the far side. Pa held to a door handle with one hand while his other grasped the seat behind May. May held to the bicycle as Clevis Harold slew into the drive. He slid to a stop near the milk wagon. Instantly May tossed the bike aside and went to the rear door. She opened the door on Pa, dragging him from his seat as he hadn't released his grip on the door handle and Pa crashed to the hard packed snow of the driveway where he lay kicking, trying to rise.

Emma rushed to him. She plopped down on the hard packed snow of the driveway and she held him close. "Robert. Robert."

"Edith," he croaked. She held him close. Terribly afraid, afraid she would lose Robert. He was frail. He was old. And she loved him. She held him close. "Edith, help," he managed to say. "She has her!"

"Who? Robert, Edith is here."

Tears streamed from Pa's eyes. "Oh, thank God," he sputtered. "Oh, thank God." Emma held him close. Rubbed his back. Kissed his cheek. She trembled at feeling his tears lovingly wet her cheek. Clydis took Edith by her hand and walked up to her Pa Groner. She knelt down at the side of him and pushed Edith gently into his arms.

"Gampah." His arms enfolded her.

"Wet in there," she explained as she looked up at her grandpa.

Pa pushed her off to arm's length. He looked up at Emma, over at Clydis. "She's wet her pants," he said. "This darling has wet her pants."

"Wet in there," she explained as grandpa began making his way to his feet. Her next comment confused him yet farther: "Emma is sleeping." Pa glanced at his wife, glanced back to Edith, and then he rested his eyes on Clydis hoping for an explanation. Edith continued: "She sleeps with Papa." Grandpa was flabbergasted. Emma and Clarence? Grabbing the car door and the edge of the front seat, and with Emma boosting, he heaved his remaining way to his feet where little Edith encircled his leg with her arms. She looked up at him as though expecting him to pick her up. He knew he could not. He pushed her hat away and ruffled his fingers through her bouncy brown hair. Edith giggled. "Wet in there," she explained, looking up at him with big round eyes.

"Robert, what happened?" Emma had her arm around him once more.

"I heard Clydis screaming."

"Screaming?" Clydis had started toward the outhouse with Edith. She turned at Pa's comment.

She rushed back to him, admitting: "It's my fault, Pa," as she approached. She placed her hands on his shoulders and she kissed his forehead. "It's my fault, Pa. I'm so sorry. It was Molly and me. We were acting foolish. We were yelling while driving the new car."

"Grown women," Pa muttered.

"Foolish grown children," she averred, "and this silly child loves you." She turned then, away from him and he missed her instantly and watched after her as she caught up with Edith, hurrying her toward the outhouse.

Chapter Twenty-six

Throughout all of the commotion in the driveway insistent hammering had dinned over the yard. Now Rik emerged from the dairy, addressing Clevis Harold as he came: "That'll do her, Pa. She's ready." Rik and Clevis Harold had been connecting the dairy to the refrigerator car. Clevis Harold had by chance looked from a window in the dairy to see Molly drive the Packard into the yard. He'd rushed from the dairy.

Clydis saw him rushing toward them shouting: "Leave it running. Leave it running!" and she jumped from the car as soon as it stopped and hurried to one side; expecting trouble that was family affairs and none of her business. Clevis Harold leaped into the car. "Show me how to drive it," he ordered.

Molly demonstrated reverse, moving the Model S limousine bodied Packard back along the driveway until it started off the drive into deep snow. Halting in time, she'd shown him low gear and spun the rear tires getting back to the hard packed drive.

She and Clevis Harold traded seats. The car commenced wearing a pattern forward and rearward along the drive. Clevis Harold was worried about Job Franklin, his father. He'd accompanied Pricilla Myra that morning over to Job Franklin and Tillie Mae's part of the house. Pricilla Myra read from the scriptures every morning and her father-in-law had always appeared to look forward to the reading. But this morning when Pricilla Myra entered the house Tillie Mae was crying and Job Franklin's face had grown fully blank. His expression did not change during the reading.

His face had first grown blank on the day, now many months past, when Red had left the farm in quest of Simon E. Lowgo, whom Red wanted to kill. Following Red's return, Job Franklin began to recover. Tillie Mae, Pricilla Myra, May, and Billie all read for him and every day he could see that Red was not dead, indeed Red was present every day for him to see, and gradually Job Franklin had managed a slight recovery. Now Red was gone! Clevis Harold was greatly troubled over his father's relapse.

When the Packard drove in he saw at once the solution. With it they could conveniently get Job Franklin a chance to see Red each day. May, not realizing where his thoughts had been, was astonished to see him take the wheel. "Come with me!" he'd then yelled at her and she handed Molly from the car and took her place in the seat beside Clevis Harold.

Edith and Clydis returned from the outhouse. All hopped into May's car. Clevis Harold pulled out onto Jericho and down into Faygard's dip. "Yaaahooo!" he shouted. Soon the car chorused a crescendo of elation as each expressed their glee. "Yaaahoooooo! Yaahoo!" Pa too shouted "Yahooo," joining their jubilee. The Packard glided smoothly along Jericho, arriving at the farm just as Sniffer was barking Clarence awake.

His first awareness on awakening was that he was not alone in the bed. Emma lay beside him on top of his covers. She'd been neatly tucked into a bright red afghan. He missed Edith immensely seeing the doll and called to her as he climbed from the bed. She didn't answer. Additionally, Sniffer was sending a confusion of signals that added to his concern as he made his way to the kitchen, pulling on his robe as he went.

The Packard flowed in past the kitchen window, heads of his family sticking out all over it and with a bicycle tied behind. Somehow he wasn't surprised to see the car. His surprise was in seeing Clevis Harold at the wheel. His family trooped inside while Sniffer dashed outside.

Clevis Harold backed the car out past the arborvitae. Quickly, he sent the car down Jericho. Sniffer ran after the car, his marking machine ready, but couldn't catch up to it. His effort carried him to the margin of the woods where his feet slid along the snow bringing him to a jolting stop. He stood alert. In many years he'd not felt this way. Now he stirred.

Her pheromone pervaded the woods. He ran to and fro, his tongue lolling. She'd wandered the woods. Now she waited near a huge tree in the forest. She was west of it and the zephyr held her scent to it. Sniffer was frantic. He bayed loudly. Suddenly his zigzag focused and he dashed toward a stand of huge trees. He didn't know of his intent to procreate a new crop of super watchdogs, but rounding a tree, he saw that she was there!

In the kitchen Clydis was telling him about the car being May's and that herself and Ma might go to The Herpolsheimer Company with May and Molly in the afternoon and would stop in to see Red and the others, but that their plans hadn't finalized. Clevis Harold's sudden attachment to the car had stunned all of them. Not one of them realized his motive.

Clydis tossed a large lump of butter into a spider and placed it atop the range. At the side sink Pa and Clarence peeled onions and potatoes. At the table Ma and Clydis diced and sliced them and as fast as they were ready Clydis dumped them into the hot fat of the spider. She placed a freshly baked loaf of bread in the warming oven and Clarence seeing this action pulled out the bread cutting board, the oleomargarine tub, along with a quarter pound of butter resplendent in its fancy T and oak leaf design, and a large jar of strawberry jam. There was coffee and skimmed milk as well.

They fell to the meal with Sniffer at his station near Edith and with Tawny nearby on Sniffer's blanket. They'd surmised she was James' dog and had let her in along with Sniffer. Pa told them of seeing the dog earlier. "Sure surprised me," Pa said. "And you'd better just keep her in here till they get back. She could run off. Or she could attract other dogs, even."

Sniffer didn't have his mind tuned for other dogs at the moment. His vigilance near Edith had just yielded a good size slice of fried potato. He thumped his tail in delight. Tawny, her interest tweaked, began walking toward him. At that moment a team passed the arborvitae. At once he was at the door, Tawny beside him, warning them of strangers.

El Stokley drew up. "Stranger," Clarence announced, looking out.

Pa joined him at the window. "El Stokley," Pa informed them. "His wife is with him."

At once Clydis and Ma looked about the room, wanting it neater, but time was against them. Clydis only managed a cursory sweep of Edith before Clarence had answered their knock. Sniffer and Tawny rushed out past them, nearly upsetting El. "Going to be dogs," El said as he entered the kitchen.

El had earlier met all but Clarence. Pa completed the introduction then El introduced them to Marquee.

"We have three children," Marquee said, "Rosalynn, Ramey, and Seth. All are in school today. Rose is six, Ramey nine, and Seth is twelve."

"They won't miss a beat coming here," El said. "They've all, every one, always been ahead of their classes. We bought the old James place from mayor Kroust. And John Clout said that I might find Robert here." He turned toward Pa. "I need help surveying the line." Pa looked to be floating on air. Did I hear right? Did he say? "I was hoping that you might be wanting a small paycheck along the way."

He'd answered Pa's prayers. Now he could keep Peanut. Now he could pay his way again. Clarence had been paying the bill for them each month at the mercantile and had seen to their fuel bill along with many other expenses, disguising some of the expenses as presents. Although it was standard procedure for a man to help out his folks, Pa'd rather carry his own weight. He grinned so that his "When do we start?" was muffled.

El beamed his own grin to Pa. "You'll be handling one end of a two hundred plus foot chain and will be holding the black and white pole that I sight upon. We could start as soon as I've drunk a cup of your daughter's coffee."

"Settled," Pa said.

El and Marquee joined them at the table. "You know, El, I helped my Pa survey. He worked with Robert E. Lee down around Toledo. Surveyed a roadway and they surveyed for the Michigan-Ohio state line."

"Great," El said. "I'm a luckier man than I thought." He glanced over at Clydis and Emma. "That's why I was over at the store this morning, to see if he could lead me to Robert. I like to hire an older man," he continued, looking again at Pa Groner. "The work is slow and kind of boring, no reflection on you Robert, so an older more patient man works best.

"I have a degree in engineering and I'm on contract with a power company. Marquee has been through high school. We marked sites for the new poles in town. Sal Perkins has jacked up two houses and is ready to move them. One will be moved over next to our house. The other one he will move out on Main. It'll be their house. They're going to build an A&P grocery store on Main where those houses are presently located, so we've marked for their poles as well."

They listened to El with interest although much of what he explained about was not new to them. "Mayor Kroust," he went on to say, "is upset because I had to tell him that the new electrical power plant he has planned for Leadford is not in the plans as a back up power generating station." They looked surprised, their ears perked. Not often was Gastoff Kroust upstaged.

"Oh, he wasn't mad at me," he explained, misinterpreting their change of expression. "It was the town council he was ticked with for moving too slow on his idea. He said he was now stuck with the building he was going to use for the generating house. He tried to sell it to me. That one that was an automobile agency, I mean. I said it would make a fine hotel but not a good house. So he wanted me to be sure there'd be the right poles set for a hotel. Forward thinker, that Kroust is."

"He is that," Robert agreed. "You say you're finished in town?"

"Ready for the townships. To mark out, that is. We can't set any poles until the thaw, but they're being sided all along from Croton to Grand Rapids. You won't need to carry any poles, Robert," he joked, "nor dig holes nor set any poles. Just the measuring chain and holding the black and white pole for me to look at, is what you'll be doing. I'll show you all of that this afternoon, if you can."

"Let's have at it," Robert declared and his cup clattered into his saucer. He felt manly, as though he would again be the man he should be, that he wanted to be. Men of such ilk bring home a paycheck!

***

Clevis Harold, after leaving his passengers and bicycle at the Groner farm, stopped in to see Sid at Faygard's. Sid, they decided, would drive the car home from Grand Rapids each morning. They would load Job Franklin into it along with anyone who wished to ride along to the city. In the afternoon they would drive back home with Job Franklin so that Sid could drive the car back to Grand Rapids.

On that next morning Molly was behind the wheel with Grandma Emma and Edith beside her. Clydis sat on the outside front with her foot braced against the finder. She held to a roof support as well. Job Franklin, May, and Prissy Myra were snuggled into the rear seat. The car moved smoothly down Jericho. Prissy Momma commenced bitching long before they reached Belmont.

"Nobody listens to me. This family is given over to pleasantries. No one reads scripture but me. We don't go to church. Here we are in too grand a car gallivanting to the city. But no one listens to me." Once into her oration, she became bitter, as though malediction fueled her thoughts. Soon she was insulting everyone. Molly pulled to a stop at an intersection near Belmont.

She turned and glared at Prissy Momma. "Prissy Momma," she said. "Get up here and drive this car."

Molly's sudden confrontation of her mother-in-law stilled her nit picking but not her venom. "Well, I declare. I don't see what's gotten into you."

"Drive or shut up. Or I leave you in Belmont."

"Snippet! I'll show you," she admonished, climbing from the car.

Molly sat next to Job Franklin. Clydis and May were up front with Prissy Momma. Edith joined her grandma in the rear seat. Prissy Momma floored the gas pedal and popped the clutch. Rear wheels screaming, the car veered out of line with the road, aiming now for a tavern porch. Painted ladies dashed from the porch as the car came on. Clydis pounded Prissy Momma on the leg in an effort to release its force on the gas pedal, to no avail. The car streaked toward the tavern. Clydis turned off the ignition. She wrenched the wheel from Prissy Momma at the same time as she forced her foot through Prissy Momma's rigidly set legs to press the brake pedal. The car slid sideways, stopping inches from the porch. "I'm not up to this," Clydis said, her voice quaking.

"You have your nerve," Prissy Momma declared.

"Pricilla, please. I'll show you how to drive this car, but not today. Tomorrow we'll do it."

"You're all against me. Did anyone ask me if we should buy a car?"

"May bought it. We're all in favor," Molly snapped at her.

"Even Reverend Sykes says that May did well," Emma commented, herself wanting to quiet Prissy Myra; and strongly wishing some one would get her out from behind the wheel. "Clydis, please drive."

"Reverend Sykes says so?" Prissy Myra asked suspiciously.

"Who?" May wanted to know.

The Reverend Harvey Sykes has returned," Emma answered. "He was in the mercantile when you bought the car. He expressed delight that you'd done so."

"I declare. He'll need me!" Prissy Myra said, not doubling that she was correct, not wondering why he hadn't looked her up the moment he'd returned to the community. Smiling now, she planked in the outside front seat while Clydis slid in under the wheel.

May sat beside Clydis and watched her every move, wanting to learn all that she could about driving her car; and wondering what she'd unleashed. Her Packard had assumed a dominant personality, able to drive decision making in the family. Already it was indispensable. She wondered when interest in and demand for the Packard may abate, affording her greater chance to drive it.

Her dream was to drive it to where her husband was interred and to put flowers on his grave in the woods near the river. She pined also driving to visit Indian friends, some living near to, some far distant from, her home at the Tobertons. She was Indian and wouldn't disregard her foundations while acting saganash. She would drive it to powwows and she would drive just for the shear fun of it.

Clydis drove smoothly toward Comstock Park, approaching the bridge to the city. She would watch Clydis drive in the bustling city. Then May would drive in it and it would be hers to claim as domain to her expanding self. Suddenly, from the rear seat:

Job Franklin laughed!

"Praise the Lord on high!" Pricilla Myra exclaimed as she looked around at him.

Glancing at her front seat companions, Clydis saw that May's lips were moving. She'd asked the Manitou for help and her god had answered. The Manitou smiled down at her and was pleased with her decision to buy the Packard. She'd asked for a sign and it'd been given.

In the rear seat Job Franklin held her against the back of the front seat and he leaned his head backward, his neck cricked, to bring focus to her beautiful sweet face and he laughed and he laughed.

It had begun in the rear seat where Edith crawled over him to get to Molly then back across him to get to Grandma Emma. During several such trips his face had remained blank, but then Edith had stopped as though suddenly discovering Job Franklin. Job Franklin had memories bad and good. The good ones pleased him and he smiled a little while they ran his mind. The bad ones put a frown on him. He'd smiled but little since the day Red had left the farm to go to the west to fight his battle. His face had stayed blank while his mind waited painfully in its not knowing what it was to remember. Since Red's return, Job Franklin's eyes sparkled whenever he could see Red and his face had perked with slight interest when anyone read to him, but he'd not truly smiled, he hadn't laughed nor had he spoken a word since Red had gone away. Now he smiled in glee and he reached her as far away from his eyes as he could so that he might focus upon the source of his delight. He saw her pretty face and he laughed!

Now he held her close. Tears streamed from his merry eyes. Her curly bouncing brown bangs stuck from under her soft blue woolen hat and tickled his face. He patted on her. He held her close. "Where is Tillie Mae?"

"She's home, Papa," Molly said. "We're going to see Red. After we see Red we're going home to see Tillie Mae."

"This baby is cute," he responded. "She is cute." Contented now, Edith sat quietly in his lap and he patted on her. His merry eyes lighted those around him. "I want to see Red," he said, "then I want to go home to Tillie Mae."

***

In Leadford, Joe and Wilma graced the bench of the mercantile porch and were making plans to marry after school let out in the spring. A stack of books rested beside them. He'd brought lessons home from school and was teaching them to Wilma, assuring that he and Wilma would graduate the eighth grade at the one room school. The lessons were unopened for a new chapter had begun. Joe was to be crowned as valedictorian. He was honored and proud for that occurrence. Even prouder he was of Wilma. She was woman. And were he a better teacher, she would be valedictorian. She leaned her battered head to his shoulder and he took her hand.

***

In late January at the mercantile Helgie and Wilma attended the birthing of Roxanne Lorraine Benson. As inexplicably as it had arisen the sciatica had eased off, affording Lorraine a comforting respite during the final days. Topping this reprieve, Roxanne had come into the world without complication. Roxy now suckled contentedly while Lorraine patted her tiny diapered bottom. Lorraine was exquisitely happy. Her little girl. Praise God, her little girl. She patted Roxy's little bottom and Roxy suckled.

***

March came in like the gentlest of lambs, warning that more of winter would ensue. At the swinery Malice Lee fretted the warm weather. Cold weather is much preferred in preparing the Easter hams, but he must get on with it. That day he needed help to sort pigs. Sandra and Lillian, at age eleven Lillian was the youngest of the three Gillis sisters, went to the pig lot to help Mal with the sorting. It was frustrating work but he must necessarily sort from the herd all of the two hundred fifty pound hogs. Those were ready to be processed into Easter hams; also into roasts and chops and into bacon, sausage, and lard. He worked the girls hard.

They were a long way out onto the farm. Malice sent Lillian to the house for a jug of cool water and, for him, a jug of hot coffee. He and Sandra were left alone with the pigs. Out amongst the pigs the pigs knew not what their grunts camouflaged. Out amongst the pigs Sandra was crying. Out amongst the pigs Mal had fueled his lust and she dared not tell of it lest she be treated worse than he'd treated Wilma. From the kitchen window Vivian saw that Lillian was on her way to the farmhouse from the pig lot.

She began loading a .22 caliber rifle, the rifle used to mortally stun pigs. She would ask Lillian to take care of her three younger siblings. Malice Lee would need her help in stunning and scalding pigs.

***

At the farm on Jericho it was Edith's second birthday and guests were expected. Naddy and Harold and Meggy would attend along with Clydene and Bernice Toberton, as would Roxy Benson. Their moms would be there, of course, as would Jill, and Wilma, Emily and Helgie. The guests were slated to arrive at two o'clock. Clarence planned to sleep until just before the time came for him to run the Alamo. This to be sure the pump motor didn't over heat in its labor to provide plenty of water for the stool.

In Leadford Lorraine had already upped the set of livery bays. Wilma sat beside her with Roxy in her lap. In the rear seat Jill held Fred on her lap and Meggy was tucked in beside Jill. Jennifer Faygard was feeling ill that day and so with regret she'd decided she must stay home. At the depot Emily hopped in beside Meggy. Emily did the hair for all the ladies who would attend the party. She would sit proudly amidst them. The livery bays snorted their impatience. It was a clear warm day and they wished to travel. Lorraine let them out. She too was impatient, wanting to show off Roxanne at the party.

At the Groners Clydis tugged pearly white brand new bloomers onto Edith then squirmed her into a white sleeveless undershirt of smooth percale. Very shiny patent leather pump shoes graced her feet and her bright new anklets matched her pretty pink dimity dress. The sparkling new pink dress hung over the back of a kitchen chair. At the last possible moment before the guests arrived she'd snuggle Edith into the dress and slip into her own matching dimity. In the kitchen Edith was busy with her baby carriage, loading it with her finest selection. In the bedroom Clydis pulled on her long smooth stockings and was attaching them to her garters when she heard Sniffer whining.

Sniffer was restless and wanted to go outside. Never before had Edith opened the kitchen door. She grasped the doorknob with both hands. She tugged and twisted. The door swung open.

Helgie sat in her lawn chair, Edith's gift in her lap. She watched along

Jericho, anxious for the first guests to appear along the road, her signal to hurry across to the Groners.

Sniffer and Edith were in the rear entry now and he whined at the door. She grasped the doorknob with both hands. She tugged and twisted. The door swung open and Sniffer dashed into the yard, leaving her at swing on the half-opened door, proud that she'd opened it. "Sniffer goes out to play," she said.

Sniffer turned around toward her and stepped a step or two toward her and whined piteously. His nose resting upon his forepaws, his eyes pleaded. She moved slightly farther out the entry doorway. He sat on his hunches, his eyes beseeching, his paws dancing, and his whine a clear invitation. The entry door swung shut. She was in the yard with him and as Sniffer danced and pleaded, she hurried after him.

He dashed into the power shed where he turned around and looked out the doorway at her, whining, eyes pleading. She ran as fast as she could, following him into the power shed.

Billie and Helen were just pulling north from Faygard's dip. Roughwater's gate loomed ahead of them. The Percherons made child's play of the heavy carriage, making a blur of the gate as they passed it. Wishing not to be late, fearing they would be, Billie pushed the Percherons. At the last moment before the intended leisurely departure Clydene did her diaper. Quickly Billie set her aright, but just then Bernice spit up. "Go Billie," Helen urged, and Billie spurred the Percherons while in the rear seat of the careening carriage, Helen snuggled Bernice into a fresh outfit.

Within the dim interior of the power shed Edith heard a whimper, a weak cry of pain. Sniffer sat on his hunches, staring off into the near dim corner of the power shed. She moved up beside Sniffer and placed her arm around him. Now she could see into the corner. Tawny lay on an old horse blanket which Clarence had left there in a sheltered place for Sniffer to rest on days when his desire and duty directed him to remain out of doors. Another pain scented whimper arose from the horse blanket. She heard other sounds now, high-pitched yips. She sat down on a small fire wood log next to Sniffer, her arm still around Sniffer.

The fire wood log was a low seat and her knees were up as she tapped her foot, first one foot then the other. Her eyes acclimated. She tapped her foot. One elbow rested on her knee. Her hand cupped her chin. With one arm she held to Sniffer. She saw the puppy struggle forward. Tawny reached for it and pulled it to her side. On the horse blanket another puppy squirmed behind Tawny. Tawny reached for it.

Having buckled her stockings to her garters, Clydis hurried toward the kitchen, worried already at the silence that greeted her ears. What is she into? Immediately her eyes fell upon the kitchen door that stood open. She ran on into the entryway. That little dickens, her mind raced as she crashed out the rear door and stood on the porch. "Edith. Edith, where are you?" She heard Sniffer answer from within the power shed. Worriedly, anxiously, she sped to the shed, soiling her fresh ecru stockings. "Edith!" Very concerned, she darted into the power shed.

At the Jameses, Claire had Naddy and Harold ready. At one minute before two o'clock they'd start out for the Groners next door, planning not to miss out on a single moment of the party.

In the dim light of the power shed she could see Edith. Edith was seated upon the small fire wood log. She was tapping a foot. A tiny beautiful hand cupped her chin and her other hand clung to Sniffer. Her curly bouncing brown hair jiggled in cadence with the steady tap-tap-tap of her foot. Clydis could see beyond Edith and Sniffer to where in the sheltering embrace of the tightly constructed power shed Tawny licked her puppies. A whimper arose from Tawny. Edith's toe tapped faster. She leaned forward the better to see and she held close to Sniffer. Clydis sat down upon the straw strewn floor of the power shed. She placed an arm around her beautiful two-year-old daughter. "Puppies," she said softly to Edith, kissing her ear. "Tawny has puppies."

"Oooh, Momma. Puppy!" Her toe tapped. Her body wriggled. "Ooooh, puppies." Sniffer thumped his tail as Tawny drew another puppy to her side and began to lick it.

He awoke while Clydis was pulling on her stockings, an event he never tired of watching, but had drifted off again before he'd time to reach for her. His eyes now popped open and he reached for her but found her missing. He hopped from the bed clad solely in his union suit and reached for his robe, the silence in the house already stimulating a charge in him. Foregoing his robe, he hurried into the kitchen where the kitchen door standing open set his heart to pounding. Have I over slept? Is she going to start the Alamo? She hadn't before attempted to start it, but he reasoned that she could; but it was his job. His duty!

"Edith! Clydis!" Sniffer's reply waft to him from within the power shed. Bare foot, clad only in his union suit, he rushed to the shed.

Ahead of her along Jericho Billie could see that Claire was just exiting her driveway. She tuned the Percherons. They bellied down. Ahead she could see a light team of bays entering Jericho from Cross. Also, she saw Helgie dashing across Jericho.

Tawny was just pulling her fifth puppy up beside her. Edith sat on her fire wood log, her foot tapping. Clydis had an arm around her beautiful daughter. Edith clung to Sniffer with one hand while with her other hand she pointed. "Puppies. Tawny has puppies." Clarence knelt behind them. He reached his arms and he embraced them. He held them close as the guests charged in past the arborvitae.

The end.

About The Author

T. F. Platt enjoyed his first writing success in grade school, discovering that he could entertain by reading aloud the story or skit that he'd written. During his years as a college professor, his articles appeared in the scientific press. He also served eleven years as a national science editor. The idea for the Jericho series of books occurred in 1975 when he visited his mother at her retirement complex. Nearby was a railroad bridge that in the author's mind became Lower Lead Bridge and a walk around the area soon identified other prominent features of the Jericho stories.

As recreation Mr. Platt flies a Piper Cherokee. He has also used an antique backhoe to landscape their four acres into ponds and leafy lanes that his children, grandchildren, and friends ply by golf cart. At the ponds, Grandma Helen or Uncle Ben may assist the little ones in fishing techniques.

Author and family reside in southern Michigan, some one hundred fifty miles from the site of his Jericho stories. They have four grown wonderful children and four marvelous grand children all of whom serve as inspiration for the writer.

Printed in the United States
41565LVS00003B/488